D0282636

QUEEN EMMA OF THE SOUTH SEAS

CAPTAIN THOMAS FARRELL, an Irish-Australian trader, de facto husband of Queen Emma.

CAPTAIN EDUARD HERNSHEIM, a Hamburg trader.

BLACK TOM, an American Negro adventurer, lover of Queen Emma.

THE HON. W. H. LYTTELTON, an English remittance man.

CHARLES MARIE BONAVENTURE DE BREIL, MARQUIS DE RAYS, a French swindler, founder of 'La Nouvelle France' in New Ireland.

CAPTAIN GUSTAVE RABARDY, master of the *Génil*, one of the de Rays ships.

DOCTOR BAUDOUIN, one of the de Rays settlers.

RICHARD HEINRICH ROBERT PARKINSON, botanist and natural historian, illegitimate son of Prince Christian August of Schleswig-Holstein, husband of Phebe Coe.

CAPTAIN AUGUSTINO STALIO, Dalmation sailor, lover of Queen Emma.

BISHOP LOUIS COUPPÉ, Sacred Heart Mission, New Britain.

COE FORSAYTH, Queen Emma's son.

HIRAM STUART, U.S. Consul to Neu Pommern (New Britain).

LIEUTENANT PAUL KOLBE, Prussian officer, husband of Queen Emma.

MR & MRS RICKARD, Wesleyan missionaries.

NELLIE DAVIDSON, daughter of Jonas Coe by his Tongan wife Litia.

COUNT RODOLPHE FESTETICS DE TOLNA, a Hungarian traveller.

DOCTOR ALBERT HAHL, Imperial Judge and late Governor of German New Guinea.

MRS ANSTRUTHER-PURDAM, an English traveller.

HEINRICH RUDOLPH WAHLEN, a Hamburg trader.

LULU MILLER, granddaughter of Queen Emma's elder sister Maria.

CONTENTS

Contents

Chapter I

PHEBE

I will soothe with the sound of names. Gunantambu. Gun-an-tambu. Emma's house over the steps over the sea. Volcanoes, clam-shells, lemons. Malapau, where we first lived. Kuradui. The plantation she gave Richard and me. Ku-ra-dui. Gun-an-tambu. Ma-la-pau. Soft native names. Emma could never learn a language. But she could speak the language of figures. And read them. And money would talk back to her, the way it never did to Richard or me. Oh she was a great reader, my sister, she was the clever one, books as well as figures. Politics, history, even medicine. *Ganz bestimmt!*

Gunantambu. We were sitting together in the big room, in our long white muslin dresses, and we each had a green and red parrot sitting on our wrists. No, it's on the verandah. There's a cool breeze, just a little bit breeze, and the parrots are turning their heads and tightening their claws on our skin. We are in our best clothes, white shoes and stockings, the German naval officers are coming to lunch. Do you know, sometimes twenty courses? Emma could never manage the kitchens, I did it all for her. *La'u pele*, my dear, we will have the Samoan feast tonight, for lunch we are European.

I will soothe with the sound of names. *Palusami, palolo, homard, asperges, canard a l'orange.* Pommery. Veuve Clicquot. Widows. Emma was a widow for forty hours. I am a widow for nearly forty years. All that food! And now, do I weigh eighty pounds? I was a big woman, we Samoans all get big when we are old. And the Japanese soldiers make us small again. *Talofa!*

'*Talofa!*' My love to you. The Japanese private said it as the old lady had taught him. Not a bad man. The corporal could never have said it, suspecting irony even if he could not have

1

explained what irony was. The Japanese soldier walked on, you could not call it marching, his rifle slung over his shoulder. There was wire round the village, but the soldier's foosteps alone in the black volcanic sand were barbed wire, electrified wire, and the jungle and the sea were walls enough. And why would those civilians interned in the village want to escape? Into the mountains of New Ireland? Or to swim to New Britain? Or to Bougainville? Or to New Guinea? The old lady was so thin she could scarcely walk across the village. She was dry as a palm leaf and maybe she crackled as she shifted her bones. The Japanese soldier sat down under the shade of banana leaves. The old woman on the floor of the thatched hut was not looking at him or the black sand or the sunrayed sea. Her head on the block of wood that was her pillow, her eyes were closed.

I will soothe with the sound of names. Phebe. P-H-E-B-E. It's spelled wrong, they'd tell me, but I'd tell them that's the name my father gave me, Jonas Myndersse Coe, American Consul in Apia, Samoa, and he was an educated man of good family. 'Phebe' was the way it was always spelled in the Coe family. And Emma and I, our mother was a Malietoa. Queen Emma they called her, 'Queen' really meant nothing, but she *was*, she ruled, Queen of Gunantambu, of Ralum, *Königin der Südsee*, the officers would say. But to be a Malietoa, that was something. To be a Princess. I don't know what they have in Samoa now, but a Malietoa was king. Or did they push him out? Send him to one of the Marshall Islands, maybe. Islands. There's always another island. Emma owned so many islands. But they murdered her brother, my brother on an island, and Stalio, her lover, the best and most handsome of all her lovers. On Nuguria. Now that is a name that soothes, but not when you think of the murders and the chief who had murdered John shooting Stalio in the chest through the walls of the hut.

Phebe. Phebe Clotilda Coe Parkinson. P-H-E-B-E. The Germans said 'Phaybe', the English 'Pheebee' and spelled it Phoebe. My husband Richard was a very learned man—yes, as a naturalist he was known to all the museums of Germany and the United States, such treasure I sent for him, It was always I who packed and sent. Richard, he said 'Phöbe' the German spelling at first, though his English was perfect. That German 'ö', I told him he sounded as if he was blowing out a candle, and he laughed (it wasn't easy to

2

make him laugh) and said it was not a candle but the moon, and no one could blow out the moon. I didn't know what he was talking about, I was only sixteen and he was twenty years older than me. He laughed again, that long, solemn face, and he said 'the good Sisters didn't educate you, don't you even know what your name means?' I said 'What, Phebe?' Like a little girl. '*Phöbe*' he said, '*Phöbe* means the moon, the name of Artemis or Diana, the goddess of the moon, Greek feminine of φοῖβος meaning "bright" '. I was really scared of all this! Imagine, a Samoan-American girl of sixteen, in Apia, in 1879. Richard was a scientist, but he knew all these things about mythology and poetry.

He held my face between his hands and said 'Phoebe' (the English way, this time, the way my father said it) 'You are my goddess excellently bright. You will always reflect but you will never be cold.'

> Tomorrow night, when Phoebe doth behold
> Her silver visage, in the watery glass . . .

Well, I suppose I did reflect him, and Emma, but it's thirty-six years since he died, and thirty years since Emma died, so who have I been reflecting all those years? I have been Miti to everyone, not Phebe or Phoebe or Phöbe. All the natives called me Miti and they liked me because I could talk to them in their languages. But it's true, I suppose I've only been carrying on what Richard and Emma left, and for the children. I had twelve children, but only four left now. He was right there, the Professor, you couldn't call me cold. But not *hot*, like Emma.

The Japanese soldier looked up, hearing the old lady laughing. He remembered his orders. He stood up and glared at her. 'White woman must not laugh in front of Japanese soldier.' But she was not laughing at him, lying still but for her shaking shoulders, her eyes closed. He nodded his head and sat down again, remembering how she had told him that although she looked and talked and acted like a white woman she was not, she was of mixed blood, a half-caste, and very proud of her Samoan blood and her American blood. The Japanese soldier had corrected her 'American blood very bad. Mixture bad. Japanese soldier not touch black woman. Or white woman.' Maybe not black or white, Phebe had thought,

3

but certainly yellow, if there's such a colour, remembering the sliding scale of screams of the Chinese women as the Japanese soldiers had taken it in turns to rape them when they were first rounded up in Rabaul.

Oh Emma, Emma. Quite unlike the moon. Emma, Emma, the heat came out of you, you drew the heat from men. You were so beautiful, so gay, and even when you were fat and forty they wanted to bathe you in champagne, and not to make you cold. This hot climate makes slide the sweat of love. Hot and cold. When Emma was a young widow, when the Forsayth husband had disappeared at sea, she was fond of that Bully Hayes, the one everyone said was a pirate, but he was always a charming man. He asked her to dinner on his boat the *Leonora*, he knew how she loved champagne. Our father would have whipped her if he had known she had gone, but he was away in Washington. Bully must have taken her for granted. She really liked him, though he was so much older, but in her time, not in his. No man ever bent Emma, she was no palm tree, no easy breeze pushed her. But that night, Le'utu my mother and I had come back to the house on Matautu Point as those other women of my father's had died or gone back to their villages, I was about ten years old I think, and lots of my half sisters were there, Caroline and Mary Ann and Laura Sophia and Lizzie and Grace, and Emma who was about twenty-three was looking after us all, together with our mother Le'utu. I was woken up by the noise of something wet on the floor mats, and then a cool hand on my shoulder and giggles. It was Emma, all wet and naked, and she was undoing her dress from her head where she had tied it. 'He thought the champagne would do the trick', she had her mouth half full of the knot she was untying in her dress, 'as if I couldn't make up my own mind. So I jumped overboard and swam ashore. He was furious, and he couldn't do anything as he had sent all his crew and his long boat ashore and I knew *he* wouldn't jump overboard. Ah, Phebe'—I was only ten, but I had often escaped from the prisons of my father and the Sisters—'the first time any man has you, it must be a sort of accident. However much you like him, don't be part of a plan. Don't let them think they can seduce you to order. Or seduce you at all! It must be what you both want.'

*

4

A ship's siren sounded, echoing off the walls of the jungle and the rocks of the green hills above the village. The soldier ran towards the centre of the internment camp where other soldiers came tumbling out of the guard hut. Outside the wire, in the main village, men, women and children ran down towards the sea and the cockeyed jetty stuck in the coral and patches of sand inside the reef.

It was hardly a ship, some sort of Japanese patrol boat with two masts for auxiliary sails. But they were not sails swinging from the yards of the forward mast. Two strange, long, dangling sacks on either side of the mast.

The corporal, the one whom Phebe and every European and Chinese in the camp hated, shouted with fury at the delay, for his slow, starving charges were being ordered to parade, and the thuds of sticks on rags and bony bodies gave a steady rhythm to his recitative of hate. He ordered four soldiers out into the village to assemble all the natives, so at last in his pleasure of order the wilted rows of Europeans and Chinese and the sturdy wildness of the natives stood on either side of the wire facing the sea.

The patrol boat was now close in to the shore and coming in alongside the planks of the jetty that were rougher than the breathless sea.

Holy Mary Mother of God, those poor young men. Alas no names can soothe them. Emma always said there was no God. 'If you doubt it, look around you, at man created in the image of God. Like the volcano across the water from Ralum, that one day created in its own image an island of steaming rock in the bay.' Yet only the other day I gave thanks to God for my good eyesight.

As the boat went hard astern by the jetty the two sacks at the yardarms swung forward and back, revealed all too clearly now as no sacks but naked men hung by their wrists, no trace of their whiteness left around the dark meat bulging out of their split skins. Flies swarmed over the bodies and crawled into the open mouths over the bridge of blackened tongues. Their buttocks and sex, those places white men keep secret from the sun, had suffered the worst of all rebirths into the parody of grilled meat. The officer in charge of the boat gave an order, and two soldiers ran with,

5

buckets, threw them on ropes into the emerald sea, and then swung their salt contents over the two corpses.

Oh God. They are *alive*. I am an old, old sick woman dying of starvation and disease. I want to die at peace with God. But how can I, when God allows such things? All I can be thankful for is that there is no priest here to tell me lies about suffering and God's will. Those poor young men.

The two bodies made slow curving movements, closer to the last twitches of dead snakes than to any conscious movement of man. If they moaned, it could have been for water or death or defiance. They were beyond all interpreters.

The Japanese officer disembarked and strode briskly down the jetty, the scabbard of his sword bumping every now and then on the uneven planks. Four soldiers with rifles came behind him.

He walked silently across the black sand and halted in front of the guards. Both sides saluted. Then he turned to the groups on either side of the wire. He was neat, with beautiful suede leather boots and gloves, quite unlike the drab guards. The races faced each other, the naked black people of New Ireland, small and scowling. The Chinese, about whom even in this terrible time you could have told nothing. The Europeans, English, German, Dutch and Australian, struck all of them with the raw fact that it had just been proved possible to find something even worse than their daily misery. And the Japanese soldiers, always prepared for anything and thus looking perfectly normal.

The officer from the boat began to speak, in that high-pitched shout that always seemed so unnecessary from those so obviously totally in command. He spoke in English, and one of his men translated into Pidgin for the benefit of the natives.

He was saying something about Japanese justice. 'All you native peoples of New Ireland and New Britain are to see these cruel men,' he pointed to the two burnt bodies that were still now, but alive as could be seen from movements of their mouths. One of them might even have been trying to jeer. 'They are Australians, your former masters who made slaves of you and beat you. They had secret radios and were bringing planes to bomb Japanese soldiers and kill innocent people. Now you see they are not your masters any more. You are now part of Japanese Co-Prosperity Sphere. No more oppression.'

6

He gave some order to the sergeant in charge of the prison guards, who gave some further order to the corporal, who took another man and went to a closed hut. From it he brought two stumbling men in Japanese uniforms.

'All villages along the coast will see these Australians. But you will also see impartiality of Japanese justice. These two soldiers have been interfering with New Ireland women, against the express orders of the Emperor. For this they must pay the penalty, and you will see that Japanese justice applies to all people, including Japanese.'

The men were manhandled into the centre of the patch of grass in front of the village, and made to kneel, heads bowed. The Japanese officer drew out his sword. He jumped slightly into the air with the electric release of all his strength into the sword. A great spurt of blood seemed to spring the head away from the stump of the neck. In a moment the second head was lying on the grass and the two twitching bodies toppled sideways. The black women screamed and ran into the village and a long drawn note came from the men as if they were trying to sing but could not form the words. An Australian woman retched, too far into starvation to vomit anything up.

With a few sharp orders the Japanese officer was back on his boat, the corpses and heads were removed, the prisoners went back to their huts, and the sailors cast off. The boat swung on full rudder and the dangling men jerked sideways. A coconut fell between the huts and the soldiers never noticed the prisoner who darted out, secured it, and dived into Phebe's hut. After a few quick movements he was offering her a drink of the milk and some pieces of the pure white meat. She shook her head. Tears were running unacknowledged down her tight cheekbones. The man nodded, and turning so she could not see, broke off a couple of pieces of the meat and left them by her wooden pillow. She stood still for a few minutes, and then knelt by the palm-leaf mat she used as a bed.

●

These are the names by which I must soothe. The sound of names. Back, back, beyond the surf on the reef. Ralum. The capital of Queen Emma's empire, the jetty and all her trading

7

ships, Stalio's *The Three Cheers*, the two-storeyed trading store with its tower and peaked hat. Simpsonhafen that they called Rabaul, Herbertshöhe that they called Kokopo, Vunapope where the Sisters were and the Mission that was called Sacred Heart Limited, with Jesus Christ owning forty-nine per cent of the shares, how Emma used to tease the Bishop Couppé about that.

Not many people's names can soothe like the names of places. Even a bad place full of fever, Likiliki, cannot kill with cruelty, like that wicked Marquis de Rays, who sent all those poor settlers there.

But it doesn't matter if people aren't good all through, there's usually something worth saving. You know, people are like the plum puddings that my dear friend Mrs Rickard was always making, and when you think of it, what could be more ridiculous than making plum puddings on the Duke of York islands almost within sight of the equator? So people are maybe a little bit ridiculous to begin with, and then the flour is musty with some, especially in the tropics, and the weevils are in others, and there's not enough fruit in others, or the worms are in the fruit, and some have been cooked by life too long and have gone mushy, and others are so stale and hard there's no nourishment in them.

But mostly I think there's a bit of good. Take Emma's husbands and lovers. What a lot of names! Young Forsayth, she really was married to him, they say he was a good man but maybe a bit dull. Then that handsome Englishman, lots of English I don't like, cold and that bad smell under the tips of their noses, but this one I still remember though I was a little bit girl when Emma took him to catch *palolo*, he was an Earl, the Earl of P— I can't remember that name.

Then Steinberger the American, we Samoans loved him whatever worms were in his sultanas. Next that rough brute Farrell, but remember it was he who with Emma began everything here after they left Samoa. No Ralum, no Gunantambu without Tom Farrell. Then Agostino Stalio, ah everything went right with his mixture when they stirred him into life. And last of all Kolbe, whom I could never like, even if he was Emma's legal husband. There were others, I forget now though I could remember if I tried.

They say that when you are starving your memory goes. So

8

even if I do not have enough to eat—that dear man, to leave those pieces of coconut meat for me—even if I know I am starving yet I *won't* starve to death if I can still remember. Isn't that right? If my *memory* hasn't gone, then I can't *really* be starving, even if I am.

We Samoans love food. That love we must live without. Richard once explained to me about a vacuum. There is a German word just the same, but another way of saying it is '*Der leere Raum*', which means 'the empty room'. Now although the room is empty the room still exists, and I am that room. We Samoans have wonderful memories. Even half Samoans, like me, but I inherited a full-Samoan memory. When you have to know all your *ainga*, all your extended family, both sides, the *tame tāne*, the male side, and the *tama fafine*, the female side, back and back and back, then you grow up with a good memory. Especially if you have no written language, no books. Of course the Sisters educated me so I have all the white things to remember too.

I will soothe with the sound of Samoan names. The islands, Upolu and Savai'i and Tutuila. The lovely little islands, Manono and Apolima. Apia, the harbour and the Beach, full of dangers for us girls, my father would say. He lived at Matautu on the east of Apia Bay, but he had land at Mulinu'u where the government is, on the west of the bay. And because my father had taken another woman my mother Le'utu went back to Falealili her village and there I was born under the Ififfi tree.

But I want to remember Emma because Emma was always the strong one. Emma Eliza Coe, born 26 September 1850, Apia, Samoa.

I will call on the dead and they will give life to the living. Or maybe I should say dying. This is 1943, I am eighty. But I am not going to die. Not just yet.

Maybe I was thirty, and Emma forty-something, when we sat on the wicker sofa in the verandah in our muslin dresses with the green parrots on our wrists. They could fly out into the sun over the grass to the lemon trees. But they would come back again. We were still beautiful, so many told us so, but not as beautiful then as all those nieces Emma brought from Samoa. She loved children and young people and Gunantambu was always full of girls. And though every ship that sailed into the South Pacific came to anchor off Ralum, and our parties at Gunantambu went on for days, and it seemed to me that half the holds in Emma's ships were full of champagne for us, yet Emma was very strict. All the girls married well. My girls, Nelly and Dolly, were the wildest of all, I think. German officers and officials, English travellers and Australian explorers, they were all in love with one or all of us.

But Emma was watching over us, as closely as she watched her money. 'Money is like a girl's virtue' she used to say. 'You must assume that every man will do all in his power to steal it, even when smiling and drinking your champagne—watch his feet!'

She inherited her father's shrewdness and his morality. You see, he was of a very old New England family, real Puritan, yet he had six wives, three more or less proper married, three *fa'aa Samoa*, that's Samoan style, and at least eighteen children, but he was a very strict man. He kept a whip for us girls!

I could not love him. I am half Samoan. He was all New England. But he loved Samoa, and so many Samoan women loved him. I can remember him, but I cannot explain him.

Chapter II

JONAS COE

I contracted a kindness for the Samoans when I drifted ashore, attached to a broken spar, at the village of Sapapali'i on the island of Savai'i in 1838, my ship having been wrecked on the reef in a storm of uncommon violence, myself being the cabin boy, aged fifteen years. What wave threw me over the reef I do not remember, but that onshore gale that was the death of our whaling ship was the life of me, for it blew me in the darkness across the lagoon to the white sand at the edge of what transpired to be the village bathing pool, for when I awoke, after lying many hours insensible, I thought myself still dreaming, for I was surrounded by maidens of a most surpassing beauty, amphibious creatures whose flashing brown limbs were encumbered by neither cotton nor calico.

They brought me to the village and made a great fuss of me and fed me with young coconut milk and baked *taro* which has a very pleasant nutty flavour. As they removed my wet clothes and wrapped me in *tapa* cloth I regained my senses with a rapidity that caused an unrestrained amusement amongst the maidens which, strangely enough, is not at all inconsistent with modesty. The beauty and courtesy of these people, from the old *matai*, the chief, down to the children, resolved me instantly to spend the remainder of my days among them after the unspeakable hardships of my three years at sea, and that, by God, have I done, and never regretted my Samoan life.

My father was Edward Morris Coe, attorney-at-law in the town of Troy in the State of New York. My ancestor was Robert Coe who sailed with his family from Ipswich on 30 April, 1634 on the *Francis*, some fourteen years after that better-known ship the *Mayflower*. I was but five years old, and my brother Edward three

11

and my sister Mary Eliza one, when my father died in 1828. My mother also dying not long after, we had the misfortune to be taken to the household of my uncle in Boston, whose purpose it was to whip badness out of us and by the openings in our flesh to let goodness in. By his great kindness I would be allowed to embark on a mercantile career in the city of New York, and by the age of fifty I would have attained to riches and a station in society consonant with that enjoyed by other distinguished members of my Puritan family. There was, for example, an example *ad nauseam*, my great-uncle the Bishop, whose pinched old face revealed perfectly the narrowness of his mind and the chill of his body, resolving me to avoid all contact, save a minimum of form, with the religion known as Christianity, a religion I am sure unknown to its founder. Another example to me was my father's cousin the Admiral, of the same name, Jonas, as myself, and a deal closer to my heart than that pious scoundrel of a Bishop. As a child I rejoiced in one particular exploit of Admiral Jonas' in some war I know not what, somewhere towards South America, when during a sharp encounter with the enemy his supply of cannon-balls became exhausted. Pressed on both sides by hostile ships he bethought himself of the cargo of Dutch cheeses he had taken on board at Curaçao. Substituting these for cannon-balls, he achieved such successful results that his ship was enabled to escape from the enemy.

At the age of twelve I was sent, as threatened, to the mercantile house in New York city, and finding life there more intolerable, if possible, than at my uncle's, I determined to run away to sea. My brother Edward was bent upon accompanying me, but fortunately allowed himself to be persuaded that he was too young. The good fellow gave me all his pocket-money, a kindness I have never forgotten. Later he did go away to sea, and in his early twenties he was awarded the gold medal of the Massachussetts Humane Society for heroism in rescuing the crew of the ship *Ocean Monarch* which had burnt at sea. I mention this to show the quality of my family. I might also mention that amongst these qualities of the Coes is that of virility. Our ancestor Robert the Puritan lived to ninety-two, and when over eighty he married his third wife.

It may not be too much to affirm, that a man who accounts

himself too old for the pleasures of the body which God has given him, puts himself in the way of being too old to live.

To return to the island of Savai'i, I speedily understood, despite my mere fifteen years, that I had come through the hell of that whaling voyage to the certainty of paradise. But the freedom of that paradise was to be denied me. I had been cast ashore, by an extraordinary chance, at the self-same little bay of Sapapali'i where, eight years before, the famous missionary, the Reverend John Williams of the London Missionary Society, had anchored in the ship he had made himself, the *Messenger of Peace*. The *Messenger of Commerce*, it had better been called, for this cunning Williams with his muskets and iron axes and looking-glasses and beads, and dressed in fine strong clothes where the Samoans had only *ti* leaves, clearly was the messenger of a God of bounty. 'Let us embrace this Christianity', said the *matai*, 'I think that the god who gave them all these things must be good, and that his religion must be superior to ours. If we receive this god and worship him, he will in time give us these things as well as them.'

So Williams told a chief who still doubted the blessings of Christianity that European vessels would not come to trade at his harbour unless he and his people became Christians. The Samoans had no powerful priestly class, no temples, no idols, lucky people, and so there was no framework of religion to be overthrown. And Williams was clever, he said that Jehovah would forbid only war and certain dances (though his book of the future had many chapters of prohibitions), and so the Samoans found Christianity an easy and tolerant religion and they accepted it. Little did they know!

Now the two Tongan missionaries at Sapapali'i took me across the strait to Malie on the island of Upolu, where there was a missionary at the head village of Malietoa Vai'inupo, who was also the high chief of Sapapali'i and other villages on Savai'i. In what Europeans would call a war of succession, he had acquired the office of Tafa'ifa, which again is what you might call that of king, though the Samoans did not have such ideas. The ridiculous social system of the Samoans is almost impossible for a European to understand; the fact that after many years I have learned to understand it does not make it any the less ridiculous. On the other hand, I have never known a less disagreeable people. All travellers have remarked on their exquisite courtesy; yet they are always making wars on one another because of their lineage disputes. They lead a life which can only be called communist, yet their old chiefs have absurd privileges and powers.

Be this as it may, I was brought to Malie, (there being no European settlement as yet at Apia), and there I was happy, and the Malietoa family showed great kindness to me. I saw much reason to congratulate myself on the fate to which I had surrendered. I, Jonas Coe, cabin-boy of a whaling ship, accustomed to ship's biscuits and the company of men on board, and twice or thrice in three years the violent debauchery ashore, was now fed on coconuts, breadfruit, bananas, *taro*, fish, lobsters and pigs at feast times. I, who had slept in the fetid air below decks of a rolling ship, now stretched on soft mats over a smooth coral floor in a *fale*, that curved Samoan hut with open sides through which the cool night wind blows, and out of which a young man can steal at night to the shores of the lagoon where all is made welcome. I from New England, who had shame and chastity beaten into me, spent my days and nights among people the missionaries had not yet corrupted, who saw no meaning in shame and no virtue in chastity, except for the *taupo* the village virgin, but who were withal happily living in family relationships of great complexity. They were pure in heart with each other because they did not think the body impure.

Malietoa was an excellent gentleman, who made me welcome and, as I was an educated lad, asked me many questions and seemed pleased with my answers, and so made me a kind of tutor for the children of Malie. But if there was teaching to be done, the missionaries wished to have the handling of it, and they wished to live their stiff lives apart and did not approve of those who like myself were only too happy to live *fa'a Samoa*, Samoan style. Some other of my old shipmates who had escaped the wreck were also given shelter by Malietoa. The missionaries now attacked him for sheltering what they described as a farrago of teachers and runaway sailors. I suppose if a farrago can have two halves, then I was both. An American ship chancing to anchor at this time in what later became the port of Apia, the missionaries seized the opportunity to acquaint the captain of the presence on Upolu and Savai'i of the survivors of the shipwreck, and we were bundled aboard, those of us they could catch, and that was the end of my free and happy life on the Navigators' Archipelago, to give Samoa its old European name.

It took me eight years of unprofitable wandering to return. In 1846 I was sailing the Pacific in an American trader bound for the port of Apia, Upolu, where by now the London Missionary Society, Catholic and Methodist missionaries, and other commercial folk, had established trading stores. In the month of August, 1846, I landed from my ship at Apia, and went to live for a few weeks at Mulinu'u Point, at the western end of Apia bay, in the hut of a white man generally addressed as Big Leg Johnnie, for he was an Englishman much afflicted with the elephantiasis, so much so he was unable to walk about much. At that time there were only two villages in the bay of Apia, the one at Mulinu'u and the other the present Apia village proper. From the fresh water stream of Mulivai to Mulinu'u was all overgrown with low wild shrub, and pandanus and coral trees and beach *mahoe* and a few of the majestic *talie* tree. Mulinu'u was the abode of innumerable crabs and rats, as was also Matautu at the other end of the bay, though in that place wild pigeons in their season were also very plentiful. At Mulinu'u the coconut trees planted by the Samoans were still quite young, only a few were full-grown and bearing nuts. The other Samoan villages were all inland, and thus there was much uninhabited beach around Apia harbour, and that is how the Europeans came to settle there. Some bought land from the Samoans, which is very difficult because so many Samoans own the one piece of land, and others got permission to live or establish a store. Runaway convicts from Australia (the worst riff-raff, these) put up huts not fit for pigs and snorted their drunken way through their empty days, but they were not typical of the beachcombers, for many of these were gentlemen, and wished for nothing but to live in peace with a Samoan girl and watch the comings and goings of the harbour, where already by 1846 some seventy ships visited in the course of a year, mostly American.

I had the gratification to be a beachcomber, being a gentleman and having brought with me a very little money, but enough withal to live on. But I lacked the temperament, being unsuited to idleness, which calls for certain spiritual qualities and I am a

15

material man. But also I lacked one essential qualification—a female companion. Despite my years at sea I was not interested in those of my own sex, though there were remarkable opportunities for those that way inclined, for some of the most beautiful Samoan girls in Apia were quite otherwise when their *lava lavas* were lifted. This is an ancient custom in many islands of the Pacific, for young men to dress as girls and indeed think of themselves as girls, and there is no prejudice against them or talk of filthy vice, despite the efforts of the missionaries to destroy such iniquitous tolerance of iniquity.

I returned therefore to my old house at Malie village, after some weeks of helping Big Leg Johnnie with his trading activities. Vai'inupo had died in 1841, and on his deathbed he had expressed the wish that the four titles of the Tafa'ifa should not again be united in the one person. By this he hoped to avoid future wars of succession. But it was already obvious that a civil war would soon break out. I should explain that so-called civilized nations might do well to copy the wars of the Samoans. A few heads are taken, but the rules of the conflict are always that not too many warriors should be killed, and no side takes unfair advantage of the other.

My old friends all welcomed me in the village by the lagoon. A Samoan village literally welcomes you with open arms, for all is open and all curved, the *fales* themselves with their oval shape and curved roof, no walls but rolled-up mats, curving out from the house of the *matai* and the ceremonial houses in the middle. The girls I had known, after eight years, were grown-up mothers of children, though no less beautiful and full of song and laughter. The Samoan I had learnt soon came back to me, and I could join in the jokes and the stories. People who think that Polynesian girls are beautiful but dumb are only those who cannot talk to them. They are highly intelligent, and very witty, and to someone brought up in Boston, wonderfully bawdy. Yet they are never improper or coarse. It contributes greatly to a man's understanding of the world to live amongst those who have been brought up in entirely different concepts from those one accepts from one's own upbringing as normal. The cardinal sin of the white man in his colonies, and in other regions of the world which in his ignorance he calls primitive, is to imagine that he is superior because he knows what the natives do not, and because his customs are different. He should remember that they also know what he does not, and that their customs may have a dignity and joy which his have lost.

I was happy amongst Malietoa Moli's people, and I especially liked his little son Laupepa, born in 1841. One day it was suggested that I accompany a party up through the green mountains behind Apia to a village called Faleaʻlili on the south coast of Upolu, the purpose of the expedition, what the Samoans call a *Malaga*, being to pay a ceremonial visit on some Malietoa cousins.

And that is how I met Le'utu Taletale, who was my wife for many years and who gave me eight children, of whom the second, Emma Eliza, was, I confess, my favourite. We were married all shipshape and legal by my friend the Reverend George Pritchard, but that was the short part of proceedings, for I was marrying into what Europeans would call the royal family, and so there was a prodigious wedding feast, and I was now established and accepted in Samoan life, and all the more so for being a gentleman in my own right. The Samoans are proud, but they have no racial resentments. One of the pleasures of Apia has always been the lack of racial tension. Perhaps one reason for this was that for many years there were no, or very few, white women living there. The Europeans all had Samoan wives, legal like mine or *fa'a Samoa*, and I should add that for the Samoans there is no such creature as an illegitimate child; whoever the mother or the father, all children are equally welcome. Into this free and natural society, yes, and this is a paradox, truly moral society, comes a poker-backed white woman, all whipped up in whalebone, and in no time she is trying to persuade everyone that the Samoans are naked, immoral savages, and those who cohabit with Samoan women are living in sin. Of course, it almost always happens that the first white woman is a missionary's wife, and that makes it all the worse.

As I could speak Samoan, and was married to a Samoan, I was the ideal person to act as intermediary between the Samoans and the traders. I was of assistance to both sides, for not only could I bring a trader in touch with new customers but also I could explain to the customers why they should not pay a thousand per cent mark-up on an axe. The Samoans do not understand about profit. I was especially helpful because the traders wanted to buy as well as sell, in particular commodities such as coconut oil or cotton. In Apia there were no duties or import restrictions of any kind, and it was soon possible for traders to make good money there.

But my function, as I saw it, was more than a mercenary one. The traders and beachcombers, and you could say I was a little of each as well as a lot more, lived along the Beach by courtesy of the Samoans. They came from America, Australia, England or Germany but they had no protection from their countries, and even had they been promised it, it should be remembered that it took four months for a letter to travel from Apia to Washington. So it was essential for the foreigners on the Beach to respect the customs of the Samoans and not interfere with them. This respect, alas, was lacking in the missionaries, although some, like Reverend George Brown, the Wesleyan, must be accounted exceptions. It is paradoxical that the missionaries, especially those learning the language of the native peoples, and translating the Bible etc., are welding link on link to the chain, which is to bind all people in social intercourse, and yet they regard the native as inferior. What is more, and I find this an entertainment, is that they regard the other christian sects not only as inferior but as wicked, the LMS despises the Catholic, the Catholic looks down on the Wesleyan, and so on. Now the Samoans are blessed with a great amount of rude intelligence, and they look on these differences and contentions, and observe the missionaries' desire for the aggrandizement and advancement of their own particular doctrine in contradiction to the advancement of Christianity. Thus as far as my experience goes, and I have looked well into the matter, there is not one Samoan in a thousand that is truly converted to Christianity.

Moreover, the Samoans, who had strictly ordered lives of decorum and dignity, whatever talk there be of 'heathen licentiousness', had only to look on certain elements among the Europeans on the Beach to see how evilly nominal Christians could behave. The chiefs did not punish transgressors. A European who ignored Samoan custom was regarded as someone of no breeding who could not be expected to know any better.

For myself, being embarked upon a household, and having a proper understanding of both the European and Samoan way of doing things, it became essential to bring up my children in the utmost strictness. I had too many opportunities of observing the results of 'going native'. Though accepted by the Samoans, I was not a Samoan. So I determined that my children should be American. Too much *fa'a Samoa* is all very well for a young man who is single, but not for a man with the responsibilities of a family.

From my marriage with Le'utu, I begat Maria, born in 1849; Emma, born in 1850; Edward, born in 1852; Mary, born in 1854 who died when she was only four years old; William, born in 1857; John, born in 1859; Ann, born in 1861 who died as an infant; and Phebe, born in 1863. I had ten other children I acknowledged from my other five wives, but they need not detain us here.

At four years old Emma was already a girl of exceptional intelligence and beauty, with a lovely brown skin, like a southern European, a shade lighter than most Samoans. On this matter of colour I would like to add that the Samoans, in common with other Polynesians, have the most beautiful of all skins, not pale and blotched like we Europeans, and eminently fitted to go bare in the sun of the tropics which turns us Europeans red and raw.

However, I was not going to have my children, whatever my pleasure in the beauty of the Samoans, running around barefooted and unclothed to be called naked savages by some Sydney barmaid giving herself airs as the wife of a trader. In my house I always saw to it that my children were properly dressed, and wearing shoes. They had to be in bed by eight o'clock, and they were not allowed out to dancing or parties unless with respectable married people. As for discipline, I made frequent use of a horsewhip. Children must learn right and wrong, and it is a father's duty to chastise them. In a Samoan village the *matai*, the chief of the household, has authority over all his extended family, but the younger children are brought up and disciplined, such as it is, by the older girls. A girl of six will look after her brother of two and her sister of three. There is merit in this, and Emma was always particularly good at looking after the younger ones, but I was the one who kept order. Le'utu did not like me to use the whip, but she never questioned my authority.

Fortunately for me, the French Catholic Sisters had established a good school near Apia. The Marist missionaries had come to

Samoa in 1845, and although (or perhaps because) they had a patron of high rank, Mata'afa Fagamanu, they had by the mid-1850s only about five hundred followers. Yet the Fathers and the Sisters were highly educated people of gentle birth, unlike most of the Protestants, who were of the level of a grocer. Now not only could they provide the best education for my children, but it amused me to send them into the house of anti-Christ and to think what would be said amongst my Episcopalian relatives in Boston, which could have been much the same as was being said by the LMS in Apia.

Emma, and the other children, were well grounded in education by the Sisters, but the facilities were of course limited, whereas by the time Emma had reached ten years of age it seemed to me that her possibilities might well be unlimited. She was already attracting attention both from the Samoans and the licentious reprobates along Apia Beach, and I feared she would have a roving eye. I was not going to lose my beauty to a grog-keeper or a Samoan villager. I used the whip, but for real safety I looked across the water. Before her eleventh birthday I sent her to Australia, to Subiaco Convent on the Parramatta River.

Chapter III

EMMA

I loved my father, the old rascal. Sometimes I wonder why, because he was very harsh with us. He'd call us into the parlour if we'd been naughty, and he'd be standing in front of the big bookcases, all those books he never read, and make us stand in front of the big mirror between the bookcases. 'Emma', he'd say, 'look at yourself in the mirror, you little savage.' There was a little girl with a hibiscus flower in her hair, a white dress muddied and ripped at the shoulder, and bare feet. Undoubtedly me.

'Emma Eliza Coe', just in case I didn't recognize her. 'Look at yourself. I'm not going to have you grow up a Samoan savage. You are going to be a young American lady. And I heard you down by the river swearing. I heard you call Edward *Puaa elo*. What does *puaa elo* mean in English?'

'Stinking pig.'

'Would you call Edward a stinking pig in English?'

Silence.

'And I heard you say to Mary Ann *"Ou te tao oe I le umu"*. What does that mean in English?'

'I shall cook you in the oven.'

'Samoans are *not cannibals*! In any case you are not a Samoan. And I heard you say to baby William, and I heard him screaming, you said *"Aia ea oa a Moso"*. And what does that mean in English?'

'Moso shall eat you.'

'And who is Moso?'

'Moso is an *aitu*, I mean a spirit, who kills and eats people, particularly children.'

'Particularly children. Poor little William. Bend over the sofa.'

This was the worst moment, as in the bottom of the big mirror you could see father's legs crossing the room, and then the cupboard open, and though you could not see the horsewhip, you knew that he had it in his hand, that tapering plaited leather devil of a whip, and then you would see the legs coming back, and stop behind you, and . . . ouch! I can still remember how it hurt and how *mad* I was that I couldn't help crying. But usually as I ran out of the house afterwards I was thankful that he had not come home half an hour earlier when he might have caught us all with all our Samoan friends swimming naked in the river. What did he mean that I was not Samoan!

Father was very, very regular. When I was about eight we moved from the old weather board house (though we really spent most of our time in the *fales* at the back in the garden) into this beautiful new white house that had come all the way from San Francisco. A portable house, they called it, it all came ready in sections to put together, on the boat from San Francisco. The floors were so elegant, narrow boards all fitting snug together. And the wall papers; different in each room. I remember the one in the parlour was white with a little gold pattern running down it. And when there was new paper to be hung we would mix up flour and boiling water for the glue. Us girls used to keep the house clean, take one room each and swap about.

I was saying, Father was so regular. Our house was on Matautu, and his office was across the river in Apia village. Early every morning he would come and wake up us children, and say 'Come on, come on, come and have your fruit,' and in a little corner on one of the verandahs he would have ripe bananas, mangoes, pawpaws, (Samoans used to feed them to the pigs but Father said they were good for us to eat), oranges and even apples, sometimes, and he would say 'Come on, come on', very briskly and then we would go and have our breakfast. He would leave at eight o'clock precise and not come home till four. So unless we were with the Sisters at the Convent we would have the whole day to ourselves, mother never used to worry us. We'd race into our rooms and tear off those dresses and shoes, then put on *lava lavas* and thread frangipani flowers and hang them round our necks, or maybe *laumaile*, sweet smelling leaves, and put hibiscus in our hair and run off into the bush. We'd make our own little *umus*, ovens, and cook breadfruit or *taro*, or climb palm trees and drink fresh milk from the nuts. We'd swim in the river or the lagoon, we were as happy in the water as on land, never got tired, I could swim for miles.

There were always lots of chiefs coming to see my father, and we knew all their sons and they were our sweethearts, the *manias*, that's the leading young men of the village. There were plenty who wanted to marry me. The chiefs wanted to get my lineage, they knew I was a Malietoa and had rights to land. But Father would roar at them and say 'What! Why in the hell do you think I go to all the trouble to bring up my children properly? Just to let them marry a Samoan and become Samoans again?' What used to make me laugh was that the Samoans would talk just the same, about their high blood and the ordinary Europeans. And they'd look down on other people from the Pacific, even Tongans, and only a street girl would marry a Solomon Islander or a Fijian.

Yes, I loved my father, although he beat me. I was always his favourite, he called me Princess, but it was not that, it was because I could make him laugh when no one else could, it was because though he did not read books himself he showed them all to me and encouraged me to read, that's why I'm such a great reader, everything from Schopenhauer to Schmidt on tropical agriculture. And we would sing together at the piano, one of the Sisters taught me, I was good at the piano, and though he was given to shouting at people he had a clear singing voice.

And I also loved Father because he showed me about another sort of book. Even when I was a little girl he could see I was interested in business, in his land deals, his buying and selling, his schooners that traded around the islands, his handling of the Samoan chiefs who came to him with their problems and needs. It amused him to let me listen while I would pretend to be playing in the corner, and then he and I would play a game afterwards.

'Well, Emma, what did you think of Dr Aaron Van Camp, United States Commercial Agent?'

'I don't think he's really a Doctor but I'm sure he's a bad man.'

This was accounted a triumph of perspicacity, as I was only five years old, and Van Camp was indeed a fake doctor, allegedly of dentistry, and he had just been trying to sell Father a ship which previously in his official capacity he had condemned and ordered to be sold, so that he himself could buy it.

I met so many types and races, and learned to watch their faces and see their motives. No one knew more than I about the *Papalangi*, the foreigners on Apia Beach. I could see how John Williams, son of the famous missionary, who was a trader and was also US Commercial Agent (which was like being Consul) made money through all his contacts with missionaries, and that missionaries created in the natives more of a hunger for goods than for God. I could see how August Unshelm, who was both Consul for Hamburg and local manager for the great trading firm of Goddefroy (a nice combination), was much more efficient than the English or the Americans, and that their big station at Matafele, on the eastern side of Apia Bay, was going to be the most important depot in Samoa.

There was an on-and-off civil war in Samoa from before I was born, from 1848 to 1857, and I could see how Father made money selling muskets to both sides, although we were Malietoas. Then, when the Samoans needed muskets and had no money or goods, they could offer to sell him land. That way he got a lot of land. And one thing he impressed was always to get a written contract, get a clear title to the land. In the early days Samoans often let Europeans use their land, even build a house on it, and they'd take some money or goods for it, but they didn't mean to sell it. Father never made this mistake, and he also made sure that the Samoan had the right to sell the land, as land belongs to families in Samoa. Finally, he had his land purchases registered in a consulate so the records would be secure. All these were lessons I never forgot.

My life as a girl in Apia was very happy, *fa'a Samoa* in the bush or the water when Father was at his office, and lots to learn and enjoy when I accompanied him to the office. They were two lives, but I could live and enjoy both.

And then he sent me to Subiaco Convent, Parramatta. All the way to Australia! I was in despair. I would be all alone, all dressed up, Sydney would be icy cold, and I would never be able to swim in the Parramatta River with a flower in my hair. I had seen a couple of Australian women. All they would ever put in their hair was a great long pin you could skewer a pig on. And Australia was full of convicts. Runaway Australian convicts had been the worst ruffians on Apia Beach.

On the ship sailing to Sydney I began to cheer up. I always love sea voyages, I'm never sick, I love wind and waves, and the sea teaches us two things, how to be strong and how to yield. Stand at the stern, and then stand at the bow, see how the copper sheath of the cutwater wounds the sea, and how already by the stern it is healing up again, the sea is too big to accept misfortune. Then when the sea shows its strength, and there is nothing in the world stronger than the sea, in storms or surf, it is only the surface of the sea that is angry, deep down it remains calm, so it never loses dignity, control. You can dive under the white water of the surf and it is green, still and clear just a few feet down.

So I stood on the ship going to Sydney, not yet eleven years old, and thought why be angry and feel betrayed. What am I, *really*? A half-caste girl on the Beach at Apia. Maybe some nice men there, but I don't want to be some small trader's wife counting out Bolivian dollars or whatever the Germans are telling us to use. Samoan men are beautiful, but I'm not going back to being Samoan. I want knowledge and power and wealth, and they've got to be my own. I don't want a rich husband. If he could buy me, well then he could sell me. My husband is going to have a rich wife. And knowledge is like money, you can and must use other people's, but only if you have your own, and to get your own you must start getting it early, and hang on to it.

Sure I was miserable at being packed off to Subiaco. But I was going to learn everything I could from those Sisters, how to be a lady, all those things I could not learn from my mother. For many years I kept the 'Introduction', as it was quaintly called, the sort of Prospectus from Subiaco that Father proudly showed me.

The Benedictine Monastry of Subiaco is pleasantly situated at the end of the Parramatta River, on an extent of land fronting a peninsula. The Monastry was founded and the Community formally installed by Archbishop Polding on February 2nd, 1849, but the School was not opened till March, 1851. The grounds, which comprise about 150 acres, are well laid out in gardens, lawns, shrubberies, a large tennis court, shady avenues, and orchards. Knots of bush lands, etc., are to be met with on this magnificent estate. Through the vista of ornamental trees glimpses and pretty peeps of the river are discernible. The large grounds, known as the vineyard, are fully taken advantage of by the young lady boarders at holiday time. A large number of cows and poultry are kept, and, therefore, an ever bountiful supply of provisions is assured. The ruddy complexions of the boarders testify to the good treatment and pure air which are here enjoyed. The health of the pupils is ordinarily so perfect that a doctor is almost an entire stranger. The class of education imparted at the Monastry is of a high order. Indeed, many of the leading Catholic ladies of the Australian States received their education there. The course of studies comprises all the usual requirements of an English education, Latin, French, Music (piano and violin), Singing, Drawing, Painting, and plain and fancy needlework.

I should explain now about Le'utu, my mother. She was a wonderful woman. The two most remarkable women I've known, and the two I've loved most, were Le'utu and my sister Phebe, Le'utu's eighth and last child. Le'utu was a Malietoa, we don't have kings and queens in Samoa like they do in Tonga or Europe, but Malietoa, Mata'afa, Tamasese, you might say these are our royal families. So she had great dignity and pride, she was a true Samoan and considered herself inferior to no one. How some foreigners who came to Apia used to hate Samoan pride! They thought the 'natives' should recognize their inferior place. Samoans! Inferior!

But Le'utu was a true Samoan in every way. She was so pretty, and gay, only seventeen when Father married her. Dance, you should have seen her dance the *siva*! Father was always making us Americans, with our buttons and sleeves and shoes and stockings and sitting down to table with knife and fork. But Le'utu was not going to let us forget we were Samoans. The missionaries had done their best to stamp out the *siva*, oh how those folk do hate anything to do with *sex*! And dancing, real dancing, is to do with nothing else. The missionaries said that Samoan dances were lascivious and the gestures indecent and the clothing, or lack of it, indecent. But that's what it meant to *them*, and they were terrified of what the dances might stir in their black trousers. For us they were a celebration of all that we thought perfectly pure and natural. At least they were to Le'utu, but not to Father when he was being the stern white paterfamilias. It was the same with food or with dancing, with Father it was just plain boiled beef and *taro*. My mother taught us how to cook all the Samoan dishes, though I never could cook myself, I left all that to Phebe, I love eating but not all that squeezing and pounding and rolling. Oh for a dish of squid in coconut milk! I knew I'd never get that at Subiaco Convent boarding school for young ladies. What I did get was indeed all those things that Le'utu could not teach me. Fine sewing, for example. I remember, long afterwards, when I was living in Apia again, little Phebe just sitting on the floor and watching me with my needle, and taking the cotton reels out of my wicker work basket and running them through her fingers. Even the way I used to bite off the thread, 'That's perfect!', she'd say.

After Samoa, Subiaco was a prison, but it was a prison that opened its doors. It had been the grand house of an Australian pioneer sheep-owner and vigneron and business man, he had the hilarious name of Hannibal Macarthur. Poor fellow, I believe his bank failed and he went bust, and that's how the Catholics got the house. It was lovely, fine old stone, (I'd never lived in a stone house before), lawns sweeping down to the Parramatta River, a drive of camphor laurels and pines, and big grounds with a paling fence around to keep the nuns in, or the amorous Australians out. But there was a big white gate in the fence, and they'd unlock that to let us go for picnics. 'Be good, girls, and don't tear your dresses,' Sister Mary Benedict would call out as we spilled out the gate into the overgrown terraces of the old vineyards. Oh the freedom of those picnics, the wild flowers (Australian wildflowers, all sharp and spiky and aromatic, not at all like our lush tropical flowers), the gum trees and the old pear tree by the creek where we'd light our fire (when it was safe, they have terrible bush fires in Australia) and boil what they call a billy, a tin of water you throw the tea into. We used to toss pancakes in a huge pan, and the little girl whose job it was to keep the fire going would always put some green wood in and the smoke would make your eyes run. But happy tears.

It was a regular prison back inside the gates at Subiaco, but the Sisters saw that I was interested in figures and in reading and they helped me. Business and book-keeping and so on weren't quite correct for young ladies then, but the Sister who did the school accounts used to show me how to manage books, double book-keeping and all. As for real books, the Mother Superior said to me 'Emma, if once your perceive a book is bad, quite unfit for a girl to read, you will shut it up immediately. No amount of amusement can make up for soiling your mind.' Nevertheless, I *was* allowed to read some real books, 'lots more than boring devotional rubbish. The lives of the saints put most girls off for life. And I can tell you that I was put off Christianity for life by having to recite, all together girls, at first and last assembly every day, the Lord's Prayer, Hail Mary, Apostle's Creed, Acts of Faith, Prayers for the Archbishop and the Queen, and the Faithful Departed. The Unfaithful Departed, I called myself when I left Subiaco.

I must own that when I left Subiaco Boarding School for Young Ladies, I left under a cloud. I had expected the white Australian Young Ladies to scoff at me because I was part Samoan, a half-caste. Father had warned me of the possibility. Attempts to import Pacific islanders into Australia as 'labourers, admittedly of a black, cannibal type, of course not Polynesians, had led to outcries of 'Preserve Australia for the white man.' 'No black, brown, yellow or brindle people.' I was undoubtedly brindle. Although fairer than most Samoans, I was very dusky compared with my school mates whose complexions were always carefully guarded from the burning Australian sun (which for much of the year I found freezing). But to my surprise there was no prejudice against me, in fact they seemed quite proud of their Pacific island savage, their Yankee Kanaka, and other names they had for me. One of the girls even made up a rude jingle about me, which she called:

> A Warning to the Gentlemen of New South Wales
>
> Beware, young man, that pretty Yankee,
> Who, just before you, dropped her hanky.
> If you pick it up to give it back her,
> You'll find she is a black Kanaka.

The brother of this girl, a handsome young fellow too, was so intrigued by the subject of this ditty that on one of our rare expeditions to Sydney town he arranged it that I was lost in the crowd at the concert we were attending. That was the first time I was kissed by an Australian, in what I think was a broom cupboard by the downstairs steps of the concert hall. I can never hear Mendelssohn's *Songs Without Words* without being reminded of the occasion. The young man was disappointed that I was not more dusky. The good Sisters never suspected anything, but praised the Lord for my safe return.

It was in my third year at Subiaco that I caused the trouble that terminated my school career. We had been that afternoon to dancing class, a species of torture I was almost beyond enduring any longer. A quadrille was the extent of our gaiety. The Sisters employed two old ladies to teach us who still (in 1864!) considered the waltz a licentious German depravity, and a polka Bohemian in spirit as well as origin. We danced with each other, of course, no boys were allowed.

That evening I said to the girls that I would show them a real dance. In no time my accomplices had stolen some coconut oil from the kitchens, some ferns and leaves and berries from the garden, and a red hibiscus — yes, how astonishing, it really was a red hibiscus. I showed the girls how to make a *lava lava* from the leaves, and to make a crown from the ferns and to plait the berries into a necklace. The materials were not quite authentic, but they were well enough. Then the girls rubbed my body with the oil and fastened the *lava lava* around my waist. For a drum we used the Sister's sewing box which had a cover of vellum painted with a scene representing the Blessed Virgin Mary ascending into heaven. I had previously instructed a friend of mine how to beat a drum, which she did tolerably well. I should explain now about the dormitory. It was enormous, with a long, barrel wooden ceiling above plain brick walls, and a huge, high framework above the beds supporting the mosquito nets behind which we disappeared, as into tents on poles, at night. At the end of the dormitory was a life-sized statue of the Virgin. Before this, by the light of a lamp, I began to dance in front of my colleagues, the young ladies of Subiaco.

Sometimes you are inspired with the certainty that you are beautiful, and it was so that night. It is not vanity, but celebration. I was thirteen, but amongst my contemporaries I looked eighteen, in fact my breasts and my hips were then at their most perfect shape. I think my shoulders and my face were much improved later. I had taught the girls how to *lomilomi*, how to massage, and they had worked the oil into my bones and joints so that my arms and legs flowed into the air and did all that my back and my thighs asked them to. I began quite chastely with the pigeon dance, calling to them softly and wooing with my breasts, until the circle of shining-eyed girls became men, it was Samoa on the coral sand under the faint shaking of palm leaves, and the dance changed, I was rapt into the frenzy of what I did not as yet fully understand but which I instinctively knew. As I shook with passion, my legs opening and closing, my curved arms drawing my lover into me, the *lava lava* flying out horizontally from my hips—into the dormitory walked Sister Monica, the Mother Superior. I did not even notice her. They told me afterwards that she had called my name several times before I heard the words 'Emma. *Emma*. You little *heathen!*'

The first thing my father knew (there were no telegrams in those days) was that a ship from Sydney arrived in Apia in August 1864 bearing a letter from the Mother Superior of Subiaco Convent Boarding School for Young Ladies, and an ex-young lady called Emma Eliza Coe.

I knew what was coming. The horse whip. Do you know, it seems odd, but I was rather looking forward to it. But things turned out quite differently. Father didn't seem cross with me at all. 'I was going to take you away in any case, and send you to your Uncle Edward's in San Francisco', he said, but almost absent-mindedly. We were waiting in the buggy by the river, for the ferry to cross to Matautu. 'You've got a little sister', he said suddenly, 'Phebe, born two months ago. Yes, your mother is well, I think she's well.'

'What do you mean, you *think?*' I couldn't bear it if anything had happened to Le'utu.

We were rattling along the coral road just before the house.

'She's not at home. Whoa! Whoa there!' He stopped the buggy at the front door and blurted out, somewhere between a roar and a gasp, really a ludicrous noise. 'Actually Emma my girl you have *three* new sisters. Yes, dammit, I said *three.*'

A very handsome young woman, taller and heavier than Le'utu, wearing a striped silk dress, came down the steps holding a girl of a year or so. 'Emma, this is your step-mother Saefaolu, from

Vaimoso village, and this is your little sister Mary Ann. That one on the steps is Caroline.'

I was always very quick with figures. Caroline looked to be about two and a half. Mary Ann, a little under a year. And my baby sister Phebe two months old. I ran right through the house, past the *fales*, through the gate in the fence, out into the hiding green of the bush and down to the river.

My brothers and sisters found me there. But by that time I had finished weeping. Some old Samoan friends had already seen me and come to talk to me. After all, it *was* Samoa, and not Sydney. Caroline and Mary Ann looked dear little girls. I didn't even mind the look of Sa, as my step-mother was familiarly called. All I wanted to do was to go and see Le'utu, my mother, wherever she was, and my baby sister Phebe. As for Father. Oh, Father! No wonder he had looked embarrassed. Father! You old *reprobate*! Why should I stop loving you?

Chapter IV

_____•◆•_____

REVEREND GEORGE BROWN

Satupa'itea, Savai'i

August 16, 1864

Reverend J. D. Frith,
Balmain,
New South Wales.

My dear James,

As you know, the mission is on the south coast of the Island, towards the eastern end. Looking from the slight elevation of our house along the coast in the evening, an uncommonly pretty sight presents itself. The coral sand is blinding white broken by the Shadows of the Palm Trees, and this makes the outcrops of volcanic rock seem even more black as they disappear into the milky water. The Natives keep pigs in little wooden Cages over the shallow sea, usually sows about to farrow, while other pigs run happily through the village. The open grass area outside the _fales_ is kept beautifully mown by men, women and little children, all wielding alarmingly long knives. Then the women regularly sweep the Grass with twig brooms, cleaning off everything from leaves to pig dung. The Samoans are a very clean People. They particularly love flowers, and plant hedges of hibiscus or croton around the _fales_, and frangipani and red and yellow acacias and many more whose names I have still to learn. The _fales_ sit on platforms of black rock, the roofpoles holding up the neatest curved thatch under which you can see the exquisite network of Beams and Laths on which the whole things depends, all bound together of course without benefit of a single nail.

We are very happy here. The Samoans are as handsome and

32

lovable a people as I have ever known, and more polite I think than any other people. They are polite in Language as well as Manner, and I fear most of the Europeans they meet must appear intolerably crude to them. I am learning the Language, or rather Languages, for there are different words according to whether you are addressing someone of high or low birth, and to make it even more complex, they in reply will speak deprecatingly of themselves, their family or possessions. For instance, if addressing a high chief you may refer to his wife as *masiofo* (queen) or *le tamitai* (lady), but in referring to her he will use the common word *ava*, or even refer to her as 'the woman of the family'.

In the highly regulated system of family life that is the basis of Samoan society, everything is shared. For a Christian observer it is very notable that the sin of Envy does not exist among them. For a Samoan the unpardonable sin is to be mean or stingy, especially with food. There are of course other sins amongst them, not only those of the flesh which so much worry my brethren and those of other sects, but I own that I think there are other sins worse. I am fortunate in having Mrs Brown with me and enjoying a happy married life.

You speak of criticism in Australia that the chief function of missionaries in the Pacific islands is not to convert the native to Christianity but to teach them that one sect is right and all the others wrong. I am no Bigot, but I will admit that there *are* some, in fact many, amongst the LMS and the Roman Catholics. Only recently, on Upolu, an LMS congregation burnt down a Methodist village. And there was the case of a Tuamasaga man who was told to pay compensation for killing a neighbour's pig. He refused, saying 'I am LMS and that was a Catholic pig.' No, I am no Bigot, but one must defend the Truth. Only recently I spoke severely to Mr J. M. Coe, a trader and land-owner, a good man in many ways, who has recently been appointed US Commercial Agent in Apia. He sent his daughter Emma to the Catholic Boarding School near Sydney, and some of his other children to the Marist school near Apia. I asked him to consider his own early education, the religion in which his Parents had trained him (especially as his Uncle is an Episcopalian Bishop), and the blessings he had received from a free Gospel, before he lightly allowed the children whom God had given him to be trained and brought up in the soul-enslaving Superstitions of Popery. I am no Bigot—I do however say without fear of contradiction that their System is a vile one.

If you can get me some real good *Australian* wine I would be obliged if you would send me one or two dozen. Some that will keep when opened will be the best. I have sent for some Taper Collars to Hordern but if you can get me some low Linen ones *good*, with Cravat ends size 15 please. Those Hordern ones sent last year are too high on the neck and I don't like the shape. The West End or Yorkshire shape like yours would do. Would you also order for us a few Tins of Sugar Lollies. We do not want Peppermint or any of that kind of Lolly but some of those Candy ones without any very strong flavour. We want them to buy things with as we sell no Fish Hooks here.

I am reading Max Müller *The Science of Language* and Lecky's *History of European Morals*. Could you please ask Robertson to send me:

Buckle	*History of Civilization in England*
Lecky	*Rise and Influence of Rationalism in Europe*
Froude	*Short Studies in Great Subjects*
Bishop Elleston	*Lectures on the Life of our Lord*
Milman	*History of Christianity*

Did you hear that Unshelm, the representative in Apia of Goddefroy, was lost at sea in a hurricane? They say that his successor, Theodore Weber, is a very remarkable and energetic man. I think the Germans will soon be the most powerful of the foreigners in Samoa, though it must be remembered that it is not a Nation that is represented in Apia, but only the City of Hamburg, so that the only warships that come here are from Britain and the United States. On their visits, these warships are called on to execute a kind of summary justice on behalf of both European residents and Samoans.

August 18: Mr J. M. Coe arrived today in his schooner and much to my surprise came ashore with a beautiful young girl of fourteen or so, whom he introduced as his daughter Emma, just come from the Papist school near Sydney. He is a blunt man and without further ado asked us if she could stay with us

34

for a while as he was on a trading voyage to Nive which is some 400 miles away among the Cook Islands. We were rather startled at the suddenness of the application, but after conferring together and asking God's advice we decided to receive her as we were unwilling to compel him to take her with him on such a long Voyage and amongst strange Natives. No agreement was made. He simply left her until he returned. He sailed away in the evening. I may say that she would happily have gone with him, protesting that she had no fears either of long sea voyages or strange natives. I believe her.

Apparently she is to be sent to his brother Edward, who is a man of substance in San Francisco, to be further educated there, let us hope not to be further enmeshed in the toils of Popery. We could understand Mr Coe's reluctance to leave her in Apia. He has with some irregularity taken himself a new Wife, the Reverend George Pritchard who married Mr Coe and his first Wife, Le'utu, having now divorced them. Mr Coe does not want to leave Emma at such a juncture at his house, nor does he wish to expose her to the Dangers and Temptations of life on Apia Beach. And I can see why. She is an exceedingly attractive young lady, outstandingly intelligent, and capable of a brisk Conversation on subjects I had not thought she would have learned of in a Convent School. She had by no means accepted the account of religious and moral History which the Nuns had attempted to foist upon her. But it was her knowledge of, and grasp of Commerce that particularly surprised us. She was well aware of the world shortage of Cotton brought about by the American Civil War, and she knew the real reason why her father was voyaging to Nive, which was not for Trade but to bring back Niveans and Raratongans on a one-year contract to work on his Cotton Plantations. (You see, Samoans will not work, they are not interested in working for wages.) What is more, she knew that Williams, the British Consul, who has about seventy acres planted in Cotton was paying ten dollars per month with rations, and that this was far too much, and that her father was hoping to sign contracts for five dollars per month with rations.

It is very surprising that a young lady of so sprightly a Disposition, blessed by God with such good looks, should be able to discuss the effects on the religion of Europe of the Thirty Years

War, and also know the current price of Cotton shipped on board at Apia (a top price of five cents a pound in seed) and the going rate for casual labour.

I perceive I have rambled on too long about this young lady, and as our boat will soon be leaving for Apia I must bring this epistle to a close.

Mrs Brown desires to be remembered to you and Mrs Frith.

Talofa!

Geo. Brown

Chapter V

EMMA

I spent five years in San Francisco and on the whole they were the most miserable of my life. My Uncle Edward I liked well enough, my Aunt Elizabeth I detested. I went to school for three years, then studied with a lady, a friend of the family, who was always known as Mrs Dr Lane. This was because she was not only a college graduate, which was rare enough in the 1860s, but the possessor of a Doctorate of Philosophy. She was also a big wheel in Society in the City, as they called San Francisco, so she was a mixture, someone after my own heart, not just a blue stocking but a woman of worldly taste. The trouble was, she was as strict as my Aunt, but having a lot more social *nous* and a lot more brains, she was more than a match for me.

Oh I used to get smoking hot with that old bitch Aunt Elizabeth. I was treated like a nursemaid. I think they agreed to have me because they thought they'd be getting a nice little coloured girl to do all the house jobs. You know what some Americans are like about colour. Well, I suppose I wasn't quite what they'd expected, not black at all, not even chocolate, and they did kind of make me one of the family, but at the same time I really worked for my keep. Father had boasted about my sewing. What a mistake! I was given the mending to do. Father had told them how wonderful I was with little children, how I just loved babies—(so I always have, as long as they've been someone else's). So I minded the babies whenever Uncle and Aunt went out. Such a *responsible* girl, Emma.

And there I was, on those high hills amid those streets like precipices, right alongside the blue Pacific, but too far for even me to swim home. Five years! My only escape was when my cousin Caroline Greene, whose mother was Aunt Elizabeth's sister, came to town from their ranch. I would beg to be allowed to visit with them when they returned, and sometimes I was told I could go. They were good times, that's when I learnt to ride a horse, and that was a kind of freedom in itself. Caroline was four years younger than me, but we were always good friends.

And in San Francisco I not only learned a lot from Mrs Dr Lane, I really enjoyed the old lady. She was far too grand to have pupils, but she agreed to take me on because she wanted to learn Samoan. She was interested in social history and primitive migrations, and she had some queer ideas about the Polynesians. So I taught her and she taught me, but most of all I learned from her that it's no shame to be a woman, but it's a hell of a battle. She told me all about American women who were trying to become doctors, lawyers and so on. Up till then I'd had a *fa'a Samoa* attitude to women. I just thought women had been made for men, and men for women, and nature had been generous with me. And I had been a special sort of woman. In Samoa we have in each village a *taupo,* the village virgin, who is of high rank and who wears special costume at dances and who is the hostess for the *matais* when there are distinguished visitors or at ceremonials, she chews the root to make the drink of *kava.* She is a princess, but her life is one of service until she marries.

I was always treated like a *taupo* at home, Father always called me Princess, and although I knew all about kissing and love making and dancing I was still a virgin. I wouldn't have been if I'd been hanging around Apia Beach after I came back from Sydney. Father knew that sure enough.

A *taupo* is at the centre of things, she has beauty, fine clothes, respect, almost even magic. But she has no power. Mrs Dr Lane taught me about power. I knew a woman has power through her womanliness and through her body. I knew how that power worked for Samoans, although they are not interested in what Europeans know as love. A grand passion, a lifetime of fidelity, Samoans think either of these absurd. Romantic love as in all those European poems is nonsense to them. But I was half Samoan and half European and I could see how much more power the concept of love gives a woman. No Samoan girl could possibly say of her lover 'He will die for me'. This much about power I understood.

Mrs Dr Lane taught me about another sort of power. 'Most women don't bother to think', she would say, 'but if they do, and think properly, with their head instead of their womb, they think more clearly and more honestly than men. Men are either choked up with envy, or else they are wanting to make good fellows of themselves. A strong woman looks beyond envy to what is worth having or not worth having. A woman does not need to flatter because she, (if she's any good) is the object of flattery.' Here she would issue a strong warning. 'But it's no use having power and being a bitch. Power is to be enjoyed and to give you a chance of making other people happy. Thus you mustn't want to have power just over one person, particularly if he's your husband, that's the surest way of being bitch-unhappy.'

And her last advice was about money. 'And women must learn about money. Men would steal the gold out of their wife's teeth while they're sleeping. Women are property, money buys property, it's as old as history. It's women's own fault that they don't know about money. Practically every damn thing that's wrong with women is women's fault, because they've been too damn prissy-genteel to do anything about it.' Apparently I did not strike her as prissy-genteel. Perhaps that's why we got on so well.

Oh I learned a lot from Mrs Dr Lane. But deep down I knew just a bit more than she did, about one thing anyway, I guess by Polynesian instinct. Sex. She used to shy off sex like those rude little magnetized dogs Caroline and I bought once downtown in San Francisco when we were supposed to be buying corsets. You know, the dog sniffs the bitch's backside and she whips around to face him. It was not that she was against sex in *theory*, she was all for it, she even had a copy of Walt Whitman's *Leaves of Grass, think* of it! But sex to her was something pure and noble and all bound up with the sanctity of marriage. I'd nothing against marriage (I hadn't tried it) but marriage to me meant the *family*, Samoan style, not necessarily monogamy. I didn't mind about Father bringing Sa home, and I suspected there were some others, as long as Le'utu was being looked after. Le'utu accepted it too. But Mrs Dr Lane couldn't see that women's freedom and power might extend to the freedom to choose their own lovers. I don't mean to be promiscuous as a matter of principle, I could see that with that grim American determination to try everything, that would probably happen to American women, just *thinking* sex. All women are different, some women want only one man, others two or a dozen or hundreds. I was good at figures. I determined to work out for myself the magic number of lovers. As I wanted them I would take them. Or I would let them take me. Strictly mutual.

But my talks and lessons with Mrs Dr Lane were my only release. Uncle Edward was all day at his office and given to playing billiards at his club in the evening, and that left me with the children and Aunt Elizabeth. The greatest excitement was a promenade with me wheeling little Edward in the pram. He was the only child I didn't like, a spoiled monster. Oh those steep streets, diving away like dry waterfalls! I could have let the pram go and watched it sail out over the Pacific. I'd have thrown Edward out and hopped in myself if I thought the pram would float.

It was Mrs Dr Lane who saw I was pining away. No, not pining, I've never been the pining type. Burning away. I was a volcano of frustration, and I don't just mean sexual frustration. There were no boys for me, no dances, no entertainment, the only outlet I had was the piano, I played that for hours each day. But it was the frozen gentility of life, ice to my fire, that was putting unbearable pressure on me. And everything so city-straight, despite the swooping curves of the hills and harbour. Straight-sided house, squared-off city blocks, streets like knives. How I longed for the curves of the *fales*, the curves of the palm trees, the breast-curves of coconut, papaw, mango, the water-curves of canoes and surf on the reef. Do you know I spent five years in San Francisco and only swam in the sea once? We were pushed out into the sea in a sort of a horse box and then entered the water dressed from neck to knee. Me, who could swim naked for miles! Once all dressed up was enough for me.

We were in the parlour one morning when Uncle Edward came home unexpectedly. He said there was a brigantine, the *Emilie Ann*, in harbour, just finishing loading, which was leaving on the next tide for Apia, Samoa. He suggested I might like to send a letter by it to my father.

It was my chance. 'I'm sending myself I cried and rushed up

to my room to pack. San Francisco, you know, is subject to earthquakes. The one that afternoon may have only happened in one house, but I guess they felt it across the Bay. Nothing was going to stop me, and Mrs Dr Lane, bless her, supported me.

I was aboard the *Emilie Ann* that evening, and after an uneventful voyage I arrived back home in Apia harbour in June 1869.

Chapter VI

————————•————————

PHEBE

It was my sixth birthday, and my father said I could come out with him on his cutter and meet the American brigantine that was anchoring inside the reef. 'Maybe there will be a letter from Emma,' he said. I was only a baby when Emma was sent away to San Francisco, but she was always the close one to me, in my imagination I was with her in San Francisco because that took me away from my father's house.

Sa, my stepmother was horrid to me. I was growing happily with my mother at Falealiʻli when my father came in the schooner and scooped me up and set me down with my brothers and half-sisters at Matautu Point.

My husband, who was a botanist, used to say that we Samoans were like plants in the rich tropic soil. *Leicht einschlagen,* easy to strike, just stick a row of hibiscus sticks in the ground and there in no time you'll have a hedge, all flowering. I didn't flower with Sa. If I had she'd have snipped the flowers off. She'd make new dresses for my half-sisters and give their old ones to me. I wasn't allowed to see my mother, Le'utu. But she came and lived with some relations on a farm nearby, and she'd send a girl for me, and I'd run off and see her and hug her and kiss her.

My father didn't waste much time on me, except to whip me for kicking the table with those hateful shoes. He seemed to be busy with another wife, or maybe two new wives, I couldn't really tell. Maybe that's why Sa was cruel to me, because she who had had my father's baby Caroline before Le'utu had me, was now being pushed out of bed by a young girl Liva from Manono Island. And then there was this other girl called Lui. My father had all that blue blood from New England but Samoa must have turned it red. Oh it doesn't take much of the hot red! Like when you're cooking in a *kasserolle* and you chop up a little tiny shiny chili and drop it in. God was always dropping another chili into my father.

Anyway, this day he was in a good mood and it was my birthday, I don't know how he remembered, there were so many of us he used to forget even our names, but this day he picked me up and put me in the stern seat of the cutter and off we flashed across Apia Bay. How I loved the sea! I've never been frightened of the sea. Emma was the same. When I was fifty, even sixty, I could swim ashore over the reef when it was too rough for the schooner to get through the passage. Once when I was maybe sixty-five, on a recruiting trip to get Buka men, in the Solomons, I was stranded in a very bad place, desolate, no water, I was all done up, ill and tired, long long way to walk to nearest village, and the little cutter rolling and tossing outside the reef in a dreadful sea. So I just floated into the lagoon, felt all calm and easy, and swam a couple of miles out to the reef, then dived under the breakers and came fine to the cutter. Maybe a shark could eat me, but I could never drown.

So it was my birthday and I was happy on the sea with my father and watching the wind lift his moustaches as the cutter keeled over making white water in the gusts. We came alongside the brigantine, *Emilie Ann*, was her name, from San Francisco. What happier sight is there than a boat from far off coming safe into a harbour! That roar and run of the anchor chain, that's a lucky noise. And there's a pretty girl I saw, leaning over the rail, waving at somebody, her red and white dress and hat, the very latest American style, how lovely she was, *wie schön!* I knew my father never missed a pretty girl and I turned to see if he was admiring her and I saw his expression! *Wie vom Donner gerührt,* knocked out with a thunderbolt, speechless! Then he began to swear, at least I suppose so, I was only six and there were a lot of strange words. The cutter came neatly up alongside the brigantine and the pretty girl was crying 'Father! Father! And that must be Phebe!'

That harsh old father of ours, Emma was the one who could soften him up, he didn't have any success at all in being angry with her.

In no time she was running our household, that is all except Le'utu who wouldn't return except when my father was away. Grumpy Sa she cheered up, telling her the next baby (she had four months to go) would surely be a boy (it wasn't, Sa never had anything but girls, six girls). Liva, she was a real Samoan, a gay *taupou*, Emma packed her off back to Manono, she could see she wan't happy between the wallpaper and the books, she told father she was bad for his liver. I liked Liva, I went to Manono once with her. Lui she made welcome, she gave her an American dress, she could see that her mat was the one my father liked to lie on. You know how many people hate to see lovers happy? Well, Emma was always in love herself and always happy to see others in bed. Father was an old man of forty-seven and Lui was the same age as her, nineteen, but she admired her father for making a young girl happy.

There was no one in Apia like Emma. 'The Princess has come home!' said my father to the family when we returned to Matautu Point. When Theodore Weber, Goddefroy's representative, the cleverest man in Apia, came to call, '*Gnädige Prinzessin!*' he bowed to her and she allowed him to kiss her hand with the wickedest spark in her eye. She knew he knew she was Joe Coe's half-caste daughter, but she knew he knew she was a Malietoa, and what's more when after a glass of *schnapps* she agreed to play the piano, she knew he knew he had not heard Mozart played like that since he had left Hamburg. And then she played *Am Brunnen vor den Tore* so he could ventilate his baritone. She had that womanly art to bring a man out to do whatever thing it is he can do well, however little a thing.

But then, you see, she turned old Weber on his head—Weber, they were all scared of him in Samoa—by asking him about copra. She knew Weber was exporting copra, the dried meat of the coconut, instead of the smelly oil in the bamboo tubes, and that it was a more reliable return than cotton. I can hear her strong, clear voice, her real rich cello voice, saying, 'Herr Weber, there is something else about this copprah'—that's the way she pronounced it, full out, 'this new process of yours of drying the coconut in a brisk oven or in the sun. It's *easier*. It's easier than all that fiddling around making coconut oil. And we Samoans do not like to work.'

44

Phebe

'*In Samoa ist nichts unpopulärer als Arbeit!*' beamed Herr Weber.

'Herr Weber, I do not speak German, although I will allow I can listen to it being sung.' A nineteen year old girl, to Herr *Weber!*

But he loved it, and apologized, and translated, rather awkwardly, 'In Samoa is nothing so unpopular than work.'

She led him on, and in no time he was telling her how many palms to the hectare, how long until they would yield, what yield to expect, how to import labour, how to discipline the labourers, whether the best copra came from being dried in the oven or the sun, where the best markets were, Sydney or Hamburg, *und so weiter.*

But when she drove with my father through Apia, along the Beach to Mulinu'u, the men who watched her were not thinking about copra. The Princess had her subjects all right, but my father did not have a palace guard. I could tell her power. I was only six years old but I was half Samoan, the palm trees had told me the secrets of the boys and girls who lay on the sand beneath them. I was afraid of that power, and other power. I envied the nuns their cool, ordered lives, I would have liked to have been a nun. There were wars too, there had been fighting right near our house, the Samoans did not touch the European houses but they burnt down each other's, or chopped the house-poles so the roof collapsed. We used to slide down the thatch. But it was sad to see all the *taro* patches burnt. Peace and order I would like, and work. Emma took over the running of the household, where my father had taken a whip she took a broom, the other children ran away, they did not care, but I wanted to work and to try so she gave them up and only beat me. We loved each other the best.

I knew she would take the broom to any man who got cheeky with her. But I also knew that she was like a volcano, all hot and bubbly inside, soon she might cause great devastation. And I could see how my father was desperate to control her. She had been bottled up with that old Aunt Elizabeth. Now she was home. It was all right for us children to be sent to bed at eight sharp and she would make sure we went. But then. . . . She and my father would play cards, or she would play the piano for him. But this was not going to last for long.

My father had married his first daughter, Maria, to a Scotsman in Pango Pango, Thomas Meredith, when she was sixteen. She was safe. But that was four years ago, and here was Emma, only a year younger than Maria, dangerously unmarried.

Just then arrived back from Tahiti on a Hort Brothers schooner a young New Zealander, James Forsayth. He was born on an island far away, called Mauritius, and he was really a Scotsman, his parents sent him back to Edinburgh and he had a lot of education. He could recite Latin poetry, maybe even read Greek. Then he had gone to New Zealand, made some money there, and was wanting to trade around the islands. My father had his eye on him, to work for him, and got him the job as mate on the Hort Brothers schooner, more or less to try him out.

But he was trying him out on more than the schooner. He was asked to dinner at our house once, twice, three times. And afternoons too. One day we little girls were going to a party at the British Consul's house, we were all dressed up like Queen Victoria's nieces, Emma had done it all, had tied all our ribbons and polished our shoes, Sa used to do nothing, just sit on the verandah on a rocking chair like any trader's fat Samoan mistress with her half-caste brats running wild. Only we did not run wild. My father came in to inspect us, he had Mr Forsayth with him.

'Well, James, are they fit for Her Britannic Majesty's representative?' he asked, knowing very well we were. Then my father, as he always did on such occasions, opened one of the glass-fronted bookcases and took out a book each for us to give to the British Consul's wife. He never read the books, so I don't know how he chose them, they just came in boxes from San Francisco. But this time Emma and Mr Forsayth looked at the books, and when they came to mine they both began to laugh. My father was in a good mood and he asked them why they were laughing, and Emma said to him 'Mrs Williams will faint, toes up, bang! if Phebe gives her this book, and Mrs Turner' (the LMS missionary's wife), 'will bust her corsets.' 'But it's poetry' said my father, 'poems are always well liked by ladies.' 'Oh ho!' said Emma, she was really enjoying herself, she turned one of the pages of the book and read:

> Hips, hip-sockets, hip-strength, inward and outward round,
>   man-balls, man-root,
> Strong set of thighs. . . .'

'Stop, stop,' my father grabbed the book. 'Not in front of the children. What the goddam hell stuff is this'—there he was, swearing in front of the children—'Walt Whitman? Never heard of the guy, this was in that case Edward sent, that Mrs Dr Lane that taught you Emma, she selected them. Christ Almighty I've just sent William and John to be educated there. *Educated!*'

We were shushed out of the house quick smart, me with another book, but I wasn't interested in the book, I could see Emma and James Forsayth, they were reading each other, not Mr Whitman.

I think it was the books that brought them together, and his manners, he was a gentleman. There was Emma, with all that beautiful body—she'd hung those tight-buttoned American clothes up in the cupboard and just wore a long loose gown, nothing underneath, cool, good for Samoa. Maybe cool underneath, but not outside, she was driving Apia Beach mad. Emma didn't care, she wanted a man all right, but with all that education she'd had she wanted a man she could *talk* to, politics, history, poetry, business, anything, oh she was a complicated one, Emma, not like me, I was the simple one. But I liked to learn.

Well, this skinny little Forsayth with his droopy moustache and his high precise voice, he could talk to her. But what else could he do, I wondered. He always looked sick to me. He must have been tough, though, otherwise he'd never have survived as mate on a Hort Brothers schooner, although he was the sort of man who always carries a belaying pin or a revolver and is quick as a lizard, you couldn't sneak up behind him. And for him, Emma was truly the Princess, he treated her not just like a gentleman, but like an officer on guard duty, trusted with something precious. There was something about that that worried me, though I liked him for knowing Emma's quality.

Well, in a couple of months they were married. My father married them, I saw him write in his big book 'Commercial Agency of the United States of America at Apia, October 23rd, 1869. Given under my hand and seal', that was very grand.

My father set them up with a schooner for trading, and away they went to Auckland and Sydney for their honeymoon, Emma always loved a sea voyage, you could add to that, you could say she loved a lover who would take her to sea. She told me she was a virgin when she married James Forsayth. There was always

47

something surprising about Emma. She said to me 'Phebe, the sea's the best place to lose your virginity. The goddess of love, Venus, came from the sea'. I couldn't keep pace with her, she'd had all that education, I was just a little Samoan girl and the Sisters never taught me anything about Venus.

While Emma went off to New Zealand I went to Manono Island with Liva, my father's third wife (they weren't really married), the gay one who was a big chief's *taupou*. Emma had really arranged for her to go, and thought up the excuse, which was that her brother was sick. Liva never came back. What a wonderful time I had with her, real Samoan life, such a gentle happy life. Oh I know Samoans can be violent, there had been a war and bloody fighting behind Apia, and they can be very hot-tempered. I once saw a man pick up a small pig and throw it at another man.

We went over to Manono from Upolu in a big canoe, the Manono people have always been very good at sea. You can walk around the island in a few hours, past villages with the grass cut so neatly, down to the coral sand. There are flowers around every house, sweet-smelling even out to sea, and when you land on the beach it's under birds singing in the palm trees. The children run up to you with sweet mangoes, calling *'Talofa'*, and there is a man all dripping from the sea with fish twitching on his spear. The pigs trot past you tip-toed, Manono pigs seem to have very long, shrewd faces and they are very jaunty. The children play on the sand a game like English hop-scotch, the old people sleep in the *fales*. All so peaceful. Two weeks I stayed there, Liva went off to stay with her sweetheart's parents, that's why she wanted to go back to Manono, and I stayed with her family and slept with the *analuma*, the unmarried girls. We wore necklaces of shells, I took off my white dress and my shoes and put on a *lava lava* and wore hibiscus in my hair. There was dancing, it was a long way from the missionary's house, and every night the boys came. We swam in the lagoon and had races, and when one girl called me a half-caste stranger I challenged her to a two-handed fight and won, I knocked her down the steps of the *fale* and she fell on top of a sleeping pig.

Emma came back from her voyage not so happy as me. She was having a baby, when it was born it was sickly and did not live long, a little girl. They know when they're wanted. Emma was strange, she surrounded herself later on with children, couldn't do enough for them, but apart from her son Coe, who was born in 1872, she didn't want any of her own. But I could see the trouble was not only the baby, it was James Forsayth, he was a worse tyrant than my father, and at least my father was manly, look at him with six wives! The Forsayth thought he had tamed Emma, he'd put her back into her San Francisco dresses after the baby, and though he was pleased to let her run the office, and she enjoyed it, he wanted Emma to have Mrs Williams and Mrs Turner to tea. Now I knew that was a mistake because Emma had told me that one of her aims in life was to have as much champagne as she wanted, and tea isn't champagne, particularly with the LMS missionary's wife. The worst thing of all he did was in Sydney, she was in the early days of having the baby, and he had to go to New Zealand, he sent her back to *school*, to the Subiaco Convent Boarding School! He said she was only nineteen and a bit more education wouldn't hurt her and the Sisters would look after her while he was away. She had nowhere else to go, no money to run away, so she had to endure the humiliation. 'Oh Phebe!' she used to tell me, putting on an oily voice of virtue, 'how Sister Monica welcomed the deliverance into her hands of a repentant sinner. Me, repentant!' For two months she endured the kindness of the Sisters. The worst thing, she would say, is that they *were* kind. She couldn't even hate them. But she really hated Mr Forsayth.

In October 1870, about a week after her birthday, a beautiful white yacht, a schooner, ran smartly into Apia harbour and anchored close in. My father was away in San Francisco, where he was taking William and John to stay with Uncle Edward while they went to school. Emma was in charge of us, and Le'utu was living with us while my father was away, and it was a very happy household. Mr Forsayth was also away on a voyage to New Zealand. Emma went out in my father's cutter to meet the yacht. Soon two gentlemen came ashore in the cutter and Emma brought them to the house. It was a great English milord and his friend, a doctor from their yacht the *Albatross*. Oh what a stir in Apia! And the British Consul and his wife were so cross that they had come to our house first, the house of the American Commercial Agent! But it was not for the sake of America or commerce that they had come to Matautu Point. They had sailed from Tahiti and Bora Bora and Raratonga, and they had heard about the Princess at Apia, and they had come to pay their respects. The Earl and the Doctor accepted an invitation to dinner on the following evening.

Chapter VII

THE EARL OF P—

10 October 1870 On a fair afternoon the Captain ran the
Albatross neatly in between the reefs to anchor in Apia Bay. As
the poor will turn out with excitement and enjoyment to see a
rich pageant of their rulers, so will a sailor, the subject of the sea,
always be enchanted to sail close to a reef, and for him there is
the added spice of observing danger and destruction from a
proximate place of safety. The great rollers of the ocean curl and
crash on the coral, and the spray blows back like the hair of
Venus. Inside the reef all is calm, and the marvellous complexities
and colours of the coral are hidden beneath the blue water
shading to green.

Safe in the arms of Apia harbour, we faced a semicircle of beach
hung over by tall coconut palms, and amongst them the pleasant,
neat white houses and trading stores of the English, American and
German residents, and the discreet thatched houses of the
Samoans. All amongst the palms and houses are flowers, red and
yellow hibiscus and many others whose names I would not
attempt. What an extraordinary landfall Apia is! Instead of the
usual stinks of a port, in this harbour the scent of flowers is
wafted to you across the sparkling water. I know of nowhere else
in the world where this is so. If the grim Puritan will forgive me,

> off at sea *south*-east winds blow
> Sabaean odours from the spicy shore
> of *Apia* the blest.

I take added liberties, for it must be remembered that the correct
pronunciation of Apia is to place the accent very lightly on the
second syllable. But let us not be ashamed to Anglicize foreign

names. What intolerable species of snob is it that returns across the English Channel from a visit to Par*ee*.

The *Albatross'* anchor chain had no sooner rattled down than the Doctor called to me to observe a trim cutter that was closing on us. It was not the lines of the cutter that took our attention but the beauteous apparition of her helmsman, a girl with long black hair flying in the wind wearing a striped blue and white *sacque* which from the pressure of the wind hid all yet revealed all. The skill with which she brought the cutter alongside was perfect. Truly the flower-soft hands of this seeming mermaid *did* yarely frame their office.

The Doctor was as entranced as I. 'Surely' he said, 'this must be the Princess Coe?'

We had come from Raiatea, where we had spent some time with Queen Moe, a wonderfully pretty girl although her King is a beast, and she repeated what we had heard in Tahiti and were to hear again in Raratonga, that there are no Kings and Queens in Samoa, but there is in the living flesh a mysterious Princess Coe.

I have always referred to her thus in my published writing, to avoid scandal, but as this may be allowed to be a private communication to those whose discretion one may trust, I will give her her real name, just as she called it up to us from her cutter, in a deep but melodious voice that had a distinctive, plangent timbre.

'Ahoy!, *Albatross*, I am Emma Forsayth, daughter of Jonas Coe, American Commercial Agent, who is absent in San Francisco.'

You may be sure we welcomed her aboard. Her figure was of the pure Grecian mould, womanly yet slender, her shoulders particularly fine, and she walked as one hopes those marble goddesses would, had they a Pygmalion to breathe life into their limbs. Her face was strong and regular, unmistakably from the South Seas and yet in the perfect balance of the bone structure it was that of Everywoman. No words, however, can capture her expression, which was of frank acceptance—we could immediately tell, the Doctor and I, that she liked us, as she was pleased by the trim elegance of our yacht, but at the same time there was a hint of amusement. She knew our faults already, and forgave them. And finally there was an immediate private communication with her. She looked me full in the eyes, she saw me as a man, dared me to

52

see her as a woman. And she was, I discovered, only a few days over twenty years old! Exactly the same age as myself!

Her complexion was brown, certainly, and no doubt would have been castigated as swarthy by the ladies of St James's. But for my taste there is no more exquisite and arousing colour than the skin of Polynesian-European half-castes. It is flawless, needing no paints or powders, and glows with the sun whose rays it does not fear. And the ladies of St James's, shielded from the sun, might with profit read that fine old poem 'The Nutbrown Maid' and take note that the *puella*, the nutbrown maid, was in fact a baron's daughter of great lineage. And so our Samoan nutbrown maid was of the Malietoa lineage, and I understand that her father, although a Beachman recently attained to riches and respectability, is in fact descended from what you might call an inverted aristocracy, the Pilgrim Fathers.

Judge the astonishment of the Doctor and myself, when we were briskly interrogated by this beauty on the subject of our victualling requirements. In no time, such a lady of business is she, we had agreed to make all our commercial arrangements with the firms of her father and husband, for it appears that our Princess Coe has recently married a Scotsman from New Zealand. Happily, he is at the moment absent in New Zealand.

We went ashore with her to her house, or rather her father's, a delightful residence reminiscent of the trim white houses of New England, where Mr Coe, who appears to be the Brigham Young of the Pacific, accommodates at least three wives, with or without benefit of matrimony. We accepted with alacrity an invitation to dine tomorrow night, and were promised a genuine Samoan dance, the *siva*, which of course is still discreetly performed despite the ferocious disapproval of the missionary in his black garb more suited to the Devil than the Apostles of Light. It also appears we have arrived, sheerly by chance, close on the two days in the year when a highly prized marine delicacy, the *polulu*, appears over the reef, and the Princess Coe promised to take us with her in her canoe for the fishing of these creatures, which are apparently a kind of worm, long black and green annelides, from two inches to two feet long and as thick as a crow-quill.

11 October It appears we have mightily offended the British Consul and the missionaries from London by calling first on Mrs

Forsayth—I cannot call her anything so prosaic—Princess Coe. We have sailed our way out of the reefs of protocol and accepted an invitation to eat what will no doubt be boiled beef, over-cooked cabbage and seeping potatoes, if they have such things. But we did not sail from England to visit its drearier reincarnations in the South Seas.

Oh, the Princess's feast! Tastes, sounds, colours,—words cannot do anything but stale their freshness. The feast was pure Samoan style, the cooking presided over by Coe's mother Le'utu, a most sprightly lady of some forty Polynesian summers which usually induce a crummy appearance, although it is a burden of honoured flesh, but in her case have left her slim and light on her feet. It was held in a native hut, a *fale*, in Mr Coe's garden. Of the many dishes I can recall most clearly the delicious squid soup, in which that creature of alarming appearance is rendered docile by being boiled in coconut milk. And then *palusami*, a coconut cream baked inside young taro leaves. But there must have been thirty dishes placed around the floor, soup, fish (most delicious when uncooked, marinaded in limes and then served with the ubiquitous coconut cream), pork and what seemed to be grubs or snails. *Kava* was the ceremonial drink, the root being masticated by the Coe's young sister. *Kava* is a mild intoxicant tasting of soap and water with a dash of horse radish. Totally harmless, it has fallen foul of the sneaking hypocrisy of Smelfungus, who has forbidden it (as the dance) for the sake of power, for the need of black killjoys to forbid *something*. It must have been a truly difficult task, needing much wearing-out of the knees of trousers in calling on God's aid, to find things to forbid amongst the courteous, charming, good-tempered Samoans.

La Coe, being only half Samoan, catered for our tastes with her American half, for as well as *Kava* she initiated me into the joys of the pure Monongahela, a sublimely different whisky. Extraordinary girl, she could always answer a question. Monongahela, it seems, is a river in Pennsylvania where the first rye whisky was produced, and in 1790-something it was the scene of a Whisky War when the farmers refused to pay a whisky tax.

But we were in the midst of revelry! In a moment my Portia was transformed to Cleopatra, the young Cleopatra Caesar knew. In a whisk the centre of the hut was cleared, the girls formed a circle and began to sing, beating their hands for the time, tossing their heads crowned in circlets of shells more delicate than the tiaras that lumber the fuzz of our society ladies. Then they sang a chorus which, in my ignorance of the Samoan language, must have incorporated witty and no doubt bawdy, judging from the looks and laughter, references to the Doctor and myself.

These songs were by way of a warming-up, for into this circle of beautiful girls suddenly erupted a creature from another level of Nature, charged with energy and grace, her only dress a soft and lissom mat, ondoyant as satin, wound round her hips, her classic torso gleaming with coconut oil, a wreath of crimson hibiscus over her dark locks, and a double row of large scarlet berries around her neck. It was our Princess. Her mother then entered, more completely clad, and together they danced a dance of exemplary propriety. Apart from La Coe's brown breasts, Smelfungus could not have faulted it. However, imperceptibly, movements of arms and hips began to alter the character of the dance, and then, with a dramatic crescendo, from the introduction of drums, the older lady vanishing into the darkness, La Coe suddenly swayed into that dance which is performed all over the world and is of the essence of love, performed by the gypsies of Seville, the Gawazee of Egypt, the Nautch girls of India, but entered into as for the first time in the Garden of Eden, when Eve, liberated of respectability by the amiable serpent, drove Adam to a frenzy of desire. But no fiery angel had held a sword over La Coe, shame has not corrupted the Samoans with fig leaves, and in these warm islands no ice of chastity can be found to freeze the pleasure of the senses.

Oh dear Doctor, so much older and wiser than I, will you forgive me for calling the lifeboat to take you back to the *Albatross*! Oh Coe, would it have been better had I accompanied the Doctor, instead of following you to the beach under the palms, where in a lighted circle of blazing coconut-leaf baskets you danced for me alone, such a dance as made those earlier dances seem like a quadrille in a girls' boarding school!

No, of course it would not, in these private pages I have no need to feel the presence of Her Majesty, Queen Victoria, peeping over my shoulder. *My* Majesty was La Coe, her servant I.

And guess my surprise, when as the last burning baskets

glimmered to coals, on the sleekest of mats on the coral sand I essayed the ultimate tribute of manhood to beauty, my Princess, laughing—*laughing*, I pray you, at such a moment—cast me off crying, I fear satirically, 'Milord P—, you are no missionary!', and in a trice we were seated face to face, my posterior a cushion for her softness, and she rode me down into darkness, my last glimpse being of the stars brushed by the feathery tops of the coco palms.

12 October Today I did nothing, and could have done nothing. Eventually aboard the yacht, I lay and let lines of poetry drift across me like the faint echoes of the ocean swell that lift and lower the boats at anchor in the harbour.

Pleasure's a sin, and sometimes sin's a pleasure.

Ah, Smelfungus, in these blest islands!—

If this be true, indeed,
Some Christians *lack* a comfortable creed.

13 October At four in the morning my Princess came alongside in an outrigger canoe. It is the day of the *polulu* fishing. In no time we are over the reef, where the water is one or two feet deep, surrounded in the dark by crowds of other canoes and the first rays of light reveal a wild, savage and larky scene, men, women and children frisking and gambadoing, old ladies chanting to some goddess of the sea, young ladies flirting, young men responding. As the light increases and the water ceases to be black, picks up colour and reveals depth, you become aware that the sea all around is pollulating—dare I say pololuting—with myriads of long thread-like creatures swimming near the surface. Immediately every sort of fishing apparatus is cast into action, as you scoop up wriggling lumps and tip them into bucket or calabash, and fish again. As soon as you catch these creatures they kick themselves into pieces, sections an inch or inch and a half long.

I have never seen such a good-natured happy crowd of people, as, instructed by La Coe, I dipped again and again for *polulu*. You are at perfect liberty to push another canoe off its spot, to splash a pretty girl who is flirting or even, if she be giving all her concentration to flirting, to empty her calabash into yours. Song and laughter are entwined as thickly as the worms.

Then the light rapidly increases and beyond the great smooth rollers breaking on the reef the sun of the tropics suddenly rises, and the dark masses of water become transparent blue. As if the light were a signal, the *polulu* instantly vanish, not to appear again for twelve months.

The rising sun has turned my Princess' splashed limbs into pure old gold and as she paddles me ashore her bare back and the play of light over her limbs gives me exquisite pleasure.

When we came ashore I found I had caught near half a gallon of inedible, fragmentated worms. I would have thrown them away, having had my enjoyment in their capture, but my Coe instructed me how to prepare them, by pounding them together with coconut meat and wrapping in *taro* leaves and baking. Then eaten with oil, vinegar and a dash of cayenne it is delicious, like a mixture of spinage and crab, and like foie gras when eaten on toast. But of course, offered by the brown fingertips of La Coe, whaleblubber would have tasted like caviare.

14 October This morning again the whole fleet turned out, but not a thimbleful of *polulu* did we catch amongst all the boats. As a consolation Princess Coe declared she would take us up into the lovely wooded hills behind Apia and show us a waterfall over which one apparently launches oneself. It sounds alarming. The Doctor examined himself and pronounced the patient unfit, but I had the fortitude to follow my fair guide.

Follow I did, but panting. We climbed a steep path through the great trees, huge sentinels knotted and gnarled with moss and orchids, past enormous ferns thirty feet high, the young fans of the fern like outstretched hands with turned-down fingertips, and higher, the very young, not yet unrolled ones like the crests of heraldic birds. Every now and then there were clearings, and vague plantings of bananas or *taro*, and a man and a woman carrying baskets on bamboo poles disappearing into the jungle. But, oh! the heat! It poured over us like hot oil down from the motionless trees, and fused into fire it radiated back from the volcanic rocks. Only the butterflies seemed cool. From nowhere two Samoan boys materialized and softly accompanied us, at every halt for breath fanning us with banana leaves and watching with sympathy my streaming face. La Coe, meanwhile, stopped only from courtesy, unaffected either by the stifling heat or the stiffness of the climb.

Emerging at last from the jungle I saw a river springing between the rocks before us, and above the roar of waters heard gay shouts and cries. Hobbling after my Princess down the burning ravine I found myself suddenly at a pool at the head of a waterfall, surrounded by wet, laughing Samoans. Old women, young children, gloriously beautiful girls and young men, all of them were taking it in turns to slide on the polished black rocks through the white, white foaming water some forty feet down into a deep dark pool. Thus our happy ancestors must have looked before superstition and shame curbed their natural joy in the created world. Garbed in absurdly unnecessary clothes as most of them are now around the island towns, up here they were their naked selves. The path was too steep and hot for old black Smelfungus, so they ran no danger of being denounced for sin.

At first there was a gasp of dismay when they saw me, a white man in my European clothes, but my Princess speedily told them I was no missionary, and they went back to their water games.

In an instant La Coe had removed her *sacque*, and had taken her turn to launch herself down the ice-smooth rock to the water far below. I must admit, to my disgust, a residual prudery which prevented me from removing all my clothes. However, arrayed only in my under linen, I now waded into the top pool—how delicious the cool water!—to take my turn. I was screwing up my courage for what, close up, looked a terrifying plunge over a precipice. As I was going to let the water carry me over the edge there was a scream from my Princess, who had just climbed up from the lower pool.

She explained to me, with that provoking deep laugh of hers, that it was extremely dangerous for a man, unless tackled in the right way, for a number of knobs and projections on the rocks on the way down, which would do no harm to a woman, might fatally damage those appurtenances of manhood which nature has so foolishly exposed on a man, unlike her neatness in the business on a woman. The art, it seemed, and she commanded a young man to demonstrate it for me, is to slide down leaning slightly over on one buttock, safeguarding the tender parts from danger.

Thus instructed, I took courage from her laughing eyes, and

let the rush of the river take me into the white foam. Down, down I went, rocking from buttock to buttock, and hit the water all of a heap, continuing under it for what seemed an infinity until I arrived at the surface again puffing and blowing. Oh, what a delicious plunge! And as I came to the edge of the pool, through this 'transparent, cool and watery wealth' and climbed to slide again, I was put in mind of the poet Vaughan, noble follower of my ancestor Herbert, in the calm of the top pool—

> As if his liquid, loose Retinue staid
> Lingering, and were of the steep place afraid,
> The common pass
> Where, clear as glass,
> All must descend
> Not to an end:
> But quickened by this deep and rocky grave.

Though I must admit my further thoughts were not mystical, but sensual.

16 October To show me further enchantments of this paradisal island, my Princess today took me to enjoy a simple, idyllic sort of sport, a species of pigeon-fancying. It would not seem possible that Smelfungus could find obscenities in such an innocent pastime, but he has, and the sport is tabood. The sport consists of going into the bush where the big blue, red-crested pigeons are, and building a bower of green leaves and branches. There, by making a booming noise like the pigeon, at which the Samoans are most adept, the birds are enticed close to the entrance to the bower, when out pops the brown paw of the concealed Samoan, and the wild pigeon is caught. This process takes time, hours of an afternoon, or maybe the bower is built of an evening to take advantage of the cool dawn when the birds are wakefully curious. Strephon would take Chloe with him, and the hours would pass happily by inside the green bower. But Smelfungus has put a stop to such immoral pursuits, and officially there is no more pigeon-fancying.

Princess Coe and I built our bower in a clearing in the jungle, where once there had been a taro field, destroyed maybe in the incessant Samoan wars. I cannot think how such a good-natured people could ever work up to fighting each other, but given their complex system of conflicting claims for the various offices of high chief, it happens pretty frequently, and the warriors will bring back baskets of 'red breadfruit' (i.e. heads) to their proud women folk.

La Coe and I made a soft mattress in our bower of leaves and grass, and we lay back to await our wild pigeons, while she most realistically imitated the deep booming note of the birds. In no time one of the beautiful smoky-blue pigeons landed near us, and peering through the opening in our bower I could see it tipping its head and raising and lowering its crest and darting its beak from side to side as its sharp eyes looked for the mate it could hear but not see.

La Coe touched my shoulder, indicating that I was the one to have the honour of catching the bird. Tense with the responsibility, being no swift Samoan, I waited until I judged it the time to strike. I shot out my hand and to my surprise and relief caught the legs of the bird. They were hard as sticks and took some hanging onto, as the bird was big and powerful and had now decided it did not wish to be drawn into its strange mate's presence.

I handed the twisting creature to my Princess. She took it, laughed, and let it go. She had said nothing, but irresistibly she reminded me of the old poem—

> I have found out a gift for my fair;
>> I have found where the wood-pigeons breed:
> But let me that plunder forbear,
>> She will say 'twas a barbarous deed.
> For he ne'er could be true, she aver'd,
>> Who would rob a poor bird of its young:
> And I loved her the more, when I heard
>> Such tenderness fall from her tongue. . . .
> Let her speak, and whatever she say,
>> Methinks I should love her the more.

But words were unnecessary, so eloquent was her gesture in freeing the pigeon and turning to me. I thought no more of pigeon-fancying, nor, I am happy to say, did she.

When I returned to normal consciousness, it seemed that the released pigeon had told all the birds in the valley what good, gentle people we were, for a *fuia*, the Polynesian blackbird, was perched on a branch of our bower regarding us cheekily and whistling shrilly, while around us like a brook flowed the soft cooing of dozens of ring-doves, *manu-tagi* the Samoans call them, the bird that cries, and there is a wistfulness in their *continuo* running under the sharp call of the blackbird, the quick clang of the paroquets and the imperious boom-boom of the blue pigeon.

After love, that is contented love, not sadness as the harsh old Roman said, but slow talk, wistful like the ring-dove. We lay in our bower and murmured to each other for hours, or so it turned out, for I had no knowledge or thought of time.

I asked her which half of her ruled, American or Polynesian, would she be content to laze life away in this delicious Samoan style, or did she feel that maddening American urge to be doing something, that guilt of idleness. At our mutual age of twenty years she had twice my energy and strength, and her saltatory disposition could never leave her satisfied with the torpid existence of genteel matrimony. And I added, hardly daring to say it in such a blissful wakening dream of love and idleness, would a constant diet of peace, freedom and enjoyment lead to spiritual indigestion? Is not true happiness born only of toil and strife?

To my surprise she vehemently agreed, lying back Venus-naked on the soft green carpet of our bower. 'I want the freedom', she said, 'to choose my own adventure, and the only way I can do this is to become rich. It's easy for you, you are an English milord, you have inherited great wealth, you are a man. I am a half-caste, my father is not rich and he already has a dozen children, and I am a woman.' Here I was unable to resist offering thanks. 'Oh yes', she continued, 'I *enjoy* being a woman, but I'm not going to be like my mother, cast off when I've had eight children. If there's any casting-off to be done, I'm going to do it. And as for this *fa'a Samoa* existence, I love it, but there are in it the black seeds of boredom. I wonder sometimes if our constant wars are not caused by boredom.'

Here we were, rapt in each other's company, talking about boredom! But my Princess was sensitive, through the soft mattress of love, as in the fairy tale, she felt the pea of ambition. 'You want power,' I suggested, 'not riches for themselves but for the power to tell the world that you, a half-caste and a woman, can do what you want with it.'

'Yes,' she answered softly. 'Look!' she pointed to a pigeon that had landed nearby. She began to call it, boom-boom, boom-boom. 'The next pigeon, the next *two* pigeons, we will eat.' She was the huntress, fair if not chaste. I had to live up to her.

18 October We left Apia this morning, our cabin so filled with presents from the generous Samoans that there was scarce room for the Doctor and myself, let alone the fair passenger I would like to have taken with us. But she had no illusions about the grim timetable of goodbye. She sailed beside us in her cutter as we ran for the entrance through the reef, came up smartly into wind, waved as she went about, and then on the other tack looked ahead to Matautu Point, her hair flying, never again turning her head.

Chapter VIII

————————•◆•————————

REVEREND GEORGE BROWN

Satupa'itea, Savai'i.

August 23, 1873

Reverend J. D. Frith,
Balmain,
New South Wales.

My dear James,

I have but recently returned from Apia where I have held much converse with a new arrival, an American, who may well turn out to be the Saviour of war-torn Samoa. As you know, I have long hoped that the Americans would take over all the Navigator's Group and make peace, as I feared the Samoans would never agree on a Government of their own, and indeed the old Club law was far better than the recent State of Affairs. But now it seems that their decision to give over fighting, in May of the year, and get up a species of confederate Government at Mulinu'u, on the west of Apia Harbour, has genuinely led to some Unity. And this will be further strengthened by the prospect of an American Protectorate held out by the arrival on August 17 of a special personal emissary from President Grant, Colonel A. B. Steinberger.

The Colonel is a man in his late thirties, of good family and well educated, and has I think the interest of the Samoans genuinely at heart. He also promises to restore some Sanity from their madness of selling Land, and particularly to bring justice to the victims fleeced by the villainous Collie and Stewart of the Central Polynesian Land and Commercial Company, which claims to have bought about half of all Samoa. On the security of these worthless titles, they borrowed much money, especially from the LMS; the firm having then been declared bankrupt, my LMS colleagues of the cloth will have had time to consider their foolishness. Behind the CPLCC, as it is known here, is a New York financier by the name of Webb who with a great flourish has been about to commence a shipping Line across the Pacific to Australia. As you are well aware, there is always a liberal proportion of Scoundrels in high places around the Government of the United States, and it is rumoured that the family of President Grant himself has an interest in Mr Webb's shipping line. Last year, by a smart move which has ironically doubled back on itself, Commander Meade of the U.S.S. *Narangansett*, attempted to assist Webb's adventures by securing to the United States exclusive rights to the harbour of Pango-Pango in Tutuila. High Chief Mauga, who has wanted to be independent of the federation at Mulinu'u, willingly signed a treaty with Commander Meade. But Congress refused to ratify Meade's Treaty, and so the whole intrigue came to nothing.

But it is clear that on a genuine basis of honest dealing, these Samoan islands would do well to come under the Protection of the United States, and especially to preserve us all from the ever-increasing power of Herr Weber and the Hamburgers. Goddefroy, whose representative Weber is, now control enormous areas of Samoa and through Weber's development of Copra and Coconut Plantations, are the biggest traders. As the German nation achieves unity, they will consider annexing Samoa. Queen Victoria is not interested, so it is best for us to have the Americans. Mr Jonas Coe, the U.S. Consular Agent, has long endeavoured to impress upon Secretary of State Hamilton Fish and President Grant that the U.S. must act quickly, and many of us signed a petition asking for U.S. protection. Mr Coe is at present in Washington urging these proposals, and also pressing his own claims. I understand that last year he bought the Land at Mulinu'u upon which the Government now meets, an extraordinary situation, but one which it appears is perfectly legal, as Mr Coe is a man to do a thing properly, having a perfect knowledge of Samoan language and customs.

You may remember some nine years ago I waxed enthusiastic in a letter to you about his Daughter Emma, whom Mrs Brown and I cared for in Mr Coe's absence on a voyage. She has now grown into a quite extraordinarily handsome and capable young Woman of twenty-three. She runs all her father's office, the acting Commercial Agent, Elisha Hamilton, the Apia port pilot, being a genial gentleman who knows little about business. She also runs the trading establishment of her husband, Captain Forsayth. There is talk in Apia that Captain Forsayth has been lost at sea on his last Voyage, but the news has not been confirmed. The young Widow, if she be that, does not seem too much concerned. She has a charming baby, a boy of a year old, named after her father. She seems to be acting in a secretarial capacity, if that be not too dry a term, for Colonel Steinberger, her intimate knowledge of all things Samoan being of inestimable help to the Colonel.

Would you kindly order for me from Horderns etc. etc. . . .

23 September, 1873

. . . Now, further to my letter to you of a month ago, more news of Colonel Steinberger. At his special request, I have recently travelled with him widely through the islands, he has won the respect and affection of all Samoans, and most Europeans, excepting the reprobates of the Beach, and perhaps the Germans. Weber is away in Hamburg, and his deputy, Poppe, has had discussions with Steinberger, but I do not know their outcome. We are to have a Constitution and a Code of Laws and, as it were, two houses of Parliament, the reigning oligarchy of *Ta'imua*, seven high chiefs, and an assembly of local representatives, the *Faipule*, numbering some two hundred. We are hoping that Steinberger, who is shortly to travel to Washington, will return with guarantees of U.S. Protection. He is certain to be appointed Premier, or some such title, by the Samoans.

Praise the Lord, we will at last through the Colonel, who leads a life of blameless rectitude, have some control of the appalling morals of the Beach. He has already called the chiefs together and told them they should not frequent the grog-shops, and it is confirmed that no liquor will be allowed to be sold on the Sabbath. Measures are being taken against the vice of prostitution, I regret to say both male and female, which flourishes abominably on the Beach. But alas the general condition of immorality in these islands is such that sailors can always find common women who do not ask payment for their services. On the extirpation of vice, at least, the sects are united. Otherwise I must report much political intrigue amongst the Popish Bigots, and double dealing amongst my 'brethren' of the LMS. . . .

20 October, 1873

. . . On 7 October Colonel Steinberger sailed for Hawaii and the U.S. on his pretty little Schooner the *Fanny*. We unite in wishing him success in Washington. . . .

. . . On 15 October, on a visit to Apia, I called on Mrs Emma Forsayth, but found that she had sailed for San Francisco a few days ago. There is still no news of Captain Forsayth, and it must be presumed that he has been lost with his Ship in some storm at sea or on one of the reefs that lie thick as shark's teeth in the smiling Pacific. Mr Coe is still in the U.S. . . .

Chapter IX

COLONEL ALBERT STEINBERGER

I've always been what people call an adventurer, but unlike many, I'm proud to accept the title. Dammit, where would our American nation be without them? Respectability is the blackguard's coat, and there are more charlatans under the alpaca of office than ever galloped after llamas in the mountains of Peru.

I come of good German-Jewish family, studied law at Princeton, fought for the North in the War and attained the rank of Colonel. I got to know the lobbies of Washington after the war, and the capitals of Europe where I found ready markets for surplus American arms after the War. I made one particularly good deal with the French at the outbreak of their war with the Prussians. I had a lot of money then and should have invested it soundly, but a bachelor in Paris is in no way to be prudent.

I returned to Washington where I eked out a living at journalism, waiting an opportunity from one of my friends in high places. By the fortunes of war, I was friendly with the man in the highest place of all, General U. S. Grant, President of the United States. I had known Sam Grant well in the army. He was a magnificent soldier and a splendid drinking companion but a damn fool when it came to advisers. There were rogues galore around him, though his Secretary of State, Hamilton Fish was straight. Sam's own family were involved in all sorts of shady deals. Well, as long as you know about these things you know how to handle them. A few presents in the right places, see where the openings are. Sam had promised to find me something, but nothing seemed to turn up.

Then on business in New York I met this fellow Webb, a friend of my brother's. He was lobbying to get U.S. support for his shipping line across the Pacific and a land company in Samoa.

My brother John was on the board of this firm, the CPLCC which I shall call the Polynesian Company. Things were in a desperate way, although it seemed they owned half of Samoa. The company was bound to be liquidated, but there was something to be salvaged from it. Sam Grant saw clearly the tremendous potential for U.S. interests in the Pacific, particularly Samoa, which could be a second Hawaii. The residents there had petitioned the U.S. for protection, but Congress had not the brains to see this as desirable. Sam advised Fish in August 1872 that I would be a competent person to visit the Navigator's Islands and report upon their condition. That old bastard Fish sat on it for seven months, when at last I was appointed Special Agent to visit Samoa.

I said I was an adventurer. Well then, I reckoned this was an adventure I was on, and I might finish up ruler of these Pacific islands, and this ought to put me in the way of restoring my fortunes, which were distinctly frayed around the edges. In fact, there were darned great holes right in the middle of them. My brother had warned me that the Polynesian Company was going bust, they had debts of $50,000 and although claimed to have bought half Samoa I gathered the titles were not too strong. But maybe there would be something to be salvaged from the wreck and I'd be the man on hand to do it. Of course the Polynesian Company directors thought I was going to save their bacon and get them their lands, but I knew what they didn't, that I had in my pocket instructions from Secretary Fish to discourage the Samoan chiefs from entering into extensive land sales. And in my head, not in any pocket, I had the words of Sam Grant, President of the United States, 'Albert, Samoa will be a second Hawaii. If you make a success of this trip, you can be U.S. Commissioner there.'

Well, I had two surprises out there in Samoa. One was that the Samoans were such damn fine people. I'll own I thought they'd be a lot of ignorant savages. I knew they wouldn't be wanting to eat me, or be bought for a few glass beads, but I thought they'd be just a simple, happy people. Well, maybe they're happy, but they sure as hell aren't *Simple*. They're a highly intelligent, civilized, cultured people, and their manners would make them at home with a Spanish grandee. And they're straight. Corruption is endless in the good old U.S.A., but out there at 172 degrees West it stops, it really does. Those damn Samoans are *different*!

Colonel Albert Steinberger

The second surprise was a woman. I've known a lot of women. My motto is travel light, and the heaviest baggage is female. My other motto is, be discreet. You can't do business with foreigners while you're knocking off their women, and if they put a woman in your bed for you, do what a gentleman should but don't talk to her, and don't talk about it afterwards. Now I knew all these stories about Polynesian women, islands of love and all that. I figured that when I came back as Commissioner I'd have plenty of time for that. This trip I had to keep my prick clean. I also knew that Samoa was stuffed tight as a roast turkey with missionaries. I knew these gentlemen wouldn't exactly offer you a whisky cocktail, but they're just as dangerous if you don't handle them right. I had to keep on the right side of them, and the same with the European traders and consuls and the big German firm, Goddefroy. The U.S. Commercial Agent was a fellow called Coe, and he was to be my first contact.

But he wasn't there, he'd gone to Washington, and here is where my second surprise came in, in the shape (and Devil take it, what a shape!) of his half-caste daughter, Emma Forsayth. She was managing his affairs for him, and I soon saw she could manage the whole of Samoa if she was given the chance. She went off under me like one of Sam Grant's mines at Vicksburg, and I went as high as that nigger who came down with the rocks after one of the blasts and they asked him how high did he go, and he answered, 'Massa, I don't rightly know, but I think mebbe it was three mile.' I still remember what she was wearing, a purple and white striped dress, kind of zig zag, covering everything up neck to wrist, but tight, so you could see that perfect figure. And her eyes, they were velvety, soft, soft, but then they'd change, turn into something liquid that the light strikes off, kind of mocking.

I came down to earth. I said to myself 'Albert. Discretion. Gravity. You are the Special Representative of the Department of State to the Samoan people.' But she was so quick she already understood all this. She offered to be my interpreter. I accepted her offer, resolving at the same time to make her my mistress. I have no doubt she had already resolved to make me her lover.

I soon found out that this convent-bred girl had acquired a singular breadth of knowledge of the world. What she thought was independent, what she said was clear, and yet with her positively masculine firmness of judgement she never lost her feminine expression nor her womanly intuition.

It seemed she had had a husband, a New Zealand trader, who had been drowned in a typhoon off China. When she spoke of him, it was in the past tense. I don't think it had been a happy marriage. She had a charming young sister called Phebe, and a pleasant brood of half-sisters, old Coe living *fa'a Samoa* with a number of wives.

In Samoa it is impossible to keep a love-affair secret, everything is open like the *fales* in which the whole family sleeps together. Yet Emma and I were discreet, and such was her character that not even George Brown, the Wesleyan missionary, looked askance at our liaison. And after all she was extremely efficient, I would never have been able to do my work without her. It was not just a matter of having a perfect interpreter, no easy matter with the courtly subtleties of the Samoan language, but of her being a larger interpreter, of Samoan life and custom. Together we travelled around the islands, much helped by her Malietoa connections. 'The Princess', all the Europeans called her in Apia, and so she was in truth amongst the Samoans. No European had moved around through all the villages as I did, and these travels contributed inestimably to my popularity amongst the Samoans.

I'll admit I'd come pretty cynically to Samoa. I'd some good deals to push through, and stood the chance of making my fortune. But between them, Emma and the Samoans made things different. I won't pretend I got soft-hearted, I could still see my opportunities and intended to take them, but at the same time they were such a damn fine bunch that, by God!, I really wanted to help them!

Back at Apia I wrote the rough draft of my report for President Grant, and assisted the Samoans to form their Government and draw up their Code of Laws. The missionaries had too much of a hand in these laws, but at this stage I intended to go along with them. A man like George Brown could be of immense assistance to me. But after some of the nights I had spent in the remoter villages, watching those oiled brown bodies dancing the *siva*, it really stabbed my vitals like a Confederate bayonet to have to agree to laws like the 'Law of Dances: Night Dances according to the old Samoan or heathen custom, that is dancing partly or quite

70

naked, committing indecency, are strictly forbidden.' Hell! When I think of those nights, and how rapturous were those indecencies! Particularly on the beach at Manono Island, Emma's strength, cavalry charges during the war, I couldn't hold her, she'd ride me, and laugh, at the moment women should be moaning she'd give a wild laugh, damn disconcerting at first, but she was really— really—laughing for joy. And the scents of her, the soft one of coconut oil, the creamy one of crushed frangipani and hibiscus, sharper ones of sweat from her dancing, and her woman scent, one night I made her laugh outright, said it reminded me of grilled kidneys. By God it did, too. You couldn't dare be too solemn or romantic with Emma, and that suited me fine.

I don't want to give the impression I came to Samoa to have a love affair, no Sir. I came to make myself Premier, or U.S. Commissioner, or something at the top. But this half-caste girl (what superb colouring, what skin!) was fascinating, not least because she could talk to you. I am a man who likes to read, particularly history. I was astounded what this girl had read, and the comparisons she could make. If you were talking about Grant and Lee, she'd bring in Scipio and Hannibal. And business, exports, imports, she was really smart. She had something more though, the gift of listening. Not that dumb, open-mouth 'Aren't you *amazing!*' look of a stupid girl, but the ability to listen of a girl to whom *you* in turn will like to listen. By listening to her I accumulated deadly accurate portraits of everybody who was anybody in Samoa. She was irreverent but she admired quality, so you got a really honest picture.

I could see that she could be very useful to me on my return to the U.S.A. in October 1873, where I aimed to get my Commission from the President before returning to Samoa. I put the notion to her, and she relished it. She shared my spirit of adventure, without wishing to be an encumbrance. She raised no objection when I said it would be indiscreet for her to travel on the *Fanny* with me. Fortunately a ship was leaving for San Francisco a few days later, and on this she took passage to stay with her Uncle and Aunt in that city.

She had no fortune, otherwise I might have proposed marriage to her. Besides, it was not absolutely certain that Captain Forsayth was dead.

71

Chapter X

---•---

JONAS COE

10 November, 1873. San Francisco   That sonofabitch Steinberger has seduced my daughter Emma. It's not safe to leave her alone in Apia. Last time I went away it was that English Earl spouting poetry at her. Now it's a goddam bogus Colonel, a Jewish adventurer, carried her off with tales of what he is going to do for her beloved Samoans. When I get back to Apia I'll tell her what I've found out about him. He has been indicted on a charge of perjury relating to a financial case of long standing. San Francisco creditors have been hounding him for months. He claims to be a friend of General Grant, but it is more to the point that he is a crony of that scoundrel Orville E. Babcock, Grant's private secretary, and that the Grant family and Steinberger's both have holdings in the infamous Polynesian Land Company. What a nest of iniquity! And now Steinberger is intriguing with the CPLCC to oust me from my post of Commercial Agent and install that louse-brained drunkard and blackguard S. S. Foster, manager for the CPLCC in Tutuila. I am to be cheated out of my legitimate land holdings and this bunch of rascals will share out Samoa between themselves, and the Samoans will find themselves dispossessed.

But the worst of it is that not only is Emma this adventurer's paramour, (after all my training), but that she is in cahoot with him in defrauding her own father. This draught of adversity would make aloes taste like Monongahela, so much a worse calamity is it. Oh ungrateful daughter!

12 November   Who should arrive in San Francisco today on the barque *Gulnare* but *my daughter Emma*! Heaven preserve an old man's sanity! She has come to the USA to assist Steinberger with his charlatan's plans. Had I my old whip at home I would have taken it to the slut. But she is a hard one to argue with. When I accused her of conspiring against me with Steinberger and the Polynesian Company, she said I had the whole story wrong, that she would never do anything against me, and that Steinberger had set the Samoans against the Polynesian Company and that Steinberger detested Foster who is ousting me from my position as Commercial Agent. She refuses to believe Steinberger is a secret agent of the Polynesian Company. 'Where does he get his funds from, then?' I asked her. 'I know it is not from the State Department.' She replied that they were his own funds. At that, I laughed. But I must admit it is hard to resist Emma. She evinces such affection for me, genuine affection. How *can* she be conspiring against me?

17 November Steinberger arrived today on the yacht *Fanny*. Although he is undoubtedly a rascal, he is a personable one, and I can see why the Samoans have fallen for him, intelligent though they are. He astounded me by saying he would write immediately to Mr Hamilton Fish against my dismissal and the appointment of S. S. Foster, whom he referred to as lazy, improvident, stupid and a foreigner from Tahiti—great qualifications for a U.S. representative! He said he had no doubt that I was most acceptable to the Samoan population. I then changed the subject and said he would be more acceptable to me as a son-in-law than as my daughter's lover, in short, what were his intentions. To which he rather too shrewdly parried by asking had I any news of Captain Forsayth? Bigamy, he said, was not a profession for a gentleman. Damn cheek, but he said it rather disarmingly. I must admit I wish we had Forsayth's bones for burying.

There is nothing for me to do but take ship as arranged for Apia, even though it means leaving Steinberger and Emma here together. At least her Aunt Elizabeth will stand no coggery.

20 November Sailed for Apia. Steinberger wrote the promised letter to Fish yesterday. Still convinced he is a rogue.

Chapter XI

---•---

EMMA

I told Aunt Elizabeth I was a widow of twenty-three, with one child living and one buried, possessed of an independent income (only just, in fact!), and that my reputation would survive my constant association with Colonel Steinberger.

I was far more worried about him, and his future prospects, and indeed my own. He truly had the interests of Samoa at heart, unlike the Congress of the United States, which had no wish to acquire one more encumbrance, and which could be counted on to be hostile to President Grant's wishes.

Albert wanted me to go east with him, to Washington, to help him with his negotiations, and to show me off at dinners and balls, to unfold for me the glittering life of New York, to introduce me to a world I had never known. 'And pay for me with the Polynesian Company's money?' I said cruelly, for Father had had very convincing arguments. But you could never get under Albert's skin that way, he just shrugged it off.

It was really my pride, though I didn't tell him. I was not going to be hawked around, to be stared at and to be the point of nudged ribs, as the Colonel's half-caste mistress. Mulatto, they'd probably call me. Father told me Albert would not propose marriage because of the uncertainty of Captain Forsayth's fate. More likely my lack of a fortune, I suspect. Some day I will be *rich*.

Let him go to Washington, New York, Hamburg, I said, let him go finish his business and let the State Department make up its mind, and then he will come back to me. Thus do powerless women challenge fate and pretend to a bravery they do not possess.

I waited a year. My cousin Caroline and all my San Francisco friends were very good to me, I had gay times in 1874, and I kept

74

myself from growing soft with idleness through handling business for Father and our firm of Forsayth on the West Coast.

In November Albert returned to San Francisco; he had been to Hamburg to see the great Cesar Goddefroy himself to ensure German co-operation in Samoa. Albert was kind to me, but pre-occupied, nervy from the Washington delays; I was prepared to wait. Early in December the letter came from Secretary of State Hamilton Fish saying that Albert was to be sent to Samoa in a U.S. warship bearing gifts from the President and assuring them of his lively interest in their welfare and happiness. No more than that. If Albert was disappointed, he did not show it.

One day Albert called for me and took me down to the docks. He wanted to show me his yacht, *his yacht, Peerless*, 45 tons, 77 feet overall, that he was fitting out to take to Samoa. I knew the cost of such a ship to be in the vicinity of $8,000. Where had he got the money? He would not answer me. 'Playing poker in New York,' he laughed. Playing something else in Hamburg, I suspected.

He took me aboard, eyes glowing, his moustaches electric with pride, and showed me the beautifully furnished stateroom and the cabins (none too large, those) with accommodation for six. 'You will travel with me', he said, 'together with my staff, as far as Honolulu, where I will transfer to the U.S. warship that will take me to Samoa.' I wanted to test him, so I said 'Say "will you", not "you will".' He looked genuinely mortified, he always had perfect manners, and subtly parodying his apology, he knelt before me, swept my feet with his grey hat, and said 'Sweet Emma, please, *will* you?' I couldn't resist him. He looked vulnerable, so proud of his yacht and yet at the mercy of someone to whom, I was sure, it really belonged, and not the tough worldly Colonel whose face he usually presented to the world. There was no one else aboard. Raising him to his feet, I whisked him into the Stateroom.

*

Early in February 1875 I sailed on the *Peerless*, but without Albert. He had received orders from Washington to delay his departure (ours too) and travel on U.S.S. *Pensacola* together with King Kalakua of Hawaii, that huge old lecher, gambler and drinker, like a Polynesian Henry VIII except he spared his wives. On the *Peerless* with me was Albert's 'staff', a rather nice if

alcoholic Major John Latrobe from an old Baltimore family who
was to drill the new Samoan militia; George Waters, some sort of
merchandise adviser, whose qualifications seemed to be a bank-
ruptcy in San Francisco; and a fellow called Charles Blake. I
learned with a sinking heart that they were both intimately connected with the Polynesian Company. I feared that that was the
true owner of the *Peerless*.

On a third ship the *D.C. Murry*, was my dear friend Caroline.
I had wanted her to travel with me on the *Peerless*, but Aunt
Elizabeth insisted that I was not moral enough a guardian, and
that she travel on the *D.C. Murry* on which her brother was mate.

I could fill pages with accounts of our junketing in Honolulu
at the Iolani Palace, and my pleasant conversations with my namesake, the widowed Queen. But my thoughts were on Samoa, and
Albert, always on official behaviour, seemed remote from me.
Champagne is the drink of festivity, and it must be cold, but the
drinker must be warm at heart. In Honolulu I was cold at heart.
Albert was already being treated as, and behaving like, the Premier
of Samoa, and he did not wish me at his side. Later, later, his
looks said.

So in a few days Commander Erben took Albert away in the
Tuscarora, and we followed after in little *Peerless*. Major Latrobe,
when he hadn't had too much whisky, was charming. Furious,
bereft, not in the least in love with him, I made him my lover.
He was a weak man, but handsome, with the real style of those
old East-coast families. I knew that in matters of love he was a
gentleman, and would not boast of my favours.

Love! I was born to be lucky with cards and money, unlucky
with love. My thin, delicate English Lord, consumptive like his
beloved Shelley, afraid of nothing though always denying it. Yes,
I loved him for those few days, but I never had any illusions he
would want to take his Princess, i.e. half-caste Mrs Forsayth, back
to his palace at Wilton. My husband I never loved. Now, damn it,
I loved this Jewish adventurer with his sleek black hair and his
bold eyes and his long, sensitive, asymmetrical moustaches. He
always had beautiful English silk cravats and shoes. But you
wouldn't call him dapper, sometimes he wouldn't look well-
dressed at all. He was a gentleman. And Father was wrong. He
really *was* a Colonel.

Chapter XII

JAMES LYLE YOUNG

June 1, 1875. Apia I arrived in this beautiful port yesterday from Fiji. How long I will stay I know not. I have funds for a year or so, but I trust that given my experience with coconut planting and copra drying I should have no trouble in finding employment with a planter, if necessary. I had expected to find Samoa in its usual state of native wars, but to my surprise it has an established Government, residing at Mulinu'u, the point of land to the east of Apia. The King is Laupepa Malietoa, an amiable man but weak, and his Premier is, astonishingly, an American, a Colonel Steinberger. Apparently he arrived just two months ago in a U.S. warship bearing a letter from President Grant, and the following gifts: 100 Springfield muzzle-loading rifle muskets, and 10,000 cartridges; one Gatling gun and carriage and 200 rounds for same; one 3-inch Parrott gun and carriage and ammunition; one forge; 100 sailors' suits and caps; 3 United States flags; instruments for a band; 12 revolvers, with ammunition; and 1 steam launch for the use of the Samoan Government. Thus does General Grant wish the peace of the United States to descend, the eagle with its beak full of arrows, on the islands of Samoa.

Colonel Steinberger also has a beautiful little private yacht, the *Peerless*, of 45 tons. I see he has mounted the Parrott gun on it.

The population of Samoa is 34,265. There are 12,539 inhabitants on the island of Savai'i; 16,568 on Upolu; 3,746 on Tutuila; 204 Europeans and Americans; 236 Polynesians; 4 Chinese; 475 imported labourers from the Gilbert Islands and Melanesia.

By far the biggest mercantile and planting interests here are German, with the firm of Goddefroy. The head of the firm here, Weber, is away in Hamburg, and an ineffectual substitute, Alfred

77

Poppe, is both acting German consul and Goddefroy manager, a fortuitous conjunction for Goddefroy's.

The British Consul, S. F. Williams, is also in an acting capacity, his father the Consul, John C. Williams, being mortally ill in Sydney. S. F. Williams is weak and unpopular.

The United States Consul is Samuel Foster, an unpleasant man given to drink, who by some intrigue succeeded Jonas Coe, a highly respected local resident who has occupied the post of Commercial Agent and Consul for many years. Mr Coe is the father of the celebrated Mrs Forsayth, a good-looking half-caste girl who has been well educated, she is now a widow with one encumbrance, and resides with her father. She is about the same age as myself. She is popularly known as 'The Princess.' She appears to be managing, although a woman, the trading firms of her father and her late husband. Mr Coe's secretary is a Mr Alvard who has been twenty-three years in Samoa, a gentleman, as is Mr Coe, of the good old New England blood, ay, and it must be remembered that that blood runs in the veins of many of the truest gentlemen, a species unfortunately too rare amongst the Americans one meets in the South Seas.

June 3 I met Colonel Albert Steinberger today. He is a man of about thirty-eight years of age, short of stature but well-built, very dark hair and complexion with black eyes and wears no beard or whiskers but a moustache only, altogether with a Spanish or Italian appearance. He seems well-informed and intelligent—rather too self-assertive and slightly egotistical but those are probably only faults of manner, and any man holding the position he does here, is a sort of 'Triton among minnows', and his self-love finds many flatterers. I am perhaps a little inclined to be suspicious of the character and motives of anyone attempting to form a native Government. Having spent most of the first twenty years of my life in Australia I am too much of a thorough-going democrat not to be suspicious of *anyone* in a position of power.

June 10 Dinner at J. M. Coe's. Everything I have heard about the celebrated Emma is true, she is a Princess who could be a Queen. Her elegance and beauty are matched by her wit, and she has an extraordinary knowledge of all aspects of commerce. When she heard of my experience of five years as a planter in Fiji she questioned me closely on all matters to do with coconut planting and the treatment of copra. I would pay court to her, but I am told she is the mistress of Steinberger. She has a young sister, Phoebe, a fine girl of about thirteen years, who is being educated by the Catholic Sisters. Harsh words were spoken about the Methodists, who will not take half-caste children in their white school. It is difficult for the half-caste population, who are amongst the most intelligent and personable of the inhabitants, when such discrimination is practised against them.

When I asked Mr Coe for some details about his successor in office, Mr Samuel Foster, I provoked an outburst. He told me Mr Foster had been a storekeeper in Tahiti and through his inefficiency and extravagance had gone bankrupt. He then ran a livery stable and abandoned himself to dissipation. After Foster had come to live in Apia, Mr Coe said he had several times seen him being driven to his home so helplessly drunk that he was incapable of setting up on the seat, he was placed in the bottom of the buggy with his head resting on the knees of the driver who with one hand supported him in that position while with the other he conducted the horse and buggy. I have heard from elsewhere that he displays an irascibility and childishness of temper most unbecoming in a man of his years. And this is the representative of the great United States! I am told he owes his appointment to the influence of the Polynesia Land Company, whose manager he was in Tutuila. Strange influence, when that Company is bankrupt! Mr Coe tells me he was absent from his office in Tutuila ten months out of nineteen.

Despite Mrs Forsayth's connection with Steinberger, Mr Coe is very much against him, it appears for personal reasons. I have not yet made up my mind about Steinberger.

16 June Away all day at a German plantation of Goddefroy's with Steinberger and three Samoan chiefs and Mrs Forsayth who acted as interpreter to investigate charges of brutality and general maltreatment of the Kingsmill Island labourers, who are clearly no better than slaves. The manager's name was Krause. When his wife (a white woman) volunteered some information in answer to a question by Steinberger, Krause struck her across the mouth.

Steinberger, much to his credit, particularly as Krause was a good deal taller than him, intervened and roundly denounced him. After several hours investigation it was clear that all the complaints were true, and that there have been floggings of both men and women, and that these ignorant islanders have been fraudulently got to work. The mortality amongst them is excessive. Krause was not better or worse than others I have met here and in Fiji. When once you give a white man unlimited power over ignorant natives he will surely misuse it and become a tyrant and a brute.

25 June I was playing billiards this evening when Steinberger came in and very rudely interrupted us to show off his admittedly considerable skill, offering no apologies. The worst of it is he was more than half drunk. He will make a nice mess of governing here if he pursues this course. His associate, Captain Latrobe, is frequently the worse for liquor. I am suspicious of Steinberger's relations with the Germans. Why has he done nothing about the well-authenticated maltreatment of labourers on the Goddefroy plantations?

30 June Colonel Steinberger dispenses free medicines every day, treating from forty to a hundred patients, almost all for trifling complaints. He is for this and many other reasons, such as his refusal to allow the alienation of their lands, much beloved of the Samoans. Yet I have heard him in his cups talking arrant nonsense and folly, boasting that he will conquer Tonga and annex the neighbouring islands. I thought him a genius, and behold! he is only a fool, that I am certain of; whether he be also a knave, is to be proved.

12 July Dinner at Mulinu'u with the high chiefs of the Government, Steinberger not present. Mr J. M. Coe, his wife and Mrs Forsayth also present. It is a curious and piquant situation. It appears that Mr Coe many years ago was the tutor of the king, Malietoa Laupepa, and that his first wife, Emma's mother, was a member of the Malietoa family. Now Mr Coe is a bitter foe of Colonel Steinberger, Laupepa's Premier, while Emma is the Colonel's mistress! Later in the evening Emma took us to the house of Malietoa Pe'a, the head of the Malietoa family, and uncle of the present king. A further amusing complication is that Mr Coe is the owner of the land at Mulinu'u on which the Government buildings stand! The origins of Mr Coe's hostility to Steinberger are probably in the fact that Steinberger refused to allow the validity of this title. But ironically, Commander Henry Erben of the *Tuscarora*, who has stood behind Steinberger in everything, in a court upset Steinberger's judgement, and allowed Mr Coe to have made a perfectly legal land purchase.

14 July I was present at the ceremony of Colonel Steinberger taking oath of office as Premier of the Samoan Government. He was dressed in a long white flannel coat (Austrian undress uniform) which was in execrable taste and in which he looked wretched, the coat being too long for him and making his naturally dark complexion look darker still. The oath was an absurdity. There was no book to swear on. Steinberger simply declared 'If I do wrong I can be removed', but he did not say who could remove him. There was a salute of seven guns, which did not work. There was a delay of ten minutes, Steinberger looking pathetic. Messages came to say the guns *won't* go off, Steinberger sends back word saying they *must* go off, amidst laughter from the spectators. I myself am from this day thoroughly convinced that Steinberger is an impostor and a shuffler. He is simply an adventurer. If he is a Special Agent of the U.S. Government, how can he take oath to the Samoan Government?

20 August Steinberger's new liquor regulations are a farce. The hotels are eleven in all, not counting shanties, the best at Matafele being Frewen's, Henry's British Lion, Cook's International, Burmeister's German, Bell's Russian Bear, Morris' Tahiti Bay, and at Apia proper, Chinaman's and Frewen's. Steinberger aims to please the Missionaries with these regulations, but at the same time he is alienating them by his loose and profligate style of living, and by his getting the natives to perform all the old forbidden dances.

Anybody who writes about the South Seas and attacks the missionaries is immediately denounced by the LMS or the Wesleyans as a beachcomber, a pirate, a kidnapper or an 'adventurer'. A very convenient phrase that last is. 'Adventurers' are the men who have made England what she is. Fighting between the sects does more harm to the general cause of religion than drinking or dancing or Sunday trading. I will back the spectacle of two ministers of the Gospel of Peace and Love contending with each other in bitterness of spirit, and refusing to shake hands with each other when they meet, to do more harm and discredit to the Bible than all the beachcombers in the Pacific, abandoned race though they be.

4 September Mr John Steinberger, the Colonel's elder brother arrived, President of a silver mining company in California, a steadier and quieter man that his brother albeit he reminds me of a master butcher. They say he has lent his brother money and has come down to see what prospect there is of it being repayed.

I am leaving Samoa shortly, with many regrets. The Samoans are a wonderfully refined people, handsome and intelligent, and their language is the Italian of the Pacific. I have experienced the greatest kindness both from the Samoans and from the white residents who are on the whole the best-hearted and most hospitable people I have met, particularly the British Consul, and Messrs J. M. Coe, Alvard and Hamilton.

In spite of this refinement, the sexual morality of the Samoans is at a very low ebb, in fact they have none. Virtue, as we understand it, absolutely does not exist. In civilized countries when a woman loses her virtue (and is known to have lost it) she becomes a pariah and outcast, and the sense of shame and sin which she feels soon drag her to the lowest depths! But here there is little shame attached to it, and certainly no sense of sin. On the whole the peculiar state of morality, and the deliciously 'free and easy' tone that pervades everything is better left undescribed in public. In private, I will happily admit that Samoa is as close to paradise as I shall attain.

24 November Happily I have returned to Samoa. I find that since my absence Colonel Steinberger has made himself even more popular with the Samoans, but that he has earned the implacable hostility of all respectable Europeans. I am told that he intends on the first available U.S. man of war to run out of the country the U.S. Consul Foster, and J. M. Coe, Hamilton, Alvard and

Parker. Foster and Coe have been forced into an uneasy alliance. Steinberger has been conducting himself in an outrageous manner, drinking constantly, and he seems to have 'gone native', walking about his place wearing nothing but a fathom of cloth or a Samoan mat, chasing the Chiefs' daughters about the beach in this rig, and running after the young girls at night in the most shameless manner, and getting up all the old heathen dances. Captain Latrobe is always beastly drunk.

16 December H.M.S. *Barracouta*, Captain Stevens, a paddle-steamer of 1000 tons, arrived—she refused to exchange salutes with *Peerless*, and Captain Stevens did not call on Colonel Steinberger. This was the result of an immediate visit on board by Consul Williams and Dr Turner of the LMS, who have made Captain Stevens's duty clear to him.

17 December The drama has commenced! *Peerless* was seized today by Mr J. M. Coe acting as 'Marshall' under the orders of the U.S. Consul, and she was sailed by Hamilton (the Pilot) from her anchorage at Matautu to the small harbour and dismantled. *Peerless* was seized for a breach of the Neutrality Laws of the U.S., in that she was an armed vessel. Immediately afterwards, Mr A. L. Poppe the German Consul came forward with a protest against the seizure, as she is mortgaged to a citizen of San Francisco named J. B. Ford and Poppe holds the mortgage as Ford's agent.

16 December It looks as if the sides are drawing up for war. Steinberger has ordered all the Cannon etc. from Mulinu'u and the ammunition stored behind Dr Turner's house to be moved to a native fort west of the town. At 2 a.m. this morning this was accomplished, the operation being superintended by Emma Forsayth! Thus her father has seized Steinberger's yacht while she is safeguarding Steinberger's guns!

Chapter XIII

————•————

JONAS COE

30 December 1875 I have been a fool, a damn, pig-headed New England fool. I have allowed my personal hostility towards Colonel Steinberger to overthrow my judgement so that I have been used as a tool by despicable people, notably Samuel Foster. I have disliked Steinberger for two reasons, viz. 1. he has obstructed my land claims, and 2. he has not behaved honourably towards my daughter. It is true that Emma says she bears no resentment towards him for his wild fornications, but he should have married her, whether *fa'a Samoa* or missionary style. She forgives him everything. Only a few days ago she was out at three o'clock in the morning organizing the removal of guns on his behalf.

But she is right. I should have trusted her judgement. Steinberger, with all his faults, is Premier of our Samoan Government, as Laupepa is our king. The missionaries are against him because of his loose living, the Consuls (except Poppe) because of his power, but the important thing for us who live here and hope to die here is that he has the almost total support of the Samoan chiefs and people. When you talk to someone like Asi Tunipopo, Emma's kinsman, a high chief and an educated man, you realize that the Samoans, although Laupepa is a weak man, are united and happy as they have never been before. They have a Constitution that works, and a set of laws which are tolerable and can be side-stepped as all laws ought to be, if without dishonesty. The Samoans give credit for this to Steinberger, and his arrival in the *Tuscarora* proved that he had the support of General Grant.

Now into Apia harbour sails, or rather paddles, a damn, jumped-up pipsqueak of a British naval officer, a Captain Stevens, who thinks he has a Divine right to take over Samoa with his blue-jackets. Over Christmas he had the King, the Premier and the

Government turn out in front of him like a bunch of sailors on a charge, and him all dressed up in his fancy uniform, demanding Steinberger's 'credentials.' I don't believe Steinberger has any, whatever they should be, but what does it matter? What matters is that Laupepa made an address saying that the Samoans did not care about credentials, if Steinberger deceived them then they could discard him.

Stevens on his own would be bad enough, but right behind him is the infamous Foster and Williams the British Consul and young Turner of the LMS, a pretty collection of crooks and bigots. Sitting on the sidelines is James Lyle Young, a pleasant enough young man who has been often to my house and has often cast an eye, in vain, towards my Emma. In September he left Samoa, but he has just returned, and Emma has it from Steinberger that he is a spy in the pay of Sir Arthur Gordon, the British Governor of Fiji. I don't know about that, but he is too damn friendly with Stevens. He has breakfasted aboard the *Barracouta*. Also he never seems to lack for money and does not seek employment. Who can one trust in these days?

Not that vile dog Foster. I have heard that he has been boasting that he will discredit me by proving that I have committed defalcations in the account books during my many years of office as Commercial Agent. Such accusations to come from *that* dishonest scoundrel! Though, in truth, God knows how many irregularities may appear if the books are examined by hostile eyes. I have never been as careful as I should have been with accounts, as Emma has pointed out to me so often. Would that I had had her running my financial affairs these past twenty years!

Now I have been duped by Foster into seizing the *Peerless* as the first step in encompassing Steinberger's downfall. I hear that the real reason for her seizure was that she was on the eve of sailing for Hawaii with letters for the State Department about the highly irregular actions of Foster, Stevens, et al. Now on the 28th these people got up a petition of 51 foreign residents to Captain Stevens asking him to protect them against the Steinberger government. In my new role of supporting Steinberger I easily persuaded all the Americans and Germans not to sign it.

2 January 1876   So desperate are this gang to stop Steinberger getting despatches away that they towed the *Satellite* out of the harbour at 4 a.m.—and in the process wrecked her on the reef! I hear Steinberger has chartered the *Vision*.

18 January They have got up another petition, which I again have countered. This one begs Captain Stevens to remove Steinberger because he is a dangerous man and neither life nor propriety can be considered as safe while he remains in the country. Whereas the only threat to our safety comes from Stevens and his blue-jackets! Of course they have no legal way of removing Steinberger, for he is Premier of the Samoan Government, and only King Malietoa Laupepa could remove him.

9 February By God! they have done it. They hauled poor weak Laupepa aboard the *Barracouta* and that verminous LMS cleric Turner worked on him until he signed a letter dictated to him (to anybody reading it the dictation is painfully patent), asking for Steinberger's removal. Laupepa I was fond of as a boy, he was my pupil, but he has always been under the thumb of the LMS. Privately I always thought it was because they told him that self-abuse, which is accounted perfectly normal in Samoa, was a deadly sin. Such trifles of the body may, if ceaselessly aggravated by moral threats, cause cankers in the soul.

So Malietoa signed on the night of the 7th, and on the 8th Captain Stevens and 75 bluejackets and marines went ashore and arrested Steinberger and took him aboard the *Barracouta*. Steinberger's friends amongst the Samoans, who are by far the majority, immediately seized Laupepa and deposed him. Emma and I were present at many noisy meetings during the night persuading the Samoans to send Laupepa away to Savai'i, for there is such anger that I fear for his safety. At 10.30 p.m. we succeeded and got him off in a boat.

Some of the Samoans want me to take over as interim Premier. I am tempted, because I could interpret their wishes, but the situation is too shifting and dangerous at the moment.

Chapter XIV

——————•——————

EMMA

12 February 1876 Albert has been publicly exposed as a villain, and by that arch-villain Samuel Foster. I always knew Albert was a devil with money and women, but they were trifles I could understand and forgive. Father said his intentions towards me were strictly dishonourable. Of course they were, and I could always read them in his black eyes and his moustaches. Sometimes he would say he would marry me if he could be sure I was a widow. James Forsayth was a handy excuse. But in love one need not forget to forgive.

He was loved by the Samoans, and he worked for their good and not his gain, and he lived and moved around among them not as a stranger from a white European house on the Beach, but as a dweller in these islands like themselves, who slept on a mat in a *fale* and wore a *lava lava*. It was funny that while Albert, the Premier, dressed like a Samoan, the King, Malietoa Laupepa, liked to dress up in a white uniform with long knee-high leggings of yellow leather, and be escorted by three white-clad soldiers with rifles. Asi Tunipopo spoke for everyone when he said that To'o (that's what they called Albert because they could not pronounce his name) was a friend they could trust because he brought the gift of himself to them. He did not belong to Jesus, or to a ship, or to copra or even to General Grant from whom he had brought so many presents.

Well, Asi was wrong. Albert belonged to Cesar Goddefroy und Sohn, Hamburg. He had sold himself to them, from the tips of his moustaches to the toes of his well-bred little feet. Imagine the relish with which the vile Foster, who had stolen all Albert's papers, called us and the High Chiefs together and read out the contract between Albert and Goddefroy. 'This iniquitous contract!'

His whisky-hoarse voice trembled with joy and the red wattles of his jowls glowed with vindictiveness. Yet, Holy Mary Mother of God, he was right, it *was* iniquitous.

I will never forget those phrases. The look on Father's face, he had only recently changed sides to support Albert. That peculiarly virtuous British smugness on the faces of Captain Stevens and Consul Williams. Yes, and the embarrassment on the fat foolish face of Poppe, Goddefroy manager and German Consul. Those awful phrases! 'Colonel Steinberger will pledge himself to the proper and legitimate interests of the establishment of Johann Cesar Goddefroy und Sohn at Apia, and to avoid all other business connexions *in toto* in Apia. He will identify the interest of the Samoan Government with that of the establishment of J. C. Goddefroy.' Oh, that was almost the worst count against him!

The terrible clauses rolled out. All copra and cocoa to be sold through Goddefroy. A coinage to be introduced and Goddefroy to be given the monopoly of coining. A. B. Steinberger to receive $2 a ton on all copra and cocoa sold, and a commission of 10 per cent on anything sold by the Samoan Government to Goddefroy.

And the money. They had bought the *Peerless* for him, and the mortgage to that American in San Francisco was really a front for them. His total debt to them was $13,982, to be repaid with 6 per cent interest. Again those phrases. 'Our agent in San Francisco will be as discreet as cautious in every respect you may rely upon it. . . . It is a difficult task you have to fulfil but having had the pleasure of your personal acquaintance we feel convinced that a failure of your mission may be considered as next to an impossibility.' Oh yes, I know the pleasures of that personal acquaintance, that damned charm while he smoked Johann Cesar's best Brazils and stroked his moustache.

'And Mr Poppe will take care that everything will be managed with great discretion in order to avoid all unnecessary comments at Samoa.' Mr Poppe ground his teeth at that.

'Our ladies unite in kind regards to you.' So. So.

Then, as if the Goddefroy agreement was not enough, horrible Foster with the grin of a vampire fastening on another rich vein, produced an agreement with Latrobe. For an undisclosed sum the family—his uncle is Governor of Maryland—sold him off to Albert, in return for a guarantee of 25 per cent of all the profits Albert made in Samoa, and a promise that Latrobe would have the best, most honourable and most lucrative office under the said Samoan Government.

Foster flourished another paper saying that Albert had been paid $25,000 by the Polynesian Land Company. That was the end. If ever there was an enemy of the Samoan people, it was that fraudulent Polynesian Land Company.

Except for the Samoans present, Father and I were the only ones who did not immediately start congratulating themselves on Steinberger's downfall. 'I always knew he was an impostor, he never took any action about slave-labour on German plantations', said that spy from Fiji, J. L. Young. What hypocrites the British are! They have shiploads of slaves running into Queensland all the time. I saw through the British, that's what caused Father to change sides and support Albert. The whole aim of Stevens and Williams in kidnapping Albert is to upset American influence in Samoa, so Sir Arthur Gordon can come in from Fiji with another warship and take over. And that Foster is such a fool he has helped them do it, even though he is U.S. Consul! He would do anything to discredit Father, I know he has had Young and some others nosing around in the Consular books, they're in a hell of a mess, you could prove anything from them, though Father never intended to embezzle a cent. This will be a case where honour among thieves is proved by branding the only honest man a thief.

13 February Despite the evidence of the documents, I had to see Albert. It was not easy, Stevens is scared of Father and myself, he knows our influence with the Chiefs. In the end we got out to the *Barracouta*, and found poor Albert confined in a cabin that could only be called a cell, with two marines outside the door. My dapper lover was a wet rag, almost insensible with the heat and lack of air. You should have heard Father bawl out Stevens with all that New England style! 'You call yourself an officer and a gentleman in the Navy of Nelson and Rodney, and you treat the Premier of Samoa and a Colonel of the United States in a way the Samoans would not treat their pigs! Go ashore and learn some courtesy from the people whose country you are plunging into ruin and confusion.' On he went, it was great style, and he soon had Stevens apologizing to Albert.

Albert admitted everything about Goddefroys, but he said it was only to get the best terms for Samoa, that in general terms he had reported his actions to the State Department. He said he had had some 'small loans' from the Latrobe family, but he angrily denied that he had ever had a dollar from the Polynesian Land Company. Do I believe him? I don't know. I ought to hate him, but now my first anger is over I am all Samoan, calm after storm. I don't love him any more. Am I without pity? Or again, is it my Samoan blood making me proof against romantic attachment? Besides, he is diminished as a man, this little sweaty fellow in captivity.

15 February I know it will not be long before Stevens and Foster move against Father. First of all, to show their power (which is really only that of the *Barracouta's* guns), they sailed off to Savai'i and brought back King Malietoa Laupepa. And I myself had written out the order by which the High Chiefs deposed him! Stevens landed him at the British Consulate (not at Mulinu'u!) with a salute of 21 guns and left him under guard. Stevens tried to stop Father and myself going down to Mulinu'u to talk to the Chiefs. Of course he had no right to do so, and we ignored his marines.

In the evening Dr C. M. Steinberger, Albert's brother, a physician, arrived from San Francisco and came to stay with us. He is a respectable person, though too fond of the Monongahela.

26 February Thanks to my Samoan friends in Foster's office, I have seen a report on Father saying there is a discrepancy of about $2000 in his fee books from 1864 to 1874. They say no proper records were kept. If so, how do they know about this discrepancy? I know that Father was always muddling his own dealings with those of the Agency. I do not doubt him. I also intercepted a letter from Stevens and Williams saying that Father and I should be arrested for 'stirring up the Natives.'

29 February That rat Foster, backed up by five marines from the *Barracouta*, entered our house by the rear and arrested Father for 'disturbing the peace of the country and inciting the Natives to oppose the Consuls.' Whose country is this? Does Samoa belong to the Samoans or to Foster and Williams?

Emma

3 March They tried to deport Father today to San Francisco on the *Ada May*, but I told them they could not do so without putting him on trial. This they threaten to do. I was much amused at an interchange between Foster and Stevens. Stevens says he wants his marines back, who are guarding Father. Foster says 'The authorities will not assist me with a guard because J. M. Coe has been their principal friend and adviser.' The marines had to stay.

14 March For two days they have had Father on trial, accusing him of endangering the peace and welfare of Samoa, and for fomenting ill-feeling on the part of the Natives against the Representative of Foreign Powers. Also for embezzling $2,361 from the Agency accounts. I knocked that one out by quoting an Act of Congress, 1866, stating that Consuls have no power to try criminal cases. Father admitted the error in the books and stated that it was not due to fraud but carelessness. Needless to say, the so-called Court found him guilty of the first charge, and ordered that he be sent to America to answer the embezzlement charge. I spent the evening with Father writing letters for San Francisco and Washington to report the illegality of all proceedings here, and to clear Father's name. We all gave evidence at the 'trial', ten high chiefs supporting Father. My favourite moment was when one witness, Mr Parker, describing the events on the night Malietoa was deposed, said that when Father heard that Foster was coming to Mulinu'u to talk to the Chiefs he waved the stick in his hand and said he'd like to knock the old son of a bitch's head off. What a pity Parker restrained him from doing so.

15 March This is the blackest day in Samoan history. Captain Stevens with a force of marines and bluejackets, a band and all the missionaries and Consuls, marched to Mulinu'u to reinstate Laupepa as King. Fighting broke out, started by the marines, and in no time a score of men on either side were killed or wounded. I was in our buggy with Phebe and Asi Tunipopo and I feared for our lives, bullets were flying everywhere. This is the first bloodshed between Samoans and Europeans in Samoan history. The fault lies entirely with Captain Stevens and the Consuls.

91

Chapter XV

JAMES LYLE YOUNG

15 March 1876   What a day! We all moved in a procession to Mu'linu'u, to reinstate Malietoa Laupepa as King. The whole population of Apia must have turned out, to trail along behind Captain Stevens and thirty-five to forty marines and bluejackets. We halted outside the church, and Captain Stevens prepared to make his announcement, while Laupepa waited to make his speech on the dismissal of Steinberger and the arrest of J. M. Coe. At this moment armed natives, of Latrobe's 'army', appeared out of the *fales* and bushes, cutting off our retreat. There was a tenseness in the air. I had always thought it foolish of Foster and Stevens to have brought Laupepa back when the Chiefs had deposed him.

Captain Stevens sent Lieutenant McLeod over to a group of soldiers to enquire the meaning of this apparent hostility. McLeod attempted to disarm a man who was threatening him. A musket went off, and immediately the marines and bluejackets began firing, the first man to fall being Josefa who had fired the first shot. One of the *Barracouta's* boats put in and took off the King, the Consuls and missionaries. Ezra Williams dropped a native dead at eighty to ninety yards, a pretty shot.

Captain Parr and I set off along the road, he armed with an umbrella, myself with a revolver. At the back of Steinberger's residence I suddenly came upon a native with a breech-loading carbine aiming at me from fifteen yards. I thought all was up. He missed. While he was attempting to reload I ran up and shot him through the jaw. A bluejacket finished him off. So ended that native's military career.

Stevens finally persuaded the natives to lay down their arms. Ten whites are wounded, one dead and two more likely to die. Eight natives are dead and twenty-five to thirty wounded. A curious feature of the whole proceedings was the presence throughout amongst the natives of many women and children. The native soldiers, trained by Latrobe, instigated the attack. Captain Stevens behaved very coolly.

Back at the house of Foster, the Consul, we prepared for an attack and barricaded the house. It was a very black night and rained horribly. It was feared that Coe would be rescued.

16 March   Coe has been safely put aboard the *Barracouta*. I gave it as my opinion to Foster and Captain Stevens that they ought also to have arrested his daughter Mrs Forsayth. She is as dangerous as her father, and she has the added lustre amongst the natives, who have by no means abandoned their loyalty to Steinberger, of being Steinberger's mistress. Or one of them, for he had a harem of Samoan girls, though obviously none of the quality of Emma. She does not like me, but I cannot help admiring her. She is dismayed at the exposure of Steinberger, but she will not publicly turn against him. Once he has been sent away, and her father also, she will be very much alone, and I may have my opportunity to pay court to her. She has prospects in Samoa, with her late husband's trading firm, but I have none, being *persona non grata* with Goddefroys and the Germans. A thought—what if Captain Forsayth should return from the sea?

29 March   The *Barracouta* left today for Auckland, carrying on board her Steinberger and Coe, who have been deported.

Chapter XVI

———————•———————

PHEBE

I was a girl of twelve when all these things happened, a little girl of twelve by Samoan standards, for the Sisters and Emma and my father had been very strict with me.

But I was the big girl who comforted Emma the night they sent my father and the Colonel away on the warship. I never knew Emma weep before, and only once since. The two men she loved most in all the world had been taken by force from her. She knew the Colonel had betrayed not only her but all of us Samoans, but she still loved him, the little smart rogue. She was taller than him, wasn't that crazy? Someone as bossy as Emma, to be loved by a man whose sleek black hair was not much higher than her eyelashes! Anyway, I couldn't blame her, the Colonel did so much for us Samoans, he was the one man who gave us unity and stopped our stupid wars, and the way the Government worked it could have kept working, even with a weak king like Laupepa.

And my father, Emma was so worried that he should clear his name in America, as if that mattered, everyone trusted him here, except a few villains like Foster, and who would trust them? My father could have succeeded the Colonel as Premier if he had wanted to, but he said he was an old man (fifty-two!) and wanted peace and quiet.

In September my father came home, and we were able to piece together everything that had happened. The *Barracouta* took them as far as Fiji, where the Colonel's brother helped them. The Governor released them from custody. The Colonel went from there to Auckland and Australia and then to London, my father direct to San Francisco. The Colonel wrote many good articles for the Australian papers, and the facts in these helped clear him and my father from the accusations against them. In May, Presi-

94

dent Grant invited my father to Washington to see him, and explain personally the intrigues of the British and the malevolence of Foster.

It's not in my nature to be vindictive, but I hugged my father for joy when we heard that Foster and Williams had both been sacked from their Consulates, and later that Captain Stevens had been relieved of his command and then dismissed from the Navy. Though none of these things could bring our dead friends back to life.

But this was much later, and I was with Emma in April 1876, when indeed things did look very bad for all of us in the Coe family. My father's affairs were not at all in good order, and Emma, who by this time looked after all our business matters, was not capable even of looking after herself. My mother Le'utu as always when there was a crisis, came back and ran the household. Those other wives of father's had gone away or died; later he took a couple more.

The Colonel had promised the Samoans he would come back, and they believed him. Not so Emma. Even when distracted by grief so that she could not see herself clearly, she could still see other people as if they were coral at the bottom of a pool inside the reef.

'No, Phebe,' she said to me, 'Albert won't come back because he *can't* come back. He has been humiliated, he has lost *mana*, even if the Samoans don't realize it yet, he knows. Did you hear that Foster seized all his goods, all his personal belongings, and auctioned them off? Lots of Samoans bought little oddments, to have a piece of To'o. When I saw Albert on board the *Barracouta* he told me it was if he had died and little pieces of his body had been spread around Samoa. He is a very proud man, and *he* knows he has lost his *mana*. He is also a very shrewd man, and he knows that the Germans, who are the most powerful traders in Samoa, will have nothing more to do with him. No, Albert won't come back. He will go to New York and very soon he will marry a rich wife.'

Emma was right. Later when we were in New Guinea she heard that he had married a wealthy widow in New York in 1878. He died in 1883. He never wrote a word to Emma. He was an adventurer, and his Samoan adventure was over.

We had a distant kinsman, a Samoan called Asi Tunipopo from Matafagatele, which is a few miles eastwards along the coast from our house at Matautu, a very pretty village, the real Samoan peace, between the white thunder of the reef and the green silence of the hills, oh you could live your life out there in joy, surrounded by good people with no money or account books, with no rich and no poor, with the old people looked after and the young ones with many mothers and fathers, not a soul amongst them lost or neglected or outcast. Now Asi asked Emma and her son Coe, and me and Caroline and Mary Ann, to come and live with him in the village, leaving Sa and baby Laura with Le'utu at Matautu.

Emma wanted to go. She indeed did feel lost, neglected, outcast. Those horrible missionaries and their wives, particularly the LMS and the Wesleyans (that nice Reverend Brown had gone away to New Guinea) had cut her dead because of the Colonel. One old bitch said of her in public, so she could hear, 'The Colonel's lady! Ha! The Colonel's whore.' These are the same missionaries who are always writing to people in England about the immorality of our Samoan life. They hate us half-castes, and except for the Catholics they will not even have us in our schools. They doubly hated Emma because she was a half-caste and the mistress of the Premier, the man they all loved at first because of his efforts to bring law and order to Samoa. In this he succeeded, but they could not forgive him because he told the Samoans there was nothing wrong with their old customs and dances, and that they should not be ashamed of them. A sense of shame is the first weapon of the missionary. Emma never did have any sense of shame, despite the efforts of the Sisters. At this moment she would not have cared about being an outcast, because she had only been cast out by people she despised. (Is it not amusing that these people are such snobs that although everyone knew she had had a love affair with the Earl of P——, they all hoped she might bring him to tea, so they never said a word!) No, Emma would not have felt an outcast, had she not been betrayed by the Colonel and bereft of her father.

So we all went to Matafagatele, and lived in *fales* by the sea, and Asi was kind to us, and Emma was kind to him. Her body was always a source of strength to her as well as the means of strength. When her fortunes were at her lowest, her undiminished sensual powers were a touchstone that brought the first gold back into her empty chest. The world of Asi's village was all of the body, all of flesh. The body was feasted, Emma and us girls coming to live in the village meant that all our kinspeople must bring presents of food, so there were feasts of pork, baked taro, raw fish, lobsters, octopus, sea eggs and all the fruits. The body was oiled and rubbed and pounded. Emma was tired and unhappy and so she needed *lomilomi*, massage, to fill the flesh full of joy and energy again. Emma's body had been forsaken by her lover, so it must be held close and loved into life again. As we young girls sat by the stream with our feet on the rocks in the brown water, threading flowers to hang around our necks, we giggled with approval as we heard how Asi had made good love to her. How when she was so limp and miserable his good strong body had made her stand up straight again. We thought that was fine, and longed for it ourselves. This is one thing the missionaries could never understand about us Samoans. I remember Emma showing me a letter that was published about us by one of the Wesleyan missionaries, not Mr Brown, a Reverend Dyson his name was. This is the sort of thing he wrote: 'The lust of the flesh pollutes the whole land. Bigamy, polygamy, adultery, and fornication are crimes which smoke from the hovels of every tribe. Lewdness meets with unblushing countenance the public eye. From their childhood the Samoans are familiar with the most obscene conversation and immorality is the natural consequence. Their ideas of virtue are low and coarse.'

Fancy calling our *fales*, so clean and airy, hovels! Truly the missionaries were serpents, because they wanted to corrupt us with the knowledge of their brand of good and evil. It was not ours. And they never doubted that this knowledge represented a 'higher' set of values than ours.

Well, the smoke of our immorality came from a fire which cleansed Emma. After a few weeks she was her old self, glowing with her own ripe, taut-skinned style of beauty, with that special tartness of hers, her wit, that was delicious at the same time, like lemons. You know how lemon juice makes everything smell clean? Well Emma when she was gay and happy was like that, her presence freshened the air. And at nights she would dance till the sweat and the coconut oil shone like wet pearl-shell under the moon.

I could have stayed in the village for ever, life was rounded out, the shape of growing, the to-and-fro circle of the sea around the island, no horrid little sharp straight lines closing like scissors, the way the missionaries like life to be, dividing the world up into black and white, right and wrong, good and bad. The Sisters were different, when I was younger I used to long to be like them, because their life was so peaceful, but not when I was thirteen. Now I see that there was an odd similarity between the life of the Sisters and the life of the village, though they seemed so different. They were both bred within circles of contentment because they obeyed strict rules, nothing upset the order of things.

But Emma was too complicated for contentment. After a month or so I could see she was getting bored with life in the village. She loved listening to the village orator, his wonderful tales and rich poetry, and she enjoyed the battles with other village orators, where the winner was rewarded not only with fine mats and food but with the honour of victory. She responded to the beauty of the Samoan language, she shared the respect everyone in the village had for the words of speech. But she was also in love with the written word, something quite foreign to old Samoa. Though Asi was an educated man he could not talk to her about books, about politics or history. And she missed her piano. She had been teaching me at home, but I knew I would never be able to play like her, I had to learn every note, whereas she could pick up a tune and put something underneath it, as well as play sonatas and things. Her education and bringing-up in Sydney and San Francisco had given her a taste for all sorts of odd pleasures you don't find in a Samoan village. Fine sewing for example. Or, something quite different, champagne! But perhaps most of all she missed what I was most glad to get away from, the world of money and business, trading, account books, battles of will with hard traders, her sharp eye seeing through shady dealers, the fun of outbuying the great firm of Goddefroy in a copra deal at Falealili, the fun of understanding the different speeds and ways in which men think, Americans, Germans, English, Samoans. You see, for her, business was *fun*, that's why she was so good at it. And she knew how to relax, so she never became a machine adding up figures and calculating profit margins. She used to read her history books late at night to put business right out of her head so she would sleep well and rise with her mind all clean and sparkling like the morning beach after the night tide has run over it.

She worried about her father too, she thought she was letting him down running away to the village and not looking after his business, and her own Forsayth interests as well, for she knew no one else would be managing as efficiently as she could. In short, her body was refreshed, and now her mind was hungry.

Chapter XVII

THOMAS FARRELL

I was sick of a life at sea, at forty a man wants to settle down on dry land, put his feet up and sleep the night through without worrying whether the anchor's dragging. I'd saved up a bit. When I went home to Sydney in 1875 from Auckland they told me Samoa's the place to go. Free for all, no customs duties, taxes. Some American running the government who'd cut out all their wars. The man to see was Coe, an American who'd married a good few Samoan wives and was cousins with everybody in the country.

So I sailed into Apia and introduced myself to him. Only a little cove, up to my shoulder, but looked at you real tough. 'An Australian, eh? Well, you look a cut above most of them, even if you are an Irish one.' If the bugger had meant to be cheeky I'd have knocked him down whatever his cousins, but he had a twinkle in his eye and said something about having been brought up in Boston, so he knew all about the Irish and thank God I hadn't started to be-jasus him. Those sort of Irish give me a pain in the cods, too.

I said I wanted to buy a pub, or something like that.

He's looking out the window, on to Apia Harbour, at a big ship that came in about the same time as us. '*Pedraya*, for Goddefroy, made a fine passage of fifty-one days around the Cape of Good Hope. Know anything about Germans?' I shook my head. 'Well then you'd better learn if you're going to settle in Apia. And if you're going to run a pub the other thing you'll need is your fists, drunkenness is getting worse among the natives, which means it's getting like it's always been among the Beach Europeans. But I guess you won't need to learn how to use your fists. You want to buy a pub?'

I nodded.

'You've timed it well, Captain Farrell. I happen to know that old Schuhmacher who runs the Familienhof wants to sell out. It's a respectable house, and if you rechristened it something like the Family and Commercial you'd keep the German clientele and get English and American as well. Even some of your Australian riff-raff, as long as you made sure they could pay first.'

And that's just what I did and in no time I had an advertisement in the *Samoa Times* soliciting custom for the Samoa Family and Commercial Hotel, Apia. Thomas Farrell prop.

That's jumping ahead. I was still in old Coe's office, thanking him for his help, when in the door bursts a creature—a woman— well now, how should I go on. She's dressed in white, but she's no angel. She's dark, dark of skin and hair, but she's no devil, or at least the devil in her would make a man risk hell for her. She was frowning with rage and sighing with love. 'They've arrested Colonel Steinberger', she says in that low voice of anger that's more deadly than a shout. 'They've kidnapped him on to the *Barracouta*.'

> Oh! think what the kiss and smile must be worth
>   When the sigh and the frown are so perfect in bliss;
> And own, if there be an Elysium on earth,
>   It is this, it is this.

I'm not one of your stage Irishmen, but I love my Tom Moore.

'What's this great bearded hulk murmuring to himself about?' she turns to her father, exiling me from Samoa with one blast of her eyes.

Coe introduces us but she takes no notice of me, going on about this cove Steinberger. I was regularly stunned. She was a boomer. I knew now why Fate had sent me to Samoa.

> Shadows of Beauty,
>   Shadows of Power,
> Rise to your duty,
>   This is the hour.

Old Tom always had the words for it.

Now was my chance. Never let yourself believe the other bugger's going to win. 'Have you got a boat, now?'

The two of them stopped talking. Coe nodded.

'Well give it to me and I'll go aboard *Barracouta* and get Colonel Steinberger off for you.'

She looked at me for the first time, bang cool in the eyes like a southerly buster. 'You would, you great red Australian, I do believe you would.' Then I saw the intelligence of her, that woman who'd been all emotion. 'No, we must avoid violence. Captain Stevens is longing to use his guns and those horrible tubes of rockets he's got pointing at Mulinu'u. Albert won't want to wade ashore through Samoan blood.' Then she went out with her father and I'd lost her.

It was a strange time to be setting up a hotel, with the country looking as if it might blow to bits. But I reckoned I'd come at the right minute, and not only for business. I heard that her husband was supposed to be lost at sea, and that she'd been Steinberger's mistress, though I'd already had no doubts on that. That was two men out of the way. I knew I wasn't within cooee of her yet, but I was in a good position to wait it out. And what if her husband wasn't in Davy Jones' locker? Sure, I'd a wife myself in Sydney, the drunken bitch. Out here in the South Seas you're a free man. You can always move on to another island, you and the one you want to take with you.

One night after they'd taken her father away too she came in to the hotel. I could see she was all stirred up, in a mad mood. She shouted drinks all round. A *woman*! Had champagne for herself. Then she sat down at the piano. Old Coe had spent a fortune on educating his Princess. She summoned me to her. Bloody well waved her hand and I went. Princess all right.

'I hear you can sing, Captain Farrell.'

I admitted to a partiality for singing, too modest to call it an ability, though I knew damn well I'd a fine voice.

'Let's have an Irish song, then.'

Well I thought she wanted me to go into something like 'In Ireland the dear land, when I was a boy,' so maybe with her troubles she could have a bit of a weep over the champagne, but hell, no! When I tried a note or two, she says 'None of your damn sentimental rubbish! Something to put spirit into us. Do you know the wicked song they taught me in Subiaco convent, thank the

Lord Sister Monica never heard us.' She struck up 'Saint Patrick was a gentleman'. Away we went, I was never in better voice.

'No wonder that we Irish boys should be so gay and frisky,
For Saint Patrick taught the happy knack of drinking
    of the whiskey.
'Twas he that brewed the best o'malt, and understood distillin',
For his mother kept a sheeban shop, in the town of Inniskillen.'

And away we went together in the chorus, she'd a clear, strong voice as well as a nimble pair of hands on the keys.

Noh! noh! noh! noh!
Success attend Saint Patrick's fist, for he's the dacent saint O,
He gave the bugs and toads a twist, he's a beauty
    without paint O!

What a night we had! She must have put two bottles of champagne away by herself when she suddenly says, all in a low voice, 'Captain Farrell, can we go into your office and talk business.'

I'd have jumped into the harbour to talk anything with her.

It was business, she meant it. It seemed she had the two trading stores, Forsayth's and Coe's, and the brig. She wanted to transfer the lot to me, in case those buggers Stevens and Foster seized her father's property like they had Steinberger's and auctioned it off. I was in fact to run the brig and the trading business for her, and share in the profits. I suggested she move in and run the hotel, but I could have bitten my tongue out, I'd rushed her. The champagne bubbles hadn't gone to her head. No, she said she wanted to go bush, sweat it out in a village with her relatives. But she added that that wouldn't be for ever. She didn't exactly give me any hopes but she didn't wipe me off like a dirty boot.

Well, you can imagine I did some quick thinking. I liked the thought of going back to sea for a voyage round the islands every now and then. But most of all, of course, it gave me the opportunity of being Emma's partner, almost. Something I'd never have dreamed of. I accepted her offer, like a shot.

I thought she'd be off then, her business done, but no, it was back to the piano for a last song. I thought I could risk something a bit more tender. I was right. I won't say she smiled at me as she played, but at least there was a smile about her.

Though fate, my girl, may bid us part,
　　Our souls it cannot, shall not sever . . .
. . . No, no; yet, love, I will not chide,
　　Although your heart were fond of roving;
Nor that, nor all the world beside,
　　Could keep your faithful boy from loving.

She went bush all right. Didn't see hide nor hair of her for weeks. I don't know whether Samoans are like our abos, suddenly drop what they're doing and have to go walkabout. I don't suppose so, because you couldn't call these Samoans a real primitive mob like our blackfellers. They're pretty civilized, and mighty proud. You'll normally find a half-caste goes for the white half and tries to cover up for the nigger half. But this wasn't the way with Emma, she was real collared on her father, but just as close to her old mother and all her Samoan relatives. And when you're Samoan you've surely got relatives!

In the meantime I'd my hands full running the pub and keeping an eye on the trading business of Coe and Forsayth. I reckoned old Coe was pretty smart and would clear himself all right back in the States on the charges those buggers Stevens and Foster had cooked up against him. Foster was a crook who was in cahoot with a whole ant's nest of crooks in that Polynesian Land Company. That was the real reason they wanted to get rid of Steinberger, they still reckoned they had titles to half the land in Samoa, and Steinberger wanted to protect the Samoans from these sharks. Steinberger really loved the Samoans, but I've heard Foster bawling the bejesus out of him for telling the world the Samoans were a civilized people when in truth 'they're but one degree removed from barbarism', I remember the exact words. No, anyone who'd knocked around a bit could have told you Foster was a bit off. As for Stevens I never met a man I took such a dislike to.

I learned a good deal more about the situation from a decent young Australian, James Young, who was knocking around the Beach looking for a job. He was a handy man with boats so I took him with me on a couple of runs around the islands in Coe's brig *Vision*. She was a useful ship, a bit lumpy in the bows in a head sea, but quick to the helm which is what you need for nicking in and out of these reefs, some of the channels are only about wide enough for a canoe. James would have been about twenty-five, he was born in the right country, in Derry as a matter of fact where my mother's people are, and his father was Captain of an East Indiaman. They'd settled in Victoria when the lad was five or so. He'd worked at most things, been a drover and a station hand in Australia and then he'd gone up to Fiji planting and skippering a schooner. So he was a real all-rounder, and educated, too.

He was feeling a bit down in the mouth about old Coe. Apparently he'd been one of the assessors who'd gone through the Consular books and then Foster had set up some sort of bush court and convicted Coe of embezzlement. James said the books were in a bit of a mess but Coe hadn't been cooking them deliberately, and he realized now Foster had been out to get Coe. It seems Coe had been very decent to James when he first arrived in Apia, and he felt he'd been used by Foster to discredit the old cove. And I tell you what, I think he was a bit shook on Emma. Though, who wasn't? But she wouldn't have a bar of him, because of what he'd done to her father and because he'd been in the fighting at Mulinu'u and had shot one of her cousins. I could see there was no harm in him, young fellows can never resist a bit of fighting.

I got him to take a run over to Tonga with me in the *Vision*. Jesus, it was good to get the sea under your feet again. It's all very well to think it's time to settle down, but a man feels cramped in a port unless he's got a ship in it waiting to take him out again. James was yarning away about where he'd like to go next, he was a real roving, restless type, and we unrolled a few charts of the Pacific and bugger me if I didn't get the roving itch myself. Look at all those islands! The Gilberts, I'd been to them, slap bang on the equator, to the north of them the equatorial current starts to get easterly. Then way up past the Gilberts there's the Marshalls, a whole bunch of atolls smothered in coconuts. Then run east on the north equatorial current and there's the Carolines, the Mortlocks, the Ladrones, hundreds of them. And what about the really big fellows further south, New Guinea, New Britain, New Ireland, nobody knows bugger-all about them. Jesus, a man could get rich in those islands! You need some capital behind you, or else you've got to work in with the Germans, and they're tough. It didn't seem possible when we heard that Goddefroys were going bust, something to do with the Franco-Prussian war. But those Ham-burgers weren't going to let it all slip, they smartly reorganized themselves into a new firm,—are you ready, take a big mouthful of air—Die Deutsche Handels-und Plantagen-Gesellschaft der Südsee Inseln zu Hamburg, the German Business and Plantation Company of the South Seas at Hamburg—we always just call it the Long-Handle Firm, or the DHPG. As well as that lot of Germans there was a trader called Hernsheim who was already well established up there amongst the islands.

James got me all worked up about those islands, how we could get old Coe and Emma to join with us, and he could stay up there and run that end of it, and I could go down to Auckland and rake up some capital for trade and buying copra. I'd have rather gone to my home town Sydney, but those stupid Australians were never interested in the South Seas the way the New Zealanders were, I knew I'd have better luck in Auckland.

Well, it all depended on Emma, on the Princess. I used to call her that as a joke, I told her we already had that old bitch Victoria sitting on top of Australia that ought to be a republic, to which she said I'd never understand about the South Seas until I under-stood ranks and titles, that her father was as much of a republican as me yet he always called her his Princess. I knew she was having me on a bit, pulling my Irish-Australian leg, but with her as my Queen we could build an empire among those hundreds and thousands of islands. Those were my thoughts as I held the bow-sprit steady for Apia. My head was full of ideas and my heart was full of hope and I told young James to crack a bottle.

> There's nothing goes wrong when the grog's mixed right,
> And I never looks dull when the liquor looks bright,—

I'd no sooner let go my cable in Apia harbour than Emma's alongside in the cutter. Jesus, a couple of months out bush had put a glow on her—she dances aboard and gives me a kiss—a kiss! —like she was Sheba bringing gold to Solomon. I was real thunder-struck. While I was standing there speechless up the companion-way comes James, and I thought, that's buggered it. But she's in a right forgiving mood and gives him her Princess' hand.

When the Lord sends you a fair wind, up sails and off! I

whipped her down to the cabin, laid the charts on the table, and told her my plans for the islands, and getting New Zealand capital, and maybe recruiting Melanesian labourers for the Samoa plantations.

'Right, Tom, right', she said to every damn thing I suggested, 'we'll be rich, we'll have an empire stretching from the Mortlocks to Bougainville.' *We*, she kept on saying, *we*. What had happened to her out in that village?

I soon heard what had happened to her when she came back from the village to Apia. She'd arranged a party, sort of welcome-home affair, at her father's house for her young sister Phebe and her half-sisters—by the holy weaver they were a pretty bunch, too—and she'd asked the daughters of the LMS missionary. And what do you think that Protestant bitch did? She came round to Emma and told her she couldn't allow her daughters in the same house as Emma. Apparently she was screaming at her, told her she was a triple-turned whore, it was bad enough being Steinberger's mistress but when she took her fornications into the very Samoan villages the missions were lifting from the dark ages of lechery, then it was the duty of every person of true religion to denounce her.

You should have seen the gunpowder flash in Emma's eye when she told me how she couldn't help herself, she'd grabbed the horse whip her father used to belt the kids with, and laid it across the bony arse of the missionary lady who went down the verandah steps squawking like an old hen with a pack of hounds after her. The only snag, said Emma, was that the old bitch had so much whalebone around her that she couldn't get a good connection with the whip.

That night Emma came to the pub and I brought out the champagne and she played the piano and I sang for her and we sang together and danced and she never went home. Yes, there was one good double bed in the house, and that's where we spent the night, and jesus, we didn't spend it sleeping.

> One hour of passion so sacred is worth
>   Whole ages of heartless and wandering bliss;
> And, oh, if there be an Elysium on earth,
>   It is this, it is this.

I loved to sing for her, you might say Tom Moore brought us together, and she said she never ceased being astonished how such a great brute of a man could have such a sweet Irish voice. But in bed! Well, I've bedded a lot of women and had no complaints, but Emma, when she should have been knocked right out, sits up and says 'No, Tom, that won't do, you're on and off like a mastiff. You don't treat me as a woman, you just think of me as a —.' God, I couldn't believe it, an educated lady using a word like that. So Tom Farrell at forty was put back to school by a girl fourteen years younger, and Jesus, what a school! My view had always been, a man's got this great big weapon all cocked up and ready to fire and a woman's there to pull the trigger. Sometimes a woman's hot, sometimes cold, they're moody the way a man never is, but that's because they don't get the pleasure out of it. Mind you, there's plenty that enjoy it, but they wouldn't knock down a locked door to get it like a man would.

That's what I thought till I met Emma. She'd show you when she wanted it, all right, she'd throw you overboard and make you take her in the sea if she felt like it. One night she did just that, when we were anchored off Mili Atoll in the Marshalls. A bit much, I thought at the time. She'd do things in bed that would make a Sydney whore blush, and yet somehow she'd make it seem natural. And she'd come up again like the bubbles in a champagne glass. You know the way some women look the next morning, as if they ought to be thrown overboard with the slops, but never Emma, no matter how heavy the night had been. I don't think she ever thought much of me as a lover, I don't know whether I really ever satisfied her. But Jesus, I had a fine time of it trying!

I wish you could have seen young James's face when he realized what had happened. I think I said he was real shook on Emma, and there's he the same age as her, and here she is on with an old bugger of forty. But he was a good lad, he knew when he was beat, and an able-bodied man needn't go to bed lonely in Apia.

Chapter XVIII

JAMES LYLE YOUNG

25 May, 1876   Sailed on the *Vision* for the Marshall's Group, with Capt and Mrs Farrell. I am to establish a trading station while Capt Farrell takes a cargo of copra down to Auckland, and there raise capital to extend our operations. J. M. Coe has not yet returned from the United States, and Alvord, who is an honest man, has been left in charge of the Coe-Forsayth business and the Commercial Hotel. I wrote Capt & Mrs Farrell but they are not married, he has an alcoholic wife in Sydney and who knows about Captain Forsayth? But Emma wishes to be referred to as Mrs Farrell, for the benefit, she says, of the missionaries resident in the islands where we intend to trade. She appears to have a very low regard for missionaries as bringers of light to darkness, but a high regard for them as precursors of trade.

I have considerable admiration for Capt Farrell, though I do not doubt that he would have few scruples when it came to a tight corner. I have met men like him on the stations and diggings in Australia who if they give you their hand will nearly break the bones of it in friendship, but if in enmity, their fists will break your head. He is a sailor half wishing to settle down, but I do not think Emma will allow him to settle in Samoa. She has been deeply affected by the Steinberger business, and insulted by some of the European women, and swears that some day she will come back and put them in their place. I find it hard to see why she is attracted to Capt Farrell, who can be very coarse and brutal. For all her wildness, she is a very cultivated and intelligent woman, and I can, and do, talk to her about things Captain Farrell has never heard of. But like many Irishmen, there is a streak of poetry in him, and he has a clear, true voice. They like to sing together.

There is a little Blackwood's ship's piano on the *Vision*, and we have many a singsong.

20 June We have been trading around the Gilbert Islands. We were much astonished on arrival at the island of Butaritari to find the whole population apparently smitten with some totally incapacitating disease. Not a soul greeted us in the villages and when we came to their meeting houses (which are of a prodigious size) we found hundreds of people lying as if under the spell of some sleeping sickness. There was something awe-inspiring if horrible about the desolation which had struck down all the inhabitants of this island, and I felt uneasy moving amongst them lest we too be felled to the ground. When Emma suddenly began to laugh it seemed almost sacrilegious. But she with her practical woman's sense had divined the cause of the mysterious malady, and picking up a bottle she waved it towards Capt Farrell and me and called out 'They're all drunk.' And indeed they were, all about us lay hundreds (literally hundreds) of empty cases of gin, emptied by the King and all his subjects. When later the natives began to return to consciousness we heard that when, after long labours, all the taro and copra had been brought in, the King declared an orgy which on our arrival had lasted for fourteen days.

There was not a sack of copra left for us as Capt Hernsheim had sailed away with the lot.

This King is an utter tyrant, who strangely enough is feared but not hated by his subjects. He's both judge and executioner, and moves about to fulfil his functions accompanied by his sixteen wives, who are also his bodyguard and the crew of his ship. He has the sole rights over all the virgins on the island, and once a month he takes to sea aboard his schooner with the latest crop of eligible girls whom he deflowers and then returns, now ready, as it were, for marriage. Should a girl claiming to be a virgin be revealed not to be so, she is immediately executed and her body thrown to the sharks.

I have never seen anything more wonderful than the enormous Council Houses of the Gilbertese, we measured one and found it 240 feet long, 120 feet wide, and 35-40 feet high, all built without a nail or bolt.

1 July We are trading around the Marshall islands. At Mili Atoll we bought 3,500 lb. of copra at 1c. a pound from 'Jack' who is trading for Hernsheim at Jaluit. I suspect 'Jack' should not have done this, and may well be somewhere else by the time Hernsheim arrives to buy copra, but Capt Farrell says that is not our business. What Capt Farrell means in fact is that whenever anything is good for our business, how we obtain it is not our business. I fear he may get into trouble one day, though I expect he will fight his way out of almost anything.

2 July Capt Farrell and Emma had a violent quarrel last night! I think arising from the purchase of the copra. Emma says Capt Farrell only got it from 'Jack' by making him drunk, and this will make an enemy of us in Hernsheim, with whom it is essential, says Emma, we should be friends. But the quarrel was about more than copra. We were ashore at 'Jack's', and Capt Farrell had been drinking, as indeed so had Emma, although it never seems to affect her. But imagine the scene when we awoke this morning, somewhat heavy in the head, to find Emma and the *Vision* gone!! She had swum out to the brig in the darkness, and has sailed off!! The Samoan crew will of course do anything for her. I have never seen a man so furious as Capt Farrell. So here we are, stranded on this tiny atoll at the dilapidated establishment of a drunken trader, alongside 3,500 lb. of copra which he has sold us, with a lot of empty bottles for company. How long will Emma leave us here? Or indeed, will she ever return?

7 July To our intense relief, the schooner *Sappho*, Capt Digby, anchored here today, having come from Majuro with the astonishing news, that felled Capt Farrell as with a club, that Emma is living there with a Negro called Black Tom, a notorious character who runs a liquor mill at Ponape and who is now on a cruise trading with his vile spirits. From Capt Digby I learned more about Eduard Hernsheim. It appears he is a Hamburg seafaring man, a gentleman, who started trading in the Pacific five or six years ago, originally from Hong Kong. He established stations at the Palan and Yap Islands, east of the Philippines, and then moving east and south has posts at Jaluit and the Duke of York Islands which are between New Britain and New Ireland. Truly, on what a vast stage are we embarked! It is two and a half thousand miles from Palan to Jaluit! And fifteen hundred from Jaluit to New Britain! Digby says Hernsheim has murdered natives at Yap. And yet we have everywhere heard good reports of Hernsheim, a hard dealer and yet a gentleman. A white man can speedily become a petty tyrant in these islands, he has so many cunning tricks the natives do not know, it is as simple as that.

12 July We have arrived in the magnificent lagoon of the great atoll of Majuro on a Hamburg brig, the *Capelle*. Capt Farrell wishing to stay here for some days, and the *Capelle* leaving shortly for Ebon Atoll, we agree that I should sail with the Germans and wait for him at Ebon. It will be good experience to get to know these German traders better. My only regret is that I shall not have more time to talk to Emma. She greeted us cool as coconut milk and as innocent, saying she has made a very advantageous purchase of copra and also taro, which is hard to come by on these barren atolls. There was no sign of Black Tom. Certainly Capt Farrell would have killed him, if Black Tom had not been quicker on the trigger. I long to hear more, but instead am forced to practise my German.

26 July Ebon. My wandering life nearly ended a few days after leaving Majuro, when we struck a reef violently in the vicinity of Mili. It seemed that certain destruction was upon us. The Germans, however, are not given to panic, and by jettisoning most of their copra we at last got off, but in extreme peril from the enormous surf. It was a miracle that we escaped. Such are the constant dangers attending all ships in these waters.

29 July Captain Farrell and Emma have arrived in the *Vision*, and it seems that they have made all necessary enquiries and have decided that it is here at Ebon, or rather on tiny Mej islet, off the tip of Ebon, that we will establish our trading station. Emma says that the real reason is that Ebon is the headquarters of the American Mission, and that trade always follows the Cross! I am to be left here to trade around the islands while Capt Farrell and Emma sail in the brig to Auckland where they will raise more capital and return together with a second ship. Were Capt Farrell on his own

I might have my doubts, but Emma will keep his business affairs in order, and as straight as possible.

31 July We have landed £800 worth of goods for me to trade with. Copra is 2 to 2½ cents a lb. My islet of Mej is half a mile long, and from 100-300 yards wide, covered in coconuts, breadfruit and pandanus. At low tide I can walk across the spit and call on Mr & Mrs Sherlock, the American missionaries. The high chiefs have promised not to sell copra to anyone else until Capt Farrell returns.

2 August I said farewell to Capt Farrell and Emma today. In a lilac dress with a white hat she looked as if the *Vision* were a gentleman's yacht and she was being taken for an afternoon's cruise with champagne and strawberries. I asked her was she not nervous of the journey of upwards of three and a half thousand miles but she laughed and asked, why? Did I want her to share my little kingdom with me? Fortunately Capt Farrell was not listening. It is true, she loves the sea and is afraid of nothing. She says her ancestor Samoans sailed here in their seventy foot canoes without a compass, so what is there to worry about in the *Vision*? Does Capt Farrell know what a lucky man he is? Well, he certainly knows how lucky he is to have her to do all his bookwork, she superintended all the buying and invoicing of the trade goods, and has left me detailed instructions of percentage rates relative to alternative prices for copra, as it is rumoured that Hernsheim may be prepared to offer 3 cents to the chiefs who have promised to sell to us. If this is to be a partnership, the brains of it will be Emma.

26 October Where is the romance of the South Seas? Alas, these islands and these islanders are a dull lot, and in the unending round of sun, sand and surf my brain is turning to the consistency of baked breadfruit. These natives of the Marshall Group are not the courteous, refined, handsome people of Samoa. Here flatness is all, we are raised at the most but a few feet above the pounding ocean, there are no cloud-hung mountains, no sheltering groves, no lacy waterfalls, no luscious tropical fruits. The climate is unhealthy and has a debilitating effect. Though I am no lover of missionaries, opponents of missionary work should come to these islands and view it with unprejudiced eyes. The climate is especially hard upon the missionary's wife (often the most valuable missionary of the two). The diet is monotonous, and the only meat preserved or salted. Their communications are but once a year. And I have been here not yet three months! Unlike Samoa, I have no friends among the native people, though I always get on well with natives. They are not emotional like the Polynesians, they possess a peculiar moral stolidity.

12 December   The *West Wind* arrived, with news that Capt Farrell has chartered the *Agnes Donald* and she is on her way. Mr Whitney, the missionary, refused to take a passenger in his small boat out to the *West Wind*, 'because he is an adulterer!!'

15 December   The *Agnes Donald* arrived, two months from Auckland, with letters. Capt Farrell should arrive soon in the *Vision*, and it seems that along the way he has bought a schooner, knowing how much the chiefs at Ebon want to buy a European boat.

10 January 1877   Capt Farrell, but without Emma. I realize that although she is not mine I am desolated not to see her, I was waiting for her presence to bring flowers and fruit to this dreary atoll. It seems she has gone to Samoa to see her son and father, who returned from the United States in August, having cleared his name of the charges Foster brought against him. I regret my part in those proceedings. I think she may be arranging to sell all her and Capt Farrell's property in Samoa. On their way to Auckland they called at Capt Hernsheim's station at Makada in the Duke of York Islands. Farrell says that it is a wild, uncivilized place but there are possibilities of trade there, and also of recruiting labour for the Samoan plantations.

12 January   *Agnes Donald* finished discharging copra, 106,000 lbs. into the brig *Vision*.

27 January   Met Capt Farrell at Ebon. Together we sold the schooner *Fortune*, 21 tons, to Chiefs Loiak and Kaiboke for $1000 cash and 150,000 lbs. copra. It is a good deal, but Capt Farrell confesses that Emma was very much against the idea. I do not see why. Capt Hernsheim anchored here yesterday, and this evening Capt Farrell went aboard with him.

31 January   Capts Farrell and Hernsheim and I all went to church, a Catholic, a Lutheran and an Anglican in an American Mission! I wonder whose prayers for the New Year would be answered, or if the Almighty, astonished at this healing of the sects, might grant all our prayers, that is assuming they were fit to be answered.

19 March   Capt Farrell is returning to Auckland. I told him I wished to leave here as soon as possible and he proposed to give me $20 a month until he returns from Auckland, when he promises I shall go west on an improved salary as Manager of a new trading station at Yap in the far western Carolines, his sponsors in Auckland being fully in agreement with his and Emma's proposition to open more trading stations in opposition to Hernsheim and Goddefroy and the Long-Handle Firm, the D.H.P.G. as the Germans call it. I will stick it out. We heard that the notorious 'Bully' Hayes, Capt W. H. Hayes, is nearby in his yacht *Lotus,* and that Ingolls nearly shot him dead in a dispute over money matters.

20 March   Capt Farrell left for Auckland via Sydney in the *Vision.* I am alone again.

14 April   Capt Hernsheim gave me full particulars of the death of Bully Hayes. He says Hayes was much maligned. He never carried a pistol, never ill-treated the natives or his crews except in cases of gross disobedience to orders, and he was consequently liked both by the native and the white members of his crew. Emma used often to talk about him, she always liked him though once I believe she had to swim ashore from the *Leonora* when not disposed to grant him her favours. Her younger brother Henry was a crew member with Bully.

24 May   I celebrated the Queen's birthday with twenty-one guns at midday, using the three 18-pounder cannon from the schooner *Fortune* which I have mounted on shore. This is the first time the Queen's birthday has been commemorated on this island.

15 September   Capt Ravekilde of the *Montiana* with letters from Yap for Capt Farrell. The muskets are selling to the natives for $4 and 250 caps for 4 shillings.

30 September   No appearance or even word of Capt Farrell. It's now six and a half months since the place has been supplied with stores and provisions, and there is nothing to be bought on any of these barren islets. I have been out of food for some time, living on breadfruit. The mission family are also in a state of semi-starvation. My nerves are frayed like old coconut fibre with the ceaseless westerly winds. I am drinking tea without sugar. I am constantly ill with dysentery, caused by the shortage of provisions. I fear some accident has happened to Capt Farrell on his way from Auckland. If so, what shall I do? And how long should I wait?

17 October   A missionary ship came from Honolulu, but she could spare me no food, it was only for the mission. No news of Capt Farrell or the brig *Vision*. I fear she is lost. I see that my writing, on which I have always prided myself for its regularity and legibility, has deteriorated sorely. I am at a loss to know what to do with myself or the trading station.

22 October   Chief Kaiboke came to say he cannot pay for the schooner *Fortune* and wants me to resume her. Emma appears to have been right about selling schooners to Marshall Island chiefs.

2 November   A report today that the *Vision* arrived at Majuro, a mere 200 miles away, a *month* ago, and that Capt Farrell is not in her, but he is insolvent!! And that a representative of his creditors is in the *Vision* to wind up his affairs! This is cheerful news with a vengeance!

9 November   The *Agnes Donald* arrived with Mr Couzens, agent for Capt Farrell's trustees, to wind up affairs. His creditors are determined to repossess Capt Farrell and close up the post here. Mr Couzens is not a bad fellow, and he gave me my first decent food and drink for many weeks. We had a bottle and he seemed to take a shine to me. In confidence he told me that it was a great

mistake of Capt Farrell's backers, a group of Auckland business-
men, to withdraw their support and force him to the wall, as he
(Couzens) could clearly see there were excellent prospects. The
trouble had been that the brains of Farrell & Co. was Mrs Farrell,
and she was away in Samoa. Without her to guide him, Capt
Farrell was apt to resort to violence. Apparently when diplomacy
and a clear balance sheet might well have won over the Auckland
business gentlemen, Capt Farrell threatened to knock their blocks
off. This approach did not succeed. Mr Couzens wants me to
proceed with him to the station at Yap and take over the
management of that place. I am undecided.

Also in the *Agnes Donald* was a member of the English aristocracy whom I had met in Fiji, where he used to lie in bed until
two o'clock in the afternoon. He is what is called a remittance
man, subsisting on funds sent by relations who would rather his
presence graced some other island than that of Britain. He plans
to learn the language here and fit himself for a diplomatic position.
He is most eccentric of manner, and in the habit of committing
the most detestable of crimes, viz. that particular one which so
largely prevailed in the Cities of the Plain as to cause the name
of one of the cities to be applied to the crime.

17 December Jaluit. Capt Hernsheim has offered me £10 a
month to go to New Britain and act as his manager there. I have
asked time to think.

18 December Mr Capelle made me an offer of £12 plus a commission of 5 per cent to take charge of his retail store here,
temporarily, with first offer of a vacancy at Guam or in the
Ladrone Islands. I accepted as I consider it likely to lead to a
better position in a more civilized community than Capt Hernsheim's offer would do. New Britain sounds excessively dangerous.
Though I am no coward I have no relish to be eaten by cannibals,
nor yet succumb to fever, both of which fates do by report await
those taking up a post in New Britain, New Ireland or the Duke
of York Islands. In addition to these hazards, there are a number
of active volcanoes which may erupt at any moment.

In the evening Capelle, Hernsheim, Ingolls and myself played
whist and drank Rheinwein until 10 p.m. Capt Hernsheim gave

his opinion that perhaps I was wise not to have accepted his offer. Last year his trading station at Matupi was attacked by natives and destroyed by fire, and this year the same station was accorded the same treatment. In addition, Matupi is directly underneath the largest volcano, which is affectionately known as The Mother, and, if this were not enough, it is flanked by two other volcanoes known as the North and South Daughters! No, life on a Marshall Group atoll may be dull, but at least it is tolerably secure.

Christmas Day 1877 I breakfasted at 11 a.m. at Capt Hernsheim's, with Capelle, Ingolls and a couple more. At 4 p.m. we adjourned to Mr Capelle's summer house. I find I get along very well with the Germans, and not only for their inexhaustible supplies of Rheinwein and excellent food. It appears that the first call on any ship of theirs is for it to be well victualled. The Germans are also well-educated gentlemen to whom one may talk on a large variety of subjects, unlike Australians such as Capt Farrell, or most of the British for that matter, who are altogether of a lower class. As I had this thought I became somewhat sentimental, and proposed a toast to Princess Emma. All who knew her responded warmly, especially Capt Hernsheim who raised his glass and said '*Keine Prinzessin—die Königin!*' So it was—to the Queen!

Capt Hernsheim retired home at 6 p.m. and we were all to go down again to his place at 7 p.m., but every one had had enough wine and so none of us went but went to bed early instead.

Chapter XIX

---------•-•---------

REVEREND GEORGE BROWN

Port Hunter,
Duke of York Islands.

10 December 1878

Reverend J. D. Frith,
Balmain,
New South Wales.

My dear James

I rejoice that you are safely returned to Sydney after your long absence, and trust that you were not corrupted by the luxuries of England and the United States. Should you have put on any extra weight, I suggest you take a short trip to stay with Mrs Brown and myself, where we will guarantee to slim you down by Fever if not by the constant exudation of the body in these humid regions, where verily one becomes a walking Bath. I am now so skinny you would scarce recognize your friend of Samoan days.

Our House is on rising ground on an isthmus between Port Hunter and Makada, which is at the north of the Duke of York Island, which lies in St George's Channel betwixt New Ireland and New Britain. These several islands are low-lying, open and amiable, reminiscent of the enchanting Manono Island in Samoa, in strong contrast to the stern, shrouded battlements of New Ireland and the volcanoes of New Britain. This truly is a savage Land about us, dark, secretive and separate, and by that I mean not only divided by chasms of custom from civilized intercourse, but separated in its parts one from another. Cross a bay, an hour's sail and you will find a Tribe whose members cannot understand the language of the tribesmen you have just left. What is more, they will never have travelled as far as each other. The men along the Coast have no contact with the men in the Mountains or the bush, except violent encounters which lead to a feast on one side or the other. There is no secret about Cannibalism. The sharp end of a spear is usually a human leg or arm bone. A man will happily say to you 'Oh man belong Saltwater he fight man belong Bush. He kaikai (eat) him. He catch him bone he go belong Spear.'

You can imagine how difficult it is to converse with the natives, even for myself, who am as you know gifted by God with an ability for languages (and, dare I add, the industry to learn them!). You cannot conceive how miserable it was when I first came to preach to these people in Pidgin which Capea interpreted to Le Bera and Le Bera interpreted to the people.

To return to Cannibal practices, I heard quite incidentally today of a man here who had killed a man from another Village a short time ago, he brought him down to the Village and sold him to Le Bera for food. It was referred to as being quite an ordinary transaction between buyer and seller.

They are indifferent to cruelty. Often those captives who are to be eaten are kept alive until the appointed day, and to prevent them from escaping the captors cut their feet off and then cauterize the stumps over a fire so they will not bleed to death before the feast. Recently I visited a Village where the Chief was called Sagina, which means 'Strong Smell', a title given him because the smell of cooked Pork or Human Flesh was always to be perceived in his Village. In one house there were thirty five Human Lower Jawbones suspended from the Rafters, most of which were blackened with Smoke but some of them quite Clean and had not been long there. A Human Hand and a Penis both smoke-dried were hanging in the same house, and just outside I counted seventy six notches in a Cocoanut Tree each notch of which the Natives proudly told me represented a Human Body which had been cooked and eaten there.

The Natives here regard all strangers as Enemies. Whether cannibalism preceded or followed the attitude is difficult to say. Our success in persuading the Natives that we come as Friends may proceed from the fact that the meat of a White man is not highly regarded! No, in truth they see that the Missionary comes in peace, not to rob them but protect them, not to shoot them but to help them to health, not to rape their women but teach them to respect them. Alas, the treatment of the women by the men is lamentable, they are beasts of burden, machines to provide food and produce children.

They are dark, secretive people, cowed by innumerable fears. How at first I longed for the sunny, gay, open Samoans! But here the Lord's task is harder, and in that I have endeavoured to rejoice.

The Natives may be accounted Savages, but they are skilled in many crafts, for instance in making great dugout canoes, fish-traps from the thorn-tree, beautiful nets, and their carvings and inlay work are very ornate if not to the usual taste of the European. The masks of the Duk-Duk, their secret society, are quite extra-ordinary, and later I will write at length about the activities of the Duk-Duk which strike terror into all.

I have been informing you about the Natives, now to the Europeans. As you know, we were the first Europeans to settle here, and the first Missionaries indeed in the whole of New Guinea. Odd whalers and traders had used the safe harbours and been tolerated by the relatively peaceful tribes of the Duke of York Islands for some years, but now Goddefroys and Hernsheim are doing well at Meoko and Makada and at Matupi on New Britain, near the Mother volcano. The development of trade has followed the establishment of our mission here. I hear Goddefroys were bankrupted in the late war and have been reconstituted under a name too long to write but usually referred to as DHPG.

Imagine my pleasure a few days ago to receive a message from my old friend of Samoan days, that fine girl Emma Forsayth, who has very recently arrived at Meoko with her husband Thomas Farrell, who is to trade and recruit labour for Goddefroy. I took the immediate opportunity to sail around the Island to Meoko and renew a most pleasant acquaintance. She is as vivacious as ever, now in her twenty-eighth year and I would say, with Mrs Brown's concurrence, in her prime of beauty. Her husband is a big Irish Australian with a red beard, and I fear he may not always maintain the highest principles in his dealings, and that he may have a strong temper, which I may be called on to endure, as I intend to obstruct him in every way in his efforts to recruit labour, which is only a form of slavery for the poor Natives who do not realize when they 'sign on' that the White man's Year is twice as long as theirs, nor how they will lay themselves open to be duped. Farrell maintains that it will be for the Natives' benefit to be removed from their savagery and superstition and to be exposed to the higher civilization of the Samoan plantations of Goddefroy, or the DHPG. This is the sort of hypocrisy, I fear, subsequent upon the Jesuitical education of the man. As you know, I am no bigot, but I have noted the ease with which Catholics allow themselves to follow such lines of thought.

Emma's plans are far different, and more ambitious. You may remember that I early noted in her a remarkable facility for figures and commerce. She and Farrell have sold all their interests in Apia (he owned a hotel, it seems) and she intends for them to trade on their own here as soon as possible. She thinks, and I have no doubt she will succeed, that while Farrell is on his voyages for the DHPG she will begin trading here. To begin with the traders here dealt with little but trochus and turtle shell, with sea slugs for the Chinese trade. Of late copra has overtaken all other articles of trade. A few thimbles full of beads will secure from the Natives a ten pound bag of copra. Copra is worth £10-16 in the overseas market, and the traders get £2 commission a ton. But she looks further than that. She asked me did I not think it absurd to ship labourers all the way from here to Samoa to work in the Cocoanut plantations, when the Cocoanut grows right here as well as it does in Samoa. She has already examined the flat and beautifully fertile coastal area of New Britain west of Meoko, known as the Gazelle Peninsula. In her keen mind's eye she can already see vast Cocoanut plantations arising there, and given her Energy and Patience she may well live not only to see them but to call them her own.

It is grand to have her as a neighbour, and I have already had the pleasure of lending her Anthony Trollope's *Australia*, a book which will interest her immensely. Farrell may well turn out to be not such a bad fellow. He has an unexpectedly mellow singing voice. Among the few furnishings which they brought from Samoa was a piano, at which Emma is expert. When Captain Hernsheim joins us with his flute, we will have a regular Concert Party.

I took the opportunity to tell her as much as I could about the

Natives, and that with ordinary Care and proper Usage there is little or no danger to be feared from them. Far more dangerous is the fever, and I saw she was well provided with quinine. Fever is the curse of these regions, particularly around swamps where the air is bad. Only recently Mrs Blohm, the wife of Goddefroy's manager, died of it. Samoans of course know nothing of it. Nature for them is bountiful and always friendly, whereas here, treachery is endemic.

Mrs Brown desires to be remembered.

Talofa! (You see, I keep some Samoan customs.)

Geo. Brown

Chapter XX

————————◆————————

EMMA

We were lucky to get out of Tom's insolvency as lightly as we did. If only I'd gone to Auckland with Tom! We lost everything at Ebon, and the *Vision*, and that damn fool schooner Tom bought. But all our belongings at Apia were safe. We sold everything up, and Tom managed to get rid of the Family and Commercial Hotel (can you imagine names more ridiculous, Tom who never had nor wanted a family, and who had no commercial sense to speak of), and we struck a deal with Weber of Goddefroy that we would trade for him out of Mioko and Tom would recruit for the Goddefroy Samoan plantations. He already had a station at Mioko, so we would be extending his operations but be allowed to trade on our own account. With any luck it would not be long before we were independent.

A Goddefroy brig was to meet us in Mioko, together with stores, provisions and some furniture. I insisted on my piano. I said farewell, I hoped not for too long, to Father and my dear Phebe, who promised to continue looking after my son Coe, a fine boy of six who knew more of her than of his mother. I love children, but you can't bring them up on a brig trading in the Pacific, let alone take such a tempting morsel to an abode of cannibals. Have I been a bad mother? Perhaps. I will be a better mother when I am older, and a very good grandmother, when I am rich.

We left Apia on 3 October, 1878, in the brig *Reconnaissance*, for Wallis Island and Sydney, where Tom fortunately still had a few assets, not to mention one alcoholic encumbrance. Oh the delights of Sydney, which will remain my favourite city and where one day I shall own a house at Vaucluse—no, a *large* house at Vaucluse and an elegant carriage and horses in which I will *not* drive to church on Sundays. Nevertheless, I went to call on my old friends and gaolers at Subiaco, and the good Sisters were enchanted that I had married a good Irish Catholic, and I did not tell them what they were so happy in not knowing, that Tom was only my lover.

By a circuitous route we came at last to Mioko's calm little harbour late in 1878. It would need to be a good harbour, as that St George's Channel has nothing saintly about it at all, devilish rough in fact. I'd seen this wild region of the world on our way down from the Marshall Islands, and had been overcome by its dangerous beauty. Beside it, Samoa seemed supinely sleepy, deserving of its ultimate fate, which is to be entirely covered by enormous white churches under whose weight it will eventually sink below the reefs. Here there were the gentle Duke of York Islands, for our temporary home, and on either side like great beasts who must be tamed, the unknown jungles and mountains of New Britain and New Ireland, with the guardian dragons (unslaughtered by St George in his Channel) of the active volcanoes. The Germans provided us with a trim cutter, the *Lelea*, and as soon as possible I took one of the three Samoans who had come with us from Apia on the brig, and I sailed over to what will surely be the future harbour, inside the arms of the bay under the volcanoes. It is splendid and dramatic, immediate green heights, immediate deep blue sea, nothing gradual or tame. Hernsheim has a post, in the corner, at Matupi. The best harbour will be at the back, where now there are mangroves. We ran down the coast of the Gazelle Peninsula to Blanche Bay and there behind the long, straight beach, on the plain before the hills, I can see clearly, in the future which is sometimes clearer than the present, plantations of thousands of coconuts, and cocoa and coffee and whatever else will grow here, for I think anything will grow in that volcanic soil.

I'm going to have trouble with Tom. He says he's a sailor and a trader and not a bloody cocky farmer, an expression I had to have explained to me, but apparently it means a small farmer who ekes out his living scratching the soil like a cockatoo. I told him I'm not going to be a farmer but a planter, and not going to be small but big. 'Be buggered to you, you stubborn bitch,' he says to me in that poetic Irish way, 'I'm not getting any sort of dirt in my finger-nails.' 'That's because you've got too much dirt there already', says I, knowing a thing or two about the slaves (no other word for it) he's aiming to ship back to Samoa. I thought he was going to hit me. I'm a strong woman but he's twice the strength of me. He only hit me once, it was at anchor in the *Vision* at Majuro Atoll in the Marshalls, I told him I'd either kill him or leave him, whichever was easiest. He knew I meant it. A woman must be independent. He didn't touch me again, though he was all bent back for another clout. We'd been having a bit of a row about my abrupt departure from Mili, when I swam out to the *Vision* and sailed her over to Majuro. Tom had been a damn fool, getting 'Jack' drunk and buying up Eduard Hernsheim's copra, but it wasn't only that, I was sick of being cooped up in the *Vision* with Tom and James Young, who's always wanting me to seduce him but I'm damned if I'm going to be the first woman to show him where to put it. We were ashore drinking with 'Jack'—I never found out his real name, but was told he is an Irish baronet which may well be true, he is certainly a gentleman and well-educated when not too drunk to speak. He kept on talking about this Black Tom, who had called in on his schooner and had only recently left for Majuro, a day's sail away. 'Black as the Duke of Wellington's boots', said 'Jack', 'but decorated for gallantry in the Civil War, led a revolution in Chile, killed a man over a woman in Tahiti, made a fortune distilling this poison'— he held up a gin bottle—'in Ponape.' He had a whole lot more stories about Black Tom, I've no idea what was true or what not, but suddenly the thought of Black Tom loomed up over me like one of those colossal South Sea thunderheads and I longed for the challenge of meeting him. So when they were snoring their heads off on Black Tom's gin I slipped off my clothes, tied them on my head and swam out to the *Vision* and sailed her to Majuro where I found Black Tom and told him how terrible his gin was. Of course he knew, but he thanked me for coming all the way from Samoa to tell him.

Oh he was a lovely man! But I won't tell you about him because I don't know what's true about him except one thing, and that's the thing you never want to talk about.

The nearest I ever got to talking about it was when Farrell and I were aboard the *Vision* and he started to abuse me for leaving him and James and sailing off to Majuro. 'A white man not good enough for you, you half-caste', he shouted, 'You want a big buck nigger.' 'Well,' I said, very coolly, 'Black Tom's prick is certainly more beautiful than that carrot of yours.' It was then he hit me. He could never bear me to use coarse language.

Later I suggested we went on deck for a breath of fresh air. Then I pushed him overboard, the great brute, and then I dived in after him. Do you know how difficult it is for a man to take his clothes off in the water? We laughed and laughed before we were both naked. I never loved him, but he was a man, and he removed me from Apia, and he'd got something in him that wasn't just crude, hungry, selfish man. I think he really did love me.

Of course he was scared stiff of losing me, not just because of loving me, but because he knew perfectly well who will be the brains of Farrell & Co.

And he was a man. I heard about him in front of old Weber in Apia, Weber, the man everyone is terrified of, when Weber asked him the questions and gave him the advice he gives every Goddefroy trader. The three questions must be answered in the affirmative. Weber: 'Can you speak the language?' Tom: 'No.' Pause. Weber: 'Can you live among natives without quarrelling with them?' Tom: 'Yes.' Weber: 'Can you keep your mouth shut?' Tom: 'Yes.' Weber went on, 'Have a woman of your own, no matter what island you take her from; for a trader without a wife is in eternal hot water. Give no assistance to missionaries either by word or deed, beyond what is demanded of you by common humanity.'

Whereupon Tom answered 'I've got a wife, I hate missionaries, I don't open my mouth, I don't quarrel with natives, but' here he broke into Pidgin 'You spik talk bilong silly bugger, and I kaikai you.' He laughed at the astonished Weber and went on 'You know as well as I do there's about 300 languages in New Guinea. I'll make do with Pidgin.'

Much happened after we arrived in Mioko. My dear old friend George Brown came to see me as soon as possible after our arrival, I hadn't the heart to tell him I was not really Mrs Farrell, but I didn't think he'd mind when he found out, he was a Christian rather than a missionary. I teazed him about the useful-ness of his missionary enterprises, and asked him to tell me honestly how many converts he has made in the five years he had been here. When pressed, and in confidence, he admitted to about a dozen. He had held a *lotu*, or religious service, and the natives walked in and out, even though he had learned to speak the local language. He told me that he asked an old chief had he been to *lotu*. 'Well,' he said, 'I went once. I went to sleep, but it was not at all comfortable. I don't think I shall go again.' I think he had imported more Fijian and Samoan teachers than he had made converts.

Only a few months ago the natives on the New Ireland mainland killed and ate four Fijian teachers. Two punitive parties went out, one led by Wilfred Powell, an Australian, and the other by Mr Brown, and burned villages and canoes and shot at least a dozen natives. Mr Brown said that had he not done so, all the Europeans here would have been massacred. Since this happened many miles away, on the north of the Gazelle Peninsula, and each tribe is enemies of the next only a few miles away, I doubt very much whether the massacre would have taken place. Mr Brown defended his actions before I had asked him about them, sure sign of a bad conscience. When he first came to see me he looked very ill indeed, and I wondered whether his sickness was in his mind as well as his body, and I had heard rumours that he was to be put on trial in Fiji for the punitive expedition.

Whatever the reasons, he left early in 1879 for medical treatment, and his place was taken by a raw young man of twenty-six, Benjamin Danks, who had only just arrived at Port Hunter. Unfortunately, Danks and Tom soon quarrelled over the recruitment of labour for Samoa. He arrived at Mioko when Blohm (the Goddefroy manager) and Tom had just returned from a very successful trip to New Ireland on the *Südsee*, with over a hundred black birds aboard. They had been celebrating before the departure of the steamer for Apia when Danks arrived and demanded to know what contracts the natives had signed. Blohm, who was even drunker than usual, threatened to knock him down. Tom, who is a very big and strong man, simply picked up the missionary and dropped him into his whale boat, to the loss of his dignity and the delight of the natives. I feared Danks would never forgive him. This was a pity, as we could not afford such enmities in such a small community. Mrs Danks was a sweet little woman, much cowed by the dangers of residence in these wild regions. I did my best to make friends with her.

Soon after this episode, Tom left for Samoa with the *Südsee*, and I was alone at Mioko. Not quite alone, as I had my dear Samoans and their wives for company inside our stout bamboo palisade, but alone in the sense that I was in command, both of the trading store and the cutter *Lelea*.

By far my best company, however, was my near neighbour Theodor Kleinschmidt and his wife. He was a botanist and naturalist sent by that remarkable man Cesar Goddefroy to gather specimens for the Goddefroy Museum in Hamburg. Imagine a business man, for no profit, sending collectors all over the Pacific and Australia to set up a private museum which for its Pacific collection is rivalled only by the British Museum! I have always had the greatest respect for the Germans, for they, although stern, always had respect for the cultures and countries of the native people they worked amongst. Consider Dr Graeffe who was in Samoa for ten years, and Amalie Dietrich in Australia, Andrew Garrett in Tahiti and the Marquesas, and Kubary in the Palaus and Ponape, who we heard much of when we were in the Marshall Islands. All these supported by Goddefroy! No wonder he went bust! I had long forgiven him for bribing Albert Steinberger.

But dear Theodor Kleinschmidt and his wife were the greatest consolation to me. I like wild life and adventure, and I need love and a man, but I have a hungry mind also, I like to talk and read and find out why the world moves in so many crazy ways. These peoples of New Britain, the Duke of Yorks, New Ireland, savages, cannibals, hating and fearing their neighbours, haunted by ghosts and spirits, scourged by loathsome skin diseases (which surely could be cured by better diet and by bathing in the mineral waters from the hot springs of the volcanoes), were they not closer to animals than men? But Theodor taught me about their beliefs and habits, and showed me their wonderfully skilled artefacts and took me with him on his collecting expeditions when he moved fearlessly among the natives who never harmed him. He analyzed for me the circumstances of attacks by natives on Europeans, and always the white man had either insolently or ignorantly transgressed native laws, or else he had brazenly robbed, raped or maltreated them until they had retaliated in outrage. I swore then to myself that if we were to prosper here then it would be because the natives regarded us as friends. These people are of an altogether lower order than Samoans, but they are human beings and I have memories enough of Europeans not treating even Samoans as human beings.

I also talked to Theodor and his wife about all the things I could never discuss with Tom who for all his good sense wouldn't know the difference between Bismarck and Beethoven. The Kleinschmidts were not of the opinion, incidentally, that Bismarck wished to establish any German colonies in the South Seas. They were overjoyed to find I had brought a piano with me, and we had many musical evenings and they taught me a lot of German songs.

A weirder neighbour was none other than that son of Sodom the Hon. W. H. Lyttelton, whom Tom and James Young had met stretched out on a mat on the beach at Ebon in the Marshalls. He had spent his time drifting around the South Seas, usually staying at some trader or missionary's expense on the strength of his noble name until he was kicked out when his unmentionable vice was discovered. It is interesting that the extent to which the mere mention of this vice outrages men like Tom or James. Buggers don't worry me. (Interesting also that Tom's favourite swear-word is 'Bugger', never stops using it.) Tolerant Mr Brown had had Lyttelton to stay at Mission House Point, but young Danks smartly booted him out, and sailed him over to Wilfred Powell's plantation at Kininigunum on Blanche Bay (which was nearby the area where I had determined to have my plantation.) One day I sailed over to enquire about the possibilities of buying land, and called on the Honourable bugger, who as usual was stretched, or rather, poured out on a mat. He was really a very dissolute-looking character. When I had lived amongst so many dark people, the extreme pallor of his skin and the ghostly scraps of his beard, as if spray had been blown on to his face, made him seem like one of the spirits so feared by the natives. His voice was higher and more precise than any I've ever heard, and his angular arms folded and unfolded towards you like the legs of a sand crab. Languidly he would invite me to unroll a mat and sit beside him.

I have often found that buggers like a pretty woman who

doesn't mind speaking her mind, and in fact they have a sort of wit that brings out the female wit which often in the presence of ordinary men is either too much shielded or barbed. He was drinking up poor Mr Powell's supply of whiskey and gin, and invited me to share in the spoils. I at least could return it later, so I accepted. We talked for hours, and in the months before he drifted on again we had many more talks, and I learned about a world I had only glimpsed through my sweet Earl in Apia, the world of power and wealth and art that never soils its hands with commerce. Myself, I love commerce, but it is the *style* of this other world that fascinates me. It is in many ways trivial, but it respects the world of art and learning, so a trader like Eduard Hernsheim (who can recite Shakespeare to you in *English*!) or a scientist like Theodor Kleinschmidt and a drone like Lyttelton (I never did know his Christian name!) could all meet on common ground, whereas a tinker like Danks (to be fair, I think he worked in a brass-foundry) had in religion or life the soul of a tradesman (which Father taught me to detest, thus reinforcing my natural Samoan inclination) and could not, for all his Christian talk, see any soul in Lyttelton at all. My Tom was not basically tradesman or trader, he had the soul of a pirate.

Lyttelton drew me out to talk about things I had scarcely even thought of, let alone discussed, and sometimes we did more than talk.

Chapter XXI

W. H. LYTTELTON

It was my great good fortune to have been cast into exile across the world to the South Seas, and there to have become a beach-comber and what is vulgarly known as a remittance man. After what without modesty I must describe as a brilliant career at Brasenose College, Oxford, where my tutor Mr Pater (who seems to have made a name for himself as a writer of essays) predicted a distinguished future as a classical scholar, I was involved, owing to my sexual tastes, in a scandal which might, had it erupted into popular view, have discredited the ancient name of Lyttelton, to the mortification of my father the Canon of Worcester, and my uncle the Baron, a mortification no doubt sharpened for both of them by the memory of the second Baron who was commonly called the wicked Lord Lyttelton. My uncle, an ardent student of colonial affairs, as of cricket, fox-hunting and Sunday School, had been instrumental in founding a province called Canterbury in New Zealand, where there is even a seaport named after him, and using one hand (which opened a little to disclose sovereigns) to quieten the scandal, he used the other to waft me out of England down to New Zealand.

With a few volumes of the Greek and Roman poets, the *Canonice* of Epicurus, and the poems of Mr Swinburne and Baudelaire as my only essential luggage, I landed in New Zealand and rapidly discovered it to be the nonconformist reformatory of the South Seas. I was expected to work with my hands, and on a sheep farm, amongst a colonial pseudo-gentry whose waspish education consisted in the denial of all pleasure in life apart from overeating on Sundays. Having endured twenty-five years of my father's homilies I was sufficiently familiar with the Christian religion. I now found that after six days of back-breaking toil among stinking sheep I was expected to ride twenty miles on Sunday to attend a vile sermon by a grocer's assistant who knew not a word of Greek and only one or two of Latin.

I soon made my escape and came to Samoa, an island whose people have a freshness of aspect and a charm of manner which would delight a visitor from Olympus, let alone one fleeing from New Zealand. I also found there was no shame attached to the love of young men. That is, among the Samoans; the missionaries, of course, thunder against Sodom, and as Samoa is plagued with those creatures of distortion, I fled again, sailing on from island to atoll through the Gilberts and Marshalls and Carolines. My remittances eventually reached me, usually by favour of the admirable Herr Hernsheim, and my life of indolent pleasure in these green gardens of the world, rimmed with coral sand and azure sea, would have earned the approval of Aristippus Cyrene, grandson of the companion of Socrates, who taught that immediate pleasure is the only true end of living. As the sun went down over the lagoon of some remote atoll I knew I had attained to that place whose reality even Aristippus was unable to conceive of, because for him it lay behind *flammantia moenia mundi*, the flaming rampart of the world.

For the pleasures of the flesh, which in those climes one pursues with a delicious, slippery languor, I had unlimited access to brown boys more beautiful than the young Harmodius. For conversation I had unexpected riches. Many a beachcomber turned out to be a man like myself, whose education and talents had been at war with the money-making or churchgoing inclination. I knew so many. An Irish baronet who had committed a murder that he thought was for the sake of his unhappy country but for which the authorities wished to award him a hempen noose. A Prussian count who had been unable to sire a son by his sow of a wife, and thus for the sake of the entail had handed over the title to his younger and more fertile brother. Now, rich irony of the Parcae, he had in the Kingsmill Islands taken him a delicious girl who had rewarded him with twins! He had my signature to a document proving his powers of paternity, but I wondered what prospects there were of a South Sea Island baby inheriting the *Schloss*. Incidentally, I have noticed an extraordinary physical resemblance between certain northern German girls and their Polynesian counterparts—how can this be? But it is.

It was at the atoll of Ebon, I think, with its huge lagoon enclosing several islets, that I first met Thomas Farrell and an attractive young man who was working for him, James Young. Mrs Forsayth was, to my disappointment, not with them. I had heard of the Princess, as she was known, in Apia, where I had some kindness from her father, Mr Coe, a gentleman from New England. Hernsheim admired her tremendously, and for him she was *Die Königin*, the Queen. Again George Brown, that rarest of birds, a missionary of education and devoid of a belief in his own superiority, sang her praises.

My curiosity was already stirring, therefore, when one of Powell's boys came running up to the hut at Kininigunum to say that Mrs Farrell (as she was then known) was coming to pay me a visit.

She was a woman with long dark hair and skin the colour but not the texture of a walnut, which was stretched smooth and tight over her body like the skin of a ripe plum. I judged she would have been about the same age as myself, in her late twenties, although she looked younger. She was dressed Samoan-style, a length of brown and white cloth wound around her breasts and kept up by a magic known only to the South Seas, leaving bare the most beautiful shoulders I have ever seen. Her face had that large and generous frankness of the Polynesians, but it also spoke wit from the mobility of the mouth and eyes. She was truly *une femme dont l'œil par sa franchise étonne*, a woman whose eyes astonish you with their candour. She walked through the garden between the banana and papaya trees, *Même quand elle marche on croirait qu'elle danse*, even when she walks you would believe she was dancing, but although Baudelaire's words were immediately in my head she was also pagan and antique in her directness, she was Dido though I was no Aeneas, she was the colour of Carthage, but unmarked by corruption or tragedy. She had come unscathed from the Samoan paradise to the inferno of New Britain. Hernsheim was right, she was *Die Königin*, and as you talked to her you could tell she was happy to accept the rights of her position, when she had a mind to do something she would look not for understanding but obedience. I remembered now a scandalous story a German trader, Capelle, retailed to me at

Ebon, that she had sailed off to Majuro to join a Negro known as Black Tom, marooning Captain Farrell and Master Young on some atoll. Splendid! She was afraid of nothing, and had the candid curiosity to embrace all forms of experience knowing that no black would rub off on her type of beauty entirely flawless and clean. This curiosity had drawn her to me, although she knew I was in no way eligible as a lover. She came searching for knowledge and needed no more than a smile to ask me to be her teacher.

I motioned her to recline on a mat beside me. She leaned forward, I thought to give me her hand in a regal gesture. Instead, she gave me a good hard shove, and said 'I thought an English gentleman always stood when a lady entered the room?'

I stumbled to my feet as if stung by my governess in the Close at Worcester, only to perceive that she was laughing at me. Well, I have never minded the laughter of my equals.

I offered her some of Mr Powell's atrocious gin, which she accepted *faute de mieux*, champagne being her favourite drink. It is odd, incidentally, in the South Seas to observe that the very first stores to arrive at some remote island, especially if brought by a German, will include Rheinwein, burgundy and champagne.

It appeared that Captain Farrell was away in Sydney, and that the Queen was lonely, so we arranged another meeting, and this led to many more, and occasionally I would sail with her over to New Ireland, or to visit the botanist Kleinschmidt. But mostly we would talk in the shade of the hut at Kininigunum, closing the gate in the bamboo stockade so that we would be entirely alone save for the huge butterflies, in our *hortus conclusus* that was more than a garden, it was in fact Epicurus's Κῆπος, a school in a garden, and you will recall that Epicurus was the first philosopher to admit women to a school of discussion.

My preference for the male sex never led me to a distaste for the female, on the contrary no Greek or Roman could have worshipped a true goddess with more fervour than I, or in the Dionysiac orgies wished the Bacchantes to rise to greater heights of abandonment. In the South Seas I had found that many different peoples, if not corrupted by missionaries, could give unrestrained expression to their primeval instincts and celebrate the union of all nature in exactly the cult of that Dionysus of whom of course they had never heard.

135

Here in Emma I found a child half of America and Europe, and half of the South Seas. She had no sense of sin or guilt, despite her extensive education with the Catholic nuns in Sydney and a prudish aunt in San Francisco. Yet she was by no means devoid of moral or ethical principles, while of course she was far removed from the taboos of her mother's people. She had no sympathy with or affinity for a 'civilized' world where pain is held to be inseparable from pleasure. A 'perfect lady' whom my mother would have graduated with honours from the ritual of tea, she would talk to me of her lovers and her pleasure in them (without any basic immodesty) in a way not possible for any educated woman in England. Nay, Dr Acton in his book on the reproductive organs has told us quite clearly, 'I should say that the majority of women (happily for society) are not very much troubled with sexual feeling of any kind.' When after some of her more bizarre disclosures I quoted this to Emma, her large eyes widened and she said innocently 'Did your Dr Acton know only the wives of the London Missionary Society?'

In her beauty she was the epitome of the whole pagan world, and there was in her body that grain of salt by which Catullus distinguished his totally beautiful Lesbia from the well-built Quintia, but I'm sure she never said 'Odi et amo', she never felt the torture the senses tear from the soul, she remained innocent and although a half-caste like Baudelaire's Jeanne Duval she never swam to her lover through the black sea of nights of horror and blasphemy. When she swam, which she did like a dolphin, it was through lagoons floored with a million emeralds.

She had no sense of sin, but she had a profound knowledge of evil which in turn made her immune to the actual horrors around her. On the face of it, what region of earth could be more terrible than New Guinea? What frightful apprehension came upon me when I awoke amongst volcanoes and cannibals and fevers worse than either, and realized how far I had come from the kindliness of Samoa or the coral purity of the atolls! I experienced the shuddering sensuality of cannibalism when I landed with George Brown on the coast of New Ireland and was offered for sale, by a smiling native, a human thigh. The ugliness of these creatures, their cruelty to their women, their callous mutilation of their captives all wound around me like the creepers of the jungle and swirled about my brain like the poisonous miasmas of the swamps, while the smell of roasting human flesh floated over all. In an obscene parody of the Eucharist I saw my father in the tranquillity of Worcester handing his lady parishioners wafers sliced from a smoked human penis. But my humour, savage or kind, failed because I had no one to share it with. In all the tropical blaze of the sun there was no light in the heart of these regions. Nor was there any passion. Though the accepting flesh could easily enough be found, one might as well be buggering a pig. Daily I felt more trapped, and was in a frenzy of wanting to escape, and yet was too lazy to attempt it, in the lethargy of heat and gin.

Then into this diabolic scenario floated Emma and my thoughts immediately took a cheerful flow and the data of sense gave instant proof of the bounty of life. She was not appalled by fevers or volcanoes, and the revolver she carried when we walked abroad was only ever used once, and that not on savages but on a brute of a German, one Rodolph, whom she shot in the groin when she caught him attempting to rape one of her Samoan servants.

Though she came to me for instruction and apologized for her vast ignorance, I was astonished at her knowledge. We talked on all topics. When I spoke of the cruelty of the New Ireland natives, and told how Mr Powell had been present when the women scraped the skin off captives preparatory to cooking them, she said surely it was not as bad as the cruelty of the Romans who in the enacting of the myth of Marsyas had flayed a man alive in the Colosseum in front of an audience of thousands. She was also in touch with the present currents of the world, always wanting to know the latest developments in politics from those like Brown or Hernsheim who were in receipt of letters and books from abroad. She had the greatest respect for the Germans, and predicted that there would be a German empire in the Pacific based on Samoa.

We talked for hours and achieved an Epicurean calm, but underneath as if in sympathy with our surroundings there were molten rocks of passion, fused beyond separate sex, and above all when she danced for me in the smoky light of a fire of coconut husks. What strange mystery was this, that I, who had no lust for the bodies of women, should have removed her robe and anointed her splendid body with sandalwood oil and set her dancing in a shimmer of skin like a still sea breathed on by the gentlest of winds in the moonlight.

God knows, though, she was no disembodied spirit. One of her Samoan servants was a magnificent fellow, and although called a servant there was nothing servile in the relationship. Transcending my pallid, emaciated self I took on the limbs of the great Dionysus myself as I released my Bacchante to the fulfilment of her dance.

And then in the morning she would be surveying the coast, making the most practical and detailed arrangements with the natives for the purchase of lands for future plantations. That same creature who had so totally abandoned herself to the spell of the moment was now living in the future, saying to me 'There's no doubt that the Germans, or possibly the British, will make this country a colony one day, and then it will be essential for any owner of land to be able to produce a proper title. My father had immense problems with his lands in Samoa, but he came through because of firm titles'. She imparted to me the astonishing intelligence that her father actually owns the land on which the Samoan Government has its offices and buildings, and that they pay him rent for it!

I attempted to dissuade her from her business activities, whether in land purchases or in running the trade store for Captain Farrell. Why not return to Samoa or to one of the atolls and live in idleness and lie in peace, instead of chancing it here against fever, volcano and savage? 'Since ambition and the pursuit of wealth are equally odious, why not embrace the unique blessing of the South Seas, the endless and inexpensive opportunity to do nothing?' 'Because, unlike yourself', she answered shortly, 'I was born neither a man nor an aristocrat. You have no insults to hurl back on the world. I'm a half-caste woman, I can't do anything about that, but I'm not going to be a victim. I'm poor, and that I can do something about. What's more, when I'm rich I'll bring my beautiful little sister Phebe here, and my old mother Le'utu who was kicked out of my father's house, and any of my brothers and nieces who can come as well. I'll have a Samoan kingdom here in New Britain, and your uncle the Baron and your father the Canon can come and drink champagne with me—and to hell with them if they ask for tea and bread and butter.'

I used to admire her hair very much, black and glossy and so long it easily covered her breasts when she let fall her robe, her nipples sometimes showing through it, like strawberries in a storm, I said jestingly to her once. It gave me intense pleasure to bury my head in it and breathe its fragrance, reminding me of some lost occasion in my earliest childhood which at the same time would call up an exotic world peopled with strange beasts and butterflies and flowers. 'All languid Asia and burning Africa, a whole distant world, absent, almost extinct, lived in the depths of this aromatic forest!' And then one day she came to me distraught, in a state in which I had never seen her, saying she had had a terrible dream in which her head had felt icy cold and in the dream she had stood in front of a mirror surrounded by a gleaming hairless cranium. She begged me to reassure her that dreams were never prophecies.

This I did, and cured her of her distress by a stroke of intuition in which I recalled that the old custom in Samoa was for women to have their heads shaved, and suggested that a childhood memory and horror of this had risen to disturb her sleep. What I did not tell her was that my ancestor the second Baron, the wicked Lord Lyttelton, had had the most famous dream in England, believed in by Dr Johnson and Horace Walpole and many more. At the age of thirty-five, in his house in Hill Street, Berkeley Square, he dreamed that a bird flew into his room and was metamorphosed into a woman, who told him that he had not three days to live. Being in perfect health, he made light of it to his friends, and when the third day came he felt very well and said he 'should bilk the ghost.' That night, just as he had settled himself in his bed and his servant was putting away his things, he died instantly.

Soon after this I left New Britain for Java, my only regret being the parting with Emma, and I never saw *die Königin* again.

Chapter XXII

—————————◆—————————

JOHN COE

I was twenty years old, just nine years younger than big sister Emma, and knocking around Apia with nothing much in the way of prospects, when in sails that tough bastard Tom Farrell saying that he and Emma are in on an almighty good proposition in the Duke of York islands, and how about I come and trade for them. 'You'll probably be cooked by cannibals', says Tom, 'but you can make your fortune and your life's your own, no bugger to tell you what to do, look at this cargo of blackbirds I've brought back. And only one mission, and that's old George Brown, a decent cove.'

'What!' I said. 'Only one mission!' That fixed it. How sweet the air would be away from those canting parasites, a man can't even get a grog in Apia on Sunday. Father was all for it, Emma was always his favourite, and he thought I'd be company for her and maybe take her side if things got too tough with Tom, Father never taking too much relish in the Irish-Australian combination.

There were drawbacks, of course. Tom had to admit the New Britain women didn't exactly look like Samoans. He was a bit Irish about this aspect. One moment he'd say it was so damn hot and humid that I wouldn't feel much like fucking anyway. Then the next moment he'd say I'd be shagging the arse off every woman in the village and they'd be queueing up for me because I'd be such a novelty. Queer thing with Tom, rough as guts with a man but I never heard him swear in front of a woman, and he'd get real wild with Emma sometimes, she never gave a bugger what she said.

'Well that won't worry me', I said, 'I've got a Samoan wife, Tau'loto, and I'll bring her with me.' Tom looked a bit surprised, but pleased too, his view was that no man can last long without a woman. 'Done', I said, 'I'll go and work for Farrell and Co., but mostly for the "and Co.".' The joke round the islands you know, of course everyone knew that Captain & Mrs Farrell weren't married at all, and the joke was that people would spell the firm 'Farrell and Coe.' A crazy bugger called Wilson, more of him later, second mate of the *Adolph*, he got a paintbrush one night and painted in an E on the end of the sign over the gate of the trading post, FARRELL & CO. Tom was up on a high rope over that, he'd have killed the man who'd done it if he'd known who it was. Pity he didn't actually.

Tom was still doing business for Goddefroys, or the DHPG as it was by this time, but he seemed to have the all-clear to build up his own firm. I think Goddefroys encouraged him to build up his own trading stations as well as theirs because this way they'd get in ahead of the missionaries in New Guinea. The traders would get copra or whatever they wanted from the Kanakas for a few blue beads, tobacco or tomahawks. But the missionaries would get at the Kanakas and make them demand piece goods so they could clothe their wicked naked bodies, and money so they could fork out for the mission funds and thus the missionaries could build those bloody great horrible churches that disfigure Samoa. Apparently there was only one missionary in New Britain, old George Brown, so it was a free for all.

When Tom was in Apia this time he was very thick with a fellow Richard Parkinson, we called him the Professor, who was working for Goddefroys as a surveyor. He was very keen on my young sister Phebe, like every other lecherous male in Apia. She was about fifteen and real pretty. Father, he kept the shotgun loaded. Also Phebe, she was real Convent-trained, the Sisters had told her to keep her legs together or the Devil'd hop in. This Parkinson was pretty old, and all filled up with education, especially botany, he could tell you all the Latin names. He was a sort of a mixture, a Dane from one of those little bits of Europe that swap around, so he was actually a German, but he had an English father and that's why he was called Parkinson. He spoke English as good as German. Him and Tom were doing a lot of talking.

Pretty soon I went off with Tom in the *Südsee*, clanking and puffing all the way from Samoa to the Duke of Yorks. The other two ships followed, the *Sophia* and the brig *Adolph*.

It was great to see Emma again. Jesus, what a looker that big sister of mine was! And fun! Hell! Soon as we arrived she's cracked open a bottle of champagne and we're drinking to the days of glory ahead. 'Take no notice of this place, John', she said. Actually they had a very trim little set-up, trading store, huts, bamboo stockade and Farrell & Co. over the gate, and Mioko was a grand little harbour. 'There it is, over there', she pointed towards New Britain, south of the volcanoes, 'we'll have our own port there, and our house, and plantations of coconuts, coffee, cocoa, chinchina.' Tom would always start to growl soon as she started to mention coconuts. His line was, why sit around seven or eight years waiting for coconuts to grow when you can buy all the copra you want from the Kanakas already? Emma would get real wild at him, tell him he was too dumb to see the future, ask him what did he think Goddefroys were doing buying all that land in Samoa and planting it up with coconuts, oh, they'd argue on. But I could tell Emma would win, I knew Emma longer than Tom had. They also talked a lot about Parkinson, and Phebe. Emma and Phebe were always very close.

Tom took me around to show me the ropes. Jesus, it was a rough turnout! The Goddefroy manager, Blohm, was a drunk, always had a bottle of schnapps, terrible fire-water. No wonder Tom was setting up his own show. George Brown was away in Sydney on sick leave, the missionary at Port Hunter was Benjamin Danks, a real prick, one of those pale-eyed bastards with a blotchy red complexion. And did he hate Tom's guts! He had a nice wife, though. Hernsheim over at Matupi, lovely harbour there only it's slap bang under a volcano, Hernsheim was a gentleman, one of those Germans who'd quote you poetry as he whipped the cork out of a bottle of white wine and then drink you under the table roaring away on those German songs. So there was the DHPG, Hernsheim and Farrell, all trading, and more than enough for all of them.

The game was rough all right. It was just about slavery, rounding up these black Melanesians to ship over to work the plantations at Samoa. A lot of them were just sold to us like pigs by a chief who'd taken them captive in these little wars they had going all the time. We didn't ask any questions, but Emma was red hot on having them all sign (what a joke!—X is a lovely signature) and say they understood the contract. Actually, whatever you hear from the British or the Americans, the DHPG treated the Kanakas well, those efficient Germans knew that was the way to get the best work out of them. (The Germans were strict, but dead consistent, the Kanakas knew where they were with them.) The Solomon islanders were the best workers. The New Britain lot were pretty small and lazy, very slow in all their movements. The New Ireland lot were better.

I could see Tom and Emma were dead set on a collision course over the right way to treat the Kanakas. Tom's instructions to me were simple: 'Kick 'em up the arse if they're cheeky. If they keep on being cheeky, shoot 'em. Pay 'em as little as you can for anything, they're only just down out of the trees and they won't notice the difference.' Now you wouldn't ever call Emma a softie, but she liked the Kanakas and always got on well with them and she said they weren't stupid, they knew when they were being cheated. Also she said they had their own customs, just as we Samoans or the Germans did, and we oughtn't to go against them. She didn't just say this for love of humanity, though she was never short of that, but because she was a good business woman. Tom had no head for business, though he could smell a good proposition when it was still over the horizon. Then he'd just take what he wanted and leave someone else to pick up the pieces.

Emma tried to impress upon all the Farrell traders that you had to treat the Kanakas well. But you can't turn a shark into a dolphin. The only sort of fellow who'd come around these islands looking for a job would be one who was too rough for civilization. And Jesus, it wasn't easy to do what Emma wanted you to out on some isolated hell-hole a couple of days sail from the nearest white man, living in a thatched hut that'd go up like a torch. They'd flush you out with the fire and then kill you. And it was so lonely it was hard not to reach for the gin bottle.

As I said, these bastards were real bad bastards. I'll give you an example. On a Sunday afternoon in the middle of October, it would have been '79, a few of us were aboard the *Südsee* in Mioko harbour having a drink. The brig *Adolph* was anchored next to us, and the second mate John Wilson and Patrick Bourke were sitting on the poop drinking. Wilson went off and lay down for a sleep. 'Come back, you bugger, there's still half a bottle to go' Bourke calls out. 'I'm going to have a sleep, pipe down,' says Wilson. 'Bugger you, you're going to have a drink' says Bourke. Wilson got up, looking annoyed, and Bourke threw a glass at him, making a great gash right across his forehead. Then there's a real ding-dong. Wilson eventually knocked Bourke down and then he grabs a great length of sugar cane and belts him over the head till Bourke's unconscious. By this time we'd realized things were getting a bit serious, and we rowed over to the *Adolph* and I hopped on board to break up the fight. Wilson whips out his revolver and tells me to stand still or he'll shoot me. Then he grabs a belaying pin and finishes off poor bloody Bourke. Then he yells to all of us to come and help him throw the sod overboard. The mate of the *Südsee* gave him a hand, and then sluiced down the decks while Wilson went below to have his interrupted sleep.

That's the sort of fellow Emma had to deal with. No wonder they weren't too polite to the bush Kanakas.

It was the same story all the time. At Kabaira, on the north of the Gazelle Peninsula, back of the Mother and Daughter volcanoes, a white trader called Southwell emptied his revolver into a village because he said they hadn't delivered the copra they'd promised. Killed a woman and blew the hand off a baby. Emma insisted that compensation be paid in *dewarra*, that's shell-money, thousands of shells strung on a string. Interesting the scale of values, incidentally.

10	fathom for a pig, approx. 120 lb.
1½	fathom for a small bag of fresh coconut meat
1	fathom for 80 taros, about 140 lb.
1	fathom for 60 yams, about 160 lb.
20	fathom for an elderly woman
50-100	fathom for a young girl
20- 50	fathom for compensation to the surviving member of the family of a murdered person.

Tom reckoned 50 fathom was plenty for an old woman and a baby's hand.

Southwell died of a fever, maybe lucky for him, and missionary Danks found him a couple of days later, stinking, and buried him. Tom put in another trader, a Frenchman, Benninger. He supplied beads, axes and other goods to the chief Tomara, in return for so much copra to be delivered in October. When the time came Tom sent Captain Murray over in the *Lelea* with a fellow called Anderson and a Buka boy, one of Tom and Emma's bodyguard from the Solomons, to collect the copra. According to Benninger, Tomara's men had not handed over the quantity promised. There was an argument, and Anderson got rough. But Tomara had the numbers, and the three white men and the Buka boy were all killed. The white men's bodies were thrown into the lagoon, and the body of the Buka was eaten. They don't like white meat as much as black.

Tom was away trading when the news reached Mioko. Emma sobered up Blohm who went over in the *Niafou* and towed the *Lelea* back. Emma, as I said, was no softie. She reckoned that four murders called for a punitive expedition, and was just setting it up when H.M.S. *Beagle* arrived and the skipper went over and held an enquiry, which found that the white men were to blame. Emma wasn't too pleased with anyone over this business. That was a bad station, that Kabaira. A year later another Farrell trader was killed there, and a few years later Hernsheim's station there was burnt. Makes you wonder why any of us took it on, doesn't it? For myself, I suppose it was the freedom, you were a real god, you could do what you wanted, no government, police, only a bit of trouble from Danks setting the Kanakas against you. And mostly the Kanakas were very friendly, and not all that bad looking. My Samoan wife Tauloto didn't last long in New Britain, she got consumption and I had to send her home. After that was when the Kanaka maries started to get better looking. I left a few kids around the coast. They tell me in Europe and America an illegitimate child has problems. None at all in Samoa or New Guinea.

I got burned out myself at a place called Kuran on New Ireland, where I was living with a Captain Clason, a Swede. I'd gone up to take over from him and a real bastard called John Knowles, Johni Mioko the Kanakas called him. This day I found the Kanakas breaking into the store and helping themselves. When I asked them what they thought they were doing they said Johni and Captain Clason had never paid them for their work, so now they were taking goods for their pay. When I told them to hand them back they burnt us out. We saved a few things in the boat, but I was glad we'd saved ourselves. We got away to Kalil to the place of one of the Wesleyan Fijian teachers. He brought us back to Mioko, but when we tried to pay him for his trouble, missionary Danks made him hand it back as he said Tom had called the missionaries dirty liars and a Jesuitical set. Bit Irish of Tom, who was a Catholic, to call Methodists Jesuits!

I mentioned those Buka boys. Jesus, were they tough! Tom and Emma brought them over as bodyguards and workers, they eventually had about 150 of them, no local treachery for them, they were devoted to Emma in particular, and the New Britain Kanakas were shit scared of them. You always felt safe if there were Buka boys around.

About this time, when I was back in Mioko for a spell, Emma arrived in a new ship, *Sea Rip*. She'd been out round the islands getting copra and trochus and tortoise shell. Sounds easy, doesn't it? But you got to remember that these islands or atolls are often only a couple of miles long, surrounded with treacherous coral reefs, and they're way off to buggery in the middle of the ocean, a couple of hundred miles one way, and three or four hundred the other. And there's Emma, with a few Buka boys and a couple of Samoans, doing the whole show herself, skippering the boat, navigating, trading, and on this trip buying the bloody islands as well! She'd bought Nuguria, or the Fead islands as the whole group is called, east nor'east of Mioko, a good 250 miles sail as you've got to go south down round Cape St George at the foot of New Ireland, she'd bought the whole bang shoot for a few boxes of beads and tomahawks. She had her usual piece of paper signed X by the chief to prove it. Then away she went 200 miles to the south-east to the Mortlock islands, which are about 150 miles north-east of Buka and Bougainville. The people there are beautiful, light-skinned Polynesians, they make canoes out of logs that float across from Buka and they sail these across to Nuguria and down to the Tasman islands. Anyway, these Mortlocks, Emma bought the lot for exactly four axes and ten pound of tobacco. She's got plans for planting coconuts there, and on her next trip she says she's going to buy the Tasmans, and the Sir Charles Hardy Group and the Carterets. She's already bought Vitu, that's a real island not a coral atoll, about two hundred miles west of the Duke of Yorks. I think she paid $50 for it and Tom was wild with her as he said it was too damn expensive.

Emma was in great spirits. She said they'd had some tricky moments rounding Cape St George as the current was running very strongly and the wind blowing on shore. She says you can never count on the currents in St George's Channel running the right way at the right time. She loves the sea, our Polynesian seafaring blood certainly flows in her veins. She says all the Kanakas are very friendly on these small islands, even though the entire crew of a whaler was massacred on the Mortlocks a few years back. But you know what some of those buggers were like, you couldn't blame the Kanakas for knocking them off. I think Emma being a woman gives them such a shock anyway that by the time they've recovered they've had time to notice that all the Bukas are carrying carbines. But Emma never has any trouble, the Kanakas know they can trust her as soon as she smiles at them. When a fellow like Tom smiles at you it's like a mastiff drawing back its upper lip. Another thing Emma says about the smaller islands, there's never any trouble about buying pigs or fowls, on the larger islands they're always going bush and the Kanakas can't catch them.

Emma wanted me to go out to Nuguria, that's the largest of the Fead islands, and set up a station there. Sounded all right to me.

Chapter XXIII

REVEREND GEORGE BROWN

Port Hunter,
Duke of York Islands.

10 November 1881

Reverend J. D. Frith,
Wesleyan Mission,
Fiji.

My dear James

You have asked me to piece together a more or less coherent account of the extraordinary events that have taken place here since my return almost exactly two years ago. I am not surprised that the Reports you have read in the *Sydney Morning Herald* and the *Telegraph* have been confusing, as several of them were written by Mr Farrell and he is not always the most reliable. Out of all the amazing and tragic events that have come to pass, Farrell and Emma are the only ones to have profited. Danks, who it must be admitted has a most un-Christian dislike of Farrell, suspects Foul Play, but I think not, though I doubt not that hard bargains were struck. Farrell indeed is not the most moral of men, but when Emma is in command, which is often, things go straight.

Please forgive that smudge on the paper. The sweat still streams off me though I thought I had long since dried out, April being our very worst month, no wind, calms to sea, and a blazing sun. Oh for a Supply of Ice, just to let us feel again what cold means. Though we have too much of cold here when the fever is on us. Mrs Danks is very poorly at the moment.

As you know, I returned here on the *Ripple* on 22 March

1880 after an absence of over a year. Only nine days later we had the startling Intelligence that there were no less than 50 to 60 white men at Cape Metlik, or Liki-Liki, at the bottom of New Ireland some 65 miles south-east of us. At first I thought they must be the advance guard of the German colonization that must one day descend on us, but we had the news through Land, a DHPG trader, and he said no, these poor wretches were French, Italians, Germans and Belgian, and that they were founding an independent Settlement to be known as New France. What Madness! It would be possible for Europeans to settle and survive almost anywhere in New Britain or New Ireland (with the goodwill of the natives), except at this little bay called Port Praslin where apparently the settlers first landed, before making their way a few miles around the coast to Liki-Liki. In this place two high mountains sweeping down directly to the shore, and the Island of Lambom off-shore, make a sort of Funnel down which the rain incessantly pours to the extent of about 200 inches a year. There is almost no flat ground, and the jungle is at its most obdurate. I can do no better than quote to you the description of Duperrey, the French navigator who many years ago called it Port Praslin. 'As soon as one steps on the foreshore the vegetation appears so active and vigorous that one sees it as overwhelming the shore and not stopping until the sea disputes the possession of the soil.'

Into this dispute of nature these poor settlers had stumbled. I sailed over to Liki-Liki in the *Ripple* to find out the truth. It was beyond Imagination. In the southerly swell we could not anchor but stood in and off while Danks and I went onshore in the boat which was immediately rushed by twenty or so wide-eyed creatures nearer skeletons than sentient beings. There were sixty-six colonists in all, to a man suffering from Fever, Malarious Dysentery and large Ulcers on their legs and other parts. Their Clothes were in the most filthy state, what there were, and stinking. Many had no clothes to wear by day nor anything to cover themselves with at night, and they had only the most miserable huts in which to sleep, if sleep they could. And all this while torrential rain poured incessantly down. They had almost nothing left in the way of stores to eat, putrid dried fish (no longer dry in this climate!), foul salted pork, rotten biscuits, and large quantities of sour Wine. There were piles of useless equipment; lamp posts; a fountain; uniforms with Brass Lions rampant, but no Axes; Rifles but no Tomahawks; and amongst the colonists plenty of Titles but no Quinine.

They had come at the instigation of a certain Marquis de Rays, who had by public subscription and clever advertisement launched an immense enterprise to found a colony, Nouvelle France, in the South Seas. Neither the Marquis nor anyone else had surveyed the spot where the Colony was to be. These poor people, who had parted with all their savings, had been brought on a ship, the *Chandernagor*, which had dumped them and bolted under cover of night, they feared never to return. More ships and colonists were expected, although it was clear that they would arrive to certain disaster.

Humanity and compassion demanded that we offer them a haven at Port Hunter where we could do our best to succour the sick and feed the starving. Our Boat was immediately rushed by the poor wretches with their pitiful belongings, and we rowed out to the *Ripple* almost gunwales under, with the heartrending cries of those left on shore floating across the water begging us to come back for them. One man rushed into the water and would have drowned himself had he not been restrained. We took forty-two back to Port Hunter, seven of whom died on the voyage, and two went mad.

Our meagre stocks of food were sorely depleted in feeding these hollow bodies, and we sent for help to Blohm and the Farrells who generously supplied Biscuits, Tea and Sugar. It was almost impossible to get nurses to wait upon the sick. They could not dress their sores as the smell was so bad, and they would not wash them because they were so full of Vermin. There was death after death, grave after grave to be dug. Emma Farrell was one who had no fear of the reek of death or the ghastly visions of fever. Many Colonists owed their lives to her. She was always a lady most amiable, sensitive and sensible of the least unkindness.

Half a dozen of the more or less able-bodied men were engaged as Traders by Hernsheim and Farrell, leaving the sick to us. One, Benninger, a Frenchman, was soon after murdered at Kabaira, a result of the previous trader being harsh and overbearing and

150

bouncing the Natives. With ordinary Care and proper Usage there is little or no damage to be feared from the Natives.

The most useful and intelligent of the Colonists was a man called Brandt, the only one who could speak German, French and English and therefore invaluable to Danks and myself in attending to the needs of the sick Colonists. But Farrell wanted to steal him away from us.

I learned from Brandt the strange principles of the Colony. They were to build three *Quartiers*, one for the *noblesse*, one for the *bourgeois*, and one for the *oeuvriers*. Frenchmen for Colonists! Despite their misfortunes many of the Colonists believed it was not the fault of the Marquis. Of the sincerity of the Marquis there is no doubt, and whatever doubts we may entertain as to the advisability or practicability of his scheme, no one can help sympathizing with him in the sorrow he must feel at the present failure of the plan he had so earnestly attempted.

In this year of tragedies, early in August kind Captain Ferguson of the *Ripple* an Australian beloved of us all and much experienced in these islands paid a trading call at Numa-Numa on north-east Bougainville. They were peacefully anchored the next morning when, for reasons not yet discovered, 300 natives swarmed aboard and murdered Captain Ferguson and three others. The *Ripple* brought back eight badly wounded to add to our list of the sick. Late in August 1880 another Ship, the *Génil*, anchored this time with no passengers, only twenty-five Malay coolies, apparently to act as a police boat and also for communications and to recruit native labour for the Colony. I shall never forget my first meeting with the *Génil's* master, Captain Rabardy on board his ship at Port-Breton, as the Marquis had rechristened Port Praslin. I think you will agree that I may, without incurring the deadly sin of Pride, think of myself as a Charitable man. I usually manage to see some good in people. Danks always maintained I was deceived in seeing any in Farrell. But Rabardy was a man whose evil was incarnate in his fiery face. I could say that his close-set Eyes and heavy blunt Nose, between mutton-chop whiskers, gave him a piggy look, but I never knew harm in a Pig. I was received in his cabin, of which he immediately locked the door. On the table was a loaded revolver. I suggested that he sail immediately to Port Hunter where his ample supplies could succour the Colonists and, incidentally, perhaps restock our sadly depleted shelves. He informed me that it was his sacred duty to remain at Port-Breton, and that I instantly arrange for the Colonists to be returned to Liki-Liki 'where they belonged.' I soon perceived there was no Rational Discourse to be had with the man, and left. After unlocking the door he retired to his cabin, locking himself in again, with his revolver for company.

His crew were a villainous riffraff, and my heart bled for those poor Coolies battened below in the stifling heat. I heard later that the whole of his original crew had deserted at Singapore, so shockingly had he punished and tortured them, his favourite mode of discipline being to suspend the victim by his thumbs from the boom for several hours. It was rumoured that two crew members who had 'died' had in fact been murdered by him. Apparently, to ensure the efficiency of his duties as police-chief, he had loaded on board in Spain a complete set of tools of torture, thumbscrews, a rack, steel-studded whips, garrotts, all the foul implements of the popish Inquisition.

On 14 October a third ship arrived, the *India*, with 340 souls mostly Italians, and 200 of them women and children. More than 100 had died on the voyage. This ship carried to this impossible Colony on this hostile coast a Cargo of items from some fantastic Dream, viz. 3000 dog collars, 22 cases of heavy writing paper stamped with the royal arms of Charles I, Emperor of Nouvelle France; a huge and magnificent altar of superbly blended Italian marbles; boxes of incense and candles and other popish knick-nackery; sufficient bricks to build a Cathedral. Nevertheless, these brave people came ashore, admittedly almost at Rabardy's gunpoint, and for a month it seemed some sort of Colony might succeed. But by the end of November supplies were running low and many were sick of Malarial Fever and other complaints. The Governor and Rabardy left in the *Génil* for Sydney to bring back supplies. The Governor, like his predecessor on the *Chandernagor*, never returned. Rabardy returned at the end of February 1881, many weeks later than promised, to find the *India* gone and the settlement deserted. The poor Italians on the *India* were eventually unloaded in Sydney.

It may seem beyond the power of belief, but shortly after this a *fourth* ship of Colonists, a steamer, the *Nouvelle Bretagne*, left Barcelona for Port-Breton. In Singapore they bought an old barque, christened it the *Marquis de Rays*, and towed it down to New Ireland. It was to be used as a floating hospital. At least this ship had two good leaders, Captain Henry and Dr Baudouin, and in addition to the cargo shipped in Spain, which included heavy machinery, a gigantic millstone, ten Punch and Judy shows, hundreds of pink and white slippers to be worn by ladies at the court of Charles I, two grandfather clocks and a set of Louis XV style drawings room tables, Henry had brought some tools and implements to build houses and till the soil.

It were tedious to relate the disasters that befell this last shipload of unfortunates, how they ran out of provisions and Captain Henry returning to Manila was told the Marquis would not honour his bills, how he defied the Spanish and sailed back, how a Spanish warship followed to seize the ship to auction it in Manila to cover the debts. Forty brave Colonists stayed, settled in at Brie Marie, near Port-Breton. Rabardy was now in command, and the *Génil* their only hope of escape, but he would have nothing to do with them, remaining on board, and every now and then sailing off for several weeks. From one such journey to Bougainville he brought back a pretty, very black little girl of thirteen or so. She used to lie at his feet like a dog, her eyes always on him. Her name was Tani and Rabardy had bought her from 'King' Kopara for two tomahawks. She was the only living creature that cared for the man.

*

10 June 1882

You must forgive me! I am finishing this letter from Sydney, if 'finishing' be the word for a document six months old, which I have only just found in my writing case. As you no doubt know, I was suddenly recalled to Sydney from Port Hunter, leaving Danks in charge, and I piece together the end of the Marquis de Rays story from Danks's letters to me.

After three or four months, and no sign of help from the Marquis, it was obvious that the Colonists would have to abandon Nouvelle France. Despite the rage of Rabardy, in a bloodless revolution King Charles I of Oceania was deposed and a Republic declared, the first object of which was to make contact with Farrell, who alone could save them. Rabardy had no course but to agree, for the key to the issue was coal, which Farrell had, while the *Génil* had almost none. An agreement was made that Farrell would provide coal and advance the Colonists £900 for a period of four months, and in return the Colonists assigned him the barque *Marquis de Rays* and all cargo in its holds. I am told that Farrell and one of his men and a crew of natives descended like vultures on to the settlements at Port-Breton and removed everything that was movable into the holds of the *Marquis de Rays* and the *Génil*, in that order. Buildings were demolished and the timber carried on board. One of the Colonists told Danks there were boxes of clothing sufficient for a hundred men for three years. They even took the altar. If there was a swindle put upon these poor Colonists, then the Catholic Church was certainly a party to it.

Apparently the infamous Captain Rabardy had an apoplexy at Mioko and suddenly died. The *Génil* eventually left in March 1882 with the surviving Colonists. Only three, a Dupré, and Mouton father and son, who elected to work for Farrell remained at Mioko. Emma and Farrell have become rich from their possession of all that the Colonists left behind.

Rusting in the jungle at Port-Breton is the machinery for a sugar-mill, a steam crane and a sawmill, unless Farrell has thought of a way to remove them. Under the trees at Port Hunter are some of the graves of the poor Colonists who never found their Paradise in the South Seas. The bodies of 250 more have been swallowed by the Sea or the Jungle. The Marquis de Rays, I am told, is to be extradited from Spain to stand trial in France for swindling and homicide through criminal imprudence. It is not for me to pass judgement on him.

I am enjoying, without guilt, some of the Pleasures of Sydney. How good it is to wear a fresh Collar and not have it instantly go limp with sweat!

Mrs Brown desires to be remembered.

Talofa!

Geo. Brown

Chapter XXIV

THOMAS FARRELL

Emma is beginning to frighten the bejesus out of me. I mean, a man's the boss, but she's getting that way she doesn't seem to think so. It's not only that I go off to Samoa with a cargo of Kanakas and I come back and she's bought half a dozen islands. It's that she's looking out there ahead somewhere she knows I can't see. Perhaps it's something to do with my chest. I didn't tell her what the quack in Sydney said, I've got about five years to live. Consumption. Jesus! A big tough bastard like me, lick anybody in the islands with the gloves off. She's that damn healthy she seems to smell out disease, like birds onto a sick one.

Yet there's more than that, she wants to be something more than I can make her. And when she wants something, nothing's going to get in her way. I don't mind a straight dirty deal, but she thinks of things no white man would. She's got no morals. Maybe no women have. Sure enough a good Catholic education made no impression on her. And there's old George Brown thinks she's so sweet and innocent and I'm the crooked one! This Rabardy business was over the fence. Jesus, it really shook me. I think she got some of these queer ideas from that Sodomite Lyttelton. I mean, no decent girl would hang around with a pervert like that. Now there was somebody who really *was* unhealthy, yet while I was away I'm told you'd think he was Solomon and she the Queen of Sheba. Disgusting.

By the holy weaver, the Rabardy business was really bad. That Dr Baudouin could have made trouble for us, though fortunately he hated Rabardy as much as anyone.

I never knew Emma take against anyone the way she took against Rabardy. Mind you, the man was a real snake, I've never met a nastier bastard, and that's saying something. He was just born that way, his brain was maggotty. Trust a swindler like de Rays to pick a madman for his police chief. One time he took me into a store-room on the *Génil*, Holy Mary Mother of God he had all the instruments of the Inquisition there. There was sulphur coming out those piggy eyes when he said to me 'We'll have no heretics and no criminals in Nouvelle France, I'll have no trouble in getting confessions.' I'll tell you a story about Rabardy that no one knows, though it's true as the Holy Cross.

He'd taken the *Génil* over to Bougainville, it was the time he brought that poor little girl Tani back with him. When he was there he heard about a white man living with the natives. This was surprising enough and even more so because they're all cannibals around the district where he was. Anyway, he found out the story was true. It was an Italian called Boero who was on the first Marquis de Rays ship, the *Chandernagor*. He and five others found it such hell at Liki-Liki that they pinched a canoe and set off for George Brown's place at Port Hunter. But the poor buggers hadn't reckoned on the St George's channel currents, and they ended up a couple of hundred miles away in the wrong direction, on Bougainville. There the natives took them captive and set up a big feast to eat them. They ate the other five but not Boero, the reason being that when they axed the first cove and strung him up over a slow fire by the heels and the women started to open his guts and scrape the skin off him the way they do, this poor sod Boero, who's only a young fellow, he bursts into tears. Well this gave the natives one hell of a shock as it was something they'd never ever seen, a man burst into tears. They poked him with a spear and made signs for him to do it again. Fortunately for Boero, he had the knack of doing it whenever he wanted to, like some of these actor coves. So they kept him on as a sort of a pet, while he watched his mates being eaten one by one, and himself weeping like a waterfall whenever they wanted him to.

Well, after a few months he began to get used to the smell of roast human flesh, and tried a few mouthfuls, and soon got as hooked on it as the natives. Then Rabardy arrived. He couldn't get anything out of Boero for a while, in some queer way he couldn't talk Italian or French any more, only the local dialect.

Anyway, Rabardy bought him for two hatchets and brought him back on the *Génil*.

Emma and I went over to see Rabardy one day. As usual he locked the cabin door, he had two revolvers on the table, and this Tani girl lying at his feet for all the world like a black kelpie sheepdog. We'd come to ask him about buying the equipment and stores rusting away on shore, but he had this horrible smile on his jowls, and he said in his disgusting lingo something like 'Pray, madam and monsewer, will you take dinner with me.' Well, this was something, to be offered a feed by Rabardy! We sat down (revolvers still there), he claps his hands and Tani brings in some crayfish and fruit and wine, very nice too, if you didn't think of those poor bloody colonists starving on shore. We're just tucking in when he claps his hands twice and Tani leads in the gibbering idiot who turns out to be Boero. The poor bugger's a hatter, quite daft. Rabardy picks up the revolver and points it at him and he bursts into tears. Rabardy cries 'Bravo' and roars with laughter. Then Rabardy claps his hands again and Tani comes back with some meat, and she gives some to Boero and tucks into the rest herself.

Rabardy hits her across the ear and points for her to offer some to us first. 'You like?' he asks, and begins to laugh, 'You like human flesh? Young girl, young man, just like young pork.' I reached for my revolver but he had his already pointing at me. I looked at Emma. She always had steadier nerves than me. She laughed right back at Rabardy and said 'We've lived here for four years, you don't think cannibals are a surprise for us? Anyway, you're only bluffing, I know pork when I see it.' Rabardy makes an obscene gesture, not at Emma but at Tani, who disappears again. A minute or two later she comes back with a covered dish, and puts it in front of Emma. Emma takes off the lid. It's a human penis, a smoked human prick, and, what's worse, a *white* one. Probably one of Boero's mates. I thought Emma was going to kill him, revolver or no. I grabbed her. Then she put the lid back on again. All this time Boero was watching us with his slobbery mouth hanging open. And then, I'll never forget it, Emma took one of Rabardy's cigars out of the box and lit it, cool as a volcano with a curl of smoke coming out of it. (She always liked cigars, but not big ones.) I could tell that

157

look on her face. She was waiting. As for Rabardy, he told Tani to take the dish away, apologized for his little joke, and began to tell us that King Charles I (viz. de Rays) would soon arrive. He was really much crazier than Boero. And there we were locked in the cabin with both of them, and that little black girl. Not a thing of it meant anything to her, except Rabardy, her master.

Emma said nothing more to me about the episode on the *Génil*, and when I mentioned it she told me to shut up. What she did do, when we got back to Mioko, was to grab a big sheet of paper and start making lists of all the material of the de Rays mob that she'd seen lying around on shore. Even a bloody altar. Then she made some calculations based on the number of colonists. Then she got another piece of paper and drafted something she said with a bit of a laugh we'd better call The Treaty of Mioko.

Finally she called me into the office. 'This is the situation now with the colonists', she said. 'The Governor, Chambaud, the one whose greatest pride, you remember, was to show us a hut filled with boxes, what he called "the chattels of the dead", Chambaud still believes in de Rays and that the *India* and the *Chandernagor* will return. The other forty, led by Dr Baudouin, know perfectly well that they've been deserted, and they want to abandon Nouvelle France and get out of it as fast as possible to Australia, before they all die of fever or starvation. Finally, there's that madman Rabardy. He's the key to the whole thing, because he's got the ship, the *Génil*, and the guns. And, he pinched the idea from us, his bodyguard of six Buka boys. So it's a deadlock. Short of murdering Rabardy, they can't get away.

'But what they don't know, and this is the hand that turns the key, your hand, Tom, is that the *Génil* has no coal. One of our Buka boys found out from one of Rabardy's Bukas. And you have coal, Tom lots of it. Our price for the coal will be all the material and stores, the old barque *Marquis de Rays* which will be very useful, and', here something hard stirred in those velvet eyes, 'Rabardy.' 'What the hell do you mean, Rabardy?' I asked. 'You'll see, Tom, you'll see.'

Well, I ran the cutter over to Port-Breton and had a yarn with Dr Baudouin. Not a bad cove. They'd just declared themselves a republic and given Governor Chambaud the chuck. They agreed to sign Emma's treaty, only they specified goods to a certain value, to be loaded on to the *Marquis de Rays*. The rest, and their personal belongings and furniture, would be stored at Mioko until they were able to send a ship for it. 'They never will', was Emma's comment. She had that one all worked out.

Next thing, after I'd gone home again, the *Génil* steamed into Mioko harbour. Dr Baudouin came ashore and said Rabardy wanted to see me and Emma. Emma wouldn't go, but it wasn't because she was scared. I went into the cabin, same old set-up, two revolvers and a cutlass on the table, Tani on the floor. I could see Rabardy was a sick man, he had a fever. What was really creepy was the way the man was always alone in his cabin, except for Tani. That poor bugger Boero had gone quite crazy and jumped overboard and the sharks had got him. The colonists hated Rabardy so much they wouldn't set foot on the *Génil*. Nor would he go ashore, in case they killed him.

Well, I told him the Treaty of Mioko had been signed, and that I'd give him enough coal to get to Sydney. He lurched to his feet and shouted at me, something like 'I do not go to Sydney. I am not a traitor. I am a loyal subject of King Charles I. I remain here. No one leaves Nouvelle France.'

I was boxed. I went ashore and told Emma the only way we'd get the *Génil* to Sydney was to shoot Rabardy. Instead, Emma dashed off a letter to Danks the missionary, who was being visited at Port Hunter by a British warship, H.M.S. *Conflict*. It did the trick. Danks wrote to Rabardy that unless he evacuated the colonists without trouble the warship would intervene. Rabardy didn't seem too keen on a naval battle.

I went back to Port-Breton in the *Génil* with a team of my boys and Dr Baudouin, and within ten days I'd organized the evacuation, and made sure all the best equipment was safe in the hold of the *Marquis de Rays*. Even all the religious gear. Emma insisted on this. 'Tom', she said, 'this disaster for the colonists has been sent by God to make our fortunes. We must show our respect for Him. We must have everything, including the altar.' She could have a real wicked sarcastic gleam in her eye, sometimes.

We brought the *Génil* and the *Marquis de Rays* back to

Mioko. The Doctor and several other colonists later told me a queer thing about that evening. When we got all snug into Mioko harbour, towing the old barque behind the steamer, it was just dark, and the lamp was on in our house, and Emma was playing the piano, it sounded like a waltz, something you'd dance to if you were feeling light-hearted. And there's these miserable buggers, half of them dying, just rescued from their hell on earth at Port-Breton where it never stopped raining, on this calm, cool evening all listening to the notes from Emma's piano like poor people being thrown golden sovereigns.

We had a sort of a sailor, a Captain Boore, lined up to take over the *Génil*. But how to get rid of Rabardy? Get him ashore, said Emma. But he wouldn't leave the cabin on the *Génil*.

He had a fever on him like the fires of Hell now. I told him how much better we could look after him on shore, and how much cooler it would be, and that was true enough, the *Génil* may have been out of coal but in Rabardy's cabin she was hot enough to raise steam. Rabardy wouldn't budge. The Doctor said it was because he was afraid of being murdered by the colonists as soon as he set foot on the beach. Then one morning Emma went out and came back with Rabardy. I don't know how she did it. She never would tell me. With him she brought his sea-chest and his terrified little black girl, Tani. Emma sent her off to be looked after by our Samoans. She made Rabardy lie down on the couch in the parlour. He was all on his own, she'd managed to get him away from his little black girl and the Bukas.

She told me to go, but I wouldn't. He didn't have his revolvers, but though he was a very sick man he was still capable of anything. God, he was a horrible creature! He had a week's growth on him, so his mutton-chop whiskers were lost in the weeds. His little eyes were red and his uniform filthy.

Emma went to the cupboard and took out a revolver. 'Holy Mary, woman,' I said 'don't shoot him here.' She waved me back, walked over to Rabardy and pointed the revolver right between his eyes and said in a real, deep, scary voice, 'Weep, Boero, weep'. He gave a little pig-blink at her, and then began to weep, with great convulsions racking him up and down on the couch.

When he quietened down Emma said, still in that deep voice, 'Boero, you have eaten the flesh of your fellow-creatures, of your

160

own white companions. You're damned and the Devil's waiting for you. You can rinse the taste of it out of your mouth with this cup,' she picked up a cup with some liquid in it, 'but what is in the cup is poison, and you'll die.'

'Let me die' he howled, and began to weep again. Then he sat bolt upright and said 'Give me the cup.'

Jesus, it was like some Black Mass, I felt all cold under my shirt, and I couldn't help crossing myself.

He drank it all down. Emma grabbed the cup. He gave a couple of tremendous convulsions and fell back, his arms flopping on either side of him. I took the cup off Emma and sniffed it. Strychnine. We always had strychnine in the medicine chest.

'Wipe out the cup,' said Emma, 'and leave it on the table alongside him. Call Dr Baudouin. He must be buried immediately. The grave has already been dug, the boys are down at the cemetery now.' She'd thought it all out.

When I came back with Dr Baudouin, who still couldn't get over the fact we'd been able to get Rabardy ashore, he wanted an autopsy. I refused. Emma said, 'Doctor, he must be buried immediately. As you know, in this climate putrefaction sets in at once. He must be properly laid out, I have had a catafalque made, and sent a boy for his uniform and sword.'

The Doctor had nothing to say, though he kept plenty back in his looks. So at three o'clock that afternoon the officers from the *Génil*, the colonists and our party all lined up to pay what you might call our last disrespects to Rabardy, all in his uniform with his hands crossed on his sword, and a Fiji preacher giving him the last rites. Only poor little Tani was sorry to see him go.

She wept for two days. Then the Doctor told me he saw her playing happily amongst the young Samoan girls. 'Where is your Capi?' he said. 'Gone, gone,' she answered and went happily back to her game.

Emma was right. We got the *Génil* away eventually, and we never saw hide nor hair of any of them ever again, except Dupré, and old Mouton and young Octave who came to work for us.

She was right too about the hardware and stores and clothing and all the rest of it, which gave us enough capital to break with the DHPG and set up on our own, and the old barque which was very useful and later served as a jetty.

The Marquis de Rays's paradise in the South Seas was a hell for all those who settled in it, but it made us independent. Emma said it was the turning point of our lives, from now on we would grow rich. She did not know how bad two things were. One, my consumption. Two, my creditors in Sydney.

Chapter XXV

PHEBE

I was a girl of fifteen, living with my father, I must have been pretty because the American Consul, Thomas Dawson, used to come just to see me, and sit on the verandah and talk to me, and my father didn't mind. Mr Dawson held my hand one evening when my sisters were inside cooking and said 'Oh Phebe, I would like you for my little wife. You come and live in my house with me and afterwards we can get married.' I always used to tell the Mother Superior everything, and when I told her this she said, 'Phebe you must stay away from that man, he is a bad man.'

Soon after this there was a dance and though I would like to have sat with Mr Dawson, for I had a little fancy for him, I went away and sat with a Mr Parkinson, a surveyor with Godde-froy, I didn't like him so much, but I had to get away from Mr Dawson.

The very next day Mr Parkinson wrote to my father and asked to marry me. I said I didn't want to get married. My father said, 'Phebe, Mr Parkinson is an old man, he is twenty years older than you maybe, but he is a good man, very well educated. And he does not drink.' 'Let him marry my sister Carrie', I said. He answered, 'It's not your sister Carrie's name in his letter. It is your name.'

I was always afraid of my father, and I thought he would beat me if I did not marry Mr Parkinson, so I said I would. The Sisters were not happy that he was a Protestant, but the Mother Superior said he was a good man, and better marry a good Protestant than a bad Catholic. I don't think many Catholics would agree with her.

So we were engaged, and I put off the wedding for six months, and I never looked at him, I did not know what colour the eyes were in his face. He didn't have any teeth in his mouth, they were all knocked out once when he fell over a fence in Africa.

I must tell you now what I found out much later about Richard Parkinson, which I didn't know then. He looked like an aristocrat, he was thin and tall with a high forehead, a long nose, a long blond beard and nice big lobes to his ears. He spoke perfect English and perfect German and read Latin and Greek as easy as doing up his bootlaces. He was always very particular about his boots being shiny, collars starched, shirts ironed without a crease, and white linen handkerchiefs. Yet he was not a dandy like Emma's colonel. The difference between them was that Richard was *fein* and Steinberger *modisch*.

Richard Heinrich Robert Parkinson spoke Danish as well, because he was born in Augustenborg in Schleswig-Holstein and his mother was a Dane. His father was the English horse-trainer for Prince Christian August and his mother was a lady-in-waiting at the court. This is what everybody was told. It was not until years later and I had had maybe six or seven children that Richard told me how the pudding was really made.

He was born on the 13th November 1844 and his father was Prince Christian August. His mother, Louise Sophie Caroline Brüning, was the daughter of a shoemaker and was twenty years old. The Prince paid Parkinson, his horse-trainer, a lot of money, and Parkinson married Louise just five weeks before the baby was born. On the wedding day, straight from the church, he left Augustenborg, and he was not there when little Richard was christened on the 18th December. Richard was given a very good education and his mother made fine embroidery and the Princess looked after her. Richard's half-brother who became Frederick VIII of Schleswig-Holstein looked just like him. Through his great grandmother, Christian VII's Queen Caroline Mathilde, he was a relative of King George II of England. Frederick's daughter, Augusta Victoria, became the wife of Kaiser Wilhelm II of Germany, so Richard was half-uncle to the Empress. How different it all is in Europe! In Samoa no one is illegitimate, though of course Richard was not illegitimate, because his father did marry his mother. Oh so complicated to be respectable!

Richard became an English teacher in Heligoland, that belonged to England. He was very musical, he played the violin beautifully, and he was choirmaster at Heligoland. He used to say music is the true sound of life, and he explained to me that in German *bei Stimmung* means both 'in tune', like a violin, and 'in good spirits.' There is an elegant little theatre there, and he used to produce Shakespeare plays there, and write plays himself. Usually love-stories, he told me, he was very sentimental. But always as well Richard had a passion for botany and ethnography, and about 1875 he met a wonderful man, Kubary, who was a collector for Goddefroy in the Caroline and Marshall Islands, bringing things back for their great museum in Hamburg. Now above everything else Richard wanted to go to the Pacific and work for Goddefroy, this became his passion. He went down to Hamburg to talk with the Goddefroys, and in the end he got his wish, first of all he went to Africa, then he was sent out to Samoa in 1878 as a surveyor for Goddefroy, and to lay out their plantations.

And there in Apia he took a fancy to little Phebe Coe and we were married in 1879. I did not want to marry him, but I was frightened of my father. When he was coming to court me I would hear his horse's hoofs and run away and hide under the bed. Or I would put on a dirty dress and mess my hair up so that Richard, being such a fastidious man, would think me disgusting. But he didn't, and we were married by the British consul when I was just sixteen, and there was a tremendous party, there were two big ships in harbour, the *Lackawana* and the *Bismarck*, and they made a great platform where we danced.

Poor Richard! When we went to bed that night I jumped in with all my clothes on and turned my back to him, and very early the next morning I got up and walked to mass. But bye and bye a baby was coming and I felt quite different about Richard. He tried to teach me German. Coming home from parties in the moonlight, he would be walking and leading my horse, he would say, 'Now Phebe, say after me "*Ich liebe dich. Du liebe mich. Er liebe sie.*"' And I would have to decline all of it, all those changes in words in that German language! Then he would stop the horse and put the bridle in my hands and hold my hands, very tall alongside the horse, and say '*Gibst mir einen Kuss*', and the first time I didn't know what the words meant but I knew he wanted me to give him a kiss.

165

I didn't know how to cook German food and when he told me he wanted me to learn I said I had not married him to be a cook. 'No', he said, 'but you must learn so that you can train the servants to cook.' There were always German warships in the harbour and we used to go to many parties with the officers, morning champagne on one ship, luncheon with many wines on another, and our nearest neighbour, Mrs Decker, who was a wonderful cook, she had us all to dinner, and afterwards Richard said 'You see why you must learn to cook, I am ashamed to ask the officers to our house where all you will give them will be beer and a little bread and a radish.' So I learned to cook by watching all the dishes he liked, and we would work out what was in them. I never learned to cook from a cook book. Richard was very particular about his food, and it must always come to the table very hot, he and the children would sit around the table, first I must serve him, and then the children, and then I could put something on a plate for myself.

It was in 1881 I think, I had had Louisa who was born in 1880 and another baby that didn't live long, that Tom Farrell came from New Britain saying that Emma wanted us to come and live with her, so Richard could lay out plantations and we would all be rich. She had plenty of land, said Tom. Richard very much wanted to go, mostly because of all those unknown peoples and butterflies and flowers he could write about. Of course I wanted to go, to be with Emma, and we were looking after her boy Coe Forsayth, who was nine now, and it would be good for him to see his mother. But somehow we kept putting off our move from Samoa, until a silly thing happened, and that just gave us the push.

A Herr August Goddefroy had come out to Samoa to be manager of the firm in Apia, the DHPG or Long Handle firm as it now was known. I think he must have been the black sheep of the family, as all the other Goddefroys were fine gentlemen. Certainly Richard did not like him at all, he offended him like dirty linen. On his way out from Hamburg, this Herr August had picked up a flash barmaid in Sydney, and from the moment she arrived in Apia she was on her high horse bossing all the employees around.

Phebe

There were at that time many New Britain and Solomon Island boys employed on the DHPG plantations, we Samoans looked down on them, they were so primitive, we called them *meauli*, black things. A lot of little stealing was going on in the building where the manager and employees lived, and where Richard had his office. Herr August told the Chinese cook to keep an eye open and report any thievery. He could easily from his kitchen at the back keep watch down the long corridor of the building.

One day he saw a young New Britain boy coming out of Frau Goddefroy's room, and reported him to Herr August, who asked him did he mean to steal. 'Me no like steal!' said the boy, but he had been caught so Herr August marched him off to the Consul, who told the black boy to tell the truth or he would get a good hiding. But the boy said again, 'Me no like steal.'

'But why did you go into the room', the Consul asked, egged on by Herr August, who wanted swift justice. 'Missis he speak me come', said the boy. 'What did Missis want from you?' asked the Consul. 'Missis,' answered the boy, 'he speak nice lapalapa belong you, me speak nice lapalapa belong me, Missis he speak me look, Missis he look, bye and bye Missis he go place belong sleep, Missis he speak me come, me come, bye and bye me go on top, me make up and down, bye and bye plenty salt water he come.'

Herr August tried to stop the enquiry, but the Consul was enjoying it so much he refused. The Consul found the boy not guilty, and had him honourably discharged.

After this all three employees, the two clerks and Richard, were disgusted and refused to work for Herr August, and resigned. So this comical little episode gave us the push and we sailed for New Britain, with a piano (which I didn't play as well as Emma), Richard's violin, a parrot, and my niece Emma Meredith, who was twelve.

We arrived safely at Mioko, a pretty little harbour with the thatched houses by the beach and Emma and I had such a happy, happy reunion. Maybe I should not say it, but she was much more pleased to see me than her son Coe, though she was very pleased to see him too. She had changed a little, which was not surprising after all those adventures, she was more a woman, more commanding. She was thirty-two, a beautiful age for a beautiful

167

woman. She was careful, and took quinine, and all the dangers of the climate had had no effect on her.

Emma was not a good mother to her own child but she was a wonderful general mother, she was born to be head of the clan, and what she wanted was to have her Samoan *ainga* there in New Britain. She already had Johnny who was out on Nuguria, then us, and her niece Emma whom she adopted, (her mother Maria, our eldest sister, had died in 1870 when little Emma was born). She had plans for our mother Le'utu to come soon, especially as my father had just married again, this time to Litia, daughter of a Tongan Methodist missionary, and this time it was a real proper marriage. In the end he had four children by her, so·that means he had eighteen in all. Emma thought with this new wife it might not be so nice at home for Sa's children, so she had plans to bring over more half-sisters as well as our brothers.

Emma and Richard were good friends at once, their brains both gave out sparks and the sparks made fire together. I am not a jealous person, that is foolishness, but with Emma and Richard who worked so close together for so many years I never would have had cause to be jealous. Emma was naughty with men, and when we arrived in Mioko I could soon she she was tired of Farrell, and this just might have been the time for her to take another man as lover, but Richard was not that man, and never would be. Richard in turn could never understand how she could live with Farrell, such a crude man. Richard was sensitive to beauty, he admired Emma for that, but he really enjoyed her mind, so fertile with ideas, so quick with answering back, and he would say to me 'What do Emma and Farrell talk about in the evenings?'

Well, maybe for the first years there hadn't been so much need for talk, Tom was a manly man, they were adventuring together in ships around the islands, and they just had simple fun together like singing at the piano. But Emma had got deeper and more thoughtful, and Tom had got cruder, I think from being amongst those Melanesians he thought of like animals, and also I was sure he was somewhere sick inside, maybe one of these strange diseases that live around New Guinea.

Tom had very little in the way of soft feelings for human beings, black or white. He treated his white traders very badly,

Richard and I soon heard about that, he just tossed them ashore in some God-forsaken island with no proper house or supplies. And they were very rough with the natives, perhaps as a result of being treated badly themselves. They weren't paid too much, but they had commission. As for pay, Richard worked for Emma to begin with for £8 a month. Emma knew about the traders, but she couldn't do much about it, and she was busy all the time running the business and being out around Blanche Bay and the Gazelle Peninsula buying land, or else buying islands far away across the sea.

Richard and I talked together immediately with Emma and said if we're going to start our own plantations at Blanche Bay, like Samoa, then we must be very straight with the natives, we must make them trust us by always keeping our word with them, both with rewards and punishments.

Richard was excited about everything, he was really a collecting scientist and here was a whole new world that had not been collected, and those strange, shy black people, withdrawing into their green jungles like sea-anemones when you poke your finger into them. We sailed over to Blanche Bay and walked through the land Emma had bought. It was even more green than Samoa, so many greens, none so vivid as the butterflies chasing one another, in love with green. And looping around a huge high tree with little white flowers were great black and grey gauze-winged moths, a brilliant wet-blood red underneath, thrusting their proboscis in and out of the blossoms. Fat kingfishers were in and out of the trees all hung with orchids and ferns, with thick creepers like sleeping pythons across their boughs. Whenever I stood on the hot black beach and watched the lovely iridescences of the sand as the wave withdrew I would think of the kingfisher's wings through the trees.

A few miles away across the bay was Matupi and all the volcanoes, a beautiful harbour where the Germans later on cleared away the mangroves and made the town of Rabaul. Over the sea in front of us were the Duke of York Islands and Mioko. Richard was so excited, digging his stick into the black soil and saying anything would grow there, coconuts, coffee, cocoa, tobacco, cotton, anything. 'But Emma,' he said, 'the Germans are going

169

to come and take over all this New Britain and New Ireland, nothing more certain, and they'll take your land away from you.'

'No they won't,' she said, 'I've watched Father all these years. I have signed agreements with all the chiefs, and now you are here we will have properly surveyed maps. As soon as you've done the maps we'll go down to Sydney and register all the land purchases at the American Consul. Don't forget that I am an American citizen. They call me Mrs Farrell here but of course I'm not.'

I watched them and listened and believed in them both and the place itself was so beautiful. But at first I hated the natives. After my lovely tall, courtly Samoans they were small, shifty, treacherous, head-hunters and cannibals, and terrible slave-traders. They would fight one of their little local wars, and the winners would take a lot of captives. They would kill and eat some, sell the able-bodied men to Tom Farrell for the labour trade, and keep the children as slaves. I made up my mind to buy as many of the children as I could. But I knew Richard would be too busy with his plants and his collections, and Emma would be too busy with her business, ever to learn even one of the local languages (there's a different one round each point in the next bay), or the language of the Buka boys at the house. So I would learn the languages, and I would go out amongst the natives and learn their customs, I thought they must be human too, and so I did.

Many labourers were needed for clearing the land and planting the coconuts, and the experimental farms where Richard was to try out all sorts of plants to see how they would grow in New Britain. Before these were recruited, Emma insisted that more Bukas be brought from Bougainville, and they would be boss boys, police boys and overseers of the working teams. I agreed with her. We had encountered Solomon Island labourers in Samoa and I had never seen anything like them, steady, quiet, earnest and uncomplaining, and yet at the same time with an independent and self-reliant spirit, they were not the kind to be put upon or oppressed, they had pluck enough. They also had the knack of working together in a disciplined way without always being fussed over. And of course as bodyguards they were always reliable, because they were hereditary enemies of the New Britain natives and thus always on the look-out for any treachery.

After several trips to Bougainville Emma and Richard had 150 Bukas working for them and gradually more and more local natives were persuaded to work for us with the Bukas. I would talk to the women, and we would get up little markets, and I went into their villages, everyone said it was very dangerous but no harm came to me. They called me Miti, and eventually all over the Gazelle Peninsula I was known as Miti. I would buy their little slave children for the price of a pig, ten fathoms of shell money, and later, when we had too many, the Catholic mission took them and educated them.

Richard surveyed all the coast and decided that the main plantation should be at Ralum, which was about half way between Cape Gazelle and Matupi. Nearby, on a bit of a cliff over the sea, was a beautiful piece of level ground, it was a place where the natives never went, called Gunantambu, which means 'forbidden to people', and there Emma decided she would have her house. It was always 'her house,' Farrell really didn't come into it much. Behind the coast there was another plantation laid out, called Malapau, and tobacco was planted there, and Richard and I lived there.

Tom Farrell really didn't approve of 'the German Professor' as he called Richard, and all this planting and waiting for years for the coconut trees to bear, though Richard put in cotton for a quick crop, but Tom knew he couldn't stop Emma. 'Phebe', he said to me one day, 'the bossiness of that woman will drive me mad one day. Thank God for my ships.' He was always away round the islands with his ships, by now he had the *Searip* and the *Golden Gate* as well as the old *Marquis de Rays*, and he was doing very well as far as money went. In other ways not so good. His old spear-wounds were troubling him, but he had this other sickness inside him, I was sure.

Emma loved to be gay, she loved music and champagne and dancing, already at Mioko we were the centre, if ships came to Hernsheim's at Matupi, or the DHPG, the officers came to see us as quick as they could, it wasn't only the pretty women, Emma, little Emma and myself, and the Samoan girls, but the parties, Emma at the piano, Richard with his violin, even Tom Farrell giving a sentimental Irish song or one of the Australian convict songs that are sad and funny at the same time. Richard was famous for that violin, he always took it with him on the horse when he went on surveying expeditions, and you can imagine the natives sitting around in a half-circle with their mouths open listening to Richard playing Mendelssohn, or the tunes of Schubert's songs, he was very fond of them.

Our parties sometimes made the other traders angry, they said how could they compete with the champagne and the music and the Samoan girls, it wasn't fair, but Emma wasn't using these things, she just loved the fun of it all.

But it was not all fun in the early days at Ralum and Gunantambu. Our house at Malapau was built first, so that Richard would have a headquarters for his planting, and I moved over with the children leaving Emma at Mioko. Oh how primitive it was, after the comforts of Mioko! Our plantation at Ralum was the first plantation in the whole of New Guinea, and Richard could leave me only a couple of Bukas and my Samoan girls as he needed all hands in the bush. I was very good friends with all the natives about, but one day a group of strange bushmen came to the house, and I saw one steal the big knife we used for cutting up the meat. I told him to put it back, but he would not, so I asked the chief to make him return it. He laughed at me, and I thought 'Phebe my girl, you are nineteen years old and you are not in Samoa, you are in wild New Britain and you must show your strength.' My strength! I didn't have any, and there were all those black bushmen with their clubs and spears, all cannibals too though that never worried me. So I told my two Bukas, I only had two, Richard had the rest, to grab the chief and put him in irons till Richard would punish him for not stopping the stealing. The Bukas seized him, and then you should have heard the howls of rage! But it was lucky they made so much noise as Richard, who was just down by the wharf, heard and came quickly with his Bukas all with their carbines. The knife was returned, and we had no more trouble.

But a while later something much worse happened to Emma, and it was the fault of the Buka boys, who were sometimes a bit rough. This day Emma was alone at Gunantambu, when a woman came in with yams for sale. Emma bought some, and went back into the house. She just happened to look through the back window in time to see the woman helping herself to clothes off the clothesline, and then running off into the bush. Emma called to the Bukas and told them to catch the woman and bring the clothes back.

Much later they came back, with the clothes. It was only later that Emma found that they had taken it in turns to rape the woman, and then they left her for dead.

Next day the men from the woman's village were all hidden, watching, and when the Bukas went down to the wharf to see a ship that had come in, they rushed the house, grabbed Emma, tied a sheet around her face to stop her cries, and then lashed her wrists and ankles together and slung her on a carrying pole, just the way they carry a pig to market. Then they ran off with her into the bush to kill and eat her.

Fortunately one of her little Samoan maids had seen it all happen, and got away, and ran like the wind down to the wharf to tell Richard. He had his horse there, and with his Bukas running beside him he rode after Emma. They could see the natives' tracks where they had left the main path, and they soon caught up with them as the natives could not make speed carrying Emma. They really feared the Bukas, and when they gave their war cry the natives dropped poor Emma and fled. She by this time was more dead than alive, from suffocation rather than fear, though even Emma, who was the bravest woman I ever knew, was certain she was going to be killed. And she would have been, if Richard had not been so close. The Bukas killed two of her kidnappers, but when the whole story came out Emma could see that it was all really the fault of the Bukas, and she paid the natives many fathoms of shell money.

It must have been 1883 that Emma took me with her down to Australia, where she was sending her son Coe and her niece, little Emma, to school. We went on a little British warship, the *Espiègle*. We landed at Cooktown in Queensland and Emma made me ride on a train, we went out to some tent town where there were gold diggings and lots of Chinese. All the Australians were very puzzled about the native boy I had with me to help look after the baby, you see his hair was dyed blond the way they often do, and his black skin and fair hair looked very odd.

In Sydney there was a big fuss made over Emma, and she was called Queen Emma in the newspapers, but I said to the dressmaker, (yes, we were all fitted out with beautiful clothes), I was very disgusted, no she is not a Queen, we are not princesses, that is just the name they have for her up in the islands because she is so good to them all. And I wouldn't go to a garden party the Admiral gave, I said it was only pushing in where we didn't belong, and I was not going to have my children called half-castes. I never liked the Australians, they are very arrogant about colour.

We came back from Sydney on a big DHPG ship, and the first officer was a tall, very handsome man, he was an Austrian but he had an Italian name, Augustino Stalio, he came from one of those towns on the Dalmatian coast. He was a very courteous man, of such charm, but strong, and a good sailor. We were only a day at sea when I knew that Emma had very much fallen in love with him.

Chapter XXVI

EMMA

To make a splash in Sydney, it is only necessary to have money. But to make a big splash that wets both sides of the Harbour, then let them think you belong to Royalty. Oh what snobs these Colonials are! As bad as the LMS missionaries in Apia. Fat old Hernsheim's name for me, *Die Königin*, had stuck, and around the islands I was always Queen Emma. So when Phebe and I and the children arrived in Sydney in 1884 in H.M.S. *Espiègle*, then the *Sydney Morning Herald* had a story, and who was I to stop the reporter improving on it? Phebe was too young and shy, but I came to Sydney to enjoy myself, and to spend some of the £2,000 we made selling our Duke of York and New Ireland land to the DHPG. It was the first time anybody had made any money out of land in New Guinea, Also our Ralum was the first plantation. I was lucky to have Richard. How Tom distrusted the Professor!

In this he was typically Australian as I have got to know them. In Sydney it was enough to be rich (which I wasn't) and a Queen (which I wasn't). Not so with the Germans, they expected a woman to know a sharp from a flat and to have read the great German playwright Shakespeare. But I had fun in Sydney, especially after the Admiral's party, when I met Tino Stalio, who was first officer on a steamer, the *Samoa* (nice name) which the DHPG had just purchased in Sydney, and was being fitted out for exploration in New Guinea, under Dr O. Finsch and Captain C. Dallman. 'Exploration', indeed! I knew perfectly well what was going on. The *Samoa* was really on a survey for Bismarck. In 1883 some pipsqueak official from Queensland had 'annexed' New Guinea. Queensland, that nest of blackbirds! Of course this was soon reduced to the nonsense it really was, but at the same time it was the final pistol that started the race between England and Germany to carve up New Guinea, New Britain, New Ireland, the Solomons and all the rest. I hoped it would be the Germans. I liked them better than the English. Well, than most English. Some are the nicest of men. But with most, they are either supercilious or boors, you make no contact with them, it's like sitting all day under a waterfall and never getting wet. And they are so colour-conscious, I could hear them calling me creole and half-caste behind my back.

Not so my big sailor from Dalmatia, Tino, who could talk German, Italian, English, all perfectly, and he was very good at swearing in some horrible language like Serb. I always thought Italians were small and dark, but he was very tall, fair, not blond but brown, with the most perfect skin I ever saw on a man. And he was very firm about his origins, 'Emma, you must learn once and for all, *una volta per sempre*, I am not an Italian, but an Italian Dalmatian, what is called a Da'lmata, from Ragusa, which is a proud and independent city that kept free of both the Turks and the Venetians. Maybe now we are part of the Austro-Hungarian Empire, but we are still Ragusans! We have an ancient civilization.' And what a dancer he was! It was like sailing, to dance with him, his body filled your arms like the wind and you floated and flew. And drink! He loved champagne almost as much as me, and he would get a little boat, and bring a basket full of champagne and shellfish, and we would find a little deserted beach in the Harbour, the loveliest harbour in the world, and he would take up his mandolin and play wild, mad Dalmatian dances, and sing those liquid Italian songs which are like syrup when sung by a fat little tenor, but like *strega* when sung directly to you by a man who can crack walnuts in the crook of his arm. That was a good trick of Tino's. We were in a restaurant in Sydney once, and a man made some remark about me, about creoles from the islands, and I thought Tino would fight him, but while the man was staring, Tino threw a walnut in the air and cracked it in his arm and offered it to the man, and he went red and stood up and apologized to me. Tino could have knocked him into the street with one blow, but he said to me, 'Always try the gentle approach first. The frightened man will not pull the trigger then, and the bully feels that little chill at the pit of his stomach.'

Dr Finsch, who was a very interesting scientist as well as the spy for Bismarck, realized I would be a good friend to have in New Britain, so he asked me and Phebe to accompany him on the *Samoa* back to Mioko. It was a terribly unseaworthy ship, and Captain Dallman was not much of a sailor, but Tino could have kept it afloat with his two hands. We arrived at Mioko on my birthday, 26 September, and what a party we had! I had been the perfect European lady in Sydney and aboard ship on the trip back, but now in my own house I gave them a Samoan evening. Phebe is a little bit proper, the influence of those damned Sisters, but this night she danced a wild *siva* with me, the Germans were bursting out of their white uniforms. Fortunately Richard was away in New Ireland, he was very strict with Phebe.

A few weeks later the English annexed New Guinea to the south, and the Germans declared their protectorate to the north.

Now would come the test of our land. Tom and I had bought, sometimes for remarkably little, land amounting in all to 400,000 acres. Tom was getting tougher and tougher. Eduard Hernsheim was, after all, a very good friend, but to Tom he was a competitor, and when he heard that Hernsheim had installed two traders in New Ireland on what Tom said was our land, he just steamed up in the *Golden Gate*, went ashore with the Bukas and sent the traders packing in their own boats with the threat of sinking them if they turned back. I thought that was a little like piracy. Then the Sacred Heart Mission, which the Methodists were doing their best to keep out anyway, established a station near Ralum at Kokopo on ten acres they said they owned. Tom disagreed. Oddly enough, they were burnt out by the natives shortly afterwards. They said Tom had bribed the natives. He said that although he was a good Catholic the natives must be Methodists. Phebe was very upset, she wanted to be able to go to mass. Later I let them have some land at Vunapope, as they called it, the place of the Pope, and Phebe used to paddle down the coast to it for mass.

The Germans set about their government indirectly, by creating something called the Neu Guinea Kompagnie, and granting it an Imperial Charter in 1885, and they sent a funny little man from

Apia, von Oertzen, to be Imperial Commissioner. His first job was to register all land claims. As he had absolutely no power to back him up, no police, no guns, all we had to do was to be nice to him, give him a glass of champagne and flirt with him. That was much easier than piracy. Old Mouton and his son, who had stayed behind when the *Génil* left, tried to claim some land that was ours, but von Oertzen quickly responded to treatment and said it was ours.

Tom was worried about the Neu Guinea Kompagnie, and even Richard was, saying that as they had the Imperial Commission they would force us to sell out to them. Not at all, I said, they will concentrate on New Guinea itself, around Finschhafen, and there is plenty more land here. I even had a long idea that Richard might go and work for them to survey their land and lay out their plantations, which would be a sure way of keeping them away from our land.

The Germans wanted new names for everything, which was very confusing. New Guinea became Kaiser Wilhemsland; New Britain, Neu Pommern; Kokopo, Herbertshöhe; and so on. The harbour behind Matupi was Simpsonhafen.

Now there came a big change in my life. For some time Tom had been feeling very poorly, and in 1885 I made him go down to Sydney to see the doctors. When he came back he said he was finished. He had tuberculosis, the new word for consumption, and he had been told he must leave New Britain immediately and live in Australia. For a long time now Tom and I had been business partners only. He had known about Tino, but not cared. Sometimes I wondered how I had lived with him so long, but now I felt that awful softness with which false emotion deadens the sharp edge of true thought and feeling. Should I leave Phebe (who was becoming so capable a manageress) and Richard behind to look after Farrell & Co., and go south and nurse Tom? I was tempted to step in front of a mirror and see the noble woman at the Dying Man's bedside. But then a voice came from my Samoan blood to say my duty was to my son and my extended family, to build up their fortunes as I knew only I could. A handy voice, that one, because I had to admit to myself that I hated nursing! It had been torture, nursing those stinking, crawling, poor devils from Port-Breton.

178

But most of all, I knew I no longer loved Tom, nor did he love me. He'd called me a bossy bitch that often, raring for a fight, but I wouldn't fight, I wouldn't split up a good business relationship. And I really knew he would be much happier with the men back in Australia, drowning the consumption in whisky, than having a woman around his neck.

So I sent him off, on the *Golden Gate,* and after him I faithfully sent half the profits of Farrell & Co. I saw him once more, in hospital in Brisbane in 1886. He was like a leatherjacket fish that's been dried out on the beach, when the skin is stretched yet hollow at the same time. Young Emma Meredith, my niece, a sweet girl who was at school in Brisbane, said they'd told her he couldn't live much longer. He died in 1887. He was fifty-seven years old. He had left me all his share of Farrell & Co.

I went down to Sydney to see about the business, and out of the woodwork all around me jumped the cockroaches, Tom's creditors. Farrell & Co. was bankrupt. Hopelessly in debt. How he had kept it from me, I don't know, as he was a fool at figures. But it was true, he had these huge debts in Sydney.

I gathered the creditors together and said to them, 'Look, you can sell up our business and our land and our ships and you won't get one per cent. You can put in a manager at Ralum and he'll either be eaten by cannibals or die of fever. Or you can let me carry on and I'll pay you seven shillings in the pound.' For a few days they hawked Farrell & Co. around Sydney while I lay low. I wasn't giving any colonial the opportunity of gloating over Queen Emma, broke. Then they came back and said they would accept my offer. 'Very well,' I said, 'then we need one more ship, a bigger one.' It was as if I had hit each of them over the head with a taro root. But there's one thing I'll give those Sydney merchants, they're gamblers. And I was looking my very best that day.

That's how Farrell & Co. that became E. E. Forsayth & Co., took the *Three Cheers* into commission, and the name of the Captain who brought her up from Sydney was Augustino Stalio.

I think maybe these next five years, 1887-92, were the happiest years of my life. But as soon as you say that, you bite your tongue, it is a stupid thing to say, because you have failed in life if you divide it up, if you say you wish you were younger, or older.

That's the life of envy and of all sins envy, and meanness that
goes hand in hand with it, is the worst. The scent of lemons
is the same when you are a little girl as when you are an old lady,
a blessing from God. Oh yes, I am a pagan as Bishop Couppé
used to tell me regularly, but that doesn't mean I don't have my
gods. At the Convent we had a hymn about life being a river,
but that's rubbish. Life's like the sea, calm underneath when
it's stormy on top, as deep on the day when you can see every
stick of coral and every fish as on the days when the sand is
churned up and you can't see a thing, life's circular like the
movement of the tides, ruled by mysteries like the moon and
women's blood. I don't know anything about deserts, but maybe
they're like the sea, for so many religious prophets came from the
deserts.

So my life these years was all part of the sea, Tino coming
and going in the *Three Cheers*, Ralum my trading station with
boats in and out all the time, and my lovely Gunantambu on
the green cliff above the sea, looking out to the Duke of York
islands.

Beyond Ralum was Kuradui, Phebe and Richard's new home.
Richard was out always, with his instruments and his horse and
his violin. Everything he planted grew just as he said it would.
And when he came back to Kuradui, the seed he planted always
grew there too. Phebe, she was always having children, always
spoiling Richard with his clothes and his food. 'Phebe', I used
to say, 'you know the right leaves of the right tree to chew so
you won't have all those babies;' but she would answer, 'Emma,
you know the Church says you musn't interfere with nature.' Oh,
I'd get exasperated and say 'Phebe, to hell with the Church!
Nature is my Church. If you chew the leaves of the tree, is not
that Nature?' And then she would say it was not for one of true
faith to argue. Oh, I'd get so cross with her! I'd say to her,
'Phebe, Richard just wants a *Hausfrau*, and that's what he's got.'
Twelve children in the end, Richard gave her. But they were
lovely children, those that survived, if a bit wild later. And she
was so beautiful, really much more beautiful than me. I told
her the reason she was so strong and beautiful was that all those
babies drained the bad and impure things out of her blood.

She was no good with figures, she would never learn book-

180

keeping. But she was wonderful with the natives. I think the reason why Ralum was such a success was that I had the business brain, and the idea; Richard had the knowledge of plants and agriculture; and Phebe managed the labour and kept us nearly always in happy relations with the natives who lived near us. Oh, yes, we had some nasty moments. Never will I forget the sky and the trees swaying above me as I was carried off to be eaten, slung on a pole like a pig and stifling for breath trying to scream into a *lava-lava* tied around my face!

Phebe was Miti to the natives, and they loved her, but she let them know her strength. She would take the baby she was suckling, and a boy to carry him, and six boys with Schneider rifles, and with her Winchester in her own hands off she would go into the bush to talk with those naked natives. She would always come back with lots of presents, friends with everybody in that village. But she never forgot to take the Winchester and the six boys, at least in the early days.

At Ralum, my own little port for my own little fleet, my buildings kept on growing, warehouse, storage sheds and so on, and my office, which was a fine two-storeyed wooden building with double verandahs, overlooking the sea, and on the side of it I had a folly, a tower as high as the top of the roof with a pointed cap on it going much higher and on top of that a flag pole. People used to say it looked a little bit Chinese, as it had three little roofs on the way up, maybe like skirts.

It was built like Gunantambu up on concrete blocks to let the cool air underneath. The house was so airy and open, arches between the rooms hung with lace curtains, the little maids kept the floors shining, never any dust on the dados around the walls or on the grand piano. After the Germans took over I put up a really big portrait of Kaiser Wilhelm looking down over his moustaches at the dining room table. The verandahs all had wooden ceilings, and the railings were made in nice patterns, and there were lots of huge wicker sofas on the verandahs, really cosy for the young people to cuddle in. My own bedroom had a huge high brass bed with immense mosquito curtains, what you need in the tropics is space and air. What used to astonish our guests was that I had a system worked by a couple of boys, that blew air into the house cooled by air blown over thorn bushes with water dripping over them. The German naval officers said they had never seen anything like that on all their cruises. The verandahs were scrubbed every day with lemon juice, and that made the wood white and the house smell fresh. There was hot water too, for washing, I had for many years the only proper hot water service in New Guinea. My favourite piece of furniture, I think, was the sideboard with its three carved doors and the mirror set between pillars.

Oh yes, there was the cabinet for drinks that I made out of the Marquis de Rays' high altar. They say it had been blessed by the Archbishop of Milan! It had so many different colours of marble, all set together and polished in that clever Italian way, how could I let such a lovely thing rot in the jungle at Port-Breton? Father Couppé would never come into the dining room because of that altar, he always took his drink on the verandah, and insisted it be poured in the parlour. 'Wine's bad enough,' he would say, 'but what about those accursed American cocktails you mix on the marble?' That used to annoy him, being a good Frenchman, that I was an American and that to be kind to my guests I would mix bitters with gin, or lemonjuice and a little sugar with whisky. But we were very good friends, and I was glad when they made him a Bishop. He was very good at business, Sacred Heart & Co., we used to call his mission, and he admired me because I was even better than him. We used to exchange lots of books, and have lovely arguments, because you see I'd been educated by the Catholics but also brought up on all George Brown's Protestant histories of Europe and religion, so I had some sharp digs to give him. We were exactly the same age, and as the years went by we'd watch each other, and I'd say 'Father Couppé, I must admit you never change', and he'd say, 'Queen Emma, that is because of the virtuous life a priest leads', and I'd say 'My old friend, I will die fat and ailing long before you, but I will be able to say like the Wife of Bath, "I have had the world and in my time".'

I was very proud of the grounds and gardens of Gunantambu. Richard took such care finding the right plants and trees for me. Coming up from Herbertshöhe the drive had frangipani on one side, and rain trees, that soon grew enormous, on the other, and the figs, with their myriad roots. Richard was always bringing new orchids from his expeditions, and they grew from every tree in the garden, I never knew all the names, but he did. In amongst the fruit and flowering trees in the grounds I had guest-houses, each with its own neat little white verandah and railings, and a real little European house for my mother, Le'utu. Each day she used to weave fans, and string up red parrots' feathers, and have a bottle of beer. She was like me, she couldn't sleep at night, so she had her brandy, her medicine she called it, at about 3 a.m. I used to read books to clear my head of figures and put me to sleep.

As the years went by I got more and more of my family from Samoa, my half-sisters Grace and Mary Ann, my brothers Henry and William, and their children, so at Gunantambu there were always lots of pretty girls and all the German officials from Herbertshöhe, and the naval officers and other visitors, they would all come to Gunantambu and we would have parties that would sometimes go on for days. But I was always very strict with those girls, and with their education, I was determined they would all make good marriages.

They were all happy because I was happy myself. All I had worked for had come to pass, and Richard's fears of the Neu Guinea Kompagnie were proved groundless and we were good friends with the Germans. I was rich. What poor old Tom could never see now came true, the coconuts started to bear, and before long I had three thousand acres of them and twelve hundred natives working for me. I was the Queen indeed, for E. E. Forsayth and Co. was all mine, and I had no trouble in paying off Tom's creditors their seven shillings in the pound. That old villain Tom would have been proud of that deal, even though he was hopeless at business.

These were all my responsibilities. But to be a Queen means also to be free to do exactly as you please, that's if you are a Queen who believes in pleasure, and not Queen Victoria. My learned and languid Sodomite, Lyttelton, gave me philosophical reasons for what I already knew in my Samoan blood, that the body is given us by the gods for all the exquisite enjoyments it can bring us. What an insult to that body not to let it love and be loved, give it the best of food and drink, offer flowers to its delicate senses. Heaven is not somewhere else, as for Christians. Touch! Touch another's body, be touched, and there is heaven. Oh, I know all about age, and sickness, and disease, but it was never my religion to let them cast a shadow on the flower in bloom.

Look at a woman's body. I know in some ways it is not as beautiful at forty as it is at fourteen, but if I were a man I know which I would rather make love to. Around forty a woman is at her best for love, if she has loved life. So for these years I was happy with my sailor, my Tino. Every now and then I would leave everything at Ralum to Richard and Phebe and sail off on the *Three Cheers* with him to my far-off islands, or even to Sydney. The sea that parted us, thus also joined us together.

I remember once, between Buka and the Mortlocks I made him stop the engines, while we watched the sea birds fishing.

There were thousands of them, totally unafraid of us, and they were feeding on millions of fish in a boiling of blood-red and white foam in the cobalt sea. The hunters were hunted, in sea, in air. The mackerel, bonito, tuna, all the big fish had rounded up the small fish and were feeding on them, and above them on different levels, like the layers of different clouds you see in the sky, were innumerable terns, and skuas and the great, majestic frigate birds. The terns would hover and dive, hover and dive, and each time come up with a fish, but often as they emerged, down would come the skua and steal the fish from the tern's beak. And then the huge frigate bird, motionless gliding five hundred feet up above them all, would suddenly close his wings and come arrowing down through the whole confusion, to sail up again with a big fish in his beak.

I can't tell why, but this dazzling, whirling thrust of life and death fairly set me afire and I became the Captain and ordering the bridge full ahead I seized Tino and almost carried him down to the cabin, and to hell with the smirks of the crew. There was absolutely nothing self-conscious or guilty about Tino, and he knew more about my body than I, who thought I knew so much about love.

He had a trick with my hair that he loved to play. On board ship I usually had it done up on top of my head, so it would not blow in the wind. As soon as we were in the cabin he would make me take out all the pins and combs and he would make me kneel above him, and he would pull it all down, it was very black and long, until I couldn't see him. Then he would part it and close it, part and close it, looking up at me, and say romantic things about my eyes being stars showing through the dark clouds of night. Oh, he knew how to talk as well as touch!

How strange that he was a Catholic too, and a much better one than Tom. He always went to Father Couppé for confession when he was in port. But whereas Australian-Irish Tom was like a stallion in a surplice, Tino with his clothes off was a naked pagan, a subtler Samoan. That lovely contrast, his hard body and all those sweet, soft words!

He was four years younger than me, but neither of us ever thought about age. He was called a Dalmata, but of course he was really very Italian, and you'd think he would have been talking about marriage, wanting *bambini,* and all that. But he had a pure heart, Tino, he never wanted to own me, nor did he covet what could obviously be a wealthy wife, he was a sailor. Once I couldn't resist it, I said 'Tino, you're a good Catholic, why don't you talk about marriage, about settling down with me at Ralum and raising children?' He just laughed, and said '*Piu tardi!*', later, and if I asked him again he would say the same, or '*Domani!*', tomorrow, or else he would say he would not give up the sea and come ashore even for me.

Now the queer thing was that I really wished he would, now at the peak of my ambitions, all my plans coming good, the consuming independence that had driven me on was beginning to leave room for a consort beside me. And I was faithful to him. Always before, I had taken any man I wanted to, happily *fa'a Samoa,* and now I knew that was because I had never been in love before. And I, who could always have any man, had to fall in love with a sailor! But he was shrewd too, under his soft songs, he had a sense of reality sharp as the strings of his mandolin. 'Emma', he said to me one day, 'You've gone to all that trouble, Mrs Forsayth, to secure all those land titles as an American citizen. You don't want to marry an Austrian, and go through all those complications with the German administration as Signora Stalio?'

I kicked him in the ankle. Maybe he was right. But truly, I did love him, oh I did love him.

Chapter XXVII

RICHARD PARKINSON

Ralum Plantation,
Bismarck Archipelago.

20 February 1890.

Mr George Le Hunte,
President of Dominica,
West Indies.

Dear Mr Le Hunte!

I was indeed agreeably surprised when I received your letter which came on the vessel that anchored off our place this morning. Mrs P. and I frequently talk about your visit to New Britain and the jolly evenings we spent in Matupi and Meoko. We note with great pleasure that you would like to return to the Pacific. Your twelve years experience in Fiji and the Western Pacific would admirably suit you for the Governorship of British New Guinea.

Here we are all German now, and not in New Britain but Neu Pommern, and the old Duke of Yorks are Neu Lauenberg, and so on. This seems to have affronted the old man below, and we have had some bad earthquakes, especially one that made me think Bismarck was going to lose his Archipelago. Mrs Farrell (who is very well) on this occasion having a number of small children sleeping in her house at Gunantambu, bravely ran into each room of the rocking house and rescued each child and dropped it to safety over the verandah. Unfortunately she had forgotten the enormous clam shells which she had recently set up as ornaments below the verandah, and some of the children suffered worse bruises and cuts by landing on the clam shells than if they had remained in their rooms where they would only have fallen out of bed. You always marvelled at Mrs Farrell's independence, well on the occasion of another earthquake, the sea receded for a good half mile in front of Ralum. This awesome spectacle without doubt presaged a tidal wave (you may recall our worst one rose forty-two feet).

My sister-in-law, however, saw an opportunity not to be missed. Tearing off her shoes and stockings, and hitching up her long white muslin dress, she seized a large native basket and ran out over the sand while I shouted to her to come back. 'Why don't you come with me?' she called back, and I gave up trying to persuade her, which is difficult enough at any time. Eventually she came running back with a basket overflowing with big fish and crayfish that had been stranded, and scrambled up the cliff. A few minutes later the returning wave rose some ten feet over high-tide level.

Since we became Germanized they claimed me as a German, and I am a real good German Subject and Citizen now and as such entitled to hold office in the Government, but the real reason they wanted me for a German is that I am the only one who at present really knows anything about the Country and they think they may make use of me. And why not? Our plantations now return a good profit, the cotton and coffee returning early crops, and the cocoa-nuts coming along well, and I have also rice and millet and many hundreds of plants in my botanical garden. So Mrs Farrell and I think it no harm for me to work for the Neu Guinea Kompagnie for a couple of years to lay out their plantations. We have a quiet laugh together, Mrs Farrell and I, because old Hernsheim and Mouton think we have quarrelled, that I should take a job with the Kompagnie, but how better to make sure there is no friction between E. E. Forsayth and Co. and the Administration? Incidentally, since Mr Farrell died in 1887 Emma has returned to using her old name, Mrs Forsayth, but I keep on forgetting.

So I will be off buying land and recruiting labour again. What a strange business it is to understand the land rights of the natives! Hernsheim always says that the natives have no concept of ownership of land at all. Kleinschmidt (you remember, the Goddefroy's naturalist on the Duke of Yorks, who bought the island of Utuan) always maintained that he had bought the fruit trees and cocoanuts on the land as well as the land, and that the natives could no longer walk across the land, but the natives did not agree. Poor Kleinschmidt, incidentally, was murdered on Utuan, some think for enforcing these ideas, but I think because he ordered some boys to row him to Birara on the Gazelle Peninsula. They refused, with good reason, because the people there were their arch-enemies. He accordingly decided to set an example and with companions began to burn their houses and destroy their canoes. Whereupon the natives massacred him and two other Europeans. Tom Farrell organized a punitive expedition.

One must endeavour to understand native customs, and explain to those logical Germans with their Prussian Law that custom also is a kind of law, and what is more, a law that can be understood by all and not only by lawyers, a pettifogging breed who think that they alone know the meaning of justice. Even to survey land is extremely difficult here. The natives will give a rock a name, but not a range of hills, a bay but not an island, a clump of trees but not a valley. And they have no concept of our straight lines and boxes. Often their ownership is more in terms of circles, what you see looking around you from a high point. So primitive law also comes round in a circle, you must always be prepared to reopen negotiations, never accept any settlement as final but as a balance of mutual requirements.

Of course all is further complicated by the fact that there are no 'chiefs' here. The natives live in groups, and often a man will speak for the group, but he is not 'chief'. When Mrs Farrell and I buy land it is necessary only to have the document signed by one or two members of the group. Maybe the land is really ownerless, maybe we will not want to use it for some time and in the meantime the ownership will just give us the rights to buy copra there. When we wish to plant an area, then Mrs P. will go amongst the natives and explain what we want to do, and maybe if there are problems she will pay more money (known as 'bribes' by our competitors) or give them credit to buy from the store at Ralum. So we get along admirably well with the natives, and we rule virtually from Cape Gazelle to Ralum and far inland, though now we make arrangements with Father Couppé and the Kompagnie, and we will have a town soon at Herbertshöhe.

In the beginnings I had some very bad scrimmages a few times with the natives but always licked them fearfully with my Buka boys (of which I have fifteen) and the consequence is that all the surrounding districts are now at peace. Off and on Mrs P. and I go as far as to the big mountain far inland and do not dream of taking any extra precautions.

We are also doing many experiments in breeding of animals. We have tried here horses, donkeys, cattle (the hump-backed strains from Asia as well as European types), goats, new breeds of pig, poultry and even sheep. Poor things, they did not like the climate!

Mrs Farrell also had the idea of cross-breeding the natives on some of the far-off atolls and islands she has bought, where the local strain is thin through inbreeding or disease or war. The best breeders, she decided, would be the Bukas or the New Irelanders, and a few ship-loads of these have been distributed about with beneficial results already. Of course in a few years there will be good teams of local labour available to pick our copra. I think she has been especially successful with her practical eugenics on the Mortlock Islands. Of course she would have preferred to send Samoans, but that proud and beautiful people would scorn to propagate with black Melanesians.

Of Samoans we have plenty more at Ralum. Mrs Farrell has now brought many members of her family here, the latest arrivals being her brother William and his new wife Utufia and his six children by his first wife Fa'uma.

Mrs Farrell's brother John, whom you met when he was living at Birara, is now living on Nuguria in the Fead Islands, where he has been managing for Emma, who owns the islands. He is a bluff but good-hearted soul. He has left several children by native women at Birara, for whom Mrs Farrell is caring. Emma has the habit of looking after everyone's stray children. Her own son Coe turned up unexpectedly a few weeks ago from Sydney, where she had confidently expected he would make a scholar and go to the University. But he, though only eighteen is of the adventuring kind and has set his heart on a life here in the islands, and she is pleased to have him with her, so here he stays. I only hope he can administer further education to himself as his mother has done to herself.

When not at work we are very gay. The English warships come no more this way, but we have many Germans. They go to Matupi, where the coaling station is, but the steam-launches run hot between Matupi and Ralum. There would be mutiny on any ship whose Captain did not call on Queen Emma at Gunantambu. That name of old Hernsheim's, incidentally, at which Emma always used to 'laugh, has stuck like the shirt to your back in this climate, and Emma is known as Queen throughout the Western Pacific. Some of the pompous new breed of German bureaucrat (how quickly they breed, so recently was there no Germany!) on arrival sneer at a title that is not *de juro* but they soon find out that it is *de facto*. There are thousands of natives who would obey her slightest order, who would think less of Bismarck than of a cassowary.

Her shipping line, now grown to a regular fleet, is in charge of an Austrian-Italian from Dalmatia, Captain Augustino Stalio, who is a gentleman of commanding physique and considerable education. You would be surprised at our Queen's court here. One night we may have a reading of Shakespeare, organized by Hernsheim, another night a concert (we muster a piano, a flute, a mandolin, and three violins including my own), and another night theatricals (my old favourite in Heligoland) for the diversion of visiting officers. That is of course apart from more obvious diversions, which for Emma begin and end with champagne. The eating arrangements, which are splendid, are invariably organized by Mrs P., who from not knowing how to roast a *taro* when I married her is now a notable cook and a past-mistress of herbs. She is a fine wife, and manages our large family with an attention to detail and economy that would not be found wanting in Leipzig.

Our chief enemy remains the climate, and disease. With regular quinine and the right food we remain healthy ourselves, but many newcomers and young people succumb, and there are already many tombstones in the little graveyard at Herbertshöhe.

190

Richard Parkinson

When a letter-writer begins to talk of death it is time for him to stop.

Please let us hear a few words from you of your family.

For the meantime I remain

Yours
Very truly

R. Parkinson

Chapter XXVIII

COE FORSAYTH

Ralum, Bismarck Archipelago

21 April, 1890

Mr Henry Holroyd,
The Sydney University,
Sydney,
New South Wales.

Dear Hal

While you are springboarding into the glewpot of Sydney University, I am catapulted into adventure!

My mother, who with justice is known as Queen Emma here, and lives in the most tremendous style, gave me as my first job the superintending of building a new road along the coast from Ralum and Gunantambu to the new German settlement at Kokopo, which is to be the centre of the administration and called Herbertshöhe. My uncle Parkinson had just been appointed officer-in-charge of this station. His wife, my aunt Phebe, I like very much and she knows more about the natives than anybody, and speaks their languages. Incidentally, it's very useful for me that my mother insisted I learn German in Sydney.

Well, I had a team of labourers, and a good overseer, Moses, a Manila man, and we were making a good coral road back of the beach above high tide mark. There were three fishermen's huts along the coast a bit, bang in the way of the road, and I told the owners a couple of weeks in advance that the huts would have to go, and how much compensation we'd pay. The huts were still there when we reached them with the road, so I rather decently took the road a little inland and gave the fishermen a last chance to get their belongings out before I burnt the huts. This they did, and at the end of the day, with old Tom, a trusty Ralum native. I payed the fisherman 15, 10, and 5 sticks of tobacco respectively for the huts, so they could build new ones. The compensation was accepted without any objections.

The next afternoon everything was going fine, and we'd got the road as far as Tokuka, when I saw Moses up ahead having a bit of a barney with 30-40 Kanakas. They looked hostile, but they didn't have any weapons, only the usual axes and knives. Moses called to me to come, and a spokesman among them demanded to know why the road was being made. 'For the use of everyone', I answered, 'whites, workers, natives, women, children.' The spokesman looked very angry and then he growled at me 'The land belongs to the natives.' 'No it doesn't', I pointed towards Ralum, 'it belongs to her.' 'No', they said, then didn't ask any more questions.

They all began to huddle together then, and then they broke up and collected all their baskets, and got together again. Well, I guessed right away what the black bastards were up to.

I must, in the best serial tradition, break off at this exciting moment to give you a brief digression on sling shots in the Bismarck Archipelago. I remember you, Hal, as being a pretty hot shot with a schoolboy catapult. My boy, believe me, a stone fired from a catapult, even with your skill behind it, has the velocity of a squashed tomato compared with a stone from a Kanaka's sling. It's their most formidable weapon. It consists of a long, indented pad made out of pandanus leaves, and in that is a carefully chosen stone, about the size of a small hen's egg. You usually can't see them loading the sling as they do it very cleverly with their toes. From the pad run two cords, three to five feet long, depending on the height of the man. One cord is hitched around the middle finger of the right hand with a running noose, the other has a lump on the end which is held between thumb and forefinger. The right arm is held well back over the right shoulder, the left is extended and the left hand holds the stone in place. Suddenly, with a very graceful gesture, the sling is jerked out of the left hand and swung several times round the head with the right hand. Then, wham! The thumb and forefinger are released and out shoots the stone.

Old Hernsheim, the fat old German trader at Matupi, told me he'd rather be shot at with a musket than one of these slings. They have a range of nearly two hundred yards, and are deadly accurate, and for the first hundred yards the stone goes so fast you can't even see it unless you're a Kanaka.

Well, I knew what was coming, and yelled to Moses and lit out down our new road to Ralum. No brave white man cowing the black fellows with a look, bugger that for a joke. You remember Coe Forsayth, the Sprinter from Samoa, school hero of the 100 and the 220? Well, there was a bend in our road about 150 yards away, and from there it followed a little bay till it curved back to the cliffs going up to Gunantambu. I reckoned if I could make that bend before they had time to load up I'd have a chance. Jesus Christ, did I move! I had on one of those stupid-looking solar topees Uncle Richard insisted I wear when working in the sun. I nearly threw it off in case it slowed me down. Thank Christ I didn't. Just as I reached the corner their first broadside reached me, one stone ricocheted off the side of the helmet, as it was, the blow nearly knocked me sideways, and I think that stumble also saved me as another stone cut through my sleeve and took a bit of meat off my arm. Then I was round the bend and still running.

The Kanakas can walk up a precipice, but they're lousy runners, and they'd had to stand to let go their slings. I was out of training, especially in this heat, and thought my lungs would burst, but I made it up to Gunantambu and scared the daylights out of mother who was playing the piano. She rang the big alarm bell and the Buka boys were out in a few seconds.

Uncle Richard appeared, mother wanted me to stay put, but to hell with that, I got my breath back and we hurried down along the road with the Bukas to see what had happened to Moses. No good. The poor old bugger, he was a real nice nigger from Manila, he'd tried to swim out to a boat, but they'd caught him in the shallow water and split his skull with an axe and carved his face in two across the mouth with a knife.

The whole thing was my fault. Shows you how you've got to know what makes these Kanakas tick. Uncle Richard and the missionary Rickard, who'd arrived by this time, had the whole story. I'd said that the road was for all, for whites, workers,

194

natives, women and children. It was the word 'women' that did it. The fishermen were Duk-Duks, members of the secret society, and the whole Duk-Duk is taboo to women.

Another digression! The Duk-Duk is a spirit which appears at regular times, always at full moon, and skips about for about three days. The old men (who really own the Duk-Duk), give a month's warning of when the Duk-Duk is to appear from the bottom of the sea, and at the appointed time vast tributes of fish, food and *diwarra* have to be ready. The day before the Duk-Duk is due all women have to go bush, or hide in their huts. It is immediate death if they see the Duk-Duk. The unfortunate women, who are the hardest workers and therefore often the best-off, have to fork out large quantities of food or cash.

At first light, singing and drumbeats are heard out to sea, and sure enough, in come five or six canoes lashed together with a platform over them. Two enormous figures, about 10 ft. high, are dancing about, the bodies all covered with leaves, looking like cassowaries, but with immense conical heads, about five feet high, made of basket plastered over and horrible faces painted on the outside. There are no arms or hands visible. The two Duk-Duks come ashore, and all the Kanakas make room quickly, as if any man touches a Duk-Duk he is tomahawked immediately. The Duk-Duk go to a secret hut in the bush, and immense quantities of food are carried there. In the evening the young men of the tribe are lined up, their hands above their heads. One Duk-Duk takes a stout cane, about 6 ft. long, the other a club, and for hours, one after the other, the young men are beaten. They must show no pain. I believe it's much worse than when the Boss used to give us six on the bare arse!

When it's all over, everything is burnt, the hut, the Duk-Duk dresses, canes, clubs, the lot. Only then do the women appear again.

And I'd put my foot right in it, for the owners of the Duk-Duk were also the owners of these three huts, and no women were allowed anywhere near, for this was the place the Duk-Duk came ashore.

Uncle Richard said the situation was very serious. He knew through a man of Rickard's who the murderers were, and we'd have to get them. At this stage Schmiele, the German Imperial

Judge, arrived and took charge, though Uncle Richard really did everything for him. Old Schmiele is one of these real clothes-horse German bureaucrats, buttoned up in his uniform with a broomstick up his arse.

He ordered a punitive expedition to be set up immediately. The way to handle the Kanakas here is to hit them hard quick, otherwise if they've had a win first round then this inspires them to commit general mayhem. You've got to lick them at once, says Uncle Richard.

The punitive expedition was really all provided by Ralum, and not Imperial Germany. There were 24 Solomon Islanders with axes, 30 New Irelanders with spears, 17 bowmen from Buka, 9 Ralum trusties with rifles, 6 police-boys and 5 whites and half-castes.

We marched quickly up to the murderers' villages behind Ralum, but they'd all cleared off, we only shot one Kanaka and captured a woman and we let her go. However we burnt 200 houses and lots of gardens and settlements.

In the evening Schmiele set guards around Ralum and we withdrew. Schmiele said we'd have no more trouble, they'd hand over the murderers. Uncle Richard wasn't so hopeful.

He was right. Two days later hundreds of Kanakas attacked Ralum and the posts on the beach. They withdrew after the guards shot three of them. Schmiele now set up a real military manoeuvre, our forces were divided into two, to make a pincer movement, one led by him and the other by Uncle Richard. Needless to say, I went with Uncle Richard. Actually this might have been the end of your old friend Coe, because we surprised the big mob of them with muskets and about fifteen of them loosed off a volley at us at point blank range. Fortunately they're such lousy shots they missed the lot of us while we dropped one of them. If the great General Dummkopf von Schmiele had only arrived with his troops then we'd have caught the lot of them, but of course he had to get lost on the other side of the valley, and they were all up into the hills as quick as cockroaches.

When he finally reached us he said we must follow them up into the mountains. Uncle Richard said he was mad, even he didn't know the terrain, and our native guide Tomakaul was out of his territory. But no, off we went, hacking our way through the jungle and making enough noise to give a tribe of cripples time to clear out, until finally we got to open grass fields and saw some Kanakas. 'Fire' says Schmiele before Uncle Richard can stop him, and a Kanaka drops. When we get there it's a mary, a woman, shot dead, they were all maries. Uncle Richard had in the meantime got round the flank and caught a mob of warriors and dropped two, and captured huge amounts of beads, clothing, guns, ammunition and over three hundred fathoms of *diwarra*. (*Diwarra* = white cowrie shells about ¼ in. long, threaded together, and a fathom is from arm to arm. Ten fathoms roughly for a pig or a man's life. In money a fathom is about 1½ German marks.) We then hot-footed it back to Ralum, so as not to be trapped by night, and the booty was distributed amongst the troops.

By 4 April the two biggest chiefs (they're not really chiefs, but the wealthiest man in the tribe) had sent rolls of 100 fathoms of *diwarra*, asking for peace. In turn, Schmiele gave each two rolls of 40 fathoms as payment for the delivering up of the murderers. He said to us that to execute a couple out of six would be enough. All in all the Kanakas lost 8 dead, houses, canoes, gardens, tools and about 600 fathoms of *diwarra*.

As two weeks later two of the inland tribes had still not paid up their share of *diwarra*, Schmiele set up what he called a demonstration march to explain to them that if they kept the peace there would be no further punishments. This time he took along Aunt Phebe.

Really, the women of our family are amazing, I don't know which astonishes me most, Mother or Aunt Phebe. I suppose there were some pretty brave Australian women out in the bush, but those tottering teacosies around Sydney wouldn't last two minutes up here. You should have seen Aunt Phebe surrounded by a couple of hundred stark naked savages coolly explaining to them in their own language that they'd better behave themselves. But no bullying, all quiet and gentle, they all know her, she's called 'Miti', and trust her. She explained to them that the road would be good for them, as they'd be able to sell their produce both to the new station at Kokopo as well as to Ralum. They asked Schmiele if any houses or coconut palms had to be removed, could they go to Aunt Phebe and discuss compensation.

197

'*Natürlich!*' Would their fishing rights be upheld? '*Natürlich!*' Would they be allowed to build houses on the other side of the road close to the shore? '*Natürlich!*' Old Schmiele was beaming like a ripe mango. Then he asks them, through Aunt Phebe, were they happy with Queen Emma's claim to own the land, or did they wish to contend it. No, perfectly happy, they all loved Queen Emma.

Thus ended the biggest uprising since 1878, the one that was suppressed by the missionary George Brown. I suppose in a way it was all my fault, though nobody holds it against me. What I really mean is that if Aunt Phebe had been with me on the road she'd have understood why they didn't want the road alongside those three huts.

From
Your old friend

Coe Forsayth

Chapter XXIX

HIRAM STUART

10 July, 1891
I joined the U.S. Consular Service to see the world, but never
dreamed I would see anything like Gunantambu!

My secret diary, only you shall know the full and naked story,
laid bare as at the confessional (though I am no Papist), of
Queen Emma's party for the 4th July and my own housewarming,
of my beautiful little white house amid the frangipani and
hibiscus of the Gunantambu garden! Even now, nearly a week
later, when all is clear in the fierce tropic sun, the bottles of
champagne and the blue haze of the finest Havanas drift across
the events in my memory causing me to wonder, were they dream
or truth? Don't be a damn fool, Hiram, you know perfectly well
they were true. This diary is not going to rise up and call you
liar. So go ahead.

Celebrations began on the 2nd, when about twenty of us
followed Queen Emma across the verandah of Gunantambu and
down the great steps to the driveway where carriages were awaiting us to take us to her port at Ralum to board her ship the
Golden Gate (named after my own dear hometown) to take
us to Matupi where we were all to dine with Eduard Hernsheim.
There must have been ten nationalities amongst us. First, of
course, with Emma was her Captain (in all respects) Stalio, that
Dalmatian Poseidon, whose safe return was perhaps the real
reason for the splendour of the celebrations of these days. For
this unbelievable man was wrecked in Queen Emma's steamer
Endora on Lihir Island off the coast of New Ireland some weeks
previously. He and the crew got ashore, and saved the small boat.
There was neither room nor provisions for all to embark in the
boat, a mere dinghy. So Stalio set off alone, on these seas that

from Gunantambu look so peaceful blue and sparkling, but as all who sail them know are surging with treacheries of currents, reefs and winds, especially in St George's Channel. For *six* days he *rowed*, no sail or engine, simply rowed with his great hands, and on the evening of the sixth day he reached Herbertshöhe, nearly dead after more than 200 miles, too exhausted to row the last couple of miles to Ralum. The last touch to this incredible story is that the relief steamer, the *Senta*, under command of Captain Boehermann, battling adverse currents and heavy seas, took fourteen days for the return journey to Lihir, a distance Captain Stalio had rowed in six! The crew were safely picked up, and the *Senta* on its return provisioned the traders on the Fead Group, where it is rumoured that Queen Emma's brother John was lost at sea between Nuguria and New Ireland.

So leading our joyful throng was Queen Emma and her brave Captain, followed by the charming Count Pfeil, the customs officer etc., and Richard and Phebe Parkinson. Then Captain Peter Hansen, the mysterious Dane who is rumoured to live in autocratic splendour on Queen Emma's island of Vitu, also known as the French Islands. Then Captain Rondahl, a solid and reliable Swede who is at present skippering the *Three Cheers* in Captain Stalio's absence. Then Octave Mouton, the Belgian owner of Kinigunan plantation nearby, a survivor of the Marquis de Rays' expedition, who has had many a row with Queen Emma, but they are good friends nonetheless. Many more followed, and Queen Emma's son Coe, and those glorious relations of Emma's of whom the most beautiful is surely her half-sister whom I shall call Euphrosyne, twenty years old.

I will never to my dying day forget the morning, a few months ago, when I first set foot inside the house at Gunantambu. Coming to this cannibal coast, on a day when a mild eruption had sent the stench of Hades from the volcano in a lowering cloud across the bay, to enter this house with the Stars and Stripes flying from its flagpole (Queen Emma is very proud of being a U.S. citizen), to stand amongst the exquisite furniture with my feet sinking into a Persian rug, fresh flowers reflected in the gleaming lid of the grand piano, to be greeted (Queen Emma was out in her plantations) by a 'Houri' of Paradise, no less. She introduced herself as Euphrosyne, Emma's sister. She was of medium height, having an oval face with a beautiful soft dark eyes guarded by long dark eyelashes; a clear olive or Mediterranean complexion, with the bust of Venus, and her true name was justified alone by the movements of her supple arms. Draped in a simple morning gown, innocent of hidden whalebone, her voluptuous figure showed to full advantage, and she stepped forth like one fresh from the Garden of Eden and held out her hand to greet me.

There, I have not trusted my shaking hand to write of this first meeting before in my diary.

We boarded the *Golden Gate* and steamed over to Matupi, where Captain Hernsheim awaited us. Queen Emma swept ashore first. She was dressed in white satin, with a long train which was borne behind her by half a dozen little dusky maidens, natives of the Solomon Islands, all dressed in fantastic costumes as birds, some as birds of paradise (with genuine plumes), others as red and green parrots, others as cassowary chicks. Above Queen Emma's jet black hair she wore a tiara of diamonds, and a necklace of alternate rubies and diamonds shone on her beautiful shoulders, held most regally. After followed her lovely female sisters and cousins, and then the rest of us. Her little maidens, all of whom owe either life or liberty to her (for they were sold to be eaten or kept as slaves when she stepped in and bought them), attend her all the time, after dinner standing behind her chair, some fanning her, others rolling the small cigars which she prefers, others handing her her coffee or cognac. This was still at the dining table, for it is not the custom in New Britain for the ladies to retire after dessert. In fact, as Queen Emma and all her female relations are exceedingly well educated, quick and witty, it would be a grievous loss to the conversation were they to leave the gentlemen alone. Who should know this better than myself, who had the good fortune to sit next to my fair Euphrosyne, who apart from her natural graces had received a first-rate education at a leading school in Sydney, was highly proficient in German, an accomplished musician and had the voice of a nightingale. I kept telling myself in amazement, 'she is a creole, a half-caste Samoan, like all the ladies here.' It is all the more amazing to me, coming from the most advanced nation on earth, to see what independence of mind these women have, and the power and authority of Queen Emma, when at home women are still so far from achieving even a minimum of their rights.

After dinner we all adjourned to Captain Hernsheim's skittle alley and then dancing was indulged in till the early hours of the morning. Though the competition was fierce, my Euphrosyne allowed me more dances than any other supplicating male.

The next day was passed in rest, in preparation for the celebrations of the Fourth of July. By the evening of the 4th all the notables from hundreds of miles around had assembled at Gunantambu, including the officers from S.M.S. *Möwe*, most opportunely anchored at that moment in Matupi for coaling. The Germans were resplendent in their uniforms, and even Imperial Judge Schmiele, a stiff stick, was beaming on all around him. The celebrations began with the firing of the cannons that line the terrace on either side of the Queen's front steps, these cannon being salvaged from the Marquis de Rays' expedition. Many guns and pistols were let off together with the cannon, and fireworks exploded over the water. Champagne was handed around by the Queen's stalwart Bukas, resplendent in livery originally destined for the high court of La Nouvelle France. For those wishing our national depravity, the cocktail, the Queen herself was concocting seductive mixtures at a great cabinet which is nothing less, in the splendour of variegated marble, than the high altar consecrated by the Archbishop of Milan, destined for the Cathedral at Port Breton. Queen Emma is not a believer in the blessings of Christianity.

In this she is the opposite of her sister Phebe, who is a devout Catholic. This remarkable lady, who would not yet be thirty years old, has the controlled beauty of a Murillo in contrast to the more opulent splendour of a Tiziano which sits so easily on her sister. Phebe's carriage is superb, her long black hair is drawn back severely but her expression is one of gentle concern. Her figure is perfect, a rather more womanly version of my slim Euphrosyne. Phebe manages everyone and everything, whether her brilliant but somewhat testy husband, the press of German officers (unlike the Queen, she speaks good German), the host of black servants, or indeed the whole feast itself, for which she had personally superintended the cooking of no less than twenty eight courses.

In such a climate it might be thought such a large gathering would be unbearably hot, but there runs in Queen Emma's blood the mechanic genius of our American race, and she has beneath the house a kind of air-pump which, by the cunning conjunction of dripping water and an ice-making plant, sends streams into the house of delicious cooled air. Were she to patent this device she would make a fortune; but she hardly has need of more than the one she already has.

Dinner was served by three comely lasses from the Admiralty Islands, dressed in nothing but brief lava-lavas, and were my eyes not already filled with the beauties of Euphrosyne, they might well have strayed in the direction of these waitresses.

After dinner Queen Emma took her seat at the piano and we all joined in the singing of 'Hail Columbia', 'The Star Spangled Banner', and 'Yankee Doodle', even the Germans making quite a good fist of it.

Then an orchestra assembled and dancing commenced, the first to take the floor being Captain Stalio and the Queen, in a rousing polka, in the solo demonstrations of which no other dancers came near them. Queen Emma is neither as young or as slim as she was, but her energy and sureness of movement are prodigious. After the languorous delights of a waltz, in which I found Euphrosyne a perfect partner, Queen Emma announced that Captain Stalio would do a solo dance from his native Dalmatia. He then appeared in the dress of his native city of Ragusa, and I will admit I have never seen a more handsome man, and he drew from those present first a breathless hush and then an eruption of applause worthy of old smokyguts across the bay.

The champagne flowed, the night rang with cries of joy, and the garden glowed with flares lighting the coral paths and flowering shrubs. But in the cool darkness, behind the lemon trees, I found occasion to walk with Euphrosyne and there essayed my first trembling kiss. To my astonishment it was not only allowed but returned with the passionate complicity of her entire, divine form. And this was the same girl who a few minutes before had been berating me for my typically Anglo-Saxon ignorance of the works of Goethe!

The 5th I cannot recall too well, but think it was generally taken as a day of rest after the celebration of the 4th. There was some soothing music in the evening, Mr Parkinson being a particularly good performer on the violin, and we sang duets (yes, Euphrosyne and I!), and trios and quartets, but left the rousing choruses alone.

On the 6th we were bidden to a Samoan feast in the gardens. A *fale*, which is the curved Samoan hut, had been built to give us shade, and the cooking had all been done under the ground. While we watched, the ovens were opened and out of the earth, wrapped in green leaves, came fish, lobsters, fowls, pigs, pigeons and a multitude of other delicacies. Phebe, who had been in charge of everything once again, pressed us to have all the Samoan dishes, of which I particularly liked the *palusami*. We all had to eat sitting on the ground, and many were the rounds of laughter as the Germans in their tight uniforms and swords creaked to a semi-reclining posture. There were no knives or forks, and coconut milk was drunk out of coconut cups. All the ladies and gentlemen of Samoan origin dressed in Samoan fashion with only a loose garment around them, and I must say that compared with us they looked light, airy and comfortable and I wondered why they did not dress thus all the time. One could not trace the slightest semblance of dark blood in them, notably my Euphrosyne, who looked bewitching with her hair loose and a red hibiscus behind her hidden ear and her exquisite shoulders and upper bosom fully exposed.

As night came on the grounds were lit up with lanterns, and Samoan dancing commenced. The men, armed with clubs, performed a war dance in which in wild gyrations and the throbbing of drums they reached such a pitch of excitement that we all expected the clubs to begin knocking out brains, but no blood was shed, only the major part of their costume, their splendid bodies gleaming in the light. Then Euphrosyne and some of her cousins danced a delicate, maidenly dance depicting the wooing of the wild wood-pigeon. Then, to our astonishment, the old lady Le'utu, Queen Emma's mother, who must be over sixty, sprang into the circle of the flares and danced a Samoan *siva* of a meaning so unmistakeable that it could only be taken as the prelude to an orgy. At this point of the entertainment Father Couppé and the Rev. and Mrs Rickard said their farewells

204

to Queen Emma, being suddenly overtaken with the need for rest.

Champagne had long since displaced coconut milk, and the beat of the drums became more insistent, and Emma and Phebe (yes, the quiet, dignified Phebe!) performed a dance which could only be said to carry on from that given by Le'utu. At the end of it Captain Stalio, whose wild energies were perhaps suppressed by his not being able to join in the Samoan dances, declared that Emma deserved after such a dance to be bathed in champagne and forthwith emptied a bottle of the best Veuve Clicquot over her, then seized her up in his arms as if she weighed no more than one of her little black hand-maidens, and ran with her up the steps of Gunantambu to the marble bath where in one gesture he divested her of her scanty clothing and deposited her gently in the bath, immediately calling for champagne which he proceeded to bathe her in. Emma entering with the utmost jollity into the spirit of the thing called to her head boy 'Bring magnums, not bottles', which I thought a splendid gesture, and a practical one too, for it needed many bottles to cover her ample flesh. When she was well bathed Stalio lifted her out and swathed her cool body in a towel, leaving the champagne sparkling invitingly in the marble, and instantly provoking a Lieutenant off the *Möwe* to whip the robe off another beautiful Samoan girl and cool her limbs in Clicquot. Shakingly I said to myself, 'Dare I?', and stood irresolute, but then, my blood afire with the drums, the dancing, the half-light from the flares in the garden, and the champagne, I swept Euphrosyne off her feet and divining her mood from her laughter and the pressure of her arms around my neck, I slipped her smooth body out of the light *lava-lava* and delicately lowered her into the marble bath where she lay as naked as ever the goddess of love came ashore to Cyprus from the sea!

Now I have written this, only for you my secret diary, does it not sound like an account of a night in some *bagnio* in the red-light district of my home town? If, so, I have betrayed you, Emma, Euphrosyne, all you Samoans. True, it was a prodigious debauch, and what the *Examiner* would call an orgy. But despite the fact that we Europeans and Americans took part, it was all Polynesian, the spirit was that of the South Seas and the spirit was pure in heart, for they see nothing sinful in the flesh. A Scotchman standing beside me said in my ear that he found old Le'utu's dance disgusting, but she saw no shame in it (nor did I), and it was her lascivious dance that gave the sanction for all the wild events of the night.

So for a whole week more the festivities continued, with new pleasures and games and trips to beauty spots provided each day by the tireless Queen, whose energy, if ever flagging, was clearly restored by her majestic consort, Captain Stalio. Since this has all been also my house-warming, I feel that the presence of the United States, in the personification of its Consular Representative, is now well established in the Bismarck Archipelago.

✱

Note, in Mrs. Parkinson's handwriting
This poor boy, only twenty-five years of age, died of blackwater fever on 28 July, 1891, and is buried in the cemetery at Herbertshöhe.

Chapter XXX

————————————◆————————————

PHEBE

Poor Emma! Poor, poor rich Emma! Richard says it is a case of
what the Greeks called *hubris*, meaning pride that tempts the
anger of the gods, but that is pagan business, there is only one
God and I do not believe he is a jealous God. Why then does
he destroy great happiness? Perhaps to show those who doubt,
that great and daring happiness is worth achieving, for when
it is cut short, there is the proof of its existence.

This sad story begins towards the end of 1890, when Emma
had sent out instructions for all our relations and friends to
gather at Gunantambu to celebrate Christmas. We Parkinsons
had our own celebration first, privately, at Kuradui on Christmas
Eve. Richard would cut the top off a young avocado tree and set
it up in a stand that contained a musical box, when you wound
it up with a key it went round and round and played 'O Tannen-
baum'. Each Christmas Richard would take one pear off the
avocado for each child, and he would dig with the spade so the
child, Louisa or Dolly or Otto or Max, would plant the pear
and he would say 'There, when you grow up you can say I
planted that tree when I was a child.' He had that big scientific
brain, but he was very sentimental. All the presents would be
heaped around the tree, surrounded by candles, and Richard
would go in and light all the candles while the children and I
stayed in another room, then he would open the double doors
and we would run in and join hands and dance around the tree
and sing carols. Later we would play Halma and Ludo. Just the
family for Christmas Eve. On Christmas day we would go for the
big party with Emma.

That Christmas we were sad because the ship that had gone to
Nuguria to bring our orother John home had returned without

him, bearing the news that the natives said he had gone off in his whale boat and never returned, so he must have perished at sea.

So Emma sent another brother, Henry, to the Fead Islands, the group of atolls which have many little islands of which Nuguria is one, to manage the flourishing copra station there. Henry was a nice, gentle quiet man, a sailor really, he'd been delicate as a boy so my father had sent him to sea as a cabin boy with Captain Hayes, the one they always called 'Bully' and said he was a pirate, though he was always a gentleman to us and we knew his wife and family well in Apia. That seemed to toughen up Henry, and he went to sea and for many years we heard nothing of him until Emma, on one of her trips to .Australia, I think in 1888, found him by chance very ill in a hospital in Cooktown in Queensland. She brought him back here where I nursed him back to health and he lived with us till he married a Samoan woman called Anga, a widow, they never had any children. Henry was a very useful and sensible man and liked by all.

So he went to the Feads and set up a station on an islet called Akani, one of over fifty islets in the group, about 125 miles east of New Ireland, or Neu Mecklenburg as the Germans rechristened it. Henry got on well at Akani. His two head boys, Puleva and Bobby, were from Nuguria, and they came to him one day and he said that their chief, known as King Soa'a and his son Pila, were planning a big feast, or sing-sing, and they would like Henry to be their guest.

Henry accepted, and they sailed over to Nuguria, and Henry was greeted by Pila and brought to the centre of the village, where King Soa'a seated him on a broad wooden bench in the shade of a tree. Pila and three other natives sat down on each side of him. Pila asked Henry what he had hanging from his belt, and Henry said it was his revolver, pulled it out and said 'Look! suppose some fellow catchem me, me shoot him!' Henry was a dead shot, and to prove it he split a coconut high on a tree above them which rained milk at their feet. Henry then waved his revolver around at Pila and the other natives, and put it back in its holster, leaving the butt exposed. The food was then brought in and the dancing began, and Henry kept his hand close to his revolver.

He did not stay very long, but took his boat back to Akani, and there a very frightened Puleva and Bobby told him that they had found out in the village that Soa'a intended to kill him just as he had killed John in 1890. Pila and the three natives were to grab him, tie him up, weight him with big rocks and throw him alive into a deep pool in the lagoon, as they had done with John. John's whaleboat was still hidden in the mangroves at the far end of Nuguria. Henry's prowess with the revolver had made them frightened to attack him.

Henry was a very practical man. As soon as he heard this story from the boys, he loaded up his boat with provisions and sailed from Akani at 4 a.m. As it was getting light they saw the canoes of Soa'a and his party arriving to murder him. Shots were fired at him, but by this time Henry's boat was out of range. Had he delayed he would have been killed in Soa'a's surprise dawn attack. He sailed on, with four labourers and the two Nuguria boys, and after two days and nights reached Cain Island, where they obtained coconuts. They then set sail for Ralum, but the S.E. winds were too strong at Cape St. George, and they turned back and sailed 250 miles up the coast of New Ireland to Kaevieng, near which they had the good fortune to sight Captain Stalio and the *Three Cheers*.

Emma swore to have vengeance on King Soa'a for the murder of John and the attempted murder of Henry, and she had the full support of Imperial Judge Schmiele, who as a military man always enjoyed the opportunity to deploy his troops. Being ill on this occasion he had to send as deputy Judge Giesler from Herbertshöhe, who took with him Bulominsky, later a famous administrator in New Ireland, and another officer and twenty-five police boys. Emma provided twenty-five Buka boys under the leadership of Henry and Captain Stalio, with J. M. Rondahl as first mate of the *Three Cheers*. The object of the punitive expedition was to bring back Soa'a and Pila and the other murderers for trial.

We dined with Emma the night in August before they sailed. Tino Stalio, that man we all loved for his strength and good spirits and for the way he made Emma so happy, we all rejoiced when the *Three Cheers* was in port, Tino said he had known

Soa'a for years and could speak his language and there would be no trouble in bringing him back to trial. What Tino said, happened; what he set out to do, he did. Do you know he rowed single-handed over 200 miles in six days, from Lihir Island to Herbertshöhe? And he was always so gentle, never like Tom Farrell in first with the fists or the gun, always the quiet talk first, during which his opponent would have the time to think about the man he was up against.

So off they went in high spirits, and reached Akani at the end of August, and sent a message to King Soa'a to come. But he did not come, so they landed at the far end of Nuguria and marched towards the village. In the centre of the island Soa'a and his men were hiding behind coconut trees, stumps and rocks and they opened fire on our party. The Judge and Captain Stalio gave orders to retaliate, and after a couple of hours three of Soa'a's men were dead. The party advanced ot the village, which was deserted, everyone had run away into the bush. Henry sent his two Nuguria boys, Puleva and Bobby, out as scouts, and they came back to say Soa'a and some of his men were hiding in the chief's 'spirit-house' at the end of the village, which they found to be all barricaded around with wood.

Henry advised burning them out. Judge Giesler said he wanted Soa'a alive to stand trial. Captain Stalio said violence was unnecessary, that if he personally explained to Soa'a that he was not going to be shot, but taken to Herbertshöhe for trial, then he would come out quietly. He had such presence that none disagreed with him.

Captain Stalio put down his rifle and revolver and walked unarmed up to the barricade and the closed hut and the hidden natives. He held up his hands to show he was unarmed, and called on Soa'a to come out and talk to him, his old friend Stalio.

His answer was a bullet through his chest. He died instantly.

The Judge ordered the hut to be set on fire. Two Ralum labourers crawled up with torches, one was shot dead, the other set the spirit-house blazing. Meanwhile Henry had moved behind the hut and lay hidden behind a stump, about 40 yards away. Soa'a ran out and Henry shot him. Then the chief's son Pila also ran out, and Henry shot him. The other native Henry missed.

Shortly afterwards, Henry remaining on Akani, the German authorities sent a gunboat which brought back the other six men involved, and after a trial they were deported for life to the mainland of New Guinea.

How strange the facts of events are! You tell them one by one, like stones. Yet they are living, and when you hand them to someone close to those events, then it is like handing them a scorpion or a kingfisher, something that will bury poison or release a rainbow. But they are not only living, they are unkillable, they cannot be suppressed.

The Judge came to me with the story, and I had to tell Emma. Only twice in her life did I see her weep, and this was the second. She wept for Tino, she wept for herself, she was utterly abandoned, she was like someone who jumps to death off a high cliff, the peak of a mountain, but Emma was casting herself down from the peak of her own life. She had achieved everything she had wanted years ago in Apia, wealth, beauty, her family around her, and the one thing she had never thought to achieve, love. She always told me she was too practical and too Samoan for that, and she knew too much about men. Love-affairs, passion, yes, but no romantic love. But Tino, her Captain, was totally unexpected, physically and mentally her perfect partner but quite beyond that, demanding nothing of her, leaving her all her freedom, simply like his ships sailing in and out of her life and embodying in his presence her love of the sea.

Her paroxysms of grief were terrifying, she rolled on the floor and banged her head on the wall as if trying to drive the evil news out of her brain. I am a strong woman, *starkgliederig*, Richard called me, strong-limbed, but I could no more hold her than straighten the coils of a python, and it took four Buka boys to bring her to her bed where I loosened her dress and hair and stroked her forehead and sang to her for five, maybe six hours and then I got her to drink half a bottle of brandy, but all the time with the Buka boys there in case she tried to kill herself.

Then she slept, while I watched her. When she woke she never cried again. The first words she said were to give me instructions for a tomb, with an angel and trumpet, to be ordered from the best Italian marble craftsmen in Sydney. It was done exactly as she said, in white marble, with the precise words carved on it that she said that morning:

'In loving Memory of Captain Augustino Stalio, who was shot by the natives of the Fead Islands, while bravely Assisting the Imperial Judge, to arrest the King and his Son, for the Massacre of John Coe.
Born at Dalmatia December, 1854. Killed at Fead Islands, 2nd Septembe., 1892.

Oh, for the touch of a vanished hand
And the sound of a voice that is still.'

Shortly after this, Emma went away to Sydney for several months, leaving me in charge of the business. I had no fears for her, but I sensed a strong, deep change in her, and knew I must wait to see what that change brought after it.

It was a time of many changes. My father Jonas Coe died in Apia in 1891, of influenza, at the age of sixty-nine, leaving several children by his last Tongan wife. My elder brother Willie came from Apia to join us in 1890, and from him we heard much of the sad events in our war-torn Samoa, where the great Powers had become involved in the rivalry between the three contenders for King, Malietoa, Mataafa and Tamasese. The Germans being the most powerful, thought they could do as they wish, and instal Tamasese with all the royal titles. Willie in the meantime was adviser to Laupepa, that same ineffectual Malietoa of the Steinberger days. Poor Laupepa, how he was humiliated! The DHPG bought the Mulinu'u land from my father, on which the Government buildings stood, and then, saying the rent had not been paid, ordered Laupepa's Government off the land. It was Willie who drafted the letter from Laupepa to Stuebel, the German Consul, as a result of which the Germans just came and took poor Malietoa Laupepa, put him on a warship and exiled him to the Caroline Islands. This made Willie very unpopular with the Germans.

In 1889 Britain, the United States and Germany all sent warships to Apia, and who knows if an international war might not have broken out in the Pacific had not a hurricane hit Apia Harbour and sunk all the ships except one. Willie was very brave in rescuing sailors from the American ships, and received official thanks from the U.S. President himself.

When Willie came here, Emma sent him out to the Mortlock Islands, where he established a very important station for copra, trochus and tortoise shell. It was Captain Stalio who suggested that he next be moved to Kaevieng at the north end of New Ireland, where he did well until his beautiful young Samoan wife, Utufia, died in 1893, when she was only twenty-one of blackwater fever. He seemed to grow very melancholic then, and resentful of the German officials. We were always good friends with the Germans until the 1890s when they sent out some men of the petty official type who thought they were twigs off the tree of Prince Bismarck and breathing in air much more pure than us creole Samoans. This was not at all so with gentlemen like old Hernsheim or young Count Pfeïl, nor Governor Hahl who came later. I think maybe Schmiele was behind it, he had the misfortune to be born a very arrogant man, and perhaps because Germany was so young a nation he thought he must throw a big weight around on her behalf, especially when he was appointed Administrator of the Protectorate in 1892. Now, although the German station was not established in Kaevieng till many years later, Schmiele on a visit told Willie he should show more respect for the German flag, and should be ashamed of himself for his conduct in Samoa. He also made some remarks which could be interpreted that half-castes would not know any better.

So next time Willie saw Schmiele's ship rounding the point he was ready to show his respect for the German flag. As Schmiele's anchor went down, up went the flag—up on a pole over the latrine, which was at the end of a little jetty over the water. Schmiele sent an armed guard to tear down the flag. He then brought a charge against Willie for insulting the German flag, and trumped up some other charge about Willie maltreating the natives, but before he could bring him to court Emma had spirited him away to Sydney. Being an American citizen, Willie got away to Guam, where he became civilian Governor. Later on he moved on the Philippines. He left all his six children behind in New Guinea, and Emma took them all in and brought them all up (with my help!).

In the early 1890s my Richard had not been at all well, Emma said it was nature's revenge for letting me do all the work while he rode around on his horse collecting birds and butterflies. She always wanted Richard to work harder at making money to support our big family, but I never minded the extra work, and I wanted him to be famous. Well, Emma said, 'let all those museums and collectors pay you for all the specimens, the rare orchids and plants, the native weapons and artefacts that you have packed up and sent, and the birds you have stuffed yourself. But no, Richard wanted that they simply go as the gift of Richard Parkinson. But if *you* hadn't done all the talking to the natives, he'd have never got the specimens, said Emma. Don't worry, don't worry, I told her, and I was glad when he went to Europe even though it was without me, so glad when in 1893 the letters came from him from all those palaces and great houses where he had been an honoured guest, from the Sultan of Johore, Prince Metternich, Dr Grundig at the Berlin Museum, Duke This, Baron That, and even Rome, where he, a Protestant, was received by the Pope. Oh, I was so glad for him, because he was really born into that world and denied his residence there, so he conquered it with his brains, and I was pleased to have been able to help.

And now came the strange events of the Herbertshöhe war, and Emma and Lieutenant Kolbe.

First I should say that Emma was not herself when she came back from Sydney after Stalio's death. She had put on a lot of weight, and her face was puffy, her skin not nice and firm. She always drank a lot but never showed it. Now sometimes I would have to put her to bed. No man could take the place of Tino, but knowing Emma as only I did, I knew she needed a man, but there was none worthy of her in the limited field of Neu Pommern. In fact, one might add, none brave enough to attempt her, they were frightened of her tongue as well as her wealth. She never tolerated fools. Her best friend in these dark days, I was pleased to see, was my dear friend too, Monsignor Couppé, or I should say, Bishop after 1890. He never forgave her for the altar she used as a drinks cabinet, but otherwise they were the best of friends and sparring partners, Emma never giving an inch in her opposition to Christianity, but the Bishop meeting her on every intellectual level from theology to business, and he learned much from her in his land-battles with Schmiele. Once when the Bishop visited Gunantambu, joining a large party drinking champagne on the verandah, I remember that he had a big boil on his neck, and Emma said to him in that deep, firm voice that dominated any conversation, pointing to his boil, 'Bishop Couppé, that's the only true religious gathering I've ever seen'.

Of course, Emma's spirits were never low for long periods, she would find some excuse for a party, and she would drive away her loneliness by her pleasure in the company of all the young people in her household. Sometimes there must have been dozens of part-time Samoans running in and out of Gunantambu and Kuradui. On one occasion when there seemed to be just too many of them, Emma scooped up ten, seven boys and three girls, and sent them with a Samoan mama over to Henry and his wife at the main station on the Fead Islands. There they lived happily, all half-castes or quarter-castes, until it was time for them to go to the mission school, when they came back to live with Emma and us.

One event we always looked forward to was the six-weekly visit of the Norddeutscher Lloyd steamer. Emma and her prettiest sisters and nieces, and all the young men from Matupi and Herbertshöhe would go aboard to drink the ice-cold champagne and dance to the ship's band. One such visit I remember very well, and afterwards the natives talked about it for years. The young things were dancing till the early hours, but Emma was more interested in drinking, I think dancing at this time always made her think of Captain Stalio, who was the best dancer I have ever seen, and she still could not bear to dance with anyone else. Finally it was time for the Captain of the steamer to catch the tide and up anchor, and all the young ladies and gentlemen went ashore, but Emma would not budge, she wanted another bottle of champagne. She was indeed Queen, her word was law, and no one dared disobey her. But the tide was on the move, and the Captain was getting frantic, for Emma was the biggest customer of the Norddeutscher Lloyd in the whole of German New Guinea, and he dreaded to offend her.

Finally, as she seemed to have dozed off, he had the ship's engines started.

She woke instantly and stormed up to the bridge where she skun that poor Captain alive. He offered then to send her ashore immediately in the ship's pinnace. 'To hell with you', said Emma, that child of the sea, and stripping off her Paris gown (which was returned, wrapped in tissue paper in a beautiful box, on the steamer's next visit), she dived from the bridge down into the deep water and struck out for home. The Captain, knowing her prowess as a swimmer and that it would be more than his life was worth to attempt to rescue her, kept his course and prayed she would not be eaten by a shark. She had been swimming happily for an hour when she was picked up by the Ralum steam-launch. This feat was talked about in every village of the Archipelago, and gave her immense prestige among the natives.

The sea always soothed her angers and allowed the bubbles of her humour to rise again. On another occasion, on the visit of the German gunboat S.M.S. *Planet*, Emma, her sister Grace and two of her nieces were dining aboard with the Captain and officers. Towards the end of the evening one of the officers made a remark to Grace that Emma considered insulting. Immediately she swept her beauties together, told the Captain to drink his cognac himself, and all four jumped over and swam ashore. Fortunately all of us Samoans could swim like bonito.

As early in the morning as was diplomatic, the Captain, his officers and the ship's band came ashore and the deputation waited on Emma at Gunantambu, where an apology was offered and accepted. Emma immediately asked me to order what she called a Dinner of Forgiveness. Then her face lit up. 'After the dinner', she said 'a ceremonial is called for! Phebe my dear I have it, I have it!' I knew from her look that somebody's dignity was going to suffer.

Now just before this, Administrator Schmiele had issued a ridiculously pompous edict that the natives must learn civilized habits of urinating and defecating. To this end, at Herbertshöhe, just near the end of the Gunantambu drive, he had ordered the erection of two corrugated iron latrines, labelled in large letters 'Damen' and 'Herren', all very separate in the interests of morality.

Of course the natives never used them, and would not have been able to read the labels, and there they stood in their pristine splendour.

So after dinner Emma gave her orders to the Captain, the ship's band formed up at the foot of Gunantambu steps, boys with lanterns and flares on either side of them, and behind them in a procession Emma placed the Captain and herself, with one of her young relations arm in arm with each of the eight officers. To a sprightly polonaise the procession moved off down the drive to the latrines, where, bowing deeply to the Captain, Emma swept in to inaugurate the *'Damen'*, while he did the same for the *'Herren'*, followed by all the rest of the party. The band then played a mazurka on the grass behind the latrines and everyone danced.

Schmiele was very chilly towards Emma when he heard of the episode, which you may be sure he did at first light the next morning. Some people will tell you the Germans have no sense of humour but this is to admit a great ignorance of Germans. There is a certain type of bureaucrat that has absolutely no sense of humour, but is he only German? The officers of S.M.S. *Planet* loved their christening of the *'Damen'* and *'Herren'*. I sometimes think the sense of humour business is an attempt to establish a monopoly by the English, who have a peculiar sense of humour by the exercise of which they recognize each other as Englishmen. (English women have no sense of humour, ever.)

In 1893 some very strange goings-on began to happen amongst the natives. When Richard retired as manager of the Neu Guinea Kompagnie at Herbertshöhe, and went to Europe, he was succeeded by a big young German, Paul Kolbe. It is important to know about him. He was born in Hildesheim in 1865 and came from a good family. He was a Lutheran. He had been in a Prussian cavalry regiment and was a brilliant rider and always very clever with horses. When he came to New Britain he was a Lieutenant of the Reserve in the Schleswigsche Field Artillery No. 9. He had been three years in Hawaii as a plantation manager, so he had had experience of tropical agriculture and managing natives. Nevertheless, he was very hot-tempered. He was a big solid man with a thick neck. He had a strong moustache maybe to make up for the fact that his hair was receding on either side of his forehead, so that if you looked at him head on you could see his moustaches going down $\wedge$ and his hair going back $\vee$. He always wore his hair cut short, quite different from Richard who had long hair and a flowing beard.

The trouble began with some of the Solomon Island labourers at Herbertshöhe pulling the bush maries, this means raping the local girls. Since that time way back when they trussed Emma up like a pig at Ralum we had been very careful of this, and we had no trouble. But Kolbe was not so careful, and two labourers were killed and then a local native shot in return. But the real trouble came from a native called Talavai, he invented a bullet-proof paint. Actually it was just red volcanic clay from Matupi like they sell in the markets. But from far and wide they came to be anointed with this paint, and always the same procedure, you had to bring a white fowl, pure white with no black or coloured feathers, and then cook it and eat it with Talavai, and pay so many fathoms of *diwarra*. Of course, Talavai got very rich. Then he would paint the man, and stand him up at the far end of the enclosure, and take his old muzzle-loader Enfield, the ones you had to ram with a ramrod, and load it and then fire it at the man. All he would feel was a little tap, and there was a little blood-red mark on his chest. He was truly bullet-proof.

But what Talavai had done was to put a little blood-red fruit like a cherry into the gun instead of a bullet—we used to grow them in the garden at Kuradui, I made a lovely red pudding from them—and of course that was the red spot on the man's chest. For a hundred fathoms of *diwarra* he let wizards from far villages in on the secret, and soon there were hundreds of bullet-proof natives. He told them that to stay bullet-proof they must eat only white fowls and not sleep with women.

So they came down to Herbertshöhe and pulled out the cotton and attacked the plantation. In July Paul Kolbe led a punitive expedition and wounded many natives. But when they came to Talavai and showed him their wounds, he said they must have slept with a woman or eaten a coloured fowl.

There was a second clash in August, and the Kompagnie made a peace offer, saying that if four of the leaders paid a shell-money fine, and Talavai was handed over, there would be peace.

But the offer was rejected. By this time Richard had come home, and Schmiele and Kolbe came to see us and said that although Ralum had not been attacked, yet if the natives succeeded in killing all the white men at Herbertshöhe, then they would kill us too. Emma and Richard and I thought this was true, so we said we would help, and Octave Mouton came with some of his boys to help too. Schmiele said his native police would carry the day, but I thought they would be useless, and so they were, firing off their ammunition wastefully in all directions.

The expedition reached a village inland and suddenly hundreds of natives charged down the hill and it might have gone very badly had not a strange thing happened. Octave Mouton who was there told me that when the natives came out into the open ground, there leaping and dancing about in front of them was Talavai, painted red and white, carrying no arms at all, in each hand he held crotons like bunches of flowers. He was singing and obviously he had come to believe in his own bullet-proof paint. Octave said he was shot immediately, then you could have heard a pin drop, then all you could hear was the rush of the natives disappearing in the bush. Octave cut off one of Talavai's ears to show all the natives that the wizard was dead.

Everyone thought this would be the end of the troubles, but the natives from other villages would not believe Talavai was dead. Peace offers were rejected. About this time, in December a cruiser, S.M.S. *Sperber*, arrived in Blanche Bay, under Captain von Arnoldi. Now a full-scale battle was planned.

Richard was to direct shelling from the warship, Kolbe was to lead one party, Schmiele another to come round in a pincer, and I was to wait with a third party in the centre. Well, Schmiele and his sixty sailors from the *Sperber* came round according to plan, and waited at the bottom of the hill for the natives who should be driven down by Kolbe's party. But what happened was this. Up in the hills they were just going to go through a narrow valley when one of Mouton's men said there was an ambush set up there. So the party came round another way and as they emerged into the open a shot was fired at them. Quickly

Kolbe and Mouton shot at the smoke, whereupon there was a tremendous volley, and immediately they knew it was the sailors, not the natives who were firing. In the silence that followed they whistled and shouted and thus the German forces were stopped from killing each other. Fortunately no one was hurt.

Meanwhile the *Sperber* shelled the inland villages, which didn't injure anyone except one native who was paralyzed with fright. The rebellion, if that's what you could call it, collapsed and the natives paid peace offerings of *diwarra* and it was all over.

But it was not all over for Schmiele, who had already had quarrels with Paul Kolbe, and wanted to put as much blame for the whole business as possible on Kolbe. Schmiele formally charged him with gross neglect of his duties, over the fracas between the sailors and the native police, and reprimanded him and fined him 100 marks (not very much really, only £5). But Paul was furious, and said he refused to accept the judgement, and would if necessary appeal to the Imperial Chancellor in Berlin. Whereupon Schmiele dismissed him from the employment of the Kompagnie.

Now the most amazing thing happened. Of course Paul was spending a lot of time at Gunantambu, drinking champagne and sympathy, for we all hated Schmiele, and it was quite obvious from Octave's account that the fault was not Paul's, but Schmiele's. And there was something appealing about Paul when he was in a good mood, (only then), he was like a big Doberman dog. He was coming to Gunantambu a great deal, and I thought he must be after one of our beautiful Samoan girls, if not my own who were still a little bit young.

But imagine, *imagine*, when Emma came to me one evening in February, 1894 and said 'Phebe, I am going to marry Paul.' My face did a landslide, I couldn't help it, and she laughed and said, 'Yes, I know he is fifteen years younger than me, I am forty-three and he is twenty-eight, but I am not ugly, am I?' She certainly was not, and she had recovered a lot of her looks and spirits. 'But the business?', I dared to say. 'Don't worry, I will remain in control. I will also pay his debts. I know he is marrying me for my money. I know I feel sorry for him, because of his treatment by Schmiele, and I know how dangerous pity is. I know all this, and I know I do not love him. Did you love

220

Richard when you married him?' I admitted I did not. 'Well, you love him now. You're luckier than me. I don't think I'll ever love Paul, I certainly won't bear any of his children. But married to him I will not be a half-caste creole of dubious background, but Frau Kolbe of good aristocratic connections, a German accepted by Germans, and rich. Phebe, it's time I showed the world who I am, and to do that a woman, even a woman like me, must have a man beside her, she can't do it on her own. I'm going to buy a big house in Sydney, in Vaucluse. Then I'm going to go back to Samoa and kick the arse of those LMS wives, and then I'm going to San Francisco and show Aunt Elizabeth and the Coes that I have servants to do the sort of things I used to do for them, and then I'm going to Berlin and the Kaiser is going to have the honour of kissing my hand!'

I'd recovered a bit by this time, so I said 'And Schmiele is not going to do you the honour of receiving you here. What's more, he's Paul's military superior and he won't give Paul permission to marry you.'

'Let him', said Emma, looking as tough as Tom Farrell.

Well, she was good as her word. On 24 February the Wesleyan schooner anchored off Ralum, with Rev. Rickard aboard. (Mrs Rickard was such a nice little woman, we used to have birthday parties together for the children, she loved Le'utu's *palusami*, and she made an awful plum pudding for the Queen's birthday the first year she was here.) The wedding party went aboard, we sailed outside German territorial waters, and Paul and Emma were pronounced man and wife. I wish I could have liked him better. I suppose I loved Emma too much.

On 26 February Paul resigned from his post in the Kompagnie, for although Schmiele had dismissed him as manager of Herbertshöhe he was still officially employed by the Kompagnie. About this time the volcano gave us a few good shakes and Emma laughed and said they would be felt in Berlin. Schmiele had refused to set foot on the soil of Ralum since the wedding, and no German officers or officials were allowed to call. This set the Administration against the Navy, as imagine what a disaster this would be to all visiting ships, who looked forward to Gunantambu parties as the brightest spot in the Pacific!

In June, Schmiele wrote to Paul and informed him that he had recommended to Berlin that Paul be expelled from German New Guinea, and that he be dishonourably discharged from the army and that he had compromised his honour as a Prussian officer by marrying a half-caste of dubious background without permission of his superior officer. (Should I mention here that Schmiele kept a Malayan mistress?)

I must admit that Paul was a fine manly-looking man and could behave like one at times. On reading this letter he called for his horse (he had a lovely seat on a horse) and galloped off to the plantation nearby that Schmiele was visiting. Emma was too much of a warrior herself to raise a finger to dissuade him. When he had gone she said to me 'Now that he is married to me they can't expel him from New Guinea anyway.'

We had of course eye-witness reports of what happened. Paul found Schmiele and dismounted, horse-whip in hand, and asked Schmiele to repeat what he had written in his letter. Schmiele did so, whereupon Paul horse-whipped him. It wasn't just a token tap, either. Schmiele, when he was able to talk again, challenged Paul to a duel.

Pastor Frobenius of the Rhenish Mission, who was standing next to Schmiele, felt constrained to tell Schmiele that a duel was murder in the eyes of the Lord. Far from being spiritually rebuked, Schmiele challenged Pastor Frobenius to a duel as well. The Pastor refused, though Paul had accepted with alacrity. Schmiele then told Hoffmann, the Mission's Senior who was also there, that unless he ordered Frobenius to give him satisfaction, Schmiele would deport both of them from German New Guinea. Hoffmann, who is an old gentleman of steady nerve and pleasant wit, told Schmiele that in view of his poor health he would enjoy a trip to Germany where he could discuss the whole matter with the Government. This seemed to quieten Schmiele down, as far as Pastor Frobenius was concerned.

All our little society in the Bismarck Archipelago was split by this quarrel between Paul and Schmiele. Not in numbers, for we had so many friends and Schmiele almost none. But these insults were based on our mixed bood. Schmiele said to Paul 'This is a German colony and I'm not going to have it run by a rabble of Samoan half-castes.' At that stage it wasn't really a colony at all, the Reich didn't take over till 1899, but Schmiele was the sort of German who makes wars.

Emma was all for the duel. Paul was a deadly shot, and Emma said it was a perfect solution for getting rid of Schmiele and restoring peace to our little society. But apparently the same thoughts had occurred to Schmiele, because over five weeks from the horsewhipping, when Paul had given up to polish his pistols any longer, one of our friends at Herbertshöhe brought us a copy of a telegram (it went by boat to the German Consul-General in Sourabaya in the Dutch East Indies, and by telegraph from there) from Schmiele to the Imperial Chancellor, Count von Caprivi, saying 'A previous employee of the Kompagnie Kolbe physically attacked and insulted me on the 9/6/94 matter has been submitted to the District Court.

(Signed) Schmiele.'

'What was the insult, Paul?' Emma asked, all giggly, like a school-girl. Paul answered 'I told him he was a pig's arse.' That particularly appealed to us Samoans.

Now the proceedings had been registered at the Court, sure enough, but Schmiele was the Judge of the Court! Paul, who knew all about the correct Prussian way of doing things, wrote to Schmiele and said the whole affair should be submitted to a Court of Honour, where officers pronounce judgement on their fellows, like something out of the times of Charlemagne—but where would he find enough officers?

The whole thing seemed as if it would fizzle out next year, when Schmiele was recalled to Berlin, and died in the arms of his Malayan mistress in Bavaria. In the meantime Emma had taken Paul off on a triumphal tour of Sydney and Samoa, where they would be in Apia for her son Coe's wedding.

Emma had wanted me to come too, but I said no, I would stay here with the children and run the plantations. Besides, I had been to Sydney and I was very unhappy there, I had to wear gloves and corsets and there was nothing to do.

Chapter XXXI

EMMA

I came back to my beloved Samoa and I could hardly see the land for churches, each little village by the sea with a great white whale stranded in the middle of it, my friends and relations still living in their *fales* working to make money to pay a fat, lazy native pastor to live in a two-storey European house.

Our ship called first at Pango-Pango on Tutuïla, where at Albert Steinberger's request I had signed away some of my land to the Americans all those years ago, and the first thing I saw was a notice-board with 'Laws and Regulations' printed and pinned up under glass. I read it out to Paul.

'Fornication is not allowed. The punishment will be to weed the road for fifty fathoms.

'All persons must obey orders.

'No pig shall be allowed to jump a fence. Any pig caught destroying plantations shall be reported to the *pulenuu*, who will then send his policeman to the owner of the pig, and if nothing is done to prevent this pig from going on such cultivations, the pig will be killed.

'No one shall be allowed to bathe without a *lava-lava* in the bathing places.

'No person shall be allowed to be tattooed within the limits of the village.

'It is forbidden for anyone to bathe naked.

'A signal will be given on the evening of Sunday. Any one disregarding this curfew will be handed over to the magistrate for punishment.

224

'It is forbidden to use bad language to strangers.

'It is forbidden for all the green products of a village to be given away free.

'Illicit cohabitation is forbidden. The punishment will be $1.00.

'No canoe shall be loaned out free to any one, except by payment of one shilling.

'No fornication is allowed and no false accusations.

'All persons must obey orders of the leader of the choir singing and must answer when his name is called on the days specified for choir singing. Anyone breaking this order will be trusted to the magistrate for punishment.

'Illicit cohabitation according to the heathen custom is forbidden.

'It is forbidden for a man not to keep in order his banana plantation.

'It is forbidden for any man not to have a taro plantation.

'It is forbidden for any man to disobey.

'No person shall be allowed to bathe naked in the bathing place which lies alongside the Government road.

'Fornication is forbidden, and eloping according to the heathen custom.

'It is forbidden for a boy and a girl to live together according to the heathen custom.

'No woman who has no husband shall fornicate with a married man. One who does so shall be punished by being required to weed the road for 100 yards; for a second offence, 200 yards.

'It is forbidden for any one woman to fail to weed the grass on their land every Wednesday and Thursday of each week.

'It is forbidden for any person to take with him a rock for the purpose of toilet. Fine $1.00 or for any one to take a rock and throw it into the woman's side of the latrine for the purpose of splashing, or for any woman to throw a rock to the men's side of the latrine. Fine $1.00

'No limit be made as to dancing or to singing or spending of the evening by chiefs and *tulafales* in Samoan *kava* drinking he'ld in the night time; that such pleasure be allowed as each person may wish, but it must not extend beyond the hour of ten in the night. Any singing or dancing or evening pleasures shall not exceed the hour of ten—the offenders will be punished before the court.

'Courting is not allowed.

'No person shall enter into the house of the village pastor, or the Catholic teacher, without obtaining permission.

'The punishment for fornication is to weed the road for eighty yards.

'Illegal cohabitation, whether a boy or a girl, sha'll be punished by weeding the road 160 yards.

'All persons must be diligent and not idling or lazy, as such will cause a person to steal.

'No person shall be seen on the Government road after the curfew is sounded.

'It is forbidden to throw missiles at domestic animals.

'It is prohibited for food and property to be taken on the birth of a child; only rejoicing will be permitted, any person who breaks this law shall be punished by a fine not exceeding $5.00.

'It is prohibited for a person to go to church with an undershirt.

'Every person must possess a Bible.

'Courting parties are prohibited, persons must obey the Government.

'It is forbidden for any one to wade naked across a ford, or to go naked to the bathing place, but he will be quickly punished.

'Public courting of girls is prohibited.

'It is prohibited for a woman to smoke a pipe.

'No person is allowed to go pleasure walking in the night time.

'It is forbidden for any person of one family to go and eat with another family.

'It is forbidden for anyone to go courting in a house where there are girls.

'It is forbidden to fornicate.'

I read all this on the noticeboard, and then I turned to Paul and said, 'It does not say it is forbidden to throw a rock at the noticeboard', and I picked up a rock and threw it bang in the centre of the glass.

Paul was very angry with me and said that was not correct behaviour for the wife of a Prussian officer. I said it was correct behaviour for a Samoan princess.

Chapter XXXII

―――――◆―――――

NELLIE DAVIDSON

Oh yes, I remember Queen Emma coming back to Samoa, I was a young girl then, she came to see my mother Litia, she was of the Royalty-family of Tonga, my mother was Jonas Coe's last wife and I was the second of four children.

Emma and her husband Paul Kolbe, they stayed at the International Hotel, they had lots of rooms because they travelled with a secretary and two maids. I had heard Emma was very rich, but when she came to the house she was wearing a mother hubbard of that cheap material you buy at the store, and a straw hat like any woman sits making in the street, she was a big woman getting some grey hair, with this big, ugly, strong husband, and I got into trouble with my mother because I said to Emma, 'You're not a Queen and you're not rich either.' But she laughed, she was real nice with a deep laugh that come all the way up from the bottom of her guts, and she said 'My dear of course I'm not a Queen, it's a joke we have in New Guinea, but don't forget that your mother and I, we're both relatives of the kings here in Samoa and in Tonga. As for rich, well my small business made your humble servant the biggest shipper of copra this season in New Guinea, last April and July about 900 tons copra and this January about 750 tons.' 'How much is that worth?' I interrupted as I was always interested how much.

'That's about half a million marks', she said, 'about 25,000 English pounds. Then there's cotton, I'm not satisfied with the Lloyd steamers, they charge me too much freight on my cotton, so I will again turn my small business to Australia and send there direct to Cooktown in my own steamer.' Yes, she had her *own* steamers! 'We received a good price for cotton, 92 in Liverpool, with the second crop we shipped maybe 210 bales. Then there's

228

the coffee, and the tobacco, but of course our trading business is very big.' My mother, her eyes were the size of coconuts, this step-daughter who was twenty-years older than her, in this cheap dress, all the Samoans had been running to us from the hotel saying 'This relative of yours, she's not rich, she wears an old mother hubbard.' But my mother and I were doing calculations, she must be a millionaire.

She said to my mother, 'Do you like to smoke?', and she drew from her bag some tobacco and some very fine leaves to roll it in, she showed them to us and said they were leaves of a special New Guinea banana, better than the finest rice paper to roll tobacco in. She was very clever at rolling these cigars. She said the beauty of these banana leaves was that if you were in the bush and had run out of tobacco, if you rolled them on their own sufficiently thick you could get a good smoke just from them.

She had a Samoan servant with her from New Guinea, she told Mr Kolbe to bring him into the house, he had a leather case with him, she made him tip it out on the table and out came golden sovereigns, hundreds of them, and she said 'Litia, that is Emma's present for you and the children, to help with their food and clothing and schooling.' I just couldn't stop picking up those golden sovereigns, they were so heavy, and taking a whole handful and letting them slither through my fingers and make a kind of a dull knock on the table, not a tinkle like ordinary money.

But my mother Litia, she began to cry, and she said 'Emma, I thought you'd be jealous of me, your father's young wife, and my children who have been left shares in his estate.' But Emma laughed and gave her a big hug, and turned to me and said 'Nellie, always remember that jealousy is only for those who have no love for other people, and envy is only for those who have no love for themselves.'

She sat down and made herself comfortable and said 'Litia, is there any of father's Monongahela left?' (that was his special rye whisky), 'tell me about Samoan politics.' All this time she didn't take much notice of Mr Kolbe, he just seemed to stand around like a sort of a bodyguard.

Well, they started in on politics, all this arguing over titles. Old Malietoa Laupepa, who was Emma's relation, was a very weak king and a sick man too, only really ruling when the German and English warships were in harbour. The Germans had exiled him once, but brought him back again, and now they had exiled his opponent Mata'afa to the Marshall Islands, but there was Tamasese making trouble too, three all wanting to be king.

That night Emma and Mr Kolbe were going to have dinner at the German Consul's, and Emma told me to come to the hotel when she was getting dressed so I could see her clothes. Well, I went, and I saw! She had just been fooling those old LMS missionary wives, walking round in her mother hubbard, so they'd say 'Emma Coe is just a poor Samoan who went to New Guinea.' She was dressed up in gold from the top to down her legs, all sorts of little leaves of gold sewn together very clever, so when she moved it all shimmered and shook. And she had beautiful jewels and gold bracelets. She never gave me a gold bracelet, or anything. But she was very good to our mother, it was not her own mother but a step-mother.

She wanted to take me with her, she said "I'll take my little sister with me, I'll take her to Sydney and send her to school there so she can have a good education, and then she can come up and live with me in New Guinea.' I liked that idea. But my mother said 'Emma I'd like her to go but you see she's the last girl here, the eldest sister is at school in Sydney now with the Methodists, and if I get sick, who's to look after me and the little boy?' And Emma said 'It's a pity you know, she's growing up and she doesn't know anything much.' She was a great believer in lots of education. I cried because I wanted to go with her, but mother said 'No, you can't, you're needed in the house here.'

Emma stayed for weeks, she paid for a real big Samoan feast in the garden behind our house, I think the whole of Apia came, all the Samoan chiefs, and the Consuls and their wives and the Chief Justice. Mr Stevenson the writer would have come but he had died just the year before, Emma bought a lot of his furniture and took it back to New Guinea.

Often she used to sleep in our house and then go back to the hotel. I used to go every night and admire her after she was dressed up, she had a different dress for every night, and so many jewels. But she never gave me a gold bracelet.

Chapter XXXIII

COUNT RODOLPHE FESTETICS DE TOLNA

Towards the end of 1895 we were sailing in my yacht *Tolna* from Bougainville to Neu Pommern, and remained four days in St. George's Channel, held up by the absence of wind and contrary currents. There was very little water left in our casks, and I was obliged to ration it severely, which some members of the crew took with a poor spirit. But I had no alternative, having under my care fourteen souls, viz., my wife, my first officer Griffiths and his wife, the stewardess Annie, eight sailors, and the cook. Jean, my French cook, an excellent servant, had deserted at Faisi in the Solomon Islands. My other cook, who despite his name of John Frank was a Japanese, was a very disagreeable fellow. It was his fault that the water casks were empty. Everyone on board was furious with him, and I was obliged to punish him severely. Shortly after this, we were all taken with vomiting and violent pains in the bowels. He had poisoned us. Fortunately we had our medicine chest, and we took emetics. I clapped him in irons and on our arrival at Herbertshöhe I handed him over to the German authorities.

The port of Herbertshöhe is very open, not all secure, and exposed to all the winds, but it occupies a most agreeable site, contrasting with the sombre and steep coast along which we had passed. The volcano at Matupi lifted its white panache of smoke into the limpid sky, and the verdant islands, scattered here and there before the background of mountains of a violent rose, were draped in the richest of tropical vegetation. A mirage made it seem as if they hung above the water trembling in the vibrant air, like garlands of leaves poised above the sea.

The little town spread out its white buildings before us, and on a hill to the north stood a magnificent house with wide steps sweeping down to a road before the sea. Undoubtedly this was the residence of the famous Queen E . . . ., a half-caste Samoan who in Neu Pommern doubles as Mme Pompadour and a colonial Mme Humbert. I understood that she welcomed visiting ships with a salvo of guns from her terrace, but silence reigned.

A few minutes later we noticed a canoe embarking towards us. It contained all the magnificent lords of the district coming to receive us. Heavy and by no means elegant, the canoe served two uses, I imagine, and without doubt carried copra as well as exalted personages. It was fleetly propelled by naked black slaves, whose anatomy revealed the wretchedness of the rations on which they subsisted. Poor devils, whose evil fate had led them to these upstart *parvenus* of colonial power, their sunken stomachs and aching shoulders proved the truth of the words of the ancient sage: 'When necessity reduces us to bondage, the best masters are those long accustomed to opulence; but those who against all hope have achieved a happy harvest, these are aways hard, always unjust to their slaves.'

It is easier to get used to poverty than to riches, and their prosperity has not yet prompted the Germans to nourish their people, not even to nourish themselves. Their reputation on this score is well established throughout the length and breadth of the Pacific, and native women, normally proud to marry a white man, unwillingly espouse a German. From Samoa to Fiji, the girls say amongst themselves, 'You know what'll happen if you marry a German, you'll get old before your time. You'll soon have a skin like the bark of a breadfruit tree from the terrible things he'll make you eat.'

The slaves heaved with skeletal arms under a rain of blows. A thousand metres away we could hear 'Pull, monkeys, or you get stick!' for the present owners of New Britain and New Ireland have never succeeded in teaching the natives two words of German. They maltreat them in English.

The threats were instantly executed. The heaving flanks and aching shoulder-blades of the rowers, covered only with a thin skin and no flesh, resounded with a dry thud under the baton which beat them at random on head or body.

To clamber up the rope ladder and heave themselves aboard

was no small matter for my visitors. From above I assisted their feeble efforts.

One of them missed his footing on the ladder and tumbled into the water, to the great mortification of his beautiful clothes of white linen, which the frugal German ladies had omitted to iron. At last they arrived on the bridge, sweating and puffing, but safe and sound.

And now began the solemnity of presentations, there were great stiff salutes, straightenings of the back, rectifications of position, feet at right angles, head bridling up on the neck in a supposedly military style. Of these bigwigs one was Harbourmaster and Station Manager, another was a young assessor bearing himself with pretentious and ridiculous gravity. Still another was a little chemist who called himself Port Doctor, and a fourth belonged to the Neu Guinea Kompagnie, who was empowered by Berlin to fulfil administrative functions.

I invited these gentlemen down to the saloon, where we would have offered them champagne; but one look at them had tipped me off: 'No', I said softly to my wife, 'give them gin . . .'

Later, when I had time to get to know the personnel of the colony, I was able to establish that my first impressions were not mistaken.

The Germans have a phrase which absolves them from reforming the abuses of their administration of their possessions. When anyone complains of an arbitrary decision, an extortion or a deni l of justice, with transcendental indifference they take a puff on their porcelain pipe and sigh, with a shrug of the shoulders, 'It's the colonies!' For them the word 'colonies' means by definition a good time for officials, rules which don't apply to friends, the collusion of employees with rich colonists, and the exploitation of foreigners.

I soon learned how much it costs to blunder into a German colony. I knew from a reliable source that a plot existed against me at Herbertshöhe to hold me at ransom. My arrival had been announced in advance by the Australian and American papers, and by the letters awaiting me at the Poste Restante. The only problem for them was to work out how much they could make me pay. 'How much can we sting him for harbour dues.'

Oh oh, says a crafty little lawyer, he stopped in the Solomon Islands. That's forbidden to merchant ships. We can't tell the difference between a yacht and a merchant ship. We'll dig up something. You'll see!

The next day the leading dignitary of the place, Herr M... went to see his great friend, Queen E... This is the name by which a certain Frau K... is known throughout the islands. It is she who pulls all the strings of the administration, and to hold the employees of the Kompagnie and the colonial magistrates in the hollow of her hand she allows them entry to a Deer Park inhabited by beautiful Kanaka girls whose lovely eyes show they know how to accommodate any demands made upon them. Frau K..., a first rate business woman, makes these fine dispositions with the complicity of the powers that be, and is possessed of an immense fortune.

Herr M... being in rapport with Mrs K..., acquainted her with his plot against me. The amiable lady thoroughly approved the idea but thought it could do with a little tightening up.

'You must have something to pin on the Captain,' she suggested, 'and then he'll have to pay us whatever we want . . . He'll be happy to get out so cheaply . . . You are shortly leaving for the Solomon Islands . . . Find out something wrong that he did there . . . The traders and the natives will say anything you want them to. How will he be able to defend himself? . . . And now, don't I have property there myself? . . . In return for all I do for you, my dear, just lay down some firm boundaries for my estate. The Kanakas are invading us . . . Just push them back a little. Those people will settle anywhere. It's all the same to them if it's somewhere a bit further away . . . Don't forget, will you? . . . I like everything to be done correctly . . . A little enlargement of the property wouldn't hurt; I have four thousand coconuts to plant this season . . .'

'*Au revoir*, my Queen,' says Herr M..., bowing, 'your orders will be attended to.'

'Ah, Herr M..., don't forget a nice dress for E...! Christmas is nearly here . . . She loves you so much, poor E...! Goodbye, but not for long . . . You won't forget to restrain those villains of Kanakas who are invading me... *Au revoir*, my dear, and *bon voyage!*'

234

This Queen E..., who speaks of herself in the third person with an infantile prettiness, is, it appears, of royal blood. She has been established for many years in New Britain, and I am told she derived vast profits from the colony of Nouvelle France at Port-Breton. Frau K... was at that time Mrs Farrell, and she knew the whole region intimately, and she could have saved many of the colonists by enabling them to leave their bay of death and settle in some more fortunate bay or island. But she and her husband kept them confined and let these unhappy people die of hunger and fever, watching their agony from afar so as to be able to take over all the possessions and equipment they had brought from France.

Being a conscientious traveller, I wanted to meet Frau K..., and had the honour of being presented to her. And how would I have been able to escape the obligation of laying my homage at her feet?

I saw at her house all the furniture and objects which came from the colony, which she made no attempt to hide.

'What a handsome sideboard you have there,' I said.

'That's the altar of the cathedral of the Marquis de Rays' colony,' she replied. 'I bought all their effects.'

With that joy in pillage and sacrilege that distinguishes women of her type, she had amused herself by turning the tabernacle into a cupboard for drinks.

I spoke about this altar to Monsignor Couppé, the bishop of the French mission, telling him how shocking I found it for his religion and his country to leave this altar in such a place; he replied that it pained him too; but he did not know how to redeem it from Frau K... I offered my services as intermediary.

'Why don't you sell this to some church?' I asked her when I returned to her house, 'You'd get a good price for it.'

'I'd certainly get a good price for it,' she replied, 'but never for a church. Nothing of mine will ever go into a church....'

It was not only the altar which was profaned. How many family treasures piously preserved from generation to generation, were stranded in Frau K...'s house. Miniatures of ladies with their hair in bows and leg of mutton sleeves, and gentlemen dressed in the style of the 1820s, with high necks and smooth shoulders; tapestry screens, worked by a great-aunt at the time of the Restoration; footstools of faded embroidery, samplers, ancestral silver sugar-bowls, clocks set in a bust of Minerva, little round tables in Louis XV style made at the time of Louis-Philippe, pins encrusted with yellow pearls, boxes made of shells, souvenirs of a holiday trip by train to the seaside, wedding presents of wood from the islands, chimney-piece ornaments evocative of a bourgeois pro-vincial *salon*, trinkets and what-nots whose touching and anti-quated ugliness has disarmed bailiffs and survived seizures! . . . The emigrants had transported them 4,500 leagues from France like household gods which would recall to them their homeland in the new land the Marquis de Rays had made for them! . . . All of these are in the corners, the servants' rooms or the attics of Frau K . . .'s house, for her taste is too good for her to wish them in her *salon*.

I must describe her. She is of slightly more than average height and wears her long hair coiled above her head. Her round and generous features are unmistakeably Polynesian, but have a Euro-pean shrewdness and intelligence. By day she wears a long white dress of simplicity but elegance, in the evening a Parisian gown and jewels display her fine shoulders and bosom. Although of a certain age, she is not, as in Byron's jest, certainly aged. She looks you in the eye as if assessing your virility.

She is married for the second time to the manager of her properties, a gentleman of formal bearing and correct dress who gives himself the airs of a man of the world. She rules him with a rod like her slaves, but at times he has flutterings of revolt.

One day, I found him with his arm bandaged up. 'What have you done to yourself, Herr K . . .,' I sympathetically asked him.

'I was bitten by one of the blacks,' he replied 'and as a result blood-poisoning has set in.'

Someone to whom I repeated the story commented, 'If he'd said he'd been bitten by a black woman, he'd have been telling the truth; it was Frau K . . . that bit him. . . .'

The elegant Frau K . . . who sets the fashion for all the ladies of Neu Pommern and Neu Mecklenburg, has the naughty habit of getting tipsy at the end of the evening. In these moments she will not suffer contradiction, and on one occasion when her husband permitted himself a comment on this, she immediately sank the teeth of a cannibal princess into his arm . . . I was told that on another occasion when she was on board a steamer visiting the islands, in a bizarre fit of anger she tore off all her elegant clothes, and leaping over the railings dived into the sea, swam to shore and returned stark naked and streaming with water to her sumptuous villa.

These little happenings scarcely worthy of history, but not to be disdained by the authors of memoirs, seemed to me worthy of setting down, to give an accurate picture of the doings of colonial society in the Pacific.

I left the *Tolna* only two days in the port of Herbertshöhe and then anchored at Matupi, in a charming bay which opened to the right onto the bare cone of the volcano. To our left, a pretty village was half hidden in the foliage of coconut palms, and the high outline of the German cruiser *Möwe* detached itself from the velvety verdure of a little island.

The officers of the German navy had nothing in common with the colonial administrators, and the Captain of the *Möwe* sent a long-boat to offer me his services, in case of need. The local agent of Hernsheim and Co., Herr Thiel, also came aboard with all his boys to offer us help. He is a charming man, who immediately invited us to his New Year's Eve party, (it was the 30th December).

He took us to his delightful house, situated on a rise over the sea and furnished in European style, where he was making preparations for his party.

I accepted his invitation and with him celebrated the arrival of 1896. All of Herbertshöhe was there, including the beautiful Frau K . . ., who on no account could one omit to invite, with a flying squadron of her young *protégées*. The food, as well prepared as if we had been in Europe, was served by black servants in elegant livery. It was a strange feeling, in the midst of the sparkling of crystal, silver and the lights of diamonds; before the table strewn with pink orchids and laden with all the refinements of a sophisticated cuisine; in the midst of conversations where one talked of art and literature, to remember that we were in the land of the cannibals and that for hundreds of miles around us, in the inaccessible jungle, human beings with hair whitened with chalk and faces zebra-striped with coloured tattooing were crouched in their huts of smokey boughs. While I chatted with the lady next

237

to me, educated at a boarding-school in Sydney, I remembered my vigils with my friends the head-hunters; I saw again the bound captives behind the trees, the chanting savages, lying on the white beach in the flickering light of the flames of a great fire, which drew the crabs out of their hiding places. . . .

The house and gardens were illuminated by a multitude of little glass lamps of different colours and shapes, imitating flowers. Their ropes and clusters hung down to the sea, casting their multi-coloured lights onto its phosphorescence, running over the waves.

The night was warm and langourous. For me it was an evocation of enchanted evenings in Hawaii and Tahiti.

Illuminated balloons glowed amongst the trees like fantastic fruits of red and blue flesh, around which danced huge moths and yellow fireflies. The perfume of mimosa and orange-blossom was distilled under the arches of palm-trees. The girls in the *salon* whirled to the sounds of the orchestra, which echoed in the sonorous air down to the port and back. At Herbertshöhe the war-ship *Falke* shot off fireworks, whose explosions sounded from afar over the promontories of the bay.

Our happy stay with Herr Thiel was marred by a tiresome incident. One morning I received an order to present myself before the judges at Herbertshöhe to answer the accusation of having sold guns and ammunition to the savages. This was the fulfilment of a plot by Frau K . . . and her friends. My yacht was searched. They did not find anything suspicious, but the Germans did not intend to let that deter them. They bore me malice, as I have already said, for having penetrated regions of their islands where their natural circumspection does not allow anyone to venture, and they were aware that I had won the favours of the chiefs and savage kings, to the point of obtaining for my collections items of which the professors sent by the Berlin Museum could only have copies made.

By fomenting a strike amongst my crew, and by playing on the jealousies aroused by the transference of Annie the stewardess' affections from my second officer Mossly to my first officer Griffith, and the affair between that Abigail Mrs Griffiths and a trader at Bougainville, the Germans extracted false witness that I had sold arms to the savages. They also dragged up the affair of my complicity with the writer R. L. Stevenson in Samoa, in our attempt to rescue the former King, Mata'afa, from Jaluit in the Marshall Islands, where he had been exiled by the Germans. Unfortunately for me, the Governor of Jaluit happened by evil chance to be in Herbertshöhe at the same time as myself, and he had not forgiven me for the insomnia I had caused him. He spoke of me in terms of a traitor and a State criminal who should be thrust into a dungeon! . . . Happily Frau K . . ., who did not lose her head, calmed their roused passions and reminded them that it was my purse and not my liberty which was of use to them. I came to terms with them by the payment of several thousand marks.

Herr Thiel gave another party for our departure: dinner, ball, illuminations. The evening was distinguished by a misadventure of which the victim was my persecutress, Frau K . . . . There is justice in heaven, even if there is none at Herbertshöhe! . . .

While everyone was dancing, Frau K . . . retired for a moment to the room available to the ladies, to satisfy a slight need; but the fragile porcelain on which she was seated broke under her weight, and suddenly her frightened cries caused consternation in the *salons*. Everyone rushed into the room to offer help . . . *Lugete, veneres* . . . Fragments of the urn were encrusted in the most intimate portion of her flesh, and no one knew how to extract them. The only pharmacologist of the colony was unhappily not amongst those invited, and the patient could not wait while he was fetched from Herbertshöhe. Men of good will had to come to the rescue. The bespectacled Germans, without setting aside their dignity, continued to stoop to frequent operations on the opulent carnation which under this rough ministration was reduced to a shuddering jelly.

It was a subject to inspire the burlesque muse of a Berni:

Piangete, destri, il caso orrendo e fiero,
Piangete, cantarelli e voi pitali . . .

(Weep, all you who wake, this horrendous, violent accident, Weep, you singers and you chamber-pots . . .)

We left Matupi, to anchor at Mioko, in the Duke of York Islands, where we were the guests of Herr Schulze, manager of a big German business. Here we came upon a souvenir from Frau K . . .'s past. Here were unrolled the last scenes of the drama of Port-Breton. Here we saw the grave of Captain Rabardy, captain of the *Génil* and acting Governor of Port-Breton, who died in the house of Mr Farrell, the former husband of Frau K...

The inventory of the dead man's effects was not held until three weeks after his decease. Mr Farrell, who held his keys, refused to deliver them any sooner. On the day of the inventory, to everyone's astonishment, there was nothing there. Among the belongings of this Captain, who was a cunning trader in tortoise-shell who had even sold it to Farrell himself, not a penny was found, not even a money-bag! . . . Mr Farrell was asked if Rabardy's funds were not perhaps in the sea-chest which had been carried ashore on the day of his death. 'The chest,' replied the trader, 'contained only some necklaces of glass beads and playthings belonging to his girl Tani.' The incident was officially closed by this declaration.

When Mr Farrell died, he left everything to his wife, the present Frau K... There are those who do not scruple to say that the contents of Captain Rabardy's sea-chest formed the cash basis of Frau K...'s immense fortune.

Chapter XXXIV

———————•———————

DR ALBERT HAHL

Herbertshöhe,
Neu Pommern

21 November 1897

Etta my dear,

You will be thinking it is not loving of a brother not to have
written to his dear sister for six months, but since my appointment as Imperial Judge last year I have been travelling incessantly
around the Islands in the Government yacht *Seestern*, and endeavouring to bring some order into the chaos of land claims and
purchases by which many of the poor natives have unknowingly
rendered themselves liable to be thrown off their ancestral (if the
word may be used) lands.

By far the largest landholder is my old friend Queen Emma
(who trades as E. E. Forsayth and Co.) with whom I have had
many a skirmish, and will have more. She has well-substantiated
claims to many hundreds of thousands of hectares in Neu
Pommern and Neu Mecklenberg, not to mention 100,000 hectares in Bougainville and whole groups of islands such as the
Feads and the Mortlocks.

I will now tell you about social life in the Bismarck Archipelago, as it is unique, and would vastly interest and entertain
you, especially you who are so involved with the dubious cause of
the emancipation of women. Could you see the conditions of life
of the native women here, you and your European sisters would
rest content for the remainder of your days with the freedom
you already have! It is clear Goethe had never visited New Guinea
when he wrote '*Das Ewig-Weibliche zieht uns an*', otherwise he
would not have written 'The eternal feminine draws us on', but

'The female is eternally driven on', when he saw these little beasts of burden stumbling under their huge loads as their lords and masters stroll behind scratching themselves.

At the other end of the social scale here, all is very, very different. When I came here I found that the centre of social (and indeed commercial) life in the Bismark Archipelago was not at the coaling station at Matupi nor at the seat of government, Herbertshöhe, but at Ralum plantation and Mrs Forsayth's house at Gunantambu and Mrs Parkinson's house at Kuradui. You are of course familiar with Richard Parkinson's book on the Bismarck Archipelago published in Leipzig in 1887; he is now at work on a massive volume of ethnographical and botanical studies of New Guinea life. He is a civilized and deeply learned man (I am told, of irregular but noble, even royal, parentage) and a veritable pearl to find in the jungles of New Guinea. I spend many enjoyable hours in his company.

But he is not the power in the land. The ladies play the dominant roles. Emma with justice is called *Königin*, a name given her in jest by Hernsheim the trader many years ago. Not only does she rule her commercial empire with total authority, but her extraordinary hospitality at Gunantambu makes her the Queen of this whole area of the Pacific. No ship would enter these waters without calling at Ralum. There is an amusing protocol to be observed with visiting ships. She has several old guns from the Marquis de Rays' lamentable expedition mounted on either side of the steps which lead down from her house to the road. If the Captain of the visiting ship meets with her favour, she has a couple of cannon fired as a signal that he and his officers are welcome at Gunantambu. Should, however, the Captain have incurred her wrath, no gun is fired, and woe betide the foolish man who ignores this hint. When the Administrator gives a dinner, she sits on his right hand. (Incidentally I have not told you the sad news that Kurt von Hagen was murdered by natives. To my disappointment, Skopnik, a very dull fellow, was appointed his successor as Administrator, and not myself. But in many ways I can be more useful as Judge.)

Now Queen Emma is a half-caste Samoan whose life has been adventurous, to say the least. Imagine the difficulties attendant on a half-caste, and a *woman*, reaching her position of wealth and power. But she is also a woman of the deepest respect for culture and education, and the finest lady in Berlin could not be a more stimulating partner in conversation. Fortunately, as you know, my English is near-perfect, as she pretends not to understand German, thus, like deaf people, hearing a lot she is not meant to. From my residence in Samoa I am familiar with her background. On her mother's side she is connected to King Malietoa Laupepa's family; her father was Jonas Coe, the U.S. Consul at Apia.

In Samoan style, she likes to have her family around her, and she has imported large numbers of brothers, sisters, nieces and nephews. By far the most remarkable is Mrs Parkinson, her full sister Phebe, who is some thirteen years younger than her. A beautiful and virtuous woman, she knows more about the natives of the Archipelago than anyone; I call her Queen Emma's 'Minister for Native Affairs.' I seek her advice constantly. She is endlessly helpful and good-natured. She has seven children living, of whom the two elder daughters are beauties, Louisa being seventeen and Nellie fourteen, very high-spirited and independent girls. I will confess to you alone, my dear sister, that I would dearly love to make Louisa my wife, but I fear my suit will not be successful.

I said Phebe was virtuous. Once again for your ears alone, I will hint to you that Emma is not. She is married now to a headstrong and violent Prussian officer, Paul Kolbe, of whom more later, but has led a very irregular life. Old Hernsheim, who knew her for twenty years, told me that she rivalled the Czarina Elizabeth in prodigies of drinking and love-making. Yet the claws of debauchery have left not a scar on her glowing face. She claims jestingly that she is so well preserved because she drinks almost nothing but champagne (she has an occasional fondness for American whisky), and that love-making is good for the skin. She is very frank in her speech. Her entertainments at Gunantambu are truly royal, sometimes lasting a week or more. Although great quantities of wine are drunk, and her many exceedingly attractive young lady relations are what you might call accessible, you must not suppose there is any presence of disorder at Gunantambu. She has the authority to bring troublemakers immediately into line.

Her influence extends far beyond the Bismarck Archipelago. Not so long ago we were visited by a large yacht belonging to a Hungarian, a Count of the Austro-Hungarian Empire bearing the odd name of Festetics de Tolna. He had spent some time cruising around the Solomon Islands and Bougainville, amongst other things amassing a large collection of native carvings and weapons and artefacts which I believe is intended for the Budapest Museum. In the course of his wanderings he had anchored at one of Queen Emma's islands, and not only had he illegally exchanged arms with the natives for artefacts, but it appears that the domestic life of her trader there, a man she had married off, in her regal way, to one of her half-caste Samoans, had been thrown into turmoil by the passion which the trader developed for the wife of Count Festetics' first officer, who has in fact remained on the island with the trader.

All these goings-on were communicated to Queen Emma long before the arrival of the Count. By then I also had intelligence that in Samoa he had been mixed up with Robert Louis Stevenson and the Mata-afa affair. When the Count's splendid yacht anchored off Herbertshöhe Emma did not accord him the salute of friendship, her usual invitation to visiting Captains, the firing of the guns outside Gunantambu. The Count, his Hungarian dignity (which was of the seam-bursting type) mortally offended, made the mistake of being rude to her, and as a result he was not made welcome at Gunantambu. Since he was obliged to spend nearly three months here, as most of his crew had deserted, he must have spent many an unhappy hour looking up to Gunantambu and hearing the sounds of revelry across the water. He turned up at Thiel's New Year's Eve party at Matupi in the most amazing uniform covered with decorations. He was a simple, boyish creature, really; his wife was the daughter of an American millionaire.

When I arrived at Herbertshöhe I found to my intense embarrassment that I had inherited a case of criminal proceedings against Captain Kolbe, brought by the former Administrator, Schmiele, whom he had horsewhipped (and I think with moral if not legal justice). I was obliged to convict him, but I have written to Berlin to urge a pardon for this man, in particular with regard to Emma, his wife, as well as for the peace of our society, and also in the interest of the undisturbed continuance of all cultural development in this small colony. I found that there had been a movement, inaugurated by Schmiele (and of course reinforced by my own verdict on Kolbe), to insulate German officers and officials from the Samoan circle centred at Ralum. On racial grounds this would be intolerable under any circumstances; if we are to build successful colonies in the Pacific whether in Samoa or here, we must draw no distinctions between white, brown, black or half-caste. Education and ability alone must be our standards. On social grounds any attempt to boycott Ralum is equally intolerable. The houses in Herbertshöhe are much too small to be made the centre of social activities, but much more important, Gunantambu is long established as the place where our officers have been able to enjoy the hospitality of the Forsayth and Parkinson families. Any disruption of these visits would be most hurtful to our naval personnel.

Moreover the large plantations as well as the trading activities of Mrs Kolbe are of the greatest advantage for the development of the colony. Her relatives and in particular the growing number of half-castes of various racial mixtures will inevitably remain as settlers in this colony. I would wish that this energetic woman, Queen Emma, who is the head of a large undertaking, be allowed to move freely in our society and without any social impediment. She also, with her American connections, is very useful in off-setting the English influence in society here, which springs from the Methodist mission, which gets its funds from Australia. The famous George Brown, the first white man to live in these regions founded the Methodist mission in the Duke of York Islands. His successors are not of his calibre, but because of his pioneering work they have a prestigious place in the colony, which they are not above exploiting. Besides they talk English, and I have made arrangements with Methodist headquarters in Sydney to send German-speaking priests, of which there are some to be had in South Australia.

To return to the Kolbes, Mr Kolbe has, I think, learned his lesson. It is doubtful whether he will ever be able completely to master his hot-blooded temperament and rash speech, but his personal behaviour has always been absolutely correct.

Outside the social area, I conceive my main duty here to lie in the protection of the interests of the natives. The early settlers, Queen Emma included, developed certain authoritarian, even tyrannical attitudes. The greater the distance from the seat of government, the more inclined were they to resort to club-law in their relations with the natives. Hence, in part the large number of traders and missionaries murdered around these Islands. The basis of my policy (unlike that of the British) will be (1) The protection of native lands, (2) the appointment of village 'chiefs', and (3) the drawing of the natives more and more into the commercial economy.

To give you an example, last year Queen Emma wished to plant 500 hectares with coconuts and expel 478 natives from the lands. I prevailed upon her not to proceed with the planting, and she and the Kompagnie and Mouton have agreed to abide by their earlier pledge to leave the natives the unimpeded use of the land they occupy. But I suspect that, while it is not legally binding, they will stick to the old 1887 land ordinance which lets them ride rough-shod over the native lands. I am drafting a new land ordinance which will put a complete ban on the alienation of occupied native land.

In the meantime I am also needling Queen Emma and the other planters over their treatment of recruited labourers. Recently I fined her fifty marks (the price of a bottle of French champagne!) for failing to supply her plantation workers with the prescribed rations (500 grammes rice, 1500 grammes yams daily, plus a weekly issue of 750 grammes meat, 60 grammes tobacco, and 1 pipe), and for retaining some of her workers after the expiration of their three-year contracts. She of course has appealed against the decision.

This and other cases in no way disrupt my friendship with her and the Parkinsons, in fact their houses are my second home. As an example I am due for dinner at Gunantambu tonight. Emma has also invited Bishop Couppé, and has promised a discussion of the latest book she has read by that strange fellow Friedrich Nietzsche, *Also Sprach Zarathustra*. She says she feels a mighty accord with his contempt for Christianity, as I foresee a lusty battle between her and the Bishop, with myself as Judge endeavouring not to deliver a verdict.

246

In any case, all differences will afterwards be healed by music. I have not told you that Queen Emma is an accomplished pianist, and Richard Parkinson plays the violin with real authority. I myself have taken up my flute again, though my fingers are almost as stiff as an English Methodist lady pouring tea.

With my fondest greetings, my dear Sister,

I remain,

Your devoted brother

Albert.

Chapter XXXV

MRS ANSTRUTHER-PURDAM

It was early in 1909 that I went to German New Guinea to see if the Germans were making as big a mess of their Colony as the Australians said they were. As an Englishwoman I·would naturally never believe an Australian, but as a fighter for women's suffrage I am well aware that South Australia gave women both the franchise and the right to sit in parliament in 1894, a lead followed by the Commonwealth of Australia in 1902, whereas three years later England was throwing Christabel Pankhurst and Annie Kenney down the Manchester Town Hall stairs, preparatory to casting them into prison.

I was confirmed in my resolve to brave fever, cannibals and Germans by hearing in Sydney that the real ruler of German New Guinea is a *woman*, a Samoan-American half-caste known throughout the Pacific as Queen Emma. Her sister, Mrs Parkinson, is also a very remarkable woman, and helps manage her sister's vast enterprises, which are known as E. E. Forsayth & Co., the headquarters being at Ralum.

To introduce German New Guinea, I cannot do better than quote from the brand-new 'Lloyd' Guide.

TRAVELLING AND EXTERNAL COMMUNICATION

A regular six-weekly communication with the Protectorate either way is kept up by a newly inaugurated line of steamers of the Norddeutscher Lloyd, trading between Australia and Asia, the nearest port of call on each continent being Brisbane and Hongkong respectively. (Vide Company's time table.)

A regular inter-island service has also been established, the Norddeutscher Lloyd steamer *Sumatra*, plying at monthly intervals between the principal islands of the Archipelago and the Northern Solomons, while a small steamer of the New Guinea

Co., and schooners of the different trading firms further effect a more or less regular communication between the islands and the mainland of New Guinea. The Government yacht *Seestern* also makes periodical tours to the different parts of the Possession, and intending passengers (subject to the sanction of the authorities) may avail themselves of that opportunity on payment of certain fixed charges.

The primitive conditions of civilization obtaining throughout the Possession, and the wild nature of the country, precludes touring in the ordinary sense of the word, with the exception of in the immediate neighborhood of the settlements. If longer overland tours are contemplated, local advice should be procured for the details of the expedition. Natives to act as carriers, as well as interpreters, can be obtained through the medium of any one of the trading or plantation firms, for a wage of about sixpence per day and their food.

Trade goods, which may be necessary for the purpose of purchasing food and as presents, should also be procured on the spot, where the requirements of the natives are best known.

HERBERTSHÖHE

Herbertshöhe, the seat of supreme Government of the German Possessions in the Western and Northern Pacific, is most picturesquely situated on the shores of Blanche Bay on the northern end of Neu Pommern in (approximately) 152° 15E. longitude and 4° 20S. latitude. It is the most important commercial centre of the Protectorate, several of the principal trading firms making it their headquarters. For the visitor it has a more than usual interest as it affords him an opportunity of seeing some of the best coconut plantations in the Pacific, among which the Ralum Plantation, already mentioned, is especially notable. Coffee, capok and cotton may also be seen growing.

The climate of Herbertshöhe resembles that of other parts of the Archipelago, but malaria fever is less prevalent here than elsewhere, and when it occurs seems to be of a milder form.

On arrival the vessel anchors about half a mile from shore in the spacious Blanche Bay, which is sheltered on the west by a projecting point of the Gazelle Peninsula, and on the north and east by the islands of Neu Lauenburg and Neu Mecklenburg. The roadstead, though otherwise excellent, is however exposed to the north-west, and it is projected to transfer the port of entry to Simpsonhafen, a completely land-locked and spacious harbour a few miles further to the westward.

The Shore is reached by means of the ship's boat which plies to and fro for the convenience of passengers.

There are two hotels at Herbertshöhe, the "Hotel Fürst Bismarck", and the "Hotel Deutscher Hof", the former being connected with the trading firm E. E. Forsayth, and the latter with the New Guinea Company.

The tariff at the "Hotel Fürst Bismarck" which is situated close to the landing pier and near the Government buildings is from 5 M. per day for room only, and from 10 M. with full board. 50 M. is charged per week, and 180 M. for monthly boarders.

The buildings of the settlement, excepting the private residences of the officials and Europeans engaged in trade or other pursuits, comprise in the order named from west to east, the stores of Messrs. E. E. Forsayth, the Government buildings, the stores of the New Guinea Company, and M. Mouton, and the large Catholic Convent of the Sacred Heart Mission, which, situated on an eminence some little distance to the left of the landing pier, looks like a little township in itself. All houses are built of weatherboard, and are surrounded by broad verandahs, and the effect produced by their pure white color standing out prominently from the dark green background of the hills, is charming.

EXCURSIONS

Though there are no natives in the immediate neighborhood of the settlement to attract the tourist, visits to the different plantations will be found to be interesting. A twenty minutes' walk to the Catholic Convent, where visitors are always made welcome, and where an opportunity is afforded of witnessing the effect of civilisation on native children, should not be omitted, the road leading through the plantation of the New Guinea Co.

For longer excursions conveyances are necessary. Buggies (seating two persons) may be hired at the hotel, the charge being 3 M. per hour, but cheaper arrangements can be made if the vehicle is required for the day. Saddle horses are charged for at the rate of 15 M. per day, or 10 M. for the half day.

A steam launch seating ten persons, can be hired for excursions at the rate of 75 M. per day. A drive through the Ralum Plantation, which extends to a considerable distance inland and along the coast to the westward, will prove a most pleasant experience. The roads are good and suitable for driving. The road to the Wesleyan Mission at Raluana (distance about one hour by buggy), where Fijian and Samoan teachers may be seen at work, also leads partly through coconut plantations.

A longer but most charming drive is that to Toma, a fort on the Varzin Mountain beyond the settlement. This military outpost, which is manned by the native armed constabulary under the supervision of a European, was established after the massacre of the wife and children of a planter, in 1902. The climate at Toma, which lies at a considerable elevation, is more bracing than that of the coast, and is said to be free from malaria. It is expected that a sanatorium will be erected there as soon as practicable.

On the way to Toma the great banyan tree at Bita Rebareba, where cannibal orgies were formerly held, is passed.

Launch trips can be arranged to the island of Kabakon, where a vegetarian colony—as yet consisting of only a few members —has been established, or to Mioko, another island of the Neu Lauenburg Group, a distance of about 14 miles from Herbertshöhe. At Mioko, which has a most charming little harbour, a station of the Wesleyan Mission, and a branch of the principal trading and plantation firm of Samoa (Deutsche Handels—and Plantagen-Gesellschaft), are established, and numerous native villages may be seen. There is also a fine coral grotto with an entrance both from the sea and the shore.

On calm days the coral reefs with their great variety of form and color, should also be visited if time permits.'

On arrival at Herbertshöhe I installed myself in surprising comfort in the Prince Bismarck Hotel, a handsome two-storey building with ornate carved balconies and towers at each corner, built and owned by Queen Emma. The dining-room opened into a big *Trinkhalle* where the Germans satisfied a thirst for beer even more prodigious than that of the Australians. There was every comfort in the hotel, fresh milk and meat and ice. It stands above lawns and gardens and a hibiscus hedge along the fine road which runs to neighbouring Gunantambu, Queen Emma's imposing house, and the many buildings of her capital, as it were, at Ralum. A magnificent flight of stone steps runs from her house down the hill-side to the road, reminding me of the huge steps in the Campo Santo in Genoa.

A few days in German New Guinea were enough to convince me that the British dislike of the Germans as colonists is based on the ignoble motives of jealousy and envy. We own the world's greatest Empire, and therefore consider no one else is entitled even to a little empire. We are notorious bumblers and therefore we resent German efficiency. What comparable British Colony could boast the roads of Neu Pommern, or the thoroughness with which the Governor, Dr Hahl, had gone into the question of native land rights, or the ethnographic and botanical and zoo-logical collections that have gone to the museums of Hamburg or Berlin? But the chief British calumny is 'The Germans are cruel colonists.' We cherish the myth that we are a kindly and just people—we, who gave the world the English Public School! It is the products of these schools who man our Empire, and it is we who read with pleasure in the *Times* newspaper that in a skirmish in some colony 'there were no casualties', meaning that only a hundred or so natives were killed and no British soldiers. We are a nation of hypocrites, so accustomed to our own brand of cruelty that we do not notice it.

The Germans are firm but just, and the natives know where they are. Corporal punishment on plantations is allowed, but must be registered in a book which is inspected at regular inter-vals. This seems to me better than the furtive and random disci-plinary cruelties practised in British Colonies I have visited. I asked various Kanakas what they thought of the Germans, and in that jargon known as Pidgin-English their reply was always the same, with a smile, 'German number one strong fella.' Inci-dentally, although I am sure the expression is well known, I enjoyed the description one of Queen Emma's Kanakas gave of her piano, 'Missus have one fellow big box, she fight him, he cry!'

The Imperial Government took over the administration in 1899 from the New Guinea Kompagnie, and the present Governor is Dr Hahl, a man of culture who speaks excellent English. He has also taken the trouble to learn some of the multitudinous local languages, and has been all around the far-flung islands in the Government yacht, *Seestern*.

He was the Judge before he became Governor, and I heard an amusing story of him and Queen Emma in the days when he took the Court in Herbertshöhe. Amongst the many half-Samoan relations Queen Emma had brought over to Gunantambu was one very pretty girl who was even wilder than most. Queen Emma's 'girls' are famous throughout the Pacific, and though not of easy virtue they are gay companions and much sought after, and many have made good marriages. This girl, who to save embarrassment I will call Gloria, was too wild even for Emma, who finally ordered her to marry (her word is law) a hideously ugly European who had lost a hand and half his face, including an eye in a dynamite explosion. He was in fact, a survivor of the infamous Marquis de Rays expedition, who had escaped from Port-Breton and had been taken in by a New Ireland tribe because of his prowess with dynamite. She promised to set the pair up on a plantation in New Ireland, that is now called Neu Mecklenburg. As the European was heavily in debt to E. E. Forsayth and Co., and Gloria had no alternative, they both accepted the offer.

Some time later, the girl brought an action against Queen Emma, claiming more land. On the day the case came up, a buggy was observed passing Gunantambu on the way to the Herbertshöhe courthouse. Queen Emma always kept a telescope at the ready on her verandah, and she examined the passengers in the buggy, who were Gloria and a servant. Gloria was magnificently attired in a white frock with balloon sleeves, with a full bosom accentuated by a frill, a high-collar neckline, black shiny shoes and a huge round straw hat stuck with feathers.

She kept herself cool with a red sunshade and a yellow fan.

Half an hour later Dr Hahl entered the court, to find Gloria and her servant (dressed in a white mother hubbard) seated in splendour, but no defendant. The court was crowded. After a minute or two Queen Emma's carriage drew up at the door.

She entered, followed by her black Buka maid. By the time they had taken their seats the assembly in the court house had moved from stunned silence to laughter, while Dr Hahl endeavoured to keep a straight face. Queen Emma was wearing a mother hubbard. Her black Buka girl was dressed exactly as Gloria, even to the white gloves and the huge hat. The only difference was that instead of shiny black shoes she wore a great black pair of seaboots.

Queen Emma meanwhile kept a straight face, and Dr Hahl was fortunate in being able to dismiss the case very quickly before the whole population of Herbertshöhe arrived in his court.

Having heard this story, I was prepared for the slightly mocking glint in the eye of the majestic lady I finally met in the central room of her spacious and splendidly furnished residence. I think she had no particular love for middle-aged English ladies (I was in my early thirties and she must have been at least twenty years older than me). But as we talked, and I did not make conventional replies to the subjects introduced by her lively mind, we soon became friends. She was going grey, and was somewhat fat, and in some indefinable way did not really look well, but still a handsome woman with a fine carriage. Her husband, Captain Kolbe, was away in Sydney. She was worth listening to on all aspects of island life, and indeed on general subjects of history, politics and morals. She berated the Australians for their 'White Australia Policy', and I fully supported her sentiments. She wanted to know the latest news of Mrs Pankhurst and the fight for woman's suffrage. The subject made her think of something, and she said 'You should have called on His Excellency before me.'

'But you are the oldest resident, I think,' was my reply. It seemed that notwithstanding my failure in complying with the usual etiquette, she was not displeased at the priority of my visit. She and Dr Hahl were on the best of terms, and it was at her house that I had the first of many meetings with him. When he made his initial appearance, I at once felt I should like him. Honest, genial, inclined to be friendly, he began at once to speak in excellent English, and we immediately carried on an animated conversation. He was of middle height, scarcely forty, inclining to be stout, but exceedingly active; in fact, he seemed to carry with him an atmosphere of latent strength. Though he had at different times had severe illnesses—even that disease nearly always fatal to Europeans in these parts—the black-water sickness —he was now used to the extreme heat.

Queen Emma in our meetings spoke at length on her plantations, her far-flung islands, her fleet of ships, the twelve hundred 'boys' she employs, and her attempts to increase and improve the population on some of the islands such as the Feads and the Mortlocks. I commented on the all-prevailing ringworm. 'It comes from poor blood,' she said. 'Some say it is the result of centuries of cannibalism, but I don't think so, and I will tell you why. I know sometimes I have cured some very bad cases by just seeing that they had regular meals and plenty of nourishing food, yams, taro, just what they are accustomed to.' Then she proceeded thoughtfully, 'I don't deny sometimes they get so diseased you can do nothing for them, then the best is that they should die out as soon as possible.'

We became very friendly. Often we would sit in the little

'Samoan house' down on the edge of the cliff, where Queen
Emma liked to write her letters, and one of the boys would bring
us a dish of pineapple and a decanter of port wine before lunch.
Sometimes we would walk through the orchard at the back of the
house, where there were mangoes, pawpaws, granadillos, oranges,
lemons, bananas, breadfruit, alligator pears, sour sop, and all sorts
of nuts. Inside the house everything was done by the little black
maries, orphans saved from slavery by Queen Emma, all beautifully dressed in white. They were very clean, always bathing in the
sea and rubbing themselves down with lemon juice, or standing
under the running water spouts in the rain, their hair was close-
cropped and they wore a *lava-lava* and blouse, with necklaces of
beads or animal's teeth. They had tiny round slender arms and
little hands like bird-claws. There were garlands of flowers on the
dining room table, and also around the headrails of the beds,
and the whole house was scented with lemon and flowers, the
one sharpening the tropical lushness of the other.

Our conversation was uninhibited. We talked of men. I told
her that in my opinion their understanding of women is on all
fours with the ordinary Anglican curate's knowledge of proto-
plasm. It simply does not exist. That women revolt at the idea
of being his chattels any longer amazes him! What does the
average man care about the better side of women? The only thing
he wants of them is to contribute to his wealth, to pander to his
selfishness.

She told me that this was because women were such weak and
underconfident creatures. They were victims of a dependence that
in secret most of them cherished. She said that money is the only
thing that can make a woman independent, not voting rights.
Beauty and intelligence can give a woman power but it is a
power dependent on man. Wealth needs no man's admiration.
(I am told she once had an argument with her husband, Captain
Kolbe, over the purchase of a group of islands. 'You must not
buy them', he said. 'Be quiet, Paul,' she interrupted, 'I bought
you.')

She told me that she had loved only two men, apart from her
father, an American, Colonel Steinberger, and a Dalmatian sailor
by the name of Stalio. Captain Stalio was employed by her, but
her wealth meant nothing to him. I asked her had she considered

marrying him. No, she said, she loved him too much to marry him. She had seen her father's wives (of which there were many) put away one after the other, sent home to their villages, to make way for a new, pretty, young one. 'There must be independence, even in love.'

I asked her were these wives of her father's willing victims? Victims of a dependence that in secret they cherished?

She laughed and said 'Touché.' She defended herself and said that she had been talking about women in a European situation, whereas her father was in Samoa, where the role of women and the family was quite different. Then she said an odd thing, 'Besides, in Samoa it is enough to be content with mere living.' I thought that, despite her obvious love of pleasure, the key to her character was the supplanting of Samoan contentment by the Puritan New England need to work which she had inherited from her father, though ironically he had fled half way round the world to escape it.

She had brought her mother, Le'utu, to New Britain and she lived until a year or two ago in a pretty little European-style house in the Gunantambu garden. She must have been a remarkable old lady. One evening, when she was over seventy, she accompanied Queen Emma to dinner at Matupi, six miles away across the bay. When it was time to take the steam-launch home, Le'utu could not be found. A search was mounted, but without success. Anxiously Queen Emma returned to Gunantambu, where she found her mother asleep in bed. The old lady had become bored with the party, and had paddled a canoe the six miles home and put herself to bed.

In only one respect did Queen Emma lag behind her subjects in the Bismarck Archipelago. She did not own a motor-car. There were two of these new-fangled contraptions clattering along the roads, one belonging to Bishop Couppé (trust the Romans!) and the other to Mr Wahlen, about whom more anon. I asked Emma why she had not bought a motor, and she said she had no intention of doing so, the horse was a much more beautiful creature. Besides, she was perfectly capable of managing a horse, and liked to take the reins, but she was too old to learn to drive a motor. I was told in Sydney that when she visits there (she has a sumptuous house in Vaucluse) her equipage is the sensation of the town, her horses being managed by two jet-black Buka boys in livery, and her little black maids attending her in the carriage.

This Mr Wahlen is a most remarkable man. He came from Hamburg in 1895 to work for Hernsheim when he was twenty-two. By 1903 he was an independent trader, and by 1905 he had taken over from Hernsheim their western islands, the Hermit and Anchorite groups. He made a fortune here from trochus shell. On one of these, a volcanic island called Maron, he built a positive *Schloss*, from a German architect's designs, of basalt and the finest woods brought from Australia. Almost outdoing Queen Emma, he had electric light and refrigeration and a huge wine cellar, and he introduced deer to the island. He also introduced (again copying Queen Emma) a large strain of outside blood to build up the population of his islands, including (I am told) a harem of Micronesian beauties. He lives like a king when he is out there, under the light on his tower which burns all night as a beacon to wandering ships. He spends much of the time here, and I had the pleasure of meeting him, a genial and forthright man still only in his mid-thirties.

A tragedy happened during the otherwise happy weeks I spent at Herbertshöhe. I had become very fond of Queen Emma's delightful sister Phebe, a beautiful woman in her forties with nine children (she had had twelve altogether), married to a scientist of international reputation, Richard Parkinson. She was of the type *Hausfrau*, and I could not interest her in the fight for women's independence, but this did not worry me unduly, for I could see, that although she tended to her husband's every whim, yet she was second only to her sister as a power in the land. It was she who managed all labour affairs, it was she to whom the Governor himself came with requests for help in the management of remote tribes, it was she who even arranged for me to see the secret Duk-Duk dances, normally forbidden to women. She was the classic example of the happy woman, who manages all from a secure domestic base. Her children were very wild, however; her sister said she gave in to them too easily.

Mr Parkinson was a man of aristocratic bearing and formidable intellect. He gave me an immense amount of information about all aspects of life and nature in the islands. Queen Emma jestingly,

257

but with some truth, I gathered, said nearly all the information was really supplied to him by Phebe.

One day Queen Emma arranged for us all to go on a picnic to Toma, a fort on Varzin mountain, where the climate is refreshingly cool after the clammy coast. Varzin plantation was the scene of a terrible massacre in 1902, in which one of Emma's favourite nieces, Carrie, twenty-two year old daughter of her brother Willie, had a miraculous escape from death. A lovely girl, she was staying with a friend, the wife of a German planter called Rudolf Wolff. Wolff had had an argument with the natives over some land on which he had laid out a new plantation. Early one morning in April he went off to the plantation, for once unarmed, and shortly afterwards some natives arrived at the house with a pig for sale. While Mrs Wolff was negotiating the sale, Carrie came out onto the verandah to join her. Suddenly there was a cry, and some natives rushed out from the back of the house and attacked the women with tomahawks. Mrs Wolff was killed instantly, and the chief of the group struck Carrie twice on the head with his tomahawk. She fell seven feet off the verandah onto the ground, but her life was saved by her thick roll of black Polynesian hair which she wore coiled on her head. This deadened the edge of the axe.

At the chief's call more natives rushed in from the bush and killed the Wolff's four months old baby and its nurse. While Carrie was unconscious the Wolff's Buka cookboy dragged her and his native wife into the kitchen and barricaded the door.

Wolff heard the cries but could not return, being unarmed, so rode to the mission station for help. Carrie and the cookboy's wife eventually escaped and reached the mission in the evening.

A punitive expedition was swiftly mounted under Dr Hahl, and the ringleader chief, Tokilang, and many others were shot. A classic epilogue was that several of Tokilang's guilty relatives sought refuge with the Taulil tribe, who perfidiously killed and ate them.

Carrie recovered completely and married Kurt Adolf Schultze, the German Government Secretary, a gentleman of culture and breeding.

The beauties of the Varzin hills are now guarded by a police station, and all is peaceful. We set off in buggies and a gig and other carriages. On our way we found the road blocked by a fallen tree; several Kanakas were endeavouring to remove it, but without success. I wondered what would happen, for our little cavalcade had come to a full stop on rising ground, much to the apparent distaste of a pair of fine horses harnessed to the high carriage wherein Queen Emma had invited me to seat myself. She, however, showed herself full of resource. She sprang out of the little low carriage she was driving, and directed the natives to hack a way through the dense bush which flanked the narrow roadway; thus we circumvented the obstruction.

After an excellent picnic lunch in beautiful surroundings, and a fascinating introduction to the birds and plants of the area from Mr Parkinson, we set off for Ralum and home. Mr Parkinson's buggy was leading, when suddenly on a long down-hill slope the horses went out of control and plunged madly to the bottom of the hill where there was a rocky ford. Here the buggy's right-hand wheel caught on a big rock and in an instant the buggy capsized and Mr Parkinson was thrown out onto his head. He was mortally injured, and died that evening. Thus poor Phebe at the age of forty-four was left a widow with nine children. It is altogether tragic, as Mr Parkinson's great book, *Thirty Years in the South Seas*, was published only recently in Stuttgart, and has already earned him immense acclaim. He was sixty-three.

I tried to be of as much assistance to Phebe as possible in the days that followed. I was full of admiration for her spirit. She was determined to carry on Richard's collecting activities, and was most concerned about a huge *tapa* standard from the Bainings, the wild and very primitive inland people formerly resident along the coast. She said to me 'Richard promised to send it to the Chicago Natural History Museum. I had spies out and I found they were going to have a big feast and dance with this. They cut a man's back specially to receive the end of the standard, and all the men hold it up there just for a minute. All that pain and work just for a little minute.' She showed it to me, and it was enormous. She was packing it with ferns and bark. What strength of character! She told me she was the first person to give the Bainings an axe. 'Oh, they were happy. Before, it had taken them two years to cut down a tree with their axes of stone.'

A few days before I left Gunantambu (Queen Emma had long

since removed me from the Prince Bismarck Hotel and installed me in a guest-house in her garden), a German warship, the *Seeadler*, came into port. The period of mourning for Mr Parkinson being over (Queen Emma not being given to prolonged formalities), several parties were given at Gunantambu for the officers. Late at night Queen Emma, having indulged a little too much in her favourite drink, dozed off while talking to a young officer. Believing that she did not speak German, and in any case was asleep, he turned to a friend and said

> 'Schlafe, mein Königin, schlaf' ein,
> Kava ist nicht so stark wie Champagner.'
>
> (Sleep, my Queen, sleep on,
> Kava is not as strong as champagne.)

It was a wretched rhyme, but quite a merry jest. The only trouble was that Queen Emma heard every word of it and understood every word of it, and there was all hell to pay for that young officer, who was ordered by his Commandant to apologize to Queen Emma.

I left Gunantambu with respect and affection for the two sisters, Emma and Phebe. Emma is the one with the decisive brain, of the type that is usually called masculine, the inference being that women are incapable of such clear intelligence. Phebe radiates warmth and love, she is intuitive and submissive and strangely impractical at times. She would find it difficult to manage her affairs without Emma, which is not to minimize the enormous help she has been to Emma, particularly in bringing about the good relations they enjoy with the natives, that is, both the local tribes, and the Kanakas who work on the plantation, as well as the Buka boys. The natives love Phebe. They call her Miti.

Where in the world would you find a parallel to this cannibal island where a woman, with another woman as her prime minister, rules over a vast enterprise and gives orders to twelve hundred blacks and more than fifty whites? And orders that are infallibly obeyed!

Chapter XXXVI

——————◆——————

HEINRICH RUDOLPH WAHLEN

Towards the end of 1907 Emma and Kolbe went on a trip to Europe. Neither of them looked at all well to me. I had heard rumours that Emma's hair was falling out, and that ·she was suffering from diabetes. She smoked cigars incessantly, and drank too much. In the old days she could drink any of us under the table, my God, she was wonderful! But now there was a heaviness in her elbow.

That *Scheisskopf* Kolbe had been down in Sydney getting all the women he never got up here. He was a pompous ass, ponderous in every respect, with no fun in him. But he also was in poor health, I was told the trouble was in his kidneys, maybe Bright's disease. He drank enough to flush anything out of his kidneys.

In September 1908 Emma returned to Gunantambu alone, having left Kolbe to make his own way. She told me she was fed up with him and all his stuffy relations. No doubt they had tried to patronize her, dear old Emma who is worth a hundred stiff-necked Prussians. She is a Hamburger in spirit. I could tell that she was getting tired. Physically she had aged a lot, though only fifty-eight she looked much older. But mentally she no longer wanted to exercise power and outwit traders and watch the price of copra. She was the Queen who wanted to abdicate. Not only did she want to retire to a quiet life in Sydney (she had bought a new house in Neutral Bay by the harbour) but she wanted to make sure her son Coe got her fortune and not Kolbe's German relations. She realized the complications of our laws regarding land inheritance. What she wanted was cash, of the liquid sort. I think part of the reason she looked so uncharacteristically tired was the immense courage needed to make the decision to sell Ralum, and with it the empire she had built. She did not ask for my sympathy for herself, but she did say sadly, 'Oh, if I go, what will become of Phebe. If only I could persuade her to come to Sydney with me. And with her, all the others, the young ones.'

The rumour that she might sell out flashed all over the Pacific in a matter of seconds. The big Australian firm of Burns, Philp made an offer but could not meet her price. I sailed for Hamburg as soon as possible and from our good people was assured of sufficient support, and forming a company called Forsayth GmGH, later converted into the Hamburgischer Südsee-Aktiengesellschaft, or HASAG, I was in 1909 able to buy Emma out for approximately one million U.S. dollars. A large portion of this was in cash, and the remainder spread through mortgages and shares in my own R. Wahlen Co.

Thus a young man who only fourteen years before had come as a penniless clerk to work for Hernsheim, was now resident in Gunantambu, the finest estate in the South Seas, with his private castle at Maron stocked with all the amenities of the good life. Truly, what a paradise it was!

Although Emma herself was leaving, she had provided well for her relations. Phebe Parkinson, that dear woman, and her children, had plantations at Kuradui and Sum-Sum and at other places, and many nieces and cousins owed their prosperity to Emma. The farewell party at Gunantambu lasted for more days than the Creation of the world, and men who had not seen each other for years came from as far as Samoa, the Marshall Islands and Australia. But it lacked the old life, because the heart was going out of it.

Emma left in style, with several of her nieces in their fashionable best. Her 'pull' with the Norddeutscher Lloyd was undiminished; the Captain of the *Prinz Waldemar* screened off the whole after part of the ship, and most of the poop-deck, so that her party would be free of unwanted visitors. But, alas, Emma herself did not look in good health, and privately I wondered how many more voyages she would make.

In the next two or three years I travelled a lot between Germany and Sweden (where I married a Swedish lady) and the South Seas. In 1912 I had the pleasure of meeting Emma again, at the Hotel Adlon in Berlin, where she and her retinue, firmly bossed around by her faithful maid Ka'ana, occupied an enormous number of rooms. She had just been received by the Kaiser, and had regained some of her old sparkle, but I feared only temporarily. She talked of returning to Sydney alone and leaving her husband, on a strict allowance, to his life of wine, women and cards, but not too much wine, as his kidneys were by now very decrepit, although he was not yet fifty.

Chapter XXXVII

————————◆————————

LULU MILLER

My mother was young Emma, daughter of Maria, Queen Emma's e'lder sister who married Tom Meredith in Samoa. My mother, she came to Duke of Yorks with the Parkinsons when she was thirteen. She married a Dutchman, Schoevres, who came to Neu Pommern to show the Germans how to grow tobacco. They went back to Sumatra and had me. I was christened Louisa but everyone calls me Lulu. Schoevres was my father, but he soon died, and mother went back to Gunantambu and soon married a German, Stensloss, he was Deputy Governor. But poor old mother, she had no luck with husbands, this one died on her of the blackwater. My father's people in Holland were real proud, it gave them a pain that their precious son had married some lousy quarter-caste Samoan, they said they'd take me on condition there was no contact with mother or my Samoan relations.

So off I went to Holland. I never got educated too good in English. Life was awful with my father's people, all corsets and buckles, hand on the table and no speaking at meals, I used to climb out the window at night.

It must have been 1910, I was about seventeen, Queen Emma went on a trip to Europe, mother begged her to get me away from the Schoevres family. Queen Emma was real fond of her namesake, used to call her her adopted daughter, by this time mother had married for a third time to Hoepfels who managed the Fürst Bismarck in Herbertshöhe.

All they o'ld Dutchmen split their wooden shoes when Queen Emma arrive, they been expecting some old black canniba'l in a grass skirt, up in a beautiful carriage and horses rolls this lady in a silk dress and a big hat pinned on with a pearl as big as a dog's nose on the end of the pin. She brought them a whole set of the best French teacups as a little present.

I don't remember good what she said to them, but she got me easy because they were real fed up with me, I was always out the window and they not able to catch me. So off we went in a party what was Queen Emma, Uncle Paul, my nice cousin Ettie Kaumann and the Samoan maid Ka'ana. I never known nothing like it, the way we lived. Suites in all the best hotels, Amsterdam, Paris, London, Berlin, Rome, the Riviera. I was fitted up in clothes that would make your mouth water, only it didn't have to, because they were on my back. Food, drink, things I'd never seen before. And lots of boring art galleries and museums because Queen Emma said it was no use being as pretty as I was unless I had something in my head. I'd rather something somewhere else.

It was mostly me and Ettie, she was about thirty, very nice but what they call a chaperone, always watching me so I couldn't sneak off. I still managed to have a lot of fun. Queen Emma and Uncle Paul had been pretty ill and didn't do much. She'd been in a clinic in Frankfort for weeks, she wasn't allowed to eat and drink some of her favourite things, but every now and then she'd say 'I'd give anything for a bottle of champagne', but Ka'ana would say 'No, remember what the doctor said.' Once when this happened Queen Emma looked so sad and turned to me and said 'Lulu life is always worth living, but I don't call this living.' Not me! I'd never lived like it! All that fuss over not being allowed to drink champagne! Beastly fizzy stuff anyway, makes you belch. But Queen Emma wasn't down all the time, not a bit of it, we had lots of fun when she was feeling good.

She looked too fat, and kind of pasty at times, though otherwise she'd hold her own with any woman of her age. But her hair was still lovely, long and black, in coils.

I could see Uncle Paul eyeing off the girls but Queen Emma didn't mind. One day she said to me, watching him talking to a pretty girl, 'Lulu I'm past it now, but you're getting right into it, and don't think I don't know what happens, you won't fool me. I'll find you a rich husband, then you can do what you want to.'

She was taking me back to New Guinea, so she told me lots of stories about all they old pioneers, specially Aunt Phebe and Mr Parkinson who was dead, and Dr Hahl the Governor, she said he helped as much as he could private people and the natives, and the German Government was a real good Government.

A terrible thing happened one night in Venice. I'd been out late with Ettie, and come round to Queen Emma's suite to say goodnight. There she was on the sofa, snoring, with an empty bottle of champagne on the table. But what was awful, real shuddery awful, was that her head had fallen back and all her hair had tumbled off. Yes, that lovely black hair was a wig, and she was bald as the monkey's bottom in the Berlin Zoo. Poor old dear! I crept out ever so quiet and she never knew I knew.

I think I know why she'd been drinking on her own. Uncle Paul had said he had to take the train up to Hanover in Germany for a few days to see his people, but Ettie and I had noticed there in Venice at the hotel was this blonde woman from Melbourne he'd met on the boat coming over, and she'd left the same day as him. Queen Emma didn't mind Uncle Paul's affairs, but this time she'd been feeling sick and had specially asked him to stay with her. I think it was diabetes she had. She shouldn't have been drinking. But she wasn't one of they drunks or anything like that.

Next day the whole trip (we were going to Constantinople) was cancelled, we left for Australia two days later, and by Heaven Uncle Paul was on the boat, he didn't want to have the money cut off. Ettie stayed behind and I didn't have no chaperone no more, so fun instead. Just near Colombo two officers got so crazy about me they were on the main deck with fists fighting. So Queen Emma locked me in my cabin and sent in the meals. This meant I miss the fancy dress ball, between Colombo and Freemantle. Well, Emma the night of the ball was seated watching the dancers, Ka'ana told me afterwards, she said the best dancer was a veiled girl dressed up as a *nautch* girl, bare belly and split skirt and a lot showing, Emma said it reminded her of her youth in Samoa. But then one of the men pulled off the girl's veil and it was Lulu. Back to the cabin. But I had the same officer to let me out.

Queen Emma was very cross and left me with her son Coe in Sydney while she and Uncle Paul went on to New Guinea, and that was very boring. But I soon came up to Rabaul, the capital had moved there from Herbertshöhe, and I am never seeing so many cousins and aunts and uncles in my life. We had parties and dancing and Mr Wahlen who had bought Ralum from Queen Emma drove me out there in his car to show it to me, it was a Daimler-Benz I remember and we ran over a pig.

Mr Wahlen was very handsome and an always happy man with much drinking but mother said he would never marry me, he would marry someone 100 per cent European and rich and would have white children, so I cried a lot, and Queen Emma sent the money and I went back to Europe to finish my education. Queen Emma sent me to Pitman's school in Breda to learn book-keeping and typing. So my English never got any better.

Chapter XXXVIII

EMMA

The sea is at my door, cut white with yachts. One big P. & O. steamer, a pack of freighters, not many square rigged ships now. This is maybe the biggest difference from Ralum and even Mioko, the boats were my boats and they came to my door. And though it is still the sea it is a harbour, Port Jackson, I can look across it and with a telescope see Vaucluse Hall, the house I bought for Coe. I spend a lot of time watching with the telescope, I know the names of all the ferries. How peaceful it is, the harbour no storms can get into, the house that never rumbles, no volcanoes, the water you can drink out of the tap (if you were fool enough to want to), the mosquitoes that don't give anyone malaria. Those scientists with their ridicuolus names, *Anopheles punctulatus punctulatus* Richard told me it's called. I always called it the punctual puncturing mosquitoe. We were all full of malaria but escaped the blackwater fever, poor Governor Hahl nearly died of it. We escaped so much. I never thought much about it at the time, too busy and too busy enjoying, but now when I think of complaining about my poor old body I look around the room and see those hungry demons that never got me and won't now, tropical ulcers, swamp typhus, enteric, elephantiasis, leprosy. How safe life is for these Australians! And those wretched blacks, they got rid of them all right.

They wouldn't let me bring any of my Bukas here to live, not even my little maids. White Australia. It's a wonder they let me in. Coe's all right, and the girls, all quarter-castes. But you can see the good old Samoan blood in me, thank God, as Phebe would say, always being grateful to God for what she'd worked so hard to do herself.

My body. Nobody desires it any more. It's going rotter blotching like an old pawpaw. Paul can have his women. I'm not wanted, I don't want. I don't want for anything, servants, stupid Irish girls, horses in the stables, I take the calèche and the four-in-hand across to the Corso at Manly, I've ordered Carrara marble for Coe for Vaucluse. Want! What should I want?

Want. Would my body look like this if Tino were still alive? I never really wanted Paul, it was just a need. I don't blame him, a man knows, you can't buy a man, though I did pay all his debts.

I had to sell to Wahlen, I had to safeguard Coe from those German relations of Paul's. I had to gather the whole thing together and feel the money in my hands. But it was like pulling a creeper, a vine off a wall, tug, there's an island, tug, there's a plantation, a boat, a trading store, and then it all gave way and it was just a huddle at my feet.

But I had to do it. There was no one to manage it all if I left, none of the men were any good. Richard with his butterflies and then he got killed. Richard was at his best and happiest as a practical botanist, planting and experimenting, as the great scientist and author he got vain and tetchy. Paul was hopeless, the Prussian officer. He had relays of horses, he could ride right across New Britain in a couple of hours, none of my managers were safe from him, he'd crash in like a coconut and start giving orders, but all the wrong orders.

Phebe said to me, 'Emma, you'll be so lonely. All those people in Sydney round you, and none of your *ainga*, none of your own family. I can stand loneliness but you always need company, the girls running in and out, the men and their talk, the champagne, the music, the dancing.'

Well, Phebe was right, I *am* lonely. I said I'd have my grandchildren, but I don't see them much. It's Christmas Eve now, when Richard and Phebe and their children always had their German Christmas, and then on Christmas Day everyone came to me. Coe and Ida and the children will come to me tomorrow, but we'll rattle around a bit. At other times I can always get people to come to a party, I'm rich and Sydney people are curious to see the Cannibal Queen or whatever they think of me.

But, do you know, I miss the conversations we had at Gunantambu, I miss the long talks at dinner and after, and the music we had together. Oh here there's the opera, and concerts, and I

269

couldn't hear Nellie Melba in New Britain I know, but these Australians don't talk to you. There's no connection between money and education, or between social position and culture. People are cultivated, not cultured. All these big houses and rich people, you go there and drink tea and talk about how terrible the servants are. With old Hernsheim or Bishop Couppé or Governor Hahl we really talked about things, and a woman could answer back. Women are in the background here, answering only when they're spoken to. If you go to a dinner party, just when the conversation is getting interesting the women are all moved off like Kanakas to the labour line. Except you don't need a whip to keep them in their place. Women are too well behaved to get cheeky. In Australia the men bought women off by giving them the vote. It was like when they freed the slaves in America, that was supposed to be enough. But they were still black.

There's nothing for an ordinary woman to do here, let alone a woman like me. Money is what guarantees that a woman will have nothing to do. True, I still play the piano. I read books all night, I scarcely sleep at all nowadays. Sometimes I spend all day on the harbour ferries just to feel a boat under me.

I haven't even a good court case coming up. Nobody seems to dispute land titles in Sydney. If Governor Hahl were here in no time he'd have the blackfellows taking the Australians to court for pinching their land off them.

I had a letter from him the other day in which he called me 'Semiramis in exile in Sydney.' Semiramis, there was a woman! She ruled Assyria and built Babylon, but also, and this is what set me thinking about Hahl's letter, when she found out that her son was plotting against her she abdicated and disappeared. I wonder if he meant anything. Coe and Paul were always getting in a huddle together. I wonder. Paul and Coe.

I remember that time in Mioko when that fellow climbed up and painted in an E after Farrell & Co. Tom was wild!

When the Sydney doctors decided I had this thing called diabetes I went to Germany where the best doctors are and they said the same thing. I made them tell me how long I would live. They said most people died within ten years. That was ten years ago.

I don't believe I've been betrayed by my body. I don't feel

resentful towards it the way white people do, it's because they're brought up as Christians and taught to hate the body. We Samoans are not like that. I just think of all the joy it has given me.

It hurts me to walk now, I seem to get a lot of sores on my feet, but when I drive down along Military Road through the bush I stop the horses and take a deep breath of that aromatic Australian bush, a little sharpness in the honey, so different from the scents of Samoa or Gunantambu.

Chapter **XXXIX**

————————◆————————

SYDNEY *TRUTH*
28/7/1913

Tragic End to Fabulous Life

Queen Emma, as she was known throughout the South Pacific, and her husband Prussian officer Paul Kolbe have both died in Monte Carlo under scandalous circumstances.

The ageing millionairess (she was in her 60's) and her handsome husband, fifteen years younger than her, were leading the *jeunesse doré* in their palatial suite in the luxurious Hotel Victoria. They had come from Berlin where the Imperial war-lord, Kaiser Wilhelm, had granted them the honour of an audience.

All the Queen's money-bags could not, however, be a nose-bag for master-horseman Paul Kolbe. He had jumped the rails of the home paddock and had cantered off with a beautiful blonde Countess from his own country.

The Queen was normally tolerant of her husband's amours, as was natural to one of her South-Sea island blood (she was, of course, despite all her wealth, of the dusky sorority), but the Countess was too much. Kolbe broke the unwritten law of old-world immorality. He told his wife he preferred his mistress to her. In the glittering world of the *bon ton*, a gentleman never insults his wife thus.

In fury Queen Emma, a deadly shot who in her day dropped many a cannibal Kanaka in his tracks, whipped out the pearl-handed revolver she always carried in her reticule, and under the horrified gaze of her black maid Ka'ana she shot him in the head.

Screaming and hysterical, Ka'ana rushed down the stairs for the *maitre d'hotel*, and when the official party arrived back in the suite they found Captain Kolbe dead and Queen Emma dying from a self-inflicted bullet.

She lingered on for sixteen agonizing hours before death sealed the pact that love had broken.

Sydney 'Truth'

Her ashes are being brought back to be buried in her private cemetery in the grounds of her fabulous palace of Gunontambo in the fetid jungles of German New Guinea.

Her colossal fortune passes to her lucky son, Coe Forsayth, of Vaucluse.

Details of her amazing life will be found on p. 12.

Chapter XL

HEINRICH RUDOLPH WAHLEN

In June 1913 the Norddeutscher Lloyd steamer *Prinz Eugen* arrived in Rabaul on her way from Sydney to Europe, and I was astonished to find amongst her passengers my old friend Queen Emma, looking much too ill to cross Sydney Harbour, let alone the oceans of the world.

Her massive good spirits had shrunk with her frame, all the roundness and radiating humour of her had sharpened and sagged, and she could not have hobbled from my motor-car up the steps of Gunantambu. I had to get two of her old Buka boys to carry her. She was much touched, as indeed·I was, to see the tears running down the cheeks of these muscular blacks, so shocked at the appearance of their old mistress.

The last twist of pathos was that she refused champagne. I could not believe it. No, she said, the doctors had strictly forbidden her her favourite drink, and she was also grievously restricted in her eating, and heaven knows she had enjoyed her food. It was because of her diabetes. 'The doctors told me that any kind of excess will kill a diabetic of many years illness,' she said, then added with some of her old sparkle, 'so think, my dear, what a curse to be pronounced on me, who all my life have believed that the road to success leads through excess.'

Now I had her comfortable in her old wicker chair on the verandah, with a cool breeze blowing from Mioko, I asked her what on earth she was doing on the *Prinz Eugen*.

She told me that she had had a cable from a friend in Monte Carlo saying that Paul Kolbe was lying dangerously ill from Bright's Disease, and that although she had allowed him to go his own way since 1912, her place was at her dying husband's side.

274

I took a deep breath (after all, I was many years her junior) and told her that such sentimentality was unworthy of her, that in fact Kolbe was unworthy of her, and she must on no account risk her life to go to him.

'He's an old stallion only fit for the knackers, I know', she said in her old forthright way, 'But I couldn't let him die alone in the gilt squalor of Monte Carlo.'

She was inflexible. She must go. Do you know, I think she cherished that *Scheisskopf* Kolbe in her heart for one thing, that he had horse whipped Administrator Schmiele for insulting her those many years ago. Her pride made her repay.

I said farewell, but I said '*Adieu*', not '*Lebewohl*', because the life was no longer in her, and she was far from well. I was sure I would never see her again. I had castigated her for being sentimental, but I must confess that her dear sister Phebe and I wept on each other's shoulders as we watched the *Prinz Eugen* sail out of Blanche Bay.

On Monday, 21 July, 1913 I received a cable forwarded by my Hamburg office, from Emma saying that Paul Kolbe had died in Monte Carlo on the 19th. The next day I received another cable from the manager of the Victoria Hotel, Monte Carlo, saying that Mrs Kolbe was also dead, and asking for instructions for the disposal of the bodies.

I immediately let Coe Forsayth know in Sydney, and telegraphed my Hamburg office to send a confidential courier to Monte Carlo to take charge and find out what had happened, and especially to interrogate Mrs Kolbe's maid Ka'ana. I also instructed him to have the bodies cremated and the ashes sent to me so they could be buried in Emma's *matmat* (cemetery) at Ralum.

This courier was of the utmost integrity, and from his report it is clear what happened. Emma arrived at Monte Carlo to find that Paul was indeed very ill, but that he was being succoured by a German woman who bluntly told her that Kolbe was her legal husband, and that she had married him in Germany in 1887, before he had left for Hawaii, where she thought he had died. Emma roundly told her that her only marriage licence was the entry in the hotel register. But, to her horror, Kolbe did not deny the German woman's claim.

To get him away from her, at least for a few minutes so they could talk in private, Emma rang for a hire car and they set off for a drive around the Corniche. The car, coming around a narrow corner on one of the steep roads along the coast, ran into a peasant's cart and Kolbe was severely injured. His resistance being heavily lowered by his kidney disease, he died on Saturday, the 19th of July.

The woman fled, not wishing to be involved in scandal and, more to the point, realizing now that Emma held the strings of the purse, and Emma was left alone with Ka'ana.

Although her maid, who was devoted to her, tried to dissuade her, she ordered three bottles of champagne and sat on the balcony of her room drinking and gazing out to sea. She would neither move nor say anything, though the manager kept demanding what he should do with Kolbe's body. The only thing she said was when Ka'ana tried to stop her drinking, reminding her that the doctor said that any excess would be fatal to her. 'The skua steals the bonito from the tern's beak, but the frigate bird is above them all.' Ka'ana remembered the exact words, but had no idea what they meant.

Some time later, Ka'ana, hearing a heavy thud, ran out to the balcony and found Emma (on the floor) in a deep coma. She was taken to hospital but never regained consciousness, dying on Monday the 21st July.

Thus died Emma Eliza Coe Forsayth Kolbe. At least her last sight was of the sea.

This is not the story of my life, but in the fateful year of 1914 I was on a trip to Germany when war broke out. I served in the army throughout the hostilities. By the inquitous Peace of Versailles, Germany lost all her Colonies, and I lost all my plantations. That, as I said, is another story. But I often wondered about woman's intuition. Emma was, though American by birth, a German citizen by her marriage. Ralum and all her plantations and business would have been expropriated, though perhaps partially restored to her after years of litigation.

Did she in 1909 scent in some flower-perfumed breeze through the groves of Gunantambu the sweeter but nauseous stench of death and acrid smoke of loss? Forgive me. The memory of the South Seas leads one too easily into hyperbole. But what drab facts and figures could describe the light on the sword of the angel who came to announce the loss of Paradise?

Chapter XLI

―――――――――◆―――――――――

PHEBE

I will soothe with the sound of names, Emma Eliza, Gunantambu, Kuradui, all gone but so good when we had them. My children's names cannot soothe. An old woman should see her children again before she dies, but I never will. Louisa, Nellie, Otto, Max, Franz, Edward, Dollie, Paul, Karl. Only four of them, maybe, alive, but I will never see them again. I never saw Coe again, Emma's son, he never came back, for him it was all finished. So much lost. I lost Kuradui in 1921, the Australians said I was a German and took my plantation away. And then I got into debt and lost the others.

Nellie, I loved Nellie. She got inflammation of the lungs and died at Buka with me, maybe 1930. Oh Nellie, Nellie, do you remember when you were locked up in the Rabaul gaol? Oh dear, it was so funny! Dolly was so pretty, but wild, a wild teenager, *phantastische*, she was asked over to Rabaul to stay with Dr Hahl at Government House. There was a Captain Richter also staying there. When everyone was asleep he sneaked down the corridor to try to make love to Dolly. But he didn't know that Dolly's Samoan maid was sleeping across the door, and he fell over her. Screams! Everyone running! When the news came back to Kuradui I was away recruiting in the hills. Nellie, she had the wild Samoan blood, Nellie jumped on her horse and rode into Rabaul to the Club and demanded to see this Captain Richter. When he came out to her she asked him for a written apology to her sister Dolly. He refused, so with her riding whip she lashed him three times across the face. Screams! Everyone running! She had struck an officer wearing the Imperial German uniform! The police chief came and locked her up on a charge of assault.

Now the Navy and Dr Hahl and the Administration they were all our good friends, but the Army not always so good. Dr Hahl cabled to the Kaiser explaining the circumstances and asking for a pardon of Nellie, but no, Nellie had to spend a month in gaol. What fun! The Navy sent in her meals three times a day, and flowers, and books, and Nellie did lots of sewing. She had 'insulted the uniform'. But Captain Richter who was inside the uniform was discharged in disgrace from the Army.

My children. Poor Otto. Otto was the handsomest of my sons, a real dandy. He used to spend too much money on clothes. It must have been 1909, he got into debt at Emma's store. Not too much money, but Emma said he must learn about money, he was twenty-four, old enough to know better she said. So she told Richard, and Richard gave Otto a good German father's dressing-down. But Otto was like the Samoan chiefs, very proud and sensitive. He was very well educated in Germany, and he was Governor Hahl's aide. Now this incident of the debt happened just after some Army officer had jeered at him for having 'Kanaka blood'. He went out amongst the coconut trees and he shot himself. It was all my fault, my fault. Before he was born, I was very unhappy, and when I was asked to guide a punitive expedition against the natives I went, though Emma said no, I ought not to go. But I did not value my life and I hoped I would be killed, and that is why my son did not value his.

That bad year 1909. That year Richard was killed when he was thrown out of the buggy. And Max who was only twenty at school in Germany, he died of T.B. there.

My children. For birthday parties we used to spread a white cloth on the grass and Emma would come and we with our children would sit around and have tea, and instead of the children enjoying tea and cakes they'd sooner a piece of roast taro.

We had so many friends. Do you remember how Emma and nice little Mrs Rickards the missionary's wife and I all went to Eduard Hernsheim's to Matupi and we were scared he'd drink too much wine and we hid the bottle and he came back in and laughed and said he could get plenty more out of the store, what fun and enjoyable hours we had with him reading Shakespeare to us. I always remember those happy times.

Franz my third boy married a Dutch girl, they lived in Java, she went insane. She took poison and killed herself. A few days later he took poison too.

It is slower poison to have no food. If there was some food here in the camp I would make a Samoan *umu* and bake Samoan dishes. I remember how you loved my mother's *palusami* and *fai'ai*, to the end she still kept making them, so good.

Emma, you were having a big party when our mother was dying. When she was sick, for seven months I slept down with her at night. After the party, Emma saw she was dying, and wept and said 'Oh, I should have been here before.' Once I had to go up to the house and see about my husband. When I came back my sister said, 'Thank God you have come. Twice Mother tried to die but she looked for you and stayed.' Then Mother looked at me and she died.

There have been two wars here, one German, one Japanese. After that first war the Australian soldiers came, so casual, they weren't a real army, just sitting around on the grass. They didn't care, not about anything, except maybe being born white. There were clerks sleeping in Gunantambu, the administration had occupied it. One night all the Australian soldiers at Kokopo got drunk, they galloped over on their big horses, walers they called them, and rode up the great steps of Gunantambu and then up on to the verandah and all through the rooms, they had lovely high wide doors a horse could fit through, cracking their whips at the clerks inside their mosquito nets. One of them, one of the Australian soldiers, said to me Queen Emma had built Gunantambu of good wood there wasn't a splinter in his horse's hooves in the morning.

My life was one wandering about since then. I managed to save three plantations along the south coast for my children so I was looking after them. But we lost them. Paul, he lost his plantation to Burns, Philp. I came over to Buka to look after my grandson Rudolf, it was right back to fifty years before when I first arrived in New Britain, Kunai grass roof, cooking on two irons, baking bread between two empty kerosene tins, but comfortable, healthy place, no mosquitoes. When I turned seventy

Phebe

I found I didn't need glasses any more. I used to say to Rudi the good Lord was good to me.

Emma used to say 'It's not the good Lord that's good to you, but me!' Well, it was true, I could never manage things like Emma did. After she went away and died everything fell to pieces, but maybe those wars didn't help too.

After Buka I lived on the Portland Islands, off New Hanover. Awful sandy soil, millions of sandflies and mosquitoes, we lived on fish and shell fish, the cutter came only every two months. I didn't mind the loneliness, only the sandflies and mosquitoes.

I often got letters from Dr Hahl and his family. He did want to marry Louisa, but she wouldn't have him.

The natives. The Japanese told them we had been exploiting them, and that we were their masters no more. Did we exploit them? Without them we would have had nothing. They used to call me Miti. People said the natives loved me. No, they didn't love me. They were grateful. I went amongst them, and spoke their languages.

I talked to the red and green parrots. They were sitting on Emma's wrist, and my wrist, and we were sitting on the verandah. Scent of lemons from the scrubbed wood.

The urn with Emma's ashes was put in a hole in a big concrete block in the *matmat*, near Agostino Stalio's tombstone. Then after the first war one night a boat came and anchored in the bay, and next day there was a hole in the concrete and Emma's ashes were gone. I heard it was her son Coe, he had someone bring them down to the cemetery in Sydney. There's just a hole in the concrete, no tombstone or anything. If it had been me, I would have scattered them into the sea. Emma always loved the sea, all her life she lived within the sound of it. She gave the sea a big dare that day when the sea went back before the tidal wave and she ran out and collected the big fish and the crayfish and raced the wave in. We were never frightened of the sea. But we respected it.

Emma's life was a hole in concrete, mine will be a hole in the sand. But that doesn't frighten me either. We had so many happy days. I'm not surprised or angry to be dying. Thank you, Emma, you have helped me keep alive. *Tele le alofa, la'u pele,* with much love, my dear.

EPILOGUE

Almost all the characters in this book existed at the times and places in which I have written of them. Almost all the events of the book are as historically accurate as I have been able to record them. In both cases I used the word 'almost' because I have invented one or two characters, and assembled others from hints and pieces, in order to tell the story.

It seemed to me best to write *Queen Emma of the South Seas* in the way I have, because the relatively large amount of historical material available about these Samoan-Americans is in fragments in unpublished letters and diaries, and in printed books, apart from the work of R. W. Robson. There are only two or three short autograph letters of Queen Emma's in existence. There are a few signed letters of Phebe's, otherwise her voice only survives in the beautifully sympathetic account of her by Dr Margaret Mead in 'Weaver of the Border'. Phebe died in a village in Japanese-occupied New Ireland in 1944, aged eighty-one.

In many cases I have incorporated into the narrative phrases or sentences from unpublished diaries and letters, e.g. of Jonas Coe, George Brown, Dr Hahl; or from books, e.g. by the Earl of Pembroke, B. Pullen-Bury, L. Overell and Margaret Mead. In two cases I have quoted at length, because of the historical importance of these obscure sources, in one, from the unpublished diaries of J. L. Young; in the other, I have translated from the French of Count Festetics de Tolna's *Vers l'Ecueil de Minicoy* (Paris, 1904). As a hostile witness, Festetics is invaluable, and his ineffable tone needed to be preserved intact. I have quoted verbatim phrases and sentences from Dr Mead's account of Phebe Parkinson. I apologize to Sydney *Truth* for inventing a 1913 news item.

I owe thanks, as anyone must who writes about Queen Emma, to R. W. Robson. His many years of pioneering research revealed many of the facts of her life, and he generously made his papers available to scholars at the Pacific Manuscripts Bureau at the

Australian National University, where Robert Langdon, its Director, is a help to all who come to him.

My personal gratitude is above all due to Bob Schultze, and his wife Doris. Bob is the son of Caroline Coe Schultze, the daughter of Emma's brother William. He has patiently helped in every aspect of research, especially to do with German documents, and the knowledge accumulated during his long residence in the New Ireland, New Britain area has been invaluable to me, and always generously shared.

I am also especially grateful to Filifilia and Taisi Tupuola Efi, and Lauitiiti and Alistair Hutchison, who helped me enormously on my visits to Samoa.

Dr Margaret Mead was kind enough to talk to me in New York about Queen Emma and Phebe, and to give me copies of invaluable photographs. I am most grateful to her and Messrs. Harper & Row for permission to publish extracts from 'Weaver of the Border', from *In the Company of Man* (ed. Joseph B. Casagrande, New York, 1960).

My thanks are due to many people, first of all to Colin and Robert Chapman, without whose initial suggestion the book would never have been written; to Robert Langdon; H. E. Maude; Peter Biskup; Stewart Firth; P. G. Sack; Douglas Lockwood; Jim Dick; the late Alex and Pat Hopper; Oscar Rondahl; Beate and George Bailey; Suzanne and Brian Ridley; Wendy Worrall; the librarians of the Mitchell Library, Sydney; the National Library, Canberra; the State Library of South Australia; the Library of the State Department, Washington; the Manuscript Division of the Library of Congress, Washington; the Alexander Turnbull Library, Wellington.

GEOFFREY DUTTON.